The PuffinCyclopedia of Children's Classics

Introduced by
Francesca Dow

PUFFIN

Acknowledgements

Many thanks to Cathy Cassidy, Charlie Higson, Geraldine McCaughrean, Louise Rennison, Meg Rosoff and Darren Shan, Kay Woodwood and Wendy Cooling for their contributions to this book.

Thanks to the Penguin and Puffin Marketing team – Robert Williams, Kirsten Grant, Emily Cox, Sarah Kettle and Reetu Kabra; Puffin Production – Katy Banyard; Puffin Design – Jacqui McDonough; and Puffin Editorial – Francesca Dow, Helen Levene and Wendy Tse. A special thank you to Dan Newman for the text design.

Finally Puffin are indebted to the following authors for their wonderful introductions to the Puffin Classics, namely Richard Adams, David Almond, Quentin Blake, Melvin Burgess, Eoin Colfer, Sophie Dahl, Cornelia Funke, Anthony Horowitz, Brian Jacques, Garth Nix, Richard Peck, Louise Rennison, Chris Riddell, Jonathan Stroud, Diana Wynne Jones and Adeline Yen Mah.

PUFFIN BOOKS

Published by the Penguin Group: London, New York, Australia, Canada, India, Ireland, New Zealand and South Africa

Penguin Books Ltd, Registered Offices: 80 Strand, London WC2R 0RL, England

puffinbooks.com

First published in Puffin Books 2008

1 3 5 7 9 10 8 6 4 2

Designed by Dan Newman

Printed in the UK by CPI Bookmarque, Croydon CR0 4TD

ISBN: 978–0–141–32481–4

Contents

Discover a new friend for life today with Puffin Classics

Welcome to *The PuffinCyclopedia*, a fun-filled tour of some of the best stories ever written. Complete with games and quizzes, celebrity articles, interviews and extracts, this little book has it all. You'll step into worlds packed with high jinx, fantasy, action and danger. You'll meet a cast of classic characters who can't wait to take you on an unforgettable journey. There's a whole range of amazing books for you out there – but it all began with the Classics. You can discover the famous authors behind these stories and find out how they inspired some of *your* favourite writers to become authors themselves. Did you know *Treasure Island* is Eoin Colfer's best-loved book or that *Little Women* inspired Louise Rennison to write her wickedly funny stories?

You can even hear your favourite Classics characters brought to life by logging on to **puffin.co.uk** and enjoying the Puffin Classics Podcasts or tuning into an audio CD.

If you love books and reading, you'll love the Puffin Classics. What are you waiting for?

Your adventure starts here . . .

PART ONE

THE BEST
Animals & Beasts
EVER WRITTEN

Jump into the saddle and ride with Black Beauty!

There was before us a long piece of level road by the river side; John said to me, 'Now, Beauty, do your best,' and so I did; I wanted no whip nor spur, and for two miles I galloped as fast as I could lay my feet to the ground; I don't believe that my old grandfather who won the race at Newmarket could have gone faster. When we came to the bridge, John pulled me up a little and patted my neck. 'Well done, Beauty! good old fellow,' he said. He would have let me go slower, but my spirit was up, and I was off again as fast as before. The air was frosty, the moon was bright, it was very pleasant; we came through a village, then through a dark wood, then uphill, then downhill, till after an eight mile run we came to the town, through the streets and into the Market Place. It was all quite still except the clatter of my feet on the stones – everybody was asleep. The church clock struck three as we drew up at Doctor White's door. John rang the bell twice, and then knocked at the door like thunder. A window was thrown up, and Doctor White, in his nightcap, put his head out and said, 'What do you want?'

'Mrs Gordon is very ill, sir; master wants you to go at once, he thinks she will die if you cannot get there – here is a note.'

'Wait,' he said, 'I will come.'

He shut the window, and was soon at the door.

'The worst of it is,' he said, 'that my horse has been out all day and is quite done up; my son has just been sent for, and he has taken the other. What is to be done? Can I have your horse?'

'He has come at a gallop nearly all the way, sir, and I was to give him a rest here; but I think my master would not be against it if you think fit, sir.'

'All right,' he said, 'I will soon be ready.'

John stood by me and stroked my neck. I was very hot. The Doctor came out with his riding whip.

'You need not take that, sir,' said John. 'Black Beauty will go till he drops; take care of him, sir, if you can, I should not like any harm to come to him.'

'No! no! John,' said the Doctor, 'I hope not,' and in a minute we had left John far behind.

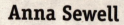

Anna Sewell

Born 30 March 1820 in Great Yarmouth, Norfolk

Died 25 April 1878 in Norwich, Norfolk

Nationality English

Lived in many different parts of England, although for health reasons she spent some time in European spas.

Married She was never married.

Children None.

Career Unable to walk due to an injury as a child, Anna worked mainly at home, helping her mother edit her writings. She also taught at Sunday School.

Hobbies Art, painting and nature, and the humane treatment of animals, particularly horses.

Famous for her one and only novel, *Black Beauty* – published in 1877, remained in print ever since, and has been quoted as being 'the most famous and best-loved animal book of all time'. Sadly, Anna Sewell died a few months after *Black Beauty* was published, so she never knew of the book's huge success.

Make room for Black Beauty and friends on your bookshelf . . .

WIN A PUFFIN CLASSICS COLLECTION!

100 prize sets of 12 books to be won – just send in the answers to ALL FOUR Classics Quiz pages for your chance to enjoy Alice's adventures, Huck Finn's riverboat rides and much, much more.

See page 101 for details on how to enter.

by **Meg Rosoff**

Despite my advanced age, I have to admit that most of my favourite literary characters are animals – often dogs, occasionally bears and not infrequently horses. I blame it all on *Go, Dog, Go!* by P. D. Eastman. Aside from the fact that I was dog crazy practically from birth, on rereading this to my five-year-old daughter, I couldn't help noticing that it (unlike me) hadn't aged a day. I still think the dog lady in the huge hats is hilarious ('Do you like my hat?' 'No, I do not like your hat.') And as for the gigantic dog party on the top of a tree? I'm still waiting for my invitation, forty-five years later.

Although I was also a confirmed *Harry the Dirty Dog* and *Yertle the Turtle* fan, it was *The Cat in the Hat* who taught me everything I know about anarchy. I loved how dangerous he was, how he made his way quietly into the house *while Mother was away*, and then calmly wreaked havoc, causing the poor feckless children no end of anxiety. And then *voila*! In waltz Thing One and Thing Two to clear up the mess, just in the nick of time. I still consider Things One and Two to be among literature's most intriguing creations. But are they animals, exactly? Perhaps someday some brilliant professor will write a thesis on the subject.

My next joyous encounter down memory lane is with Winnie the Pooh and Eeyore. Poor, long-suffering Eeyore ('Don't mind me, it's all I deserve, surely?') still makes me laugh out loud, and I've met so many of his human relatives over the years that I've lost count. I even dated one for a while! As for dear Pooh, I identified strongly with his enormous appetite for honey – well, his enormous appetite in general – and his earnest confusion about the world.

Then came chapter books. The first five hundred or so that I read during my American childhood all featured horses as protagonists – *The Black Stallion* and his twenty or so sequels started things off, and I actually remember experiencing a deep, enduring sorrow when I finished the last of the fifty-nine Marguerite Henry horse books. (Has anyone in Britain even heard of *King of the Wind* or *Misty of Chincoteague*? If not, I thoroughly recommend them!) Even *Little House on the Prairie* had some good animals – Jack the dog, and Pet and Patty, the two plough horses.

Everyone waited for me to outgrow this stage and move on to more mature books – *Little Women*, perhaps, or *Ballet Shoes*. But no, it was *Just So Stories*, *The Call of the Wild* and *The Incredible Journey*. I adored Gerald Durrell's *My Family and Other Animals*. Dolphin books took centre stage for a while (*Dolphin Island* and *Island of the Blue Dolphins*), and of course there was the wonderful autobiography of a horse, featuring the unforgettable Black Beauty. A sense of great moral outrage about the use of bearing reins has stayed with me to this day, despite the fact that they are, so far as I can tell, pretty much extinct.

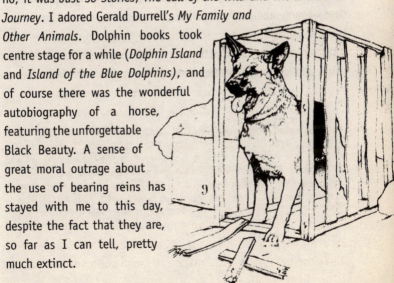

Even today, my favourite adult novels often feature animals – *All the Pretty Horses* by Cormac McCarthy, for example, or Rory Stewart's *The Places In Between*, in which he walks across Afghanistan with only a large golden mastiff for company. I'm sure my greatest folly as a writer was to invent the wise, serene greyhound in *Just in Case* and then fall in love with him to such an extent that I found myself (as if in a trance) driving home from a trip to Gloucestershire with two scruffy lurcher puppies in a cardboard box.

Today, while most sane writers are just sitting down to that first invigorating hour of morning work with a cup of a coffee in a wonderfully silent house, I'm tramping up and down Hampstead Heath chasing squirrels with my two hairy lunatics in the rain. Will I ever learn? Probably not. I've written two picture books featuring wild boars, and my new novel's protagonist is a girl who runs away from home on her wedding morning, taking her beautiful white horse with her. These days, when I should be working, I find myself daydreaming about the feasibility of keeping a beautiful white horse in London.

It's not feasible. I know that for a fact. So, for now, I'll stick to books and keep my fantasies literary. But maybe someday . . .

Meg Rosoff moved from New York City to London in 1989 where she lives with her husband, daughter and two lurchers. Her first novel, *How I Live Now*, won the Guardian Children's Fiction Prize 2004 and the Brandford Boase Award, and is being made into a film. Her second book, *Just in Case*, won the 2007 Carnegie Medal. Meg's third book, *What I Was*, has been shortlisted for the Costa Book Award. It is due out in paperback in Spring 2008.

Puffin Classics on Film

The Call of the Wild was first filmed in 1935 and starred American heart-throb Clarke Gable. In 1972 a new film was made with another of America's leading male actors, Charlton Heston, who played Buck's firm but loving master, John Thornton. It's now considered a classic on DVD. More recently a film was made for television called *The Call of the Wild: Dog of the Yukon*.

There have been numerous film adaptations of *White Fang*, the most popular one produced by Walt Disney.

Black Beauty has been adapted for film and television several times. The first was a silent movie made in 1921! Fifty years later, another film was made starring Mark Lester (the child star of the film *Oliver!*) and is now considered to be the best adaptation of Anna Sewell's book. And in 1972 it was made into a long-running television series called *The Adventures of Black Beauty*. The latest film was made in 1994 and starred Sean Bean.

Kenneth Grahame's *The Wind in the Willows* is one of the best-loved children's books in English literature. It has been adapted many times for stage, from A. A. Milne's (author of *Winnie-the-Pooh*) successful musical stage version, *Toad of Toad Hall*, in 1929 to Alan Bennett's play for the National Theatre in London. In 1983 a brilliant film animation was made with lots of famous actors doing the voices, including David Jason as Toad. And in 2006 a new live-action adaptation was made for television, starring Matt Lucas as Toad and Mark Gatiss as Ratty.

Take a trek with Buck the dog and await the call of the wild!

For two days and nights Buck never left camp, never let Thornton out of his sight. He followed him about his work, watching him while he ate, saw him into his blankets at night and out of them in the morning. But after two days the call in the forest began to sound more imperiously than ever. Buck's restlessness came back on him, and he was haunted by recollections of the wild brother, and of the smiling land beyond the divide and the run side by side through the wide forest stretches. Once again he took to wandering in the woods, but the wild brother came no more; and though he listened through long vigils, the mournful howl was never raised.

He began to sleep out at night, staying away from camp for days at a time; and once he crossed the divide at the head of the creek and went down into the land of timber and streams. There he wandered for a week, seeking vainly for fresh signs of the wild brother, killing his meat as he travelled and travelling with the long, easy lope that seems never to tire. He fished for salmon in a broad stream that emptied somewhere into the sea, and by this stream he killed a large black bear, blinded by the mosquitoes while likewise fishing, and raging through the forest helpless and terrible. Even so, it was a hard fight, and it aroused the last latent remnants of Buck's ferocity. And two

days later, when he returned
to his kill and found a dozen
wolverenes quarrelling over the spoil,
he scattered them like chaff; and
those that fled left two behind who
would quarrel no more.

The blood-longing became stronger than ever
before. He was a killer, a thing that preyed, living on the things
that lived, unaided, alone, by virtue of his own strength and
prowess, surviving triumphantly in a hostile environment
where only the strong survived. Because of all this he became
possessed of a great pride in himself, which communicated
itself like a contagion to his physical being. It advertised itself
in all his movements, was apparent in the play of every muscle,
spoke plainly as speech in the way he carried himself and
made his glorious furry coat if anything more glorious. But
for the stray brown on his muzzle and above his eyes, and for
the splash of white hair that ran midmost down his chest, he
might well have been mistaken for a gigantic wolf, larger than
the largest of the breed. From his St Bernard father he had
inherited size and weight, but it was his shepherd mother who
had given shape to that size and weight. His muzzle was the
long wolf muzzle, save that it was larger than the muzzle of
any wolf; and his head, somewhat broader, was the wolf head
on a massive scale.

His cunning was wolf cunning, and the wild cunning; his
intelligence, shepherd intelligence and St Bernard intelligence;
and all this, plus an experience gained in the fiercest of schools,
made him as formidable a creature as any that roamed the wild.

❧

Trivia

Windy words

All of the following are names for wind around the world (and possibly in the Willows too):

Berg • Bora • Brickfielder • Buran
Chinook • Föhn • Gregale
Habob • Harmattan • Helm
Khamsin • Levanter • Leveche
Libeccio • Marin • Meltemi
Mistral • Pampero • Reshabar
Seistan • Shamal • Simoon
Sirocco • Southerly Buster
Tramontana • Vendavales

Did you know...?

The Call of the Wild tells the story of a dog that turns wild. And *White Fang* is the story of a wolf-dog that ... well, can you guess?

Famous horses in fact and fiction

Black Beauty – the star of Anna Sewell's famous – and only – novel.

Black Bess – a magnificent, black thoroughbred, and the beloved mount of the legendary eighteenth-century highwayman, Dick Turpin.

Champion the Wonder Horse – the wild stallion who starred in the 1950s US television series of the same name. Champion (played by four different horses) really was a Wonder Horse. He was incredibly heroic and could perform tricks, such as untying rope knots.

Man O' War – the greatest (and feistiest) US thoroughbred horse of the twentieth century. He won twenty of the twenty-one races that he competed in, and sired sixty-four stakes winners and 200 other champions.

Pegasus – the winged horse of Greek mythology. It is said that wherever he struck his hoof a spring would appear.

Red Rum – the first horse to win the Grand National at Aintree in England and the only horse to win the race three times (and come second twice).

Five **grrrrreat** facts about wolves

1 A wolf howl is a continuous sound lasting up to ten seconds and is used to bring the pack together and as a long-distance call expressing their territory.

2 The Inuit tribe of North America were the first to use dogs to pull sledges.

3 Wolves are carnivores and use their strong sense of smell to hunt large prey, such as moose, reindeer, elk and bison.

4 Wolves breed in January and after sixty to sixty-five days the female gives birth to an average of five to nine cubs.

5 All dogs are descendants of wolves (Latin name: *Canis lupus*).

The Klondike Gold Rush . . .

. . . was the greatest ever. In 1896 Skookum Jim Mason, Dawson Charlie and George Washington Carmack found gold in Rabbit Creek – later renamed Bonanza Creek – a tributary of the Klondike River in the Yukon in northwest Canada. Many gold-prospectors made their fortune, but many returned empty-handed – like Jack London. Luckily, the author did bring back stacks of ideas for his bestselling novels including *The Call of the Wild* and *White Fang*.

Which creature does NOT appear in *The Wind in the Willows*?

a) A rat
b) A skunk
c) A toad
d) A badger
e) An otter

Answer: b) A skunk!

Travel back to where it all began . . .

n the High and Far-Off Times the Elephant, O Best Beloved, had no trunk. He had only a blackish, bulgy nose, as big as a boot, that he could wriggle about from side to side; but he couldn't pick up things with it. But there was one Elephant – a new Elephant – an Elephant's Child – who was full of 'satiable curtiosity, and that means he asked ever so many questions. *And* he lived in Africa, and he filled all Africa with his 'satiable curtiosities. He asked his tall aunt, the Ostrich, why her tail-feathers grew just so, and his tall aunt, the Ostrich, spanked him with her hard, hard claw. He asked his tall uncle, the Giraffe, what made his skin spotty, and his tall uncle, the Giraffe, spanked him with his hard, hard hoof. And still he was full of 'satiable curtiosity! He asked his broad aunt, the Hippopotamus, why her eyes were red, and his broad aunt, the Hippopotamus, spanked him with her broad, broad hoof; and he asked his hairy uncle, the Baboon, why melons tasted just so, and his hairy uncle, the Baboon, spanked him with his hairy, hairy paw. And *still* he was full of 'satiable curtiosity! He asked questions about everything that he saw, or heard, or felt, or smelt, or touched, and all his uncles and his aunts spanked him. And still he was full of 'satiable curtiosity!

One fine morning in the middle of the Precession of the Equinoxes this 'satiable Elephant's Child asked a new fine question that he had never asked before. He asked, 'What does the Crocodile have for dinner?' Then everybody said, 'Hush!' in a loud and dretful tone, and they spanked him immediately and directly, without stopping, for a long time.

By and by, when that was finished, he came upon Kolokolo Bird sitting in the middle of a wait-a-bit thornbush, and he said, 'My father has spanked me, and my mother has spanked me; all my aunts and uncles have spanked me for my 'satiable curtiosity; and *still* I want to know what the Crocodile has for dinner!'

Then Kolokolo Bird said, with a mournful cry, 'Go to the banks of the great grey-green, greasy Limpopo River, all set about with fever-trees, and find out.'

Rudyard Kipling

Name (Joseph) Rudyard Kipling

Born 30 December 1865 in Bombay, India

Died 18 January 1936 in London, and buried in Poet's Corner in Westminster Abbey

Nationality British

Lived in India, London, the south of England, USA and South Africa.

Married to Caroline 'Carrie' Balestier in 1892.

Children Josephine (who died from influenza at an early age), Elsie and John (who was tragically killed in action during World War I).

Career Journalist, editor, poet and novelist.

Hobbies Reading, writing, travelling and the Scouting movement.

Famous for stories, poems, and novels for children, including *The Jungle Book* (1894) which was made into a much-loved Disney film, and *Just So Stories* (1902). He was the first English author to receive the Nobel Prize for Literature. In 1995 Rudyard Kipling's poem 'If' was voted Britain's favourite poem.

Switch on to the Classics!

Now Playing
Alice's Adventures in Wonderland

▼ **Puffin Classics**

A Little Princess
► Alice's Adventures in Wonderland
Anne of Green Gables
Black Beauty
Five Children and It
Little Women
Peter Pan
The Railway Children
The Secret Garden
The Wind in the Willows
The Wizard of Oz
White Fang

Hear the best stories ever written.
Puffin Classics on audio.

Classic Connections

We're said to be a nation of animal lovers – if you are one too then all these books are for you. Follow the links from books you know to books you don't – yet.

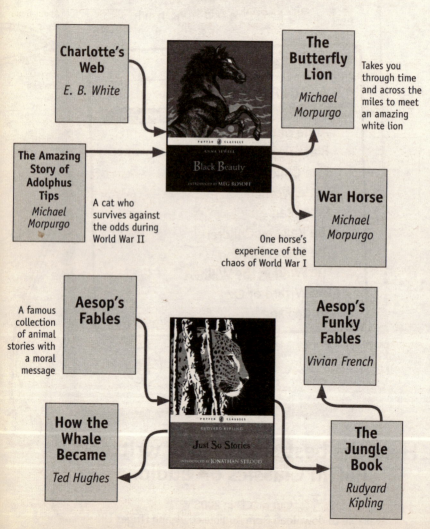

Charlotte's Web

E. B. White

The Amazing Story of Adolphus Tips

Michael Morpurgo

A cat who survives against the odds during World War II

The Butterfly Lion

Michael Morpurgo

Takes you through time and across the miles to meet an amazing white lion

War Horse

Michael Morpurgo

One horse's experience of the chaos of World War I

A famous collection of animal stories with a moral message

Aesop's Fables

Aesop's Funky Fables

Vivian French

How the Whale Became

Ted Hughes

The Jungle Book

Rudyard Kipling

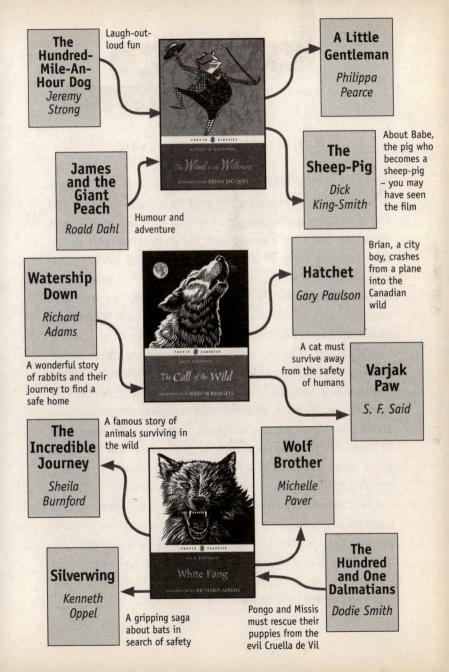

The Hundred-Mile-An-Hour Dog
Jeremy Strong

Laugh-out-loud fun

A Little Gentleman
Philippa Pearce

James and the Giant Peach
Roald Dahl

Humour and adventure

The Sheep-Pig
Dick King-Smith

About Babe, the pig who becomes a sheep-pig – you may have seen the film

Watership Down
Richard Adams

A wonderful story of rabbits and their journey to find a safe home

Hatchet
Gary Paulson

Brian, a city boy, crashes from a plane into the Canadian wild

A cat must survive away from the safety of humans

Varjak Paw
S. F. Said

The Incredible Journey
Sheila Burnford

A famous story of animals surviving in the wild

Wolf Brother
Michelle Paver

Silverwing
Kenneth Oppel

A gripping saga about bats in search of safety

The Hundred and One Dalmatians
Dodie Smith

Pongo and Missis must rescue their puppies from the evil Cruella de Vil

Run wild with White Fang!

Kiche licked White Fang soothingly with her tongue, and tried to prevail upon him to remain with her. But his curiosity was rampant, and several minutes later he was venturing forth on a new quest. He came upon one of the man-animals, Grey Beaver, who was squatting on his hams and doing something with sticks and dry moss spread before him on the ground. White Fang came near to him and watched. Grey Beaver made mouth-noises which White Fang interpreted as not hostile, so he came still nearer.

Women and children were carrying more sticks and branches to Grey Beaver. It was evidently an affair of moment. White Fang came in until he touched Grey Beaver's knee, so curious was he, and already forgetful that this was a terrible man-animal. Suddenly he saw a strange thing like mist beginning to arise from the sticks and moss beneath Grey Beaver's hands. Then, amongst the sticks themselves, appeared a live thing, twisting and turning, of a colour like the colour of the sun in the sky. White Fang knew nothing about fire. It drew him as the light in the mouth of the cave had drawn him in his early puppyhood. He crawled the several steps toward the flame. He heard Grey Beaver chuckle above him, and he knew the sound was not hostile. Then his nose touched the flame, and at the same instant his little tongue went out to it.

For a moment he was paralysed. The unknown, lurking in the midst of the sticks and moss, was savagely clutching him by the nose. He scrambled backward, bursting out in an astonished explosion of ki-yi's. At the sound, Kiche leaped, snarling, to the end of her stick, and there raged terribly because she could not come to his aid. But Grey Beaver laughed loudly, and slapped his thighs, and told the happening to all the rest of the camp, till everybody was laughing uproariously. But White Fang sat on his haunches and ki-yi'd and ki-yi'd, a forlorn and pitiable little figure in the midst of the man-animals.

It was the worst hurt he had ever known. Both nose and tongue had been scorched by the live thing, sun-coloured, that had grown up under Grey Beaver's hands. He cried and cried interminably, and every fresh wail was greeted by bursts of laughter on the part of the man-animals. He tried to soothe his nose with his tongue, but the tongue was burnt too, and the two hurts coming together produced greater hurt; whereupon he cried more hopelessly and helplessly than ever.

And then shame came to him. He knew laughter and the meaning of it. It is not given us to know how some animals know laughter, and know when they are being laughed at; but it was this same way that White Fang knew it. And he felt shame that the man-animals should be laughing at him. He turned and fled away, not from the hurt of the fire, but from the laughter that sank even deeper, and hurt in the spirit of him. And he fled to Kiche, raging at the end of her stick like an animal gone mad – to Kiche, the one creature in the world who was not laughing at him.

From cover to cover . . .

The FIRST ever Puffin Storybook was published as long ago as 1941. That book was *Worzel Gummidge*, the much-loved walking, talking scarecrow by Barbara Euphan Todd. Since then many other great stories have appeared on the Puffin list. Take a look at the covers of these wonderful classics and see how styles have changed from the early years of Puffin Books right up to present day!

THE WIND IN THE WILLOWS

Kenneth Grahame

pictures by
John Burningham

1983

PUFFIN CLASSICS

The Wind in the Willows
KENNETH GRAHAME

1994

PUFFIN CLASSICS
KENNETH GRAHAME

THE WIND IN THE WILLOWS

1983

PUFFIN CLASSICS
KENNETH GRAHAME
The Wind in the Willows
INTRODUCED BY BRIAN JACQUES

2008

Puffin Classics then and now!

Classics Quiz
Part One

Answer the questions on all four Classics Quiz pages and enter our competition to win a 12-copy set of Puffin Classics! *Details of how to send in your answers are on page 101.*

1 Which animal carol-singers visit Mole's House in *The Wind in the Willows*?
a) Mice
b) Otters
c) Moles
d) Badgers

2 In *Alice's Adventures in Wonderland*, what is the name of Alice's cat?
a) Diana
b) Dinah
c) Daisy
d) Dorothy

3 What was Black Beauty's mother's name?
a) Bess
b) Starlight
c) Duchess
d) Lady

4 Who was *not* at the Mad Hatter's tea party in *Alice's Adventures in Wonderland*?
a) The March Hare
b) The White Rabbit
c) The Mad Hatter
d) The Dormouse

5 What kind of animal is Shere Khan?
a) A leopard
b) A giraffe
c) A panther
d) A tiger

6 Who wrote *Charlotte's Web*?
a) E. B. White
b) Dick King-Smith
c) Dodie Smith
d) E. Nesbit

7 What kind of animal is Babe?
a) A sheep
b) A dog
c) A pig
d) A horse

8 In *Aesop's Fables*, which two animals have a race?
a) Lion and mouse
b) Hare and tortoise
c) Fox and crow
d) Wolf and goat

Kenneth Grahame

Born 8 March 1859 in Edinburgh, Scotland

Died 6 July 1932 in Pangbourne, Berkshire; buried in Holywell Cemetery, Oxford, with his son, Alastair.

Nationality Scottish

Lived in Inverary, Argyll, and in Cookham Dene and other villages by the river Thames in Berkshire.

Married to Elspeth Thomson in 1899.

Children One son, Alastair, born in 1900. On Alastair's fourth birthday his father began to tell him the stories that later became *The Wind in the Willows*. Alastair's nickname was Mouse.

Career He began as a clerk at the Bank of England, rising to Secretary of the Bank of England in 1898.

Hobbies Kenneth Grahame was a good sportsman, and particularly excelled at rugby. He loved nature, boating on the river Thames and walking in the woods.

Famous for *The Wind in the Willows* (published 1908) which remains one of the world's best-loved classics.

Spend a season on the river bank and take a walk on the wild side . . .

Poor Mole found it difficult to get any words out between the upheavals of his chest that followed one upon another so quickly and held back speech and choked it as it came. 'I know it's a – shabby, dingy little place,' he sobbed forth at last, brokenly: 'not like – your cosy quarters – or Toad's beautiful hall – or Badger's great house – but it was my own little home – and I was fond of it – and I went away and forgot all about it – and then I smelt it suddenly – on the road, when I called and you wouldn't listen, Rat – and everything came back to me with a rush – and I wanted it! – O dear, O dear! – and when you wouldn't turn back, Ratty – and I had to leave it, though I was smelling it all the time – I thought my heart would break. – We might have just gone and had one look at it, Ratty – only one look – it was close by – but you wouldn't turn back, Ratty, you wouldn't turn back! O dear, O dear!'

Recollection brought fresh waves of sorrow, and sobs again took full charge of him, preventing further speech.

The Rat stared straight in front of him, saying nothing, only patting Mole gently on the shoulder. After a time he muttered gloomily, 'I see it all now! What a pig I have been! A pig – that's me! Just a pig – a plain pig!'

He waited till Mole's sobs became gradually less stormy and more rhythmical; he waited till at last sniffs were frequent and sobs only intermittent. Then he rose from his seat, and, remarking carelessly, 'Well, now we'd really better be getting on, old chap!' set off up the road again, over the toilsome way they had come.

'Wherever are you (hic) going to (hic), Ratty?' cried the tearful Mole, looking up in alarm.

'We're going to find that home of yours, old fellow,' replied the Rat pleasantly; 'so you had better come along, for it will take some finding, and we shall want your nose.'

'O, come back, Ratty, do!' cried the Mole, getting up and hurrying after him. 'It's no good, I tell you! It's too late, and too dark, and the place is too far off, and the snow's coming! And – and I never meant to let you know I was feeling that way about it – it was all an accident and a mistake! And think of River Bank, and your supper!'

'Hang River Bank, and supper too!' said the Rat heartily. 'I tell you, I'm going to find this place now, if I stay out all night. So cheer up, old chap, and take my arm, and we'll very soon be back there again.'

AND

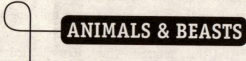

If you like stories about

ANIMALS & BEASTS

then you should also try these classic stories...

- [ ] *Watership Down* RICHARD ADAMS
- [ ] *Greyfriar's Bobby* ELEANOR ATKINSON
- [ ] *The Incredible Journey* SHEILA BURNFORD
- [ ] *Fantastic Mr Fox* ROALD DAHL
- [ ] *The Sheep-Pig* DICK KING-SMITH
- [ ] *The Jungle Book* RUDYARD KIPLING
- [ ] *Lassie Come-Home* ERIC KNIGHT
- [ ] *Winnie-the-Pooh* A. A. MILNE
- [ ] *Mrs Frisby and the Rats of Nimh*
      ROBERT C. O'BRIEN
- [ ] *Gobbolino the Witch's Cat*
      URSULA MORAY WILLIAMS
- [ ] *The Hundred and One Dalmatians*
      DODIE SMITH
- [ ] *Charlotte's Web* E. B. WHITE

Tick if you've read it!

MARK TWAIN
The Adventures of
Huckleberry Finn
INTRODUCED BY DARREN SHAN

L. M. MONTGOMERY
Anne of Green Gables
INTRODUCED BY LAUREN CHILD

FRANCES HODGSON BURNETT
A Little Princess
INTRODUCED BY ADELINE YEN MAH

LOUISA MAY ALCOTT
Little Women
INTRODUCED BY LOUISE RENNISON

FRANCES HODGSON BURNETT
The Secret Garden
INTRODUCED BY SOPHIE DAHL

PART TWO

THE BEST
Friends & Family
EVER WRITTEN

Board the raft with Huck and Jim and drift downriver . . .

The fifth night below St Louis we had a big storm after midnight, with a power of thunder, and lightning, and the rain poured down in a solid sheet. We stayed in the wigwam and let the raft take care of itself. When the lightning glared out we could see a big straight river ahead, and high rocky bluffs on both sides. By-and-by says I, 'Hel-lo, Jim, looky yonder!' It was a steamboat that had killed herself on a rock. We was drifting straight down for her. The lightning showed her very distinct. She was leaning over, with part of her upper deck above-water, and you could see every little chimbly-guy clean and clear, and a chair by the big bell, with an old slouch hat hanging on the back of it when the flashes come.

Well, it being away in the night, and stormy, and all so mysterious-like, I felt just the way any other boy would a felt when I see that wreck laying there so mournful and lonesome in the middle of the river. I wanted to get aboard of her and slink around a little, and see what there was there. So I says:

'Le's land on her, Jim.'

But Jim was dead against it, at first. He says:

'I doan' want to go fool'n 'long er no wrack. We's doin' blame' well, en we better let blame' well alone, as de good book says. Like as not dey's a watchman on dat wrack.'

'Watchman your grandmother!' I says; 'there ain't nothing to watch but the texas and the pilot-house; and do you reckon anybody's going to resk his life for a texas and a pilot-house such a night as this, when it's likely to break up and wash off down the river any minute?' Jim couldn't say nothing to that, so he didn't try. 'And besides,' I says, 'we might borrow something worth having, out of the captain's stateroom. Seegars, I bet you – and cost five cents apiece, solid cash. Steamboat captains is always rich, and gets sixty dollars a month, and they don't care a cent what a thing costs, you know, long as they want it. Stick a candle in your pocket; I can't rest, Jim, till we give her a rummaging. Do you reckon Tom Sawyer would ever go by this thing? Not for pie, he wouldn't. He'd call it an adventure – that's what he'd call it; and he'd land on that wreck if it was his last act. And wouldn't he throw style into it? – wouldn't he spread himself, nor nothing? Why, you'd think it was Christopher C'lumbus discovering Kingdom-Come. I wish Tom Sawyer *was* here.'

Mark Twain

Name Samuel Langhorne Clemens; better known as Mark Twain

Born 30 November 1835 in Missouri, USA

Died 21 April 1910 in Connecticut, USA

Nationality American

Lived in Hannibal, Missouri, and all over the United States and Europe.

Married to Olivia (Livy) Langdon in 1870.

Children A son, Langdon, and three daughters – Olivia Susan, Clara Langdon and Jane Lampton (sadly, only Clara outlived Twain).

Career and hobbies Mark Twain had a wide range of jobs and interests. He trained as a printer's apprentice, was a gold prospector and a timber prospector, spent several years as a pilot on the Mississippi riverboats, volunteered as a soldier during the Civil War, and became a successful novelist and short-story writer.

Famous for his children's classics, including *The Adventures of Huckleberry Finn*, *The Adventures of Tom Sawyer* and *The Prince and the Pauper*. Mark Twain is America's best-loved classic author.

Classics Quiz
Part Two

Answer the questions on all four Classics Quiz pages and enter our competition to win a 12-copy set of Puffin Classics! *Details of how to send in your answers are on page 101.*

1 Who leads Mary Lennox to the key in *The Secret Garden*?
a) A robin
b) Her uncle
c) The gardener
d) A cat

2 Prince Edward Island is the home to which children's book character?
a) Sara Crewe
b) Robinson Crusoe
c) Long John Silver
d) Anne Shirley

3 Who was the youngest sister in *Little Women*?
a) Beth
b) Amy
c) Jo
d) Meg

4 Down which river do Huckleberry Finn and Jim travel?
a) The Missouri
b) The Ohio
c) The Mississippi
d) The Ouachita

5 What are the names of the three 'Railway Children'?
a) Sarah, Clara and Tom
b) Amy, Beth and Jack
c) Roberta, Phyllis and Peter
d) Elizabeth, Jane and Michael

6 In *Little Women*, what present does Mr Laurence give to Beth?
a) A book
b) A violin
c) A piano
d) A coat

7 Which book tells the story of a little girl from India who comes to live with her rich uncle?
a) *A Little Princess*
b) *Heidi*
c) *The Secret Garden*
d) *Pollyanna*

8 Who are Ann, Julian, Dick, Georgina and Timmy?
a) The Family from One End Street
b) The Borrowers
c) The Famous Five
d) The Children of the New Forest

Families come in all shapes and sizes. Some are cool and clever, some warm and welcoming, some fiery, some funny, and some just plain weird! Family life is not always perfect. Families can fight and argue, and sometimes they break up and join themselves together again in a different shape, a stepfamily. Sometimes, your friends can be a kind of family, too!

When I was little, I lived with my mum, dad and brother in an ordinary semi-detached house in a Midlands city. We were a slightly offbeat, eccentric family, and certainly had our share of ups and downs, but we were happy. My dad and I used to haunt the local libraries, and I always loved reading about other families and how they handled the dramas that life threw at them.

One of my favourite books back then was *Anne of Green Gables* by L. M. Montgomery, the story of an orphan girl sent to live with an elderly farming couple in Canada about a hundred years ago. Things don't start well for Anne – the couple are expecting a boy, to help out on the farm, but Anne soon wins their hearts and the unlikely threesome quickly weave themselves into a close and caring family.

Anne is a character I really identified with – well-meaning, but always getting into scrapes! She has red hair and is often teased for it. At one point in the story she tries to dye her hair and turns it green by mistake – not unlike what happens in my own book *Scarlett*! It makes me smile to think that the inspirations for that story reach right back to a book I read when I was eleven!

Another favourite, *What Katy Did* by Susan Coolidge, also featured a girl who couldn't stay out of trouble. A terrible accident finally stops Katy's tomboyish adventures, but nothing can squash her love of life, her enthusiasm, spirit and determination. That really made an impression on me, and to this day, in my own books, I try to show that life has its own special magic – no matter what hardships you may have to face.

Reading about families from other times and places was fascinating for me as a child . . . I loved *Little Women* by Louisa May Alcott, a book about four teenage girls in nineteenth-century Boston. I loved that the girls were not perfect – and that I could read about the little details of their everyday lives, as well as their big dramas and tragedies. Jo was my favourite character – like me, she was a tomboy and loved writing!

One of the best things about all of these books was that the end of the book was not the end of the story – each one had sequels so you could find out what happened next!

I also loved stand-alone books like *A Little Princess*, *The Railway Children* and *The Secret Garden* . . . each one was like a passport into a different world, mysterious, dangerous, scary, sad, but always exciting, addictive, a place to escape to.

What I learned from these books was that great characters are rarely angelic or perfect, and that real life isn't always happy-ever-after. Like the writers I admired, I choose not to shy away from difficult subjects and instead try to show that friendship and families can get you through the toughest of times. Life isn't always fair or easy, but that's all the more reason to make every day count . . . fix a smile on your face, dream big, work hard and go for it!

Cathy Cassidy worked as an editor and teacher before becoming a full-time writer. Her most recent book, *Lucky Star*, follows the massive success of *Dizzy*, *Indigo Blue*, *Driftwood*, *Scarlett* and *Sundae Girl*.

Make some mischief with Anne down at the farm

Anne came running in presently, her face sparkling with the delight of her orchard rovings; but, abashed at finding herself in the unexpected presence of a stranger, she halted confusedly inside the door. She certainly was an odd-looking little creature in the short, tight wincey dress she had worn from the asylum, below which her thin legs seemed ungracefully long. Her freckles were more numerous and obtrusive than ever; the wind had ruffled her hatless hair into over-brilliant disorder; it had never looked redder than at that moment.

'Well, they didn't pick you for your looks, that's sure and certain,' was Mrs Rachel Lynde's emphatic comment. Mrs Rachel was one of those delightful and popular people who pride themselves on speaking their mind without fear or favour. 'She's terrible skinny and homely, Marilla. Come here, child, and let me have a look at you. Lawful heart, did anyone ever see such freckles? And hair as red as carrots! Come here, child, I say.'

Anne 'came there', but not exactly as Mrs Rachel expected. With one bound she crossed the kitchen floor and stood before Mrs Rachel, her face scarlet with anger, her lips quivering, and her whole slender form trembling from head to foot.

'I hate you,' she cried in a choked voice, stamping her foot on the floor. 'I hate you – I hate you – I hate you –' a louder stamp with each assertion of hatred. 'How dare you call me skinny and ugly? How dare you say I'm freckled and red-headed? You are a rude, impolite, unfeeling woman!'

'Anne!' exclaimed Marilla in consternation.

But Anne continued to face Mrs Rachel undauntedly, head up, eyes blazing, hands clenched, passionate indignation exhaling from her like an atmosphere.

'How dare you say such things about me?' she repeated vehemently. 'How would you like to have such things said about you? How would you like to be told that you are fat and clumsy and probably hadn't a spark of imagination in you? I don't care if I do hurt your feelings by saying so! I hope I hurt them. You have hurt mine worse than they were ever hurt before even by Mrs Thomas' intoxicated husband. And I'll *never* forgive you for it, never, never!'

Stamp! Stamp!

'Did anybody ever see such a temper!' exclaimed the horrified Mrs Rachel.

'Anne, go to your room and stay there until I come up,' said Marilla, recovering her powers of speech with difficulty.

Anne, bursting into tears, rushed to the hall door, slammed it until the tins on the porch wall outside rattled in sympathy, and fled through the hall and up the stairs like a whirlwind. A subdued slam above told that the door of the east gable had been shut with equal vehemence.

'Well, I don't envy you your job bringing *that* up, Marilla,' said Mrs Rachel with unspeakable solemnity.

Who was your favourite author when you were little?

Good point. Well made. Erm . . . I'm not entirely surprised I have grown up as I have because my early reading was weird encyclopedias. Not little books about fluffy rabbits in mittens. 'Pictorial History' I think they were called. And it has given me a very peculiar view of the world indeed.

One of the history bits was about the boys of Sparta being so brave (or remarkably stupid, some might say). Two of them went out and stole a couple of chickens because they didn't get fed at home and then the farmer came along and said (in Latin probably), 'Oi, you two-us, have you seeneth my chicken-us?' They said, 'No nottus, mate-us!'

And because their mum had said, 'Come home with your shield or on it,' they stood there while the chickens pecked them underneath their togas, and they didn't moan or anything. And they went home with the chickens and one of them died from chicken injuries.

And you wonder why I think that boys are odd.

Oh, and the only other books were about girls becoming airhostesses or nurses (Florrie Nightingale and so on).

The nice thing is I don't blame my parents. I just look at them and think . . . erm, are you mad?

What type of books do you like to read today?

For escapey dapeys I read detective books. I luuurve Raymond Chandler and Aggie Christie. I am always reading a comedy book at the same time, though. I've got *The Bumper Book of Fads and Crazes* and a naughty slang book at the moment. And *Just William* and a P. G. Wodehouse for backup. I do, and this is true, read all the classics if I want to feel cosy and happy.

I think Richmal Compton is far and away one of the funniest writers I have read.

What is your favourite film/music/food?

Oh, shut up about films. I once said to a group of friends some years ago when they said, 'Let's go to the late night cinema,' I said, 'No, I hate films! They are WUBBISH.' And they have never let me forget it. I don't actually think all films are wubbish. I cried for about forty years over Christmas at *Gone with the Wind*.

However, on the whole, I like more live things. I like going to the theatre A LOT. My mate was in a play this weekend and he said I had to come because he was wearing a special comedy moustache and he would do secret moustache twitch that only I would know about. And he did and it made me laugh so much I had to go and pay an emergency piddly-diddly department visit.

I *luurve* all food. Apart from slimy things. I don't like slimy cold soups or slimy-type slimy creatures. Oh, of course you know what I mean. Also, because I am from Yorkshire, I do like comedy puddings – spotty dick for instance.

I like loads of music and I like going to gigs. I am not a big fan of the 'moaning on' sort of stuff. I get up and jig about in the mornings to the radio. Not in the nuddypants. Well, rarely in the nuddypants.

What do you see yourself doing in years to come?

Being Empress of the Universe. But it's only a little private dream I have.

What books do you think will become the classics of the future?

Blimey. I suppose it's a bit swotty-knickers to say my own!!

No, not really, I am thrilled as a thrilled person that people like them. And that is a fact. I wonder if people ever do sit down and think, *Do you know what? I am going to write a classic today, I can feel one coming on . . .*

I don't think even Billy Shakespeare would have thought that. He probably thought, *Blimey, thank goodness they like it. What shall I write next? I know, something a bit depressing . . . I shall call it* Macuseless.

Who is your all-time hero?

I don't know I haven't had all my time yet (I hope). But I have some faves – an odd collection really (I don't know what it suggests about my personality).

My grandfather was a hero to me even though he did say about my Irish dancing: 'She's a good turn but she's on too long.'

My priest was a big hero of mine. On the bigger stage the Dalai Lama, Archbishes of Canterbury and York (I wrote to the Archbish of Canterbury and told him I was worried that he didn't have enough mates. He wrote back and said it was OK he had mates who were not 'beardist' and thanked me for my concern.), Gordon Smith the psychic barber, my mum and sis, Sophia Loren.

Goodnight and thank you.
Georgia Nicolson

Georgia Nicolson is the creation of Louise Rennison, bestselling and award-winning author of the angst-filled *Confessions of Georgia Nicolson*, published by HarperCollins. Louise lives in Brighton, the San Francisco of England (apart from the sun, Americans, the Golden Gate Bridge and earthquakes).

E. Nesbit

Name Edith Nesbit; better known as E. Nesbit (as author); Daisy (as nickname)

Born 15 August 1858 in London

Died 4 May 1924 in Kent

Nationality British

Lived all over Europe during her childhood, then mainly in Kent and London as a teenager and adult.

Married to Hubert Bland, 1880–1914, and to Thomas Tucker, 1917 onwards.

Children Paul, Iris and Fabian (Bland) were her own children, but she brought up Hubert Bland's other children, Rosamund and John, also as her own.

Career At the age of seventeen she began to write poems and short stories for magazines and then went on to write children's stories.

Hobbies Both Edith and her husband Hubert Bland were actively involved in politics and were founder members of the Fabian Society – a socialist group which led to the formation of the Labour Party.

Famous for some of the best-known books for children, including *The Story of the Treasure Seekers* (published in 1898), *Five Children and It* (1902) and *The Railway Children* (1906).

*Step into Sara's shoes as fate
determines her fortune . . .*

'Put down your doll,' said Miss Minchin. 'What do you
mean by bringing her here?'

'No,' Sara answered. 'I will not put her down. She is all I have.
My papa gave her to me.'

She had always made Miss Minchin feel secretly
uncomfortable, and she did so now. She did not speak with
rudeness so much as with a cold steadiness with which Miss
Minchin felt it difficult to cope – perhaps because she knew
she was doing a heartless and inhuman thing.

'You will have no time for dolls in future,' she said. 'You will
have to work and improve yourself and make yourself useful.'

Sara kept her big, strange eyes fixed on her, and said not a
word.

'Everything will be very different now,' Miss Minchin went
on. 'I suppose Miss Amelia has explained matters to you.'

'Yes,' answered Sara. 'My papa is dead. He left me no money.
I am quite poor.'

'You are a beggar,' said Miss Minchin, her temper rising at the
recollection of what all this meant. 'It appears that you have no
relations and no home, and no one to take care of you.'

For a moment the thin, pale little face twitched, but Sara
again said nothing.

'What are you staring at?' demanded Miss Minchin sharply. 'Are you so stupid that you cannot understand? I tell you that you are quite alone in the world, and have no one to do anything for you, unless I choose to keep you here out of charity.'

'I understand,' answered Sara, in a low tone; and there was a sound as if she had gulped down something which rose in her throat. 'I understand.'

'That doll,' cried Miss Minchin, pointing to the splendid birthday gift seated near – 'that ridiculous doll, with all her nonsensical, extravagant things – I actually paid the bill for her!'

Sara turned her head toward the chair.

'The Last Doll,' she said. 'The Last Doll.' And her little mournful voice had an odd sound.

'The Last Doll, indeed!' said Miss Minchin. 'And she is mine, not yours. Everything you own is mine.'

'Please take it away from me, then,' said Sara. 'I do not want it.'

If she had cried and sobbed and seemed frightened, Miss Minchin might almost have had more patience with her. She was a woman who liked to domineer and feel her power, and as she looked at Sara's pale little steadfast face and heard her proud little voice, she quite felt as if her might was being set at naught.

Classic Connections

If you like friends and family stories then you'll want to read these books.

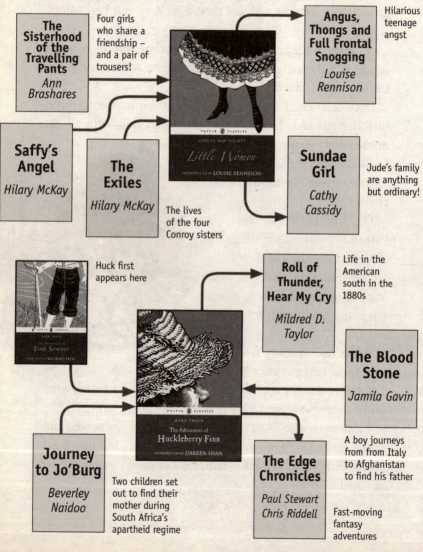

The Sisterhood of the Travelling Pants
Ann Brashares

Four girls who share a friendship – and a pair of trousers!

Angus, Thongs and Full Frontal Snogging
Louise Rennison

Hilarious teenage angst

Saffy's Angel
Hilary McKay

The Exiles
Hilary McKay

The lives of the four Conroy sisters

Sundae Girl
Cathy Cassidy

Jude's family are anything but ordinary!

Huck first appears here

Roll of Thunder, Hear My Cry
Mildred D. Taylor

Life in the American south in the 1880s

The Blood Stone
Jamila Gavin

Journey to Jo'Burg
Beverley Naidoo

Two children set out to find their mother during South Africa's apartheid regime

The Edge Chronicles
Paul Stewart
Chris Riddell

A boy journeys from from Italy to Afghanistan to find his father

Fast-moving fantasy adventures

A true tale of a cruel childhood

Chinese Cinderella
Adeline Yen Mah

The Princess Diaries
Meg Cabot

Mia, a modern princess, is at school in New York

Journey to the River Sea
Eva Ibbotson

Orphan Maia's journey to South America

Millions
Frank Cottrel Boyce

Two boys coping with great sadness

Pollyanna
Eleanor H. Porter

The Railway Children
E. Nesbit

Heidi
Johanna Spyri

His Dark Materials trilogy
Philip Pullman

Step into another world

The Story of Tracy Beaker
Jacqueline Wilson

Boy Overboard
Morris Gleitzman

Two children leave Afghanistan for a new life in Australia and are parted from their parents

Step by Wicked Step
Anne Fine

Skellig
David Almond

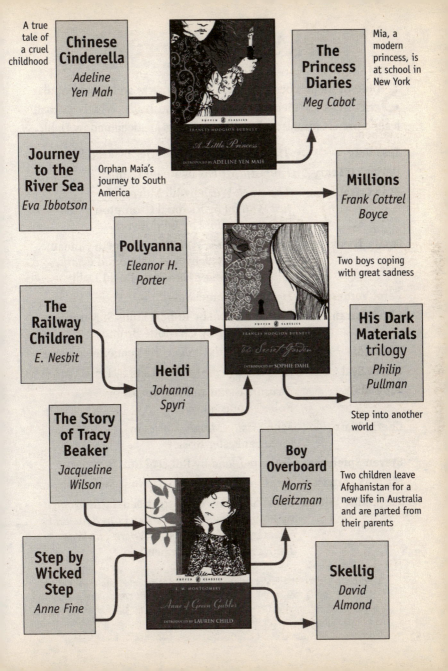

Celebrity Favourites

Some of today's best-loved children's writers and most-popular celebrities list their favourite childhood reads. Which football legend prefers pirates and which presenters are delighted by Dahl?

Tess Daly	*The Folk of the Faraway Tree* by Enid Blyton
Dermot O'Leary	*Fantastic Mr Fox* by Roald Dahl
Ellie Crisell	*The Worst Witch* by Jill Murphy, *Just William* by Richmal Crompton and *The Famous Five* by Enid Blyton
Jamie Theakston	*The Wind in the Willows* by Kenneth Grahame, *Winnie-the-Pooh* by A. A. Milne and *Charlie and the Chocolate Factory* by Roald Dahl
Carol Vorderman	*Heidi* by Johanna Spyri
Chris Tarrant	*Treasure Island* by Robert Louis Stevenson and *Jane Eyre* by Charlotte Brontë
Bill Oddie	*The Wind in the Willows* by Kenneth Grahame
Meera Syal	*Alice Through the Looking-Glass* by Lewis Carroll
Tony Blair	*Treasure Island* and *Kidnapped* by Robert Louis Stevenson
Cherie Blair	*Milly-Molly-Mandy Stories* by Joyce Lankester Brisley
Steven Spielberg	*Treasure Island* by Robert Louis Stevenson
Sir Alex Ferguson	*Treasure Island* by Robert Louis Stevenson
Jacqueline Wilson	*Ballet Shoes* by Noel Streatfeild, *Little Women* by Louisa May Alcott, *Family From One End Street* by Eve Garnett and *Where The Wild Things Are* by Maurice Sendak

Northern Lights, the first part of His Dark Materials by Philip Pullman, was crowned the Carnegie of Carnegies, the world's most prestigious children's literary award, having been voted the very best of all the Carnegie Medal winners since the award began in 1937.

Eoin Colfer	*The Adventures of Huckleberry Finn* by Mark Twain, *Stig of the Dump* by Clive King and *The Hobbit* by J. R. R. Tolkien
Philip Pullman	*The Magic Pudding* by Norman Lindsay and *Finn Family Moomintroll* by Tove Jansson
Morris Gleitzman	*Just William* by Richmal Crompton
J. K. Rowling	*The Story of the Treasure-Seekers* by E. Nesbit
Michael Morpurgo	*Just So Stories* by Rudyard Kipling
Cornelia Funke	*The Adventures of Tom Sawyer* by Mark Twain, *The BFG* by Roald Dahl, *Just So Stories* by Rudyard Kipling, *Peter Pan* by J. M. Barrie and *The Wizard of Oz* by L. Frank Baum
Michael Rosen	*Each Peach Pear Plum* by Janet and Allan Ahlberg, *In the Night Kitchen* by Maurice Sendak and *Alice's Adventures in Wonderland* by Lewis Carroll
David Almond	*The Adventures of Tom Sawyer* by Mark Twain, *Charlotte's Web* by E. B. White and *The Adventures of King Arthur* by Roger Lancelyn Green
Dick King-Smith	*Tarka the Otter* by Henry Williamson
Paul Stewart	*The Phantom Tollbooth* by Norton Juster
Chris Riddell	*The Shrinking of Treehorn* by Florence Parry Heidi, *The Incredible Adventures of Professor Branestawm* by Norman Hunter and *Alice's Adventures in Wonderland* by Lewis Carroll

Britain's favourite book is *The Lord of the Rings* by J. R. R. Tolkien. It came out top in two surveys – one in 1997 conducted by Waterstone's and the second in 2003 by BBC television. And in 2007 it was chosen by the public in a survey to coincide with the 10th anniversary of World Book Day as 'one of the ten books the nation can't live without'.

Meg – the sweet-tempered one.
Jo – the smart one. Beth – the shy one.
Amy – the sassy one.

'You know the reason Mother proposed not having any presents this Christmas was because it is going to be a hard winter for everyone; and she thinks we ought not to spend money for pleasure when our men are suffering so in the army. We can't do much, but we can make our little sacrifices, and ought to do it gladly. But I am afraid I don't'; and Meg shook her head, and she thought regretfully of all the pretty things she wanted.

'But I don't think the little we should spend would do any good. We've each got a dollar, and the army wouldn't be much helped by our giving that. I agree not to expect anything from Mother or you, but I do want to buy *Undine and Sintram* for myself; I've wanted it *so* long,' said Jo, who was a bookworm.

'I planned to spend mine on new music,' said Beth, with a little sigh, which no one heard but the hearthbrush and kettle-holder.

'I shall get a nice box of Faber's drawing pencils; I really need them,' said Amy, decidedly.

'Mother didn't say anything about our money, and she won't wish us to give up everything. Let's each buy what we want, and have a little fun; I'm sure we work hard enough to earn it,' cried

Jo, examining the heels of her shoes in a gentlemanly manner.

'I know *I* do – teaching those tiresome children nearly all day when I am longing to enjoy myself at home,' began Meg, in the complaining tone again.

'You don't have half such a hard time as I do,' said Jo. 'How would you like to be shut up for hours with a nervous, fussy old lady, who keeps you trotting, is never satisfied, and worries you till you're ready to fly out of the window or cry?'

'It's naughty to fret; but I do think washing dishes and keeping things tidy is the worst work in the world. It makes me cross; and my hands get so stiff, I can't practise well at all'; and Beth looked at her rough hands with a sigh that anyone could hear that time.

'I don't believe any of you suffer as I do,' cried Amy; 'for you don't have to go to school with impertinent girls, who plague you if you don't know your lessons, and laugh at your dresses, and label your father if he isn't rich, and insult you when your nose isn't nice.'

'If you mean *libel*, I'd say so, and not talk about *labels*, as if Papa was a pickle-bottle,' advised Jo, laughing.

'I know what I mean, and you needn't be *statirical* about it. It's proper to use good words, and improve your *vocabulary*,' returned Amy, with dignity.

'Don't peck at one another, children. Don't you wish we had the money Papa lost when we were little, Jo? Dear me! how happy and good we'd be, if we had no worries!' said Meg, who could remember better times.

1983

1953

1983

1994

2008

Puffin Classics then and now!

1951

From cover to cover . . .

Here are the covers of some early and recent Puffin editions of *The Secret Garden* and *The Adventures of Huckleberry Finn*. Which cover style do you like the best?

1982

1994

2008

Trivia

Best of friends

Tom Sawyer has the starring role in Mark Twain's *The Adventures of Tom Sawyer*, but he also appears in *The Adventures of Huckleberry Finn*. And Huck Finn returns the favour by appearing in *The Adventures of Tom Sawyer* too. The pair get together again in *Tom Sawyer, Abroad* and *Tom Sawyer, Detective*.

True *or* **false?**
Frances Hodgson Burnett's *A Little Princess* was originally entitled *Sara Crewe: or, What happened at Miss Minchin's boarding school.*

Who *said* **what?**

Can you match the famous phrase with the character who said it?

I feel pretty nearly perfectly happy. **1**

. . . please, sir, I want some more. **2**

I'll teach you how to jump on the wind's back, and then away we go. **5**

What is the use of a book . . . without pictures or conversation? **3**

Humbug! **4**

Peter
Peter Pan

Anne Shirley
Anne of Green Gables

Alice
Alice in Wonderland

Ebenezer Scrooge
A Christmas Carol

Oliver
Oliver Twist

Spot the Puffin Classic

Meg, Jo, Beth and Amy are the famous March sisters from *Little Women*. Can you match these groups of characters with their books?

- *A Christmas Carol*
- *The Wind in the Willows*
- *The Secret Garden*
- *King Arthur and his Knights of the Round Table*
- *Peter Pan*
- *Black Beauty*

Ginger and Merrylegs

Mary Lennox, Colin Craven and Dickon Sowerby

Mole, Ratty, Toad and Badger

Ebenezer Scrooge, Marley and Tiny Tim

Sir Launcelot, Queen Guinivere and Sir Galahad

Captain Hook and the Lost Boys

Some Yorkshire words in *The Secret Garden*

aye – yes

clemmin' – going hungry

graidely (sometimes spelt **gradely**) – good or very good

lass – girl or young woman

moithered (sometimes spelt **mithered**) – bothered, annoyed

mun(not) – must (not)

nesh – weak, delicate

nowt – nothing

wick – alive, lively

Did you know . . . ?

Anne of Green Gables was rejected by four publishers. The book's author – L. M. Montgomery – became so fed up that she packed it away in a hatbox for a year. When it was finally published, it was a huge success. And one of its greatest fans was author Mark Twain.

Open the door and step into the garden
with Mary . . .

Mary Lennox had heard a great deal about Magic in her Ayah's stories, and she always said what happened almost at that moment was Magic.

One of the nice little gusts of wind rushed down the walk, and it was a stronger one than the rest. It was strong enough to wave the branches of the trees, and it was more than strong enough to sway the trailing sprays of untrimmed ivy hanging from the wall. Mary had stepped close to the robin, and suddenly the gust of wind swung aside some loose ivy trails, and more suddenly still she jumped towards it and caught it in her hand. This she did because she had seen something under it – a round knob which had been covered by the leaves hanging over it. It was the knob of a door.

She put her hands under the leaves and began to pull and push them aside. Thick as the ivy hung, it nearly all was a loose and swinging curtain, though some had crept over wood and iron. Mary's heart began to thump and her hands to shake a little in her delight and excitement. The robin kept singing and twittering away and tilting his head on one side, as if he were as excited as she was. What was this under her hands which was square and made of iron and which her fingers found a hole in?

It was the lock of the door which had been closed ten years, and she put her hand in her pocket, drew out the key, and found it fitted the keyhole. She put the key in and turned it. It took two hands to do it, but it did turn.

And then she took a long breath and looked behind her up the long walk to see if anyone was coming. No one was coming. No one ever did come, it seemed, and she took another long breath, because she could not help it, and she held back the swinging curtain of ivy and pushed back the door which opened slowly – slowly. Then she slipped through it, and shut it behind her, and stood with her back against it, looking about her and breathing quite fast with excitement, and wonder, and delight. She was standing *inside* the secret garden.

AND

If you like stories about ....

FRIENDS & FAMILY

then you should also try these classic stories ...

- ☐ *Good Wives* LOUISA MAY ALCOTT
- *Pride and Prejudice* JANE AUSTEN ☐
- ☐ *What Katy Did* SUSAN COOLIDGE
- *The Family from One End Street* EVE GARNETT ☐
- ☐ *Bridge to Terabithia* KATHERINE PATERSON
- *Pollyanna* ELEANOR H. PORTER ☐
- ☐ *Swallows and Amazons* ARTHUR RANSOME
- *Heidi* JOHANNA SPYRI ☐
- ☐ *Roll of Thunder, Hear My Cry* MILDRED D. TAYLOR
- *The Prince and the Pauper* MARK TWAIN ☐
- ☐ *Mary Poppins* P. L. TRAVERS
- *The Swiss Family Robinson* J. D. WYSS ☐

Tick if you've read it!

ROGER LANCELYN GREEN
King Arthur
and his Knights of the Round Table
INTRODUCED BY DAVID ALMOND

MARK TWAIN
The Adventures of
Tom Sawyer
INTRODUCED BY RICHARD PECK

JULES VERNE
JOURNEY to the
CENTRE of the EARTH
INTRODUCED BY DIANA WYNNE JONES

CHARLES DICKENS
Oliver Twist
INTRODUCED BY GARETH NIX

ROBERT LOUIS STEVENSON
Treasure Island
INTRODUCED BY EOIN COLFER

PART THREE

THE BEST
Heroes & Danger
EVER WRITTEN

As a child I was only interested in reading books in which the central character carried a sword, preferably one with magic powers that could disembowel scores of non-heroes with one swipe. If a hero isn't able to wade into battle and set about himself with gusto, his blade dripping with blood, he has no right to call himself a hero. Not for me sporting heroes or boring explorers, and certainly no one contemporary. Heroes have to have swords!

I loved adventure stories, stories that would take me out of my humdrum world of school and parents and *Coronation Street* and grey skies. I lost myself in the myths and legends of ancient Greece and Rome, or stories of the Norse gods. Achilles, now there was a

hero. Perseus, Jason, Theseus . . . Thor! (Admittedly he had a war hammer rather than a sword, and was more of a god than a hero, but, boy, could he do some damage). It didn't end with myths and legends, though, there were the fantasy books of Tolkien, pirate stories, historical novels set in the middle ages, and of course stories about Robin Hood and King Arthur's knights.

I don't know what it is about swords. We're genetically programmed to think they're cool. Show any small boy a stick and he will pick it up and try to hit someone with it. It needn't be a stick, though; anything vaguely stick-shaped will stand in as a sword – wooden spoons, rulers, Lego, even cheese strings. I was no different; I would play for hours, using the arm of a sofa as a horse, riding into battle and decapitating the enemy – knights, Napoleonic infantry, orcs . . . I wasn't fussy.

Of course there's no room in the modern world for real heroes – with swords. I've been in danger a few times, and on no occasion would things have been any easier if I'd been accompanied by a mighty warrior with a battle axe. The closest I ever came to death, for instance, was in a road accident, and I notice they don't equip AA men with swords. I suppose there were times at school when it would have been nice to have had Achilles at my side, but in the end most problems are much better sorted out with a quiet, sensible chat than with a magic sword. Let's face it, if Achilles showed up today he'd probably be arrested as a dangerous psychopath.

Charlie Higson is a well-known writer of screenplays and adult thriller novels. He's also a performer and co-creator of *The Fast Show*. He has written four bestselling novels about Young Bond – *SilverFin*, *Blood Fever*, *Double or Die* and *Hurricane Gold*.

Step up to the Round Table and join the Knights of the Realm

'Well, put the sword back into the anvil, and let us see you draw it out,' commanded Sir Ector.

'That's easily done,' said Arthur, puzzled by all this trouble over a sword, and he set it back easily into the anvil.

Then Sir Kay seized it by the hilt and pulled his hardest: but struggle and strain as he might, he could not move it by a hair's breadth. Sir Ector tried also, but with no better success.

'Pull it out,' he said to Arthur.

And Arthur, more and more bewildered, put his hand to the hilt and drew forth the sword as if out of a well-greased scabbard.

'Now,' said Sir Ector, kneeling before Arthur and bowing his head in reverence, 'I understand that you and none other are the true-born King of this land.'

'Why? Oh, why is it I? Why do you kneel to me, my father?' cried Arthur.

'It is God's will that whoso might draw forth the sword out of the stone and out of the anvil is the true-born King of Britain,' said Sir Ector. 'Moreover, though I love you well, you are no son of mine. For Merlin brought you to me when you were a small child, and bade me bring you up as my own son!'

'Then if I am indeed King,' said Arthur, bowing his head over the cross-hilt of the sword, 'I hereby pledge myself to the service of God and of my people, to the righting of wrongs, to the driving-out of evil, to the bringing of peace and plenty to my land . . . Good sir, you have been as a father to me since ever I can remember, be still near me with a father's love and

a father's counsel and advice . . . Kay, my foster-brother, be you seneschal over all my lands and a true knight of my court.'

After this they went to the Archbishop and told him all. But the knights and barons were filled with rage and jealousy, and refused to believe that Arthur was the trueborn King. So the choice was put off until Easter; and at Easter once more until Whitsun, or Pentecost as it then was called: but still, though many kings and knights came to try their strength, Arthur alone could pull out the sword.

Then all the people cried: 'Arthur! We will have Arthur! By God's will he is our King! God save King Arthur!' And they knelt down before him, the noble and the humble together, the rich and the poor, and cried him mercy for delaying him so long. And Arthur forgave them readily, and kneeling down himself he gave the wondrous sword to the Archbishop and received of him the high and holy order of Knighthood. And then came all the earls and the barons, the knights and squires, and did homage to Arthur, swearing to serve and obey him as was their duty.

King Arthur now gathered together all the hosts of Britain, and with the pick of the older knights who had served his father and the younger knights whose chief desire was to show their courage and loyalty, he set out to do battle with the Saxons and to punish all those thieves and robbers who had ravaged the land for many years, doing cruel and shameful deeds.

Before long he had brought peace and safety to the southern parts of Britain, making his capital at Camelot. But the other kings who ruled then in and about Britain – the Kings of Orkney and Lothian, of Gwynedd and Powys, of Gorre and Garloth – grew jealous of this unknown boy who was calling himself King of all Britain, and sent word that they were coming to visit him with gifts – but that their gifts would be given with sharp swords between the head and shoulders.

Then Merlin came suddenly to Arthur and led him to the city of Caerleon in South Wales, into a strong tower well provisioned for a siege. The hostile kings came also to Caerleon and surrounded the tower: but they could not break in, to kill Arthur and his faithful followers.

Merlin came out of the tower after fifteen days, stood upon the steps in the gateway and asked all the angry kings and knights why they came in arms against King Arthur.

'Why have you made that boy, that Arthur, our King?' they shouted.

'Be silent and listen, all of you!' commanded Merlin, and a great quiet fell upon all who were gathered together, an awe and a wonder as the good enchanter spoke to them.

'I will tell you of wondrous things,' he said.

Classics Quiz
Part Three

Answer the questions on all four Classics Quiz pages and enter our competition to win a 12-copy set of Puffin Classics! *Details of how to send in your answers are on page 101.*

1 When Oliver Twist first leaves the workhouse, what job does he do?
a) Chimney sweep
b) Newspaper seller
c) Road sweeper
d) Undertaker's assistant

2 Which author created Long John Silver?
a) Frances Hodgson Burnett
b) L. Frank Baum
c) Robert Louis Stevenson
d) L. M. Montgomery

3 From which country does Professor Lidenbrock begin his journey to the centre of the earth?
a) Norway
b) Iceland
c) Sweden
d) Denmark

4 Which character lived at 221b Baker Street?
a) Sherlock Holmes
b) Dr Frankenstein
c) James Bond
d) Jane Eyre

5 In *Twenty Thousand Leagues Under the Sea*, who was the captain of the *Nautilus*?
a) Captain Blythe
b) Captain Cook
c) Captain Nemo
d) Captain Smollett

6 In *Tom's Midnight Garden*, Tom has to stay with his aunt and uncle because his brother has:
a) chicken pox
b) scarlet fever
c) mumps
d) measles

7 Name the famous book that begins with the line: *Marley was dead: to begin with. There is no doubt whatever about that.*
a) *Treasure Island*
b) *A Christmas Carol*
c) *Robinson Crusoe*
d) *Oliver Twist*

8 What is the name of King Arthur's realm?
a) London
b) Lille
c) Logres
d) Lyon

An interview with

Darren Shan

Who was your favourite author as a child?
Probably Enid Blyton – I loved The Famous Five and The Secret Seven books! But my favourite book was *The Secret Garden* by Frances Hodgson Burnett.

What do you like to read today?
A mix of adult's and children's books. On the children's side I read Eoin Colfer, Anthony Horowitz, J. K. Rowling, Marcus Sedgwick and a variety of others, though my favourite is Philip Pullman.

What made you decide to become a writer?
I've always loved making up stories – it's as simple as that!

Where do you get your ideas from?

The same place as everybody else – life and all that I experience.

If you weren't a writer, what do you think you'd be?

I'd probably be working in something to do with computers, but even if I wasn't getting paid to write, I would still be writing. For me there was never an option NOT to write – it was simply a question of whether I could get paid doing it. If I couldn't, I'd support myself with another job, but writing would still be the most important thing in my life.

What's your favourite film/music/food?

The Wizard of Oz is one of my fave films. The Smiths were my favourite band as a teenager. I like all types of food, though I do have a soft spot for sweet and sour chicken, or fish and chips!

What books (apart from your own, of course!) do you think will become the classics of the future?

I think Philip Pullman's His Dark Materials trilogy will be read for a long time to come.

Who is your all-time hero?

Stephen King. He writes great books, he works hard, and *Salem's Lot* opened my eyes to what a really good, modern horror story could do.

Darren Shan is the award-winning author of The Saga of Darren Shan series and The Demonata series, both published by HarperCollins.

Escape with Tom and a terrible secret . . .

When they reached the haunted house, there was something so weird and grisly about the dead silence that reigned there under the baking sun, and something so depressing about the loneliness and desolation of the place, that they were afraid, for a moment, to venture in. Then they crept to the door and took a trembling peep. They saw a weed-grown, floorless room, unplastered, an ancient fire-place, vacant windows, a ruinous staircase; and here, there, and everywhere, hung ragged and abandoned cobwebs. They presently entered softly, with quickened pulses, talking in whispers, ears alert to catch the slightest sound, and muscles tense and ready for instant retreat.

In a little while familiarity modified their fears, and they gave the place a critical and interested examination, rather admiring their own boldness, and wondering at it, too. Next they wanted to look upstairs. This was something like cutting off retreat, but they got to daring each other, and of course there could be but one result – they threw their tools into a corner and made the ascent. Up there were the same signs of decay. In one corner they found a closet that promised mystery, but the promise was a fraud – there was nothing in it. Their courage was up now, and well in hand.

They were about to go down and begin
work when – 'Sht!' said Tom.

'What is it?' whispered Huck, blanching with fright.

'Sh! There! Hear it?'

'Yes! Oh, my! Let's run!'

'Keep still! Don't you budge! They're coming right towards
the door.'

The boys stretched themselves upon the floor with their eyes
to knot-holes in the planking, and lay waiting in a misery of
fear.

'They've stopped – No – coming – Here they are. Don't
whisper another word, Huck. My goodness, I wish I was out
of this!'

Classic Connections

If you enjoy the fast and furious adventure stories of today, such as those of Eoin Colfer's **Artemis Fowl**, young James Bond by Charlie Higson in **SilverFin** and more, or Alex Rider's adventures by Anthony Horowitz that began in **Stormbreaker**, you will devour these great stories.

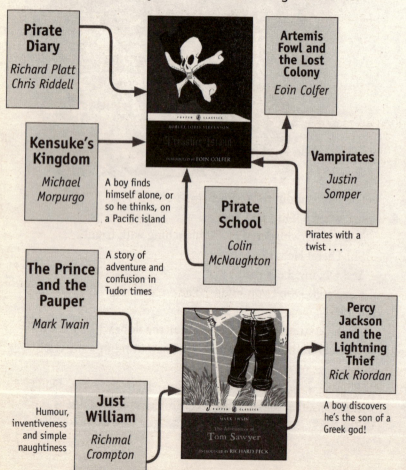

Pirate Diary

Richard Platt
Chris Riddell

Artemis Fowl and the Lost Colony

Eoin Colfer

Kensuke's Kingdom

Michael Morpurgo

A boy finds himself alone, or so he thinks, on a Pacific island

Pirate School

Colin McNaughton

Vampirates

Justin Somper

Pirates with a twist . . .

A story of adventure and confusion in Tudor times

The Prince and the Pauper

Mark Twain

Percy Jackson and the Lightning Thief
Rick Riordan

A boy discovers he's the son of a Greek god!

Humour, inventiveness and simple naughtiness

Just William

Richmal Crompton

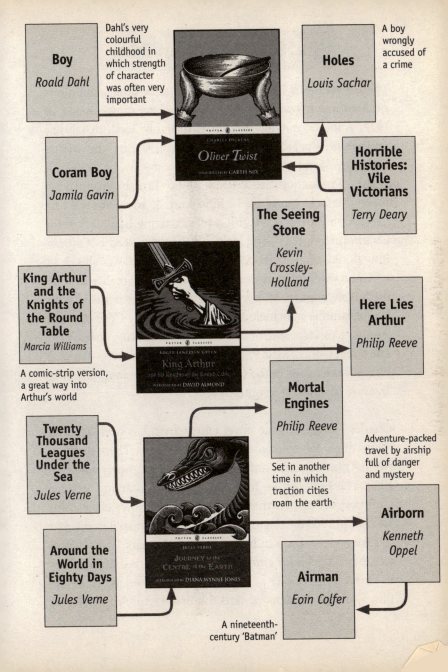

Boy

Roald Dahl

Dahl's very colourful childhood in which strength of character was often very important

Holes

Louis Sachar

A boy wrongly accused of a crime

CHARLES DICKENS

Oliver Twist

INTRODUCED BY GARTH NIX

Coram Boy

Jamila Gavin

Horrible Histories: Vile Victorians

Terry Deary

The Seeing Stone

Kevin Crossley-Holland

King Arthur and the Knights of the Round Table

Marcia Williams

A comic-strip version, a great way into Arthur's world

ROGER LANCELYN GREEN

King Arthur

and his Knights of the Round Table

INTRODUCED BY DAVID ALMOND

Here Lies Arthur

Philip Reeve

Mortal Engines

Philip Reeve

Set in another time in which traction cities roam the earth

Twenty Thousand Leagues Under the Sea

Jules Verne

JULES VERNE

JOURNEY to the CENTRE of the EARTH

INTRODUCED BY DIANA WYNNE JONES

Adventure-packed travel by airship full of danger and mystery

Airborn

Kenneth Oppel

Around the World in Eighty Days

Jules Verne

Airman

Eoin Colfer

A nineteenth-century 'Batman'

Puffin Classics on Film

There have been over fifty film and television adaptations of *Treasure Island*. The first was a silent movie made in 1912. Another notable version is a highly acclaimed black-and-white film made in America in 1934 by the Metro-Goldwyn-Meyer (MGM) production company. In 1950 Walt Disney Productions and RKO Radio British Productions made *Treasure Island* in Technicolour. It was Disney's first live-action movie. A television film, starring legendary actor Charlton Heston as Long John Silver, Oliver Reed as Captain Billy Bones and Christian Bale as Jim Hawkins, was shown in 1990 and was filmed in Devon, Cornwall and Jamaica. In 1996 the hugely popular *Muppet Treasure Island* was released, with lots of famous stars including Tim Curry, Billy Connolly and Jennifer Saunders and, of course, Kermit the Frog, Fozzie Bear, The Great Gonzo, Miss Piggy and more. And in 2003 *Treasure Planet* was released in the USA – a Disney animated version of *Treasure Island* – set in outer space!

Charles Dickens' classic novel *Oliver Twist* has been adapted many times for cinema, television and stage. There are over twenty film versions – the first was a silent movie made in 1909. The 1948 feature film by David Lean, starring Sir Alec Guinness as Fagin, is thought to be the definitive classic film version. In 1960 the stage musical *Oliver!* by Lionel Bart opened to rave reviews and ran in London for six years. The musical was then adapted for cinema in 1968 and starred Mark Lester as Oliver, Ron Moody as Fagin and Oliver Reed as Sikes. The film won the Academy Award for Best Picture in 1969 and is still among the best-loved classic films today. A new film was released in 2005, directed by award-winning film-maker Roman Polanski and starring Ben Kingsley as Fagin. Filmed in and around Prague, this version is over three hours long. More recently, in 2007, a new BBC adaptation, written by Sarah Phelps (one of Britain's top screenwriters) and with an all-star cast, was broadcast in five episodes over the Christmas holidays. And finally, *Oliver!* will return to London's West End in 2008, with the BBC's new show *I'd Do Anything* searching for new performers to play the roles of Nancy and Oliver.

The great sci-fi novel **Journey to the Centre of the Earth** has been made into several film versions. In 1959 it was a movie starring great actor James Mason. This version was noted for its special effects and nominated for three Academy Awards. And, coming soon, *Journey to the Centre of the Earth 3D* is a live-action remake with photo-real 3D technology (to be shown on special digital screens) due for release in summer 2008.

The Adventures of Tom Sawyer by Mark Twain has been filmed numerous times over the last century – from the first silent movie in 1907, to the first sound adaptation in 1930 made by Paramount Studios, to the Technicolour 1938 version, and the musical film adaptation in 1973. In 1995 Walt Disney Pictures produced a new movie under two names, *The Adventures of Tom and Huck* and just plain *Tom Sawyer*. Two years prior to this, the studio had released a film adapatation of *The Adventures of Huckleberry Finn*, which starred Elijah Wood (who went on to play Frodo in *The Lord of the Rings* trilogy).

Descend into the crater!

At that moment I distinctly heard an unfamiliar sound travelling through the granite walls, a sort of dull rumbling, like distant thunder. During this first half-hour of our walk, seeing no sign of the promised spring, my fears had been reawakened, but now my uncle explained the origin of the noise I could hear.

'Hans was not mistaken,' he said. 'What you can hear is the roar of a torrent.'

'A torrent?' I exclaimed.

'There's no doubt about it. A subterranean river is flowing around us.'

We hurried on, spurred on by hope. I no longer felt tired: this murmur of running water had already refreshed me. The torrent, which for some time had been over our heads, was now roaring and leaping along inside the lefthand wall. I kept passing my hand over the rock, hoping to find traces of moisture or damp, but in vain.

Another half-hour went by, and another mile and a quarter was covered.

It now became clear that the guide had gone no further during his absence. Guided by an instinct peculiar to mountaineers and water-diviners, he had as it were felt this torrent through the rock, but he had certainly not seen any of the precious liquid or quenched his thirst with it.

Soon indeed it became clear that, if we went on, we should be getting farther away from the stream, the noise of which was becoming fainter.

We turned back. Hans stopped at the exact spot where the torrent seemed closest to us. I sat near the wall, where I could hear the water rushing past me with extreme violence about two feet away. But a granite wall still separated us from it.

Without thinking, without asking myself whether there might not be some way of obtaining this water, I gave way to a feeling of despair.

Hans looked at me, and I thought I saw a smile appear on his lips.

He stood up and took the lamp. I followed him. He went up to the wall while I watched him. He pressed his ear against the dry stone and moved it slowly to and fro, listening intently. I realized that he was trying to find the exact spot where the noise of the torrent was loudest. He found that spot three feet up from the floor.

I was tremendously excited, though I scarcely dared to guess what the guide intended to do. But I understood and clasped my hands and hugged him when I saw him seize his pickaxe and attack the rock.

'We are saved,' I cried.

DID YOU KNOW…?

Some pirates really did have hooks as hands (like Cap'n Hook in *Peter Pan*) or wooden legs (like Long John Silver in *Treasure Island*), because they'd lost limbs in battle.

19 September is **International Talk Like a Pirate Day. Oooh-arrr, Jim lad!**

It was actually Robert Louis Stevenson's twelve-year-old stepson who gave him the idea for *Treasure Island*, when the two of them sketched a map of a treasure island together.

The traditional pirate flag of European and American pirates is called the Jolly Roger. But it isn't very jolly – it shows a skull and crossbones …

Dickensian London …

… was the biggest city in the world. In 1800, the population was about a million. By 1871, it was over three million.

… was horribly overcrowded. Poor people lived in dreadful, dirty, cramped conditions.

… was very smelly. There were no sewers and deadly diseases such as cholera were rife.

… wasn't a very nice place to live, especially if your name was Oliver Twist.

Pen names

Authors do not always publish books under their own names. Some use a pen name or pseudonym or *nom de plume* – fancy words that mean 'fictitious name'.

Pen name	Real name
Currer Bell	Charlotte Brontë
George Eliot	Mary Anne Evans
George Orwell	Eric Arthur Blair
J. K. Rowling	Joanne Rowling
Lewis Carroll	Charles Lutwidge Dodgson
Mark Twain	Samuel Langhorne Clemens

Trivia

Fantastic journeys

Intrepid travellers have yet to go on a Journey to the Centre of the Earth in real life, but they have been on many other amazing journeys.

Camelot

According to legend, Camelot was the beautiful castle where King Arthur and his Knights gathered round the equally legendary Round Table. But where was it? Many have linked Camelot with sites in England, Wales and Scotland. Some even think that it might have been at Windsor, the home of Queen Elizabeth II. But no one really knows . . .

Norwegian explorer Roald Amundsen became the first person to journey to the bottom of the Earth, when he reached the South Pole in 1911.

Edmund Hillary from New Zealand and Sherpa Tenzing Norgay from Nepal were the first to climb 8,848 metres (29,029 feet) to the top of the world. They reached the summit of Mount Everest in 1953.

A Journey to the Centre of the Earth would be about 6,367 km or 3,956 miles.

British adventurer Jason Lewis travelled around the world by human power alone. He cycled, hiked, rollerbladed, kayaked and travelled by pedal boat, dodging crocodiles and pirates on the way. He started out in 1994 and originally thought the journey might last three and a half years. But he ran into so many problems (including breaking both legs) that it eventually took thirteen years, two months and twenty-three days.

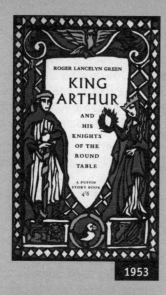

1953

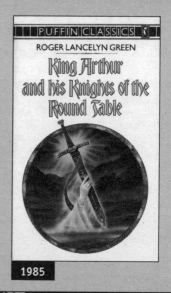

1985

1994

2008

Puffin Classics then and now!

MARK TWAIN
The Adventures of Tom Sawyer

1950

1994

PUFFIN CLASSICS

MARK TWAIN

The Adventures of

Tom Sawyer

INTRODUCED BY RICHARD PECK

2008

From cover to cover . . .

These Puffin editions of two great adventures – *King Arthur* and *Tom Sawyer* – have changed considerably from the 1950s!

Sneak into a den of villains and thieves with Oliver Twist . . .

'Stop thief! Stop thief!' There is a passion for hunting something deeply implanted in the human breast. One wretched breathless child, panting with exhaustion; terror in his looks; agony in his eyes; large drops of perspiration streaming down his face, strains every nerve to make head upon his pursuers; and as they follow on his track, and gain upon him every instant, they hail his decreasing strength with still louder shouts, and whoop and scream with joy. 'Stop thief!' Ay, stop him for God's sake, were it only in mercy!

Stopped at last! A clever blow. He is down upon the pavement; and the crowd eagerly gather round him: each new-comer jostling and struggling with the others to catch a glimpse. 'Stand aside!' – 'Give him a little air!' – 'Nonsense! he don't deserve it.' – 'Where's the gentleman?' – 'Here he is, coming down the street.' – 'Make room there for the gentleman!' – 'Is this the boy, sir!' – 'Yes.'

Oliver lay, covered with mud and dust, and bleeding from the mouth, looking wildly round upon the heap of faces that surrounded him, when the old gentleman was officiously dragged and pushed into the circle by the foremost of the pursuers.

'Yes,' said the gentleman, 'I am afraid it is the boy.'

'Afraid!' murmured the crowd. 'That's a good 'un!'

'Poor fellow!' said the gentleman, 'he has hurt himself.'

A police officer (who is generally the last person to arrive in such cases) at that moment made his way through the crowd, and seized Oliver by the collar.

'Come, get up,' said the man, roughly.

'It wasn't me indeed, sir. Indeed, indeed, it was two other boys,' said Oliver, clasping his hands passionately, and looking round. 'They are here somewhere.'

'Oh no, they ain't,' said the officer. He meant this to be ironical, but it was true besides; for the Dodger and Charley Bates had filed off down the first convenient court they came to. 'Come, get up!'

'Don't hurt him,' said the old gentleman, compassionately.

'Oh no, I won't hurt him,' replied the officer, tearing his jacket half off his back, in proof thereof. 'Come, I know you; it won't do. Will you stand upon your legs, you young devil?'

Oliver, who could hardly stand, made a shift to raise himself on his feet, and was at once lugged along the streets by the jacket-collar, at a rapid pace. The gentleman walked on with them by the officer's side; and as many of the crowd as could achieve the feat, got a little ahead, and stared back at Oliver from time to time.

The best books ever written

PENGUIN CLASSICS

SINCE 1946

If you've enjoyed any of the books in this guide, or just enjoy reading the very best from around the world, why not try a Penguin Classic? There are over 1,400 brilliant titles, containing everything from daring exploits, iconic heroes and heroines, and hilarious misadventures to fresh chances, exotic villains and heartbreaking friendships ...

The Best Animal & Beasts Ever Written

Monkey Wu Ch'eng-En
Prince Tripitaka is on a dangerous mission, accompanied by Pigsy, Sandy and the irrepressible trickster Monkey, who rides the clouds and holds the secrets of heaven and earth.

A Kestrel for a Knave Berry Hines
Billy Casper is a failure at school and unhappy at home, but discovers a new passion in life when he finds Kes, a kestrel hawk. How long can this happiness last?

The Complete Fables Aesop
In these fables, Aesop created a vivid cast of characters to demonstrate different aspects of human nature, including a wily fox outwitted by a quick-thinking cicada, and a tortoise triumphing over a self-confident hare.

Animal Farm George Orwell
When the downtrodden animals of Manor Farm overthrow their master, they imagine it is a life of freedom – until a cunning, ruthless group of pigs start to take control ...

The Best Friends & Family Ever Written

Of Mice and Men **John Steinbeck**
George and his simple-minded friend Lennie have nothing in the world except each other and a dream – but their hopes are doomed when Lennie becomes a victim of his own strength.

Three Men in a Boat **Jerome K. Jerome**
Martyrs to imaginary illness, J. and his friends decide that a jaunt up the Thames is the best cure, but troubles lie ahead with tow-ropes, unreliable weather-forecasts and tins of pineapple chunks . . .

Le Grand Meaulnes **Henri Alain-Fournier**
When Meaulnes first arrives at school, loyal Francois is captivated by his daring and charisma. But when Meaulnes starts to speak of a strange party at a mysterious house and a beautiful girl, it is clear that something has changed him forever.

Mapp and Lucia **E. F. Benson**
Emmeline Lucas is an arch-snob of the highest order – and in Miss Elizabeth Mapp, Lucia has met her match; between these two genteel society ladies, there is no plan too devious in order to win the battle for social supremacy.

The Best Heroes & Danger Ever Written

The 39 Steps **John Buchan**
Adventurer Richard Hannay is thoroughly bored with his London life – until a murder is committed in his flat. An obvious suspect for the police, Hannay must use all his wits to stay one step ahead of the game . . .

Casino Royale **Ian Fleming**
Bond – suave, chillingly ruthless and licensed to kill – is sent to a casino to disgrace the lethal Russian agent 'Le Chiffre' by ruining him – but his quarry is not content to go without a fight.

She **H. Rider Haggard**
On his twenty-fifth birthday, Leo Vincey and his companions travel to Zanzibar, and discover Ayesha, She-Who-Must-Be-Obeyed:

dictator, femme fatale, tyrant and beauty, who has been waiting for the true descendant of her murdered lover to arrive ...

The Day of the Triffids John Wyndham

Bill Masen wakes up to find civilization in chaos, and the triffids – huge, venomous, and carnivorous – having their day. Together with the beautiful novelist Josella Playton, he must battle the deadly plants – as well as the other human survivors.

The Best Make-Believe Ever Written

The Odyssey Homer

Odysseus faces a ten-year journey home after the Trojan War, and must do battle with shipwrecks, sirens, battles, monsters and the implacable enmity of the sea-god Poseidon to return to his wife and child.

Gulliver's Travels Jonathan Swift

Shipwrecked and cast adrift, Lemuel Gulliver wakes to find himself on Lilliput, an island inhabited by little people. His subsequent encounters – with crude giants, the philosophical Houyhnhnms and the brutish Yahoos – give Gulliver new, bitter insights into human behaviour.

Perfume Patrick Suskind

Jean-Baptiste Grenouille is abandoned on the filthy Paris streets as a child, but grows up to discover he has a sense of smell more powerful than any other human's. Soon, he is creating the most sublime fragrances – but there is one odour he cannot capture ...

Tales from the Thousand and One Nights

The tales told by Scheherazade over a thousand and one nights to delay her execution by the vengeful King depict a fabulous world of all-powerful sorcerers, jinns imprisoned in bottles and enchanting princesses.

Discover ... the best books ever written

penguinclassics.co.uk

Robert Louis Stevenson

Name Robert Louis Balfour Stevenson

Born 13 November 1850 in Edinburgh

Died 3 December 1894 in Apia in the Samoan Islands

Nationality Scottish

Lived all over the world, including Scotland, France, Switzerland, the US, Australia and the South Pacific.

Married to Fanny Osbourne, an American.

Children Two stepchildren, Lloyd and Belle.

Career His father wanted him to be an engineer, but he wasn't particularly scientific. He studied law at university but never practised, and instead went on to a brilliant career in literature and writing.

Hobbies Forced to stay indoors for long periods due to illness as a child, Robert Louis Stevenson spent his time making up stories and writing. Later he loved to travel and explore different countries.

Famous for *Treasure Island* which was the Harry Potter of its day! He wrote over fifty books, including poetry. *A Child's Garden of Verses* (1885) is regarded as one of the finest collection of poetry for children still in print today. He also wrote the infamous *Dr Jekyll and Mr Hyde*.

EXTRACT: Treasure Island

by Robert Louis Stevenson

Set sail aboard the Hispaniola, *with fearless Jim and the formidable Long John Silver!*

'And now, men,' said the captain, when all was sheeted home, 'has any one of you ever seen that land ahead?'

'I have, sir,' said Silver. 'I've watered there with a trader I was cook in.'

'The anchorage is on the south, behind an islet, I fancy?' asked the captain.

'Yes, sir; Skeleton Island they calls it. It were a main place for pirates once, and a hand we had on board knowed all their names for it. That hill to the nor'ard they calls the Fore-mast Hill; there are three hills in a row running south'ard – fore, main, and mizzen, sir. But the main – that's the big 'un with the cloud on it – they usually calls the Spy-glass, by reason of a look-out they kept when they was in the anchorage cleaning; for it's there they cleaned their ships, sir, asking your pardon.'

'I have a chart here,' says Captain Smollett. 'See if that's the place.'

Long John's eyes burned in his head as he took the chart; but, by the fresh look of the paper, I knew he was doomed to disappointment. This was not the map we found in Billy Bones's chest, but an accurate copy, complete in all things – names and heights and soundings – with the single exception of the red crosses and the written notes. Sharp as must have been his annoyance, Silver had the strength of mind to hide it.

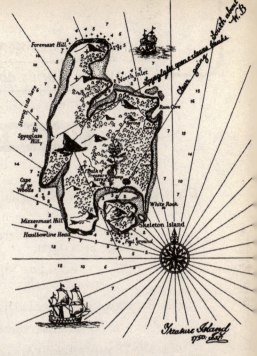

'Yes, sir,' said he, 'this is the spot to be sure; and very prettily drawn out. Who might have done that, I wonder? The pirates were too ignorant, I reckon. Ay, here it is: "Capt. Kidd's Anchorage" – just the name my shipmate called it. There's a strong current runs along the south, and then away nor'ard up the west coast. Right you was, sir,' says he, 'to haul your wind and keep the weather of the island. Leastways, if such was your intention as to enter and careen, and there ain't no better place for that in these waters.'

'Thank you, my man,' says Captain Smollett. 'I'll ask you, later on, to give us a help. You may go.'

I was surprised at the coolness with which John avowed his knowledge of the island; and I own I was half frightened when I saw him drawing nearer to myself. He did not know, to be sure, that I had overheard his council from the apple barrel, and yet I had, by this time, taken such a horror of his cruelty, duplicity, and power, that I could scarce conceal a shudder when he laid his hand upon my arm.

AND

If you like stories about ....

HEROES & DANGER

then you should also try these classic stories...

☐ *The Great Adventures of Sherlock Holmes*
ARTHUR CONAN DOYLE

*Sindbad the Sailor and Other Tales
from the Arabian Nights* N. J. DAWOOD ☐

☐ *Robinson Crusoe* DANIEL DEFOE

Great Expectations CHARLES DICKENS ☐

☐ *The Three Musketeers* ALEXANDRE DUMAS

Tales of the Greek Heroes
ROGER LANCELYN GREEN ☐

☐ *The Adventures of Robin Hood*
ROGER LANCELYN GREEN

Moonfleet JOHN MEADE FALKNER ☐

☐ *King Solomon's Mines* H. RIDER HAGGARD

Stig of the Dump CLIVE KING ☐

☐ *Kidnapped* ROBERT LOUIS STEVENSON

Around the World in Eighty Days JULES VERNE ☐

Tick if you've read it!

PART FOUR

THE BEST
Make-Believe
EVER WRITTEN

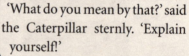

by Lewis Carroll

Join Alice in Wonderland, where nothing is quite as it seems…

The Caterpillar and Alice looked at each other for some time in silence: at last the Caterpillar took the hookah out of its mouth, and addressed her in a languid, sleepy voice.

'Who are *you*?' said the Caterpillar.

This was not an encouraging opening for a conversation. Alice replied, rather shyly, 'I – I hardly know, sir, just at present – at least I know who I *was* when I got up this morning, but I think I must have been changed several times since then.'

'What do you mean by that?' said the Caterpillar sternly. 'Explain yourself!'

'I can't explain *myself*, I'm afraid, sir,' said Alice, 'because I'm not myself, you see.'

'I don't see,' said the Caterpillar.

'I'm afraid I can't put it more clearly,' Alice replied very politely, 'for I can't understand it myself to begin with; and being so many different sizes in a day is very confusing.'

'It isn't,' said the Caterpillar.

'Well, perhaps you haven't found it so yet,' said Alice; 'but when you have to turn into a chrysalis – you will some day, you know – and then after that into a butterfly, I should think you'll feel it a little queer, won't you?'

'Not a bit,' said the Caterpillar.

'Well, perhaps your feelings may be different,' said Alice; 'all I know is, it would feel very queer to *me.*'

'You!' said the Caterpillar contemptuously. 'Who are *you*?'

Which brought them back again to the beginning of the conversation. Alice felt a little irritated at the Caterpillar's making such *very* short remarks, and she drew herself up and said, very gravely, 'I think you ought to tell me who *you* are, first.'

'Why?' said the Caterpillar.

Here was another puzzling question; and as Alice could not think of any good reason, and as the Caterpillar seemed to be in a *very* unpleasant state of mind, she turned away.

'Come back!' the Caterpillar called after her. 'I've something important to say!'

This sounded promising, certainly: Alice turned and came back again.

'Keep your temper,' said the Caterpillar.

'Is that all?' said Alice, swallowing down her anger as well as she could.

'No,' said the Caterpillar.

Alice thought she might as well wait, as she had nothing else to do, and perhaps after all it might tell her something worth hearing. For some minutes it puffed away without speaking, but at last it unfolded its arms, took the hookah out of its mouth again, and said, 'So you think you're changed, do you?'

by **Geraldine McCaughrean**

I can remember the family copy of *Peter Pan and Wendy* on the bookshelf when I was little: the feel of it, the smell, the pictures. Who read it to me? I don't recall. In fact I don't remember a time when I didn't know the story of the Boy-Who-Never-Grew-Up. My first theatre trip was to see *Peter Pan*. Forty years later, it was my daughter's too. So I am understandably fond of Peter.

Not that he's loveable. He's sulky, bad-tempered, self-centred and a show-off. But what a hero! And what a character! The Disney cartoon is pretty cute, but the original book is dark and scary, what with spiteful, jealous Tinker Bell, killer mermaids and murderous pirates. And did you know that if the Lost Boys grew too big, Peter *killed* them? Hardly cute. But then J. M. Barrie understood: what boy wants to be 'cute'?

Tinker Bell is the tiny – and very rude – fairy that causes mischief in *Peter Pan*. But did you know how she got her name? She was named Tinker Bell because her special magic is mending pots and pans. In J. M. Barrie's time, a person who did this for a living was called a tinker.

He got on better with children than with grown-ups – maybe because he was only 140 centimetres tall – and loathed the whole idea of being grown up. He said that, after the age of two, life just gets worse and worse. For him, sadly, that was true: his own life was horribly unhappy. But James Barrie knew the cure for unhappiness. He knew how to climb inside his imagination and go somewhere better. It was his escape chute! That's what *Peter Pan* is really all about: flying off to somewhere bigger and better than the here-and-now. In Neverland the colours are brighter, the heroes and heroines are braver, the villains are more villainous.

When I won the chance to write the official sequel to *Peter Pan*, that was the one thing I shared with Barrie: a passion for climbing inside my head and becoming everything I'm not in real life – brave, clever, resourceful, powerful, amazing.

I was a bit scared people would hate my sequel. I could picture them clapping their hands to their foreheads and crying, 'Who does this woman think she is?' Still, no point in being scared: if I don't enjoy writing a book, no one is going to enjoy reading it. So I went to work.

The writing bit was easy. Barrie's magical world sucked me in. Those terrific characters wrote the story for me. It was enormous fun, too, to try to copy Barrie's odd, quirky style and sideways sense of humour. I created a couple of new characters and argued with Barrie about the awfulness of mothers and growing up.

If he were alive today, would he mind some writer woman continuing his beloved story? I don't think so. Not when the idea for the book came from Great Ormond Street Children's Hospital.

Barrie 'gave' *Peter Pan* to the hospital so that they, not he, would get all the money it earned. That's how much the hospital meant to him. In the book, Peter rescues the Lost Boys, the Darlings and Tiger Lily. But *in real life* he has saved the lives of many thousands of sick children . . . just because of Barrie's gift.

Geraldine McCaughrean is the author of 141 stories, plays, retellings and picture books, for every age of reader from four to ninety-four. Her work has been read in more than forty countries so she has been able to make writing her full-time career. *Peter Pan in Scarlet* is soon to be filmed.

Classic Connections

Have you been reading **Harry Potter**, **The Lord of the Rings** or **His Dark Materials**? If they're your sort of books then these are all worth a read too!

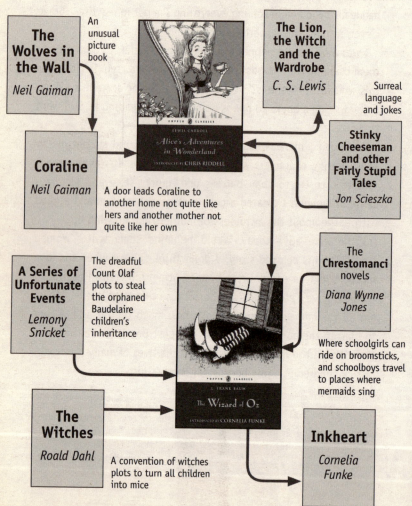

The Wolves in the Wall
Neil Gaiman

An unusual picture book

The Lion, the Witch and the Wardrobe
C. S. Lewis

Surreal language and jokes

Coraline
Neil Gaiman

A door leads Coraline to another home not quite like hers and another mother not quite like her own

Stinky Cheeseman and other Fairly Stupid Tales
Jon Scieszka

A Series of Unfortunate Events
Lemony Snicket

The dreadful Count Olaf plots to steal the orphaned Baudelaire children's inheritance

The Chrestomanci novels
Diana Wynne Jones

Where schoolgirls can ride on broomsticks, and schoolboys travel to places where mermaids sing

The Witches
Roald Dahl

A convention of witches plots to turn all children into mice

Inkheart
Cornelia Funke

How To Live Forever
Colin Thompson

Peter Pan
J. M. Barrie

Peter Pan in Scarlet
Geraldine McCaughrean

Tuck Everlasting
Natalie Babbit

The story of a family who are destined to live forever

The **Lion Boy** trilogy
Zizou Corder

Magical cat-speaking Charlie Ashanti

The Phoenix and the Carpet
E. Nesbit

PUFFIN CLASSICS
E. NESBIT
Five Children and It
INTRODUCED BY QUENTIN BLAKE

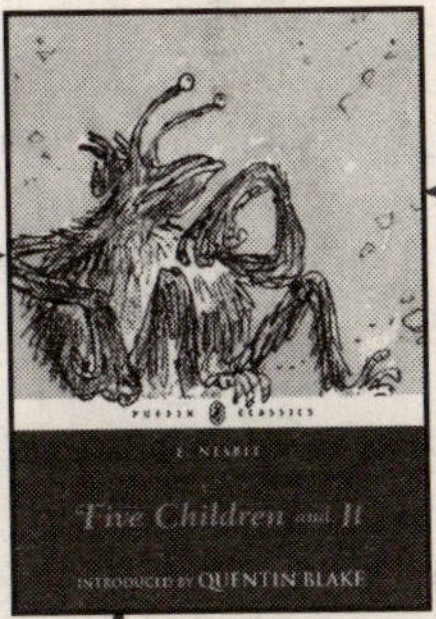

The Magician's Nephew
C. S. Lewis

The Worst Witch
Jill Murphy

A school for young witches

The Story of the Amulet
E. Nesbit

A Handful of Magic
Stephen Elboz

About a boy in a Victorian London ruled by magic

The Amulet of Samarkand
Jonathan Stroud

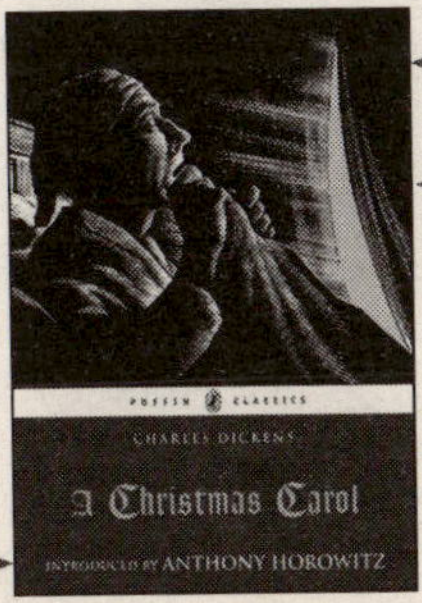

PUFFIN CLASSICS
CHARLES DICKENS
A Christmas Carol
INTRODUCED BY ANTHONY HOROWITZ

Horrible Histories: Vile Victorians
Terry Deary

The Haunting of Alaizabel Cray
Chris Wooding

Classics Quiz
Part Four

Answer the questions on all four Classics Quiz pages and enter our competition to win a 12-copy set of Puffin Classics! *Details of how to send in your answers are opposite.*

1 In *The Wizard of Oz*, what is the name of Dorothy's dog?
a) Fido
b) Tito
c) Toto
d) Joey

2 Which girl inspired Lewis Carroll to write *Alice's Adventures in Wonderland*?
a) Alice Lomax
b) Alice Landers
c) Alice Liddell
d) Alice Lennox

3 How many ghosts visit Ebenezer Scrooge in *A Christmas Carol*?
a) One
b) Two
c) Three
d) Four

4 Who is known as 'the boy who never grew up'?
a) Tom Sawyer
b) Peter Pan
c) Tiny Tim
d) Oliver Twist

5 In *The Wizard of Oz*, what does Dorothy steal from the Wicked Witch of the West?
a) Her hat
b) Her cat
c) Her broomstick
d) Her shoes

6 Which of the following stories is *not* a fairy tale by Hans Christian Andersen?
a) *The Snow Queen*
b) *The Little Mermaid*
c) *Cinderella*
d) *Thumbelina*

7 Who was the stranger who came to look after Jane and Michael Banks?
a) Maria
b) Nurse Matilda
c) Mary Poppins
d) Nana

8 Which children's book features Tweedledum and Tweedledee?
a) *Alice's Adventures in Wonderland*
b) *Alice Through the Looking-Glass*
c) *The Wizard of Oz*
d) *The Borrowers*

Want to be in with a chance to win?

Here's how to enter our Puffin Classics give-away:
Send your **name, age, address and answers** for ALL FOUR
Classics Quiz pages in *The PuffinCyclopedia* to:

Puffin Classics Competition,
c/o Puffin Marketing,
80 Strand, London WC2R 0RL

Don't forget to number your answers. For example, if you
think the answer to the first quiz's Question 1 is 'a' and the
answer to Question 2 is 'b', write:

Quiz One
1   a) Mice
2   b) Dinah

until you have answered all the questions in all four quizzes.
There are 32 questions in total. Or email your name, age,
address and answers to **puffinclassics@uk.penguingroup.com**

The first **100** correct entries that we draw at random
will win a 12-copy set of Puffin Classics containing: *The
Adventures of Huckleberry Finn, Alice's Adventures in
Wonderland, Black Beauty, The Call of the Wild, Just So Stories,
A Little Princess, Little Women, Oliver Twist, The Secret Garden,
Treasure Island, The Wind in the Willows* and *The Wizard of Oz.*

Closing date for the competition is **31 December 2008.**

See page 122 for the rules of the competition.

The Puffin yclopedia
of Children's Classics

DODO BOOKS

Published by the Pengrin Group

Pengrin Books Ltd, 80 Strand, London WC2R 0RL, England
Pengrin Group (USA) Inc., 375 Hudson Street, New York, New York 10014, USA
(a division of Pearson Penguin Canada Inc.)
Pengrin Group (Canada), 90 Eglinton Avenue East, Suite 700, Toronto, Ontario, Canada M4P 2Y3

Pengrin Ireland, 25 St Stephen's Green, Dublin 2, Ireland (a division of Pengrin Books Ltd)
Pengrin Group (Australia), 250 Camberwell Road, Camberwell, Victoria 3124, Australia
(a division of Pearson Australia Group Pty Ltd)
Pengrin Books India Pvt Ltd, 11 Community Centre, Panchsheel Park, New Delhi – 110 017, India
Pengrin Group (NZ), 67 Apollo Drive, Rosedale, North Shore 0632, New Zealand
(a division of Pearson New Zealand Ltd)
Pengrin Books (South Africa) (Pty) Ltd, 24 Sturdee Avenue, Rosebank, Johannesburg 2196, South Africa

Pengrin Books Ltd, Registered Offices: 80 Strand, London WC2R 0RL, England

pengrin.co.uk

First published 2008
1

Text copyright © Puffin Books 2008
Article copyright © Red Queen 2008
Article copyright © Catherine Earnshaw 2008
Article copyright © Ali Baba 2008

Lewis Carroll

Name Charles Lutwidge Dodgson; better known as Lewis Carroll

Born 27 January 1832 in Daresbury, Cheshire

Died 14 January 1898 in Guildford, Surrey

Nationality English

Lived in Cheshire, Yorkshire, Oxfordshire and Surrey.

Married He was never married.

Children None.

Career Charles was a brilliant scholar and went to Oxford University where he gained a First Class Honours degree in Mathematics. He stayed on at Christ Church College, Oxford, as a tutor in mathematics. He also took holy orders and became known as the Reverend Charles Lutwidge Dodgson, but he never went into the priesthood.

Hobbies He was a keen photographer and became one of the best portrait photographers of his time. He enjoyed theatre and opera, and loved playing games such as croquet, billiards and chess. He created logic puzzles and games, and made up stories and rhymes for his many child friends. He wrote letters and kept diaries and was very meticulous, making lists and keeping records of everything that he did.

Famous for *Alice's Adventures in Wonderland* and *Through the Looking Glass*. Next to the Bible and the works of Shakespeare, these are among the world's most widely translated works of literature. Also renowned for his poems including 'Jabberwocky', 'You Are Old Father William' and 'The Hunting of the Snark'.

Go on a ghostly journey with Ebenezer Scrooge

'Are you the Spirit, sir, whose coming was foretold to me?' asked Scrooge.

'I am!'

The voice was soft and gentle. Singularly low, as if instead of being so close beside him, it were at a distance.

'Who, and what are you?' Scrooge demanded.

'I am the Ghost of Christmas Past.'

'Long past?' inquired Scrooge: observant of its dwarfish stature.

'No. Your past.'

Perhaps, Scrooge could not have told anybody why, if anybody could have asked him; but he had a special desire to see the Spirit in his cap; and begged him to be covered.

'What!' exclaimed the Ghost, 'would you so soon put out, with worldly hands, the light I give? Is it not enough that you are one of those whose passions made this cap, and force me through whole trains of years to wear it low upon my brow!'

Scrooge reverently disclaimed all intention to offend, or any knowledge of having wilfully 'bonneted' the Spirit at any period of his life. He then made bold to inquire what business brought him there.

'Your welfare!' said the Ghost.

Scrooge expressed himself much obliged, but could not help thinking that a night of unbroken rest would have been more conducive to that end. The Spirit must have heard him thinking, for it said immediately:

'Your reclamation, then. Take heed!'

It put out its strong hand as it spoke, and clasped him gently by the arm.

'Rise! and walk with me!'

It would have been in vain for Scrooge to plead that the weather and the hour were not adapted to pedestrian purposes; that bed was warm, and the thermometer a long way below freezing; that he was clad but lightly in his slippers, dressing-gown, and nightcap; and that he had a cold upon him at that time. The grasp, though gentle as a woman's hand, was not to be resisted. He rose: but finding that the Spirit made towards the window, clasped his robe in supplication.

'I am mortal,' Scrooge remonstrated, 'and liable to fall.'

'Bear but a touch of my hand *there*,' said the Spirit, laying it upon his heart, 'and you shall be upheld in more than this!'

As the words were spoken, they passed through the wall, and stood upon an open country road, with fields on either hand. The city had entirely vanished. Not a vestige of it was to be seen. The darkness and the mist had vanished with it, for it was a clear, cold, winter day, with snow upon the ground.

'Good Heaven!' said Scrooge, clasping his hands together, as he looked about him. 'I was bred in this place. I was a boy here!'

The Spirit gazed upon him mildly. Its gentle touch, though it had been light and instantaneous, appeared still present to the old man's sense of feeling. He was conscious of a thousand odours floating in the air, each one connected with a thousand thoughts, and hopes, and joys, and cares long, long, forgotten!

'Your lip is trembling,' said the Ghost. 'And what is that upon your cheek?'

Scrooge muttered, with an unusual catching in his voice, that it was a pimple; and begged the Ghost to lead him where he would.

'You recollect the way?' inquired the Spirit.

'Remember it!' cried Scrooge with fervour – 'I could walk it blindfold.'

'Strange to have forgotten it for so many years!' observed the Ghost. 'Let us go on.'

They walked along the road; Scrooge recognising every gate, and post, and tree; until a little market-town appeared in the distance, with its bridge, its church, and winding river. Some shaggy ponies now were seen trotting towards them with boys upon their backs, who called to other boys in country gigs and carts, driven by farmers. All these boys were in great spirits, and shouted to each other, until the broad fields were so full of merry music, that the crisp air laughed to hear it.

'These are but shadows of the things that have been,' said the Ghost. 'They have no consciousness of us.'

The jocund travellers came on; and as they came, Scrooge knew and named them every one. Why was he rejoiced beyond all bounds to see them! Why did his cold eye glisten, and his heart leap up as they went past! Why was he filled with gladness when he heard them give each other Merry Christmas, as they parted at cross-roads and bye-ways, for their several homes!

What was merry Christmas to Scrooge? Out upon merry Christmas! What good had it ever done to him?

'The school is not quite deserted,' said the Ghost. 'A solitary child, neglected by his friends, is left there still.'

Scrooge said he knew it. And he sobbed.

They left the high-road, by a well remembered lane, and soon approached a mansion of dull red brick, with a little weathercock-surmounted cupola, on the roof, and a bell hanging in it. It was a large house, but one of broken fortunes; for the spacious offices were little used, their walls were damp and mossy, their windows broken, and their gates decayed. Fowls clucked and strutted in the stables; and the coach-houses and sheds were over-run with grass. Nor was it more retentive of its ancient state, within; for entering the dreary hall, and glancing through the open doors of many rooms, they found them poorly furnished, cold, and vast. There was an earthly savour in the air, a chilly bareness in the place, which associated itself somehow with too much getting up by candle-light, and not too much to eat.

They went, the Ghost and Scrooge, across the hall, to a door at the back of the house. It opened before them, and disclosed a long, bare, melancholy room, made barer still by lines of plain deal forms and desks. At one of these a lonely boy was reading near a feeble fire; and Scrooge sat down upon a form, and wept to see his poor forgotten self as he had used to be.

1946

1962

1985

1994

2008

From cover to cover . . .

Some more favourite
classic Puffin editions from
as early as the 1940s!

1967

1986

1988

2006

Puffin Classics then and now!

Make a wish with the Sand-fairy

'Quick,' said the Sand-fairy crossly. No one could think of anything, only Anthea did manage to remember a private wish of her own and Jane's which they had never told the boys. She knew the boys would not care about it – but still it was better than nothing.

'I wish we were all as beautiful as the day,' she said in a great hurry.

The children looked at each other, but each could see that the others were not any better-looking than usual. The Psammead pushed out its long eyes, and seemed to be holding its breath and swelling itself out till it was twice as fat and furry as before. Suddenly it let its breath go in a long sigh.

'I'm really afraid I can't manage it,' it said apologetically; 'I must be out of practice.'

The children were horribly disappointed.

'Oh, *do* try again!' they said.

'Well,' said the Sand-fairy, 'the fact is, I was keeping back a little strength to give you the rest of you your wishes with. If you'll be contented with one wish a day amongst the lot of you I daresay I can screw myself up to it. Do you agree to that?'

'Yes, oh yes!' said Jane and Anthea. The boys nodded. They did not believe the Sand-fairy could do it. You can always make girls believe things much easier than you can boys.

It stretched out its eyes farther than ever, and swelled and swelled and swelled.

'I do hope it won't hurt itself,' said Anthea.

'Or crack its skin,' Robert said anxiously.

Everyone was very much relieved when the Sand-fairy, after getting so big that it almost filled up the hole in the sand, suddenly let out its breath and went back to its proper size.

'That's all right,' it said, panting heavily. 'It'll come easier tomorrow.'

'Did it hurt much?' asked Anthea.

'Only my poor whisker, thank you,' said he, 'but you're a kind and thoughtful child. Good day.'

It scratched suddenly and fiercely with its hands and feet, and disappeared in the sand. Then the children looked at each other, and each child suddenly found itself alone with three perfect strangers, all radiantly beautiful.

They stood for some moments in perfect silence. Each thought that its brothers and sisters had wandered off, and that these strange children had stolen up unnoticed while it was watching the swelling form of the Sand-fairy. Anthea spoke first –

'Excuse me,' she said very politely to Jane, who now had enormous blue eyes and a cloud of russet hair, 'but have you seen the two little boys and a little girl anywhere about?'

'I was just going to ask you that,' said Jane. And then Cyril cried:

'Why, it's *you*! I know the hole in your pinafore! You *are* Jane, aren't you? And you're the Panther; I can see your dirty handkerchief that you forgot to change after you'd cut your thumb! Crikey! The wish has come off, after all, I say, am I as handsome as you are?'

Puffin Classics on Film

The Wizard of Oz was released in 1939 and directed by Victor Fleming. This was not the first film version of the popular book, but it is by far the most famous.

Sixteen-year-old Judy Garland starred as Dorothy. She was too old for the part and MGM (the studio) originally wanted child-star Shirley Temple, but Garland won it with her vocal abilities and was made to look younger than her actual age. This film made her into a star and, over the years,  Garland's Dorothy gained her iconic status. She was given an honorary juvenile Academy Award for her performance and the song 'Over the Rainbow' is thought to be, to this day, one of the greatest movie songs ever.

Interestingly, the film which is considered one of the all-time classic family movies was not widely well received in 1939. It was thought to be technically advanced (the Kansas scenes were shot in black and white, whilst the Oz scenes were filmed in Technicolour) – but it was a slow burner. It gathered popularity after subsequent cinema re-releases but it was not until the film was shown on television in the 1950s that it became a real hit. *The Wizard of Oz* is still shown annually on television (and sometimes twice), usually around the holidays.

Although essentially the same story, there are numerous differences between the original book and the 1939 movie. These include:

- Glinda (the Good Witch of the South) appears at beginning of film in the Land of the Munchkins, i.e. as the Good Witch of the North, and gives Dorothy a pair of ruby slippers rather than silver shoes.
- Dorothy is often portrayed as a damsel in distress in the film, whereas in the book she is frequently rescuing her companions.
- The film suggests that the whole adventure is a dream, unlike the book in which Dorothy actually travels to Oz.

Peter Pan, first adapted for film in 1924, was one of the most popular films during the silent-movie era. And if you love Disney films, then the 1953 Walt Disney animation of *Peter Pan* is considered to be a classic.

In 2003 a new film was made starring Jeremy Sumpter as the boy hero, and Rachel Hurd-Wood who was chosen to play Wendy from hundreds of hopefuls.

The story of Peter Pan has sparked numerous spin-offs, including *Hook*, directed by Steven Spielberg and released in 1991 starring Robin Williams and Dustin Hoffman, about a grown-up Peter Pan who has forgotten his childhood, and *Finding Neverland*, which starred Johnny Depp as the author J. M. Barrie and tells of how he came to write *Peter Pan*.

Fly across the sky with Peter and Wendy

His sobs woke Wendy, and she sat up in bed. She was not alarmed to see a stranger crying on the nursery floor; she was only pleasantly interested.

'Boy,' she said courteously, 'why are you crying?'

Peter could be exceedingly polite also, having learned the grand manner at fairy ceremonies, and he rose and bowed to her beautifully. She was much pleased, and bowed beautifully to him from the bed.

'What's your name?' he asked.

'Wendy Moira Angela Darling,' she replied with some satisfaction. 'What is your name?'

'Peter Pan.'

She was already sure that he must be Peter, but it did seem a comparatively short name.

'Is that all?'

'Yes,' he said rather sharply. He felt for the first time that it was a shortish name.

'I'm so sorry,' said Wendy Moira Angela.

'It doesn't matter,' Peter gulped.

She asked where he lived.

'Second to the right,' said Peter, 'and then straight on till morning.'

'What a funny address!'

Peter had a sinking. For the first time he felt that perhaps it was a funny address.

'No, it isn't,' he said.

'I mean,' Wendy said nicely, remembering that she was hostess, 'is that what they put on the letters?'

He wished she had not mentioned letters.

'Don't get any letters,' he said contemptuously.

'But your mother gets letters?'

'Don't have a mother,' he said. Not only had he no mother, but he had not the slightest desire to have one. He thought them very over-rated persons. Wendy, however, felt at once that she was in the presence of a tragedy.

'O Peter, no wonder you were crying,' she said, and got out of bed and ran to him.

'I wasn't crying about mothers,' he said rather indignantly. ' I was crying because I can't get my shadow to stick on. Besides, I wasn't crying.'

'It has come off?'

'Yes.'

Then Wendy saw the shadow on the floor, looking so draggled, and she was frightfully sorry for Peter. 'How awful!' she said, but she could not help smiling when she saw that he had been trying to stick it on with soap. How exactly like a boy!

Wondrous facts

Alice's Adventures in Wonderland was originally called *Alice's Adventures Under Ground*. Which title do you prefer?

'**Mad as a hatter**' was a common phrase in nineteenth-century England. This is probably because many hatters really did go stark-staring mad from exposure to mercury, a highly dangerous chemical that was used in the process of making felt hats.

As well as being a children's author, Lewis Carroll was a top mathematician and a skilled code-breaker.

True *or* **false?**
Charles Dickens hated Christmas.

Did you know ... ?

The Wicked Witch of the West in the 1939 film version of *The Wizard of Oz* was nearly played by someone else. But the first choice – a beautiful, glamorous actress – refused to wear make-up that made her look ugly. And so American actress Margaret Hamilton got the part.

In L. Frank Baum's classic novel, the Good Witch of the North gives Dorothy a pair of **silver** shoes. These became **ruby** slippers in the film, because they were more vivid in glorious Technicolor.

The Wizard of Oz has thirteen sequels!

Christmas carol quiz

Lots of Christmas carols were written in the nineteenth century. Can you spot the odd one out?

1818 – *Silent Night*
1843 – *O Come All Ye Faithful*
1843 – *A Christmas Carol*
1848 – *Once in Royal David's City*
1857 – *We Three Kings of Orient Are*
1868 – *O Little Town of Bethlehem*
1883 – *Away in a Manger*

Trivia

What is It?

'Its eyes were on long horns like a snail's eyes, and it could move them in and out like telescopes; it had ears like a bat's ears, and its tubby body was shaped like a spider's and covered with thick soft fur; its legs and arms were furry too, and it had hands and feet like a monkey's.'

Clue: the answer's in the question.

Famous wizards of fiction

Coriakin – a wizard from *The Voyage of the Dawn Treader* by C. S. Lewis

Gandalf – J. R. R. Tolkein's wizard from *The Lord of the Rings*

Harry Potter – no wizarding list would be complete without him

Merlin – a prophet and magician from Arthurian legend

The Wizard of Oz – a famous wizard and the title of the magical book by L. Frank Baum

A birthday to treasure

Robert Louis Stevenson's birthday was on 13 November. But one of his friends was born on Christmas Day and longed to have a different birthday. So, it is said that the author of *Treasure Island* left the friend a gift in his will – his own birthday!

A special present

When he died, J. M. Barrie left the copyright for *Peter Pan* to the Great Ormond Street Hospital for Sick Children in London. Every time the book is published or the play is performed in Great Britain, the famous children's hospital receives money. No one knows how much, because J. M. Barrie wanted this to be kept a closely guarded secret. Thanks to the author's generosity, the boy who would not grow up has been helping other children for over seventy years.

Follow the Yellow Brick Road!

As for the little old woman, she took off her cap and balanced the point on the end of her nose, while she counted 'One, two, three' in a solemn voice. At once the cap changed to a slate, on which was written in big, white chalk marks:

LET DOROTHY GO TO THE CITY OF –
EMERALDS

The little old woman took the slate from her nose, and having read the words on it, asked, 'Is your name Dorothy, my dear?'

'Yes,' answered the child, looking up and drying her tears.

'Then you must go to the City of Emeralds. Perhaps Oz will help you.'

'Where is this city?' asked Dorothy.

'It is exactly in the centre of the country, and is ruled by Oz, the Great Wizard I told you of.'

'Is he a good man?' inquired the girl anxiously.

'He is a good Wizard. Whether he is a man or not I cannot tell, for I have never seen him.'

'How can I get there?' asked Dorothy.

'You must walk. It is a long journey, through a country

that is sometimes pleasant and sometimes dark and terrible. However, I will use all the magic arts I know of to keep you from harm.'

'Won't you go with me?' pleaded the girl, who had begun to look upon the little old woman as her only friend.

'No, I cannot do that,' she replied, 'but I will give you my kiss, and no one will dare injure a person who has been kissed by the Witch of the North.'

She came close to Dorothy and kissed her gently on the forehead. Where her lips touched the girl they left a round, shining mark, as Dorothy found out soon after.

'The road to the city of Emeralds is paved with yellow brick,' said the Witch, 'so you cannot miss it. When you get to Oz do not be afraid of him, but tell your story and ask him to help you. Good-bye, my dear.'

The three Munchkins bowed low to her and wished her a pleasant journey, after which they walked away through the trees. The Witch gave Dorothy a friendly little nod, whirled around on her left heel three times, and straightaway disappeared, much to the surprise of little Toto, who barked after her loudly enough when she had gone, because he had been afraid even to growl while she stood by.

But Dorothy, knowing her to be a witch, had expected her to disappear in just that way, and was not surprised in the least.

Charles Dickens

Full name Charles John Huffam Dickens

Born 7 February 1812 in Portsmouth, Hampshire

Died 9 June 1870 in Chatham, Kent, and buried in Poet's Corner in Westminster Abbey

Nationality English

Lived mainly in and around London.

Married to Catherine (Kate) Thomson Hogarth in 1836; separated 1858.

Children Ten children: Charles, Mary, Kate, Walter, Francis, Alfred, Sydney, Henry, Dora and Edward.

Career At the age of twelve he worked in a shoe polish factory to help with the family's debts. At fifteen he began work in a lawyer's office and went on to reporting on court cases. From there he began selling stories to newspapers and magazines, and when a selection of these were printed as a book, his career as a novelist began.

Hobbies Charles Dickens edited a monthly magazine, gave readings and explored London.

Famous for being one of the English language's greatest writers. His many famous novels include *A Christmas Carol*, *Oliver Twist*, *Great Expectations* and *David Copperfield*.

AND

If you like stories about

MAKE-BELIEVE

then you should also try these classic stories...

☐ *Alice Through the Looking-Glass*
LEWIS CARROLL

Pinocchio CARLO COLLODI ☐

☐ *Charlie and the Chocolate Factory*
ROALD DAHL

A Wrinkle in Time MADELEINE L'ENGLE ☐

☐ *The Princess and the Goblin*
GEORGE MACDONALD

The Chronicles of Narnia C. S. LEWIS ☐

☐ *Hans Andersen's Fairy Tales*
RETOLD BY NAOMI LEWIS

The Phoenix and the Carpet E. NESBIT ☐

☐ *The Story of the Treasure Seekers* E. NESBIT

Gulliver's Travels JONATHAN SWIFT ☐

☐ *The Lord of the Rings* J. R. R. TOLKIEN

The Happy Prince and Other Stories
OSCAR WILDE ☐

Tick if you've read it!

Puffin Classics Competition Rules

1. No purchase necessary to enter this promotion.
2. This competition is open to all UK residents aged 9 or over, with the exception of employees of the Promoter, their immediate families and anyone else connected with this promotion. Entries from those under 13 years of age must be accompanied by the written consent of their parent/guardian.
3. Entries must be received by 31 December 2008. The Promoter accepts no responsibility for any entries that are incomplete, illegible or fail to reach the Promoter by the relevant closing date for any reason. Proof of posting or sending is not proof of receipt. Entries via agents or third parties are invalid. Entries become the property of the Promoter and cannot be returned.
4. Only one entry per person. No entrant can win more than one prize.
5. To enter the promotion, answer all of the questions on the four Classics Quiz pages in *The PuffinCyclopedia of Children's Classics*. Answers can be emailed to puffinclassics@uk.penguingroup.com with the subject heading 'Puffin Classics Competition' or, alternatively, send your answers along with your name, address, age and email address to Puffin Classics Competition, c/o Puffin Books, 80 Strand, London, WC2R 0RL.
6. All correctly completed entries will be entered into a prize draw, which will take place on 2 January 2009. The first 100 entries drawn at random will be the winners.
7. The winners will each receive one full set of 12 Puffin Classics consisting of a copy each of: *The Adventures of Huckleberry Finn, Alice's Adventures in Wonderland, Black Beauty, The Call of the Wild, Just So Stories, A Little Princess, Little Women, Oliver Twist, The Secret Garden, Treasure Island, The Wind in the Willows* and *The Wizard of Oz*.
8. The decision of the Promoter as to the winners will be final and no correspondence will be entered into.
9. The winners will be notified by email within 4 weeks of the closing date. The winners must claim their prize within 30 days of the Promoter sending notification. If the prize is unclaimed after this time, it will lapse and the Promoter reserves the right to offer the unclaimed prize to a substitute winner selected in accordance with these rules.
10. Prizes are subject to availability. In the event of unforeseen circumstances, the Promoter reserves the right (a) to substitute alternative prizes of equivalent or greater value and (b) in exceptional circumstances to amend or foreclose the promotion without notice. No correspondence will be entered into.
11. To obtain a list of winners for the prize draw please email puffin@uk.penguingroup.com within 4 weeks of the closing date, stating the name of the prize draw in the subject heading.
12. The Promoter will use any data submitted by entrants only for the purposes of running the prize draw, unless otherwise stated in the entry details.
13. The winners agree to take part in reasonable post-event publicity and to the use of their names and photographs in such publicity.
14. By entering the prize draw each entrant agrees to be bound by these Terms and Conditions.
15. These Terms and Conditions shall be governed by English law and the courts of England and Wales shall have exclusive jurisdiction.
16. The Promoter is Penguin Books Limited, 80 Strand, London WC2R 0RL.

Sources

This list includes the Internet sites and publications
which were considered helpful for the purposes of this guide:

amazon.co.uk
Books for Keeps magazine
booktrusted.co.uk
guardian.co.uk/arts
Metro newspaper
readingmatters.co.uk

authors' own websites
Carousel magazine
carnegiegreenaway.org.uk
lovereading4Kids.co.uk
penguinclassics.co.uk

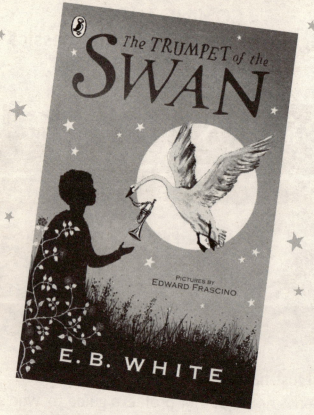

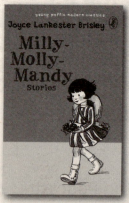

From master storyteller E. B. White,
the original and best

The magical
much-loved
classic

puffin.co.uk

AN A–Z OF ADVENTURE…

Alice, Black Beauty, Cathy, Dracula, Estella, Fagin, Gulliver,
Huckleberry Finn, It, Jim Hawkins, King Arthur, Long John Silver, Mowgli,
Nancy, Oliver, Pollyanna, the Queen of Hearts, Ratty, Sara Crewe,
Tom Sawyer, Uriah Heap, Rip Van Winkle, the Wizard of Oz,
the PhoeniX, the Yahoos and Zeus …

Some of these you might know. Others you won't. Some you'll know without
even knowing how you know them. They're from a cast of classic characters
who have travelled through time – in their ships or motor cars, or even tumbled
down rabbit holes – to come to life for your grandparents, your parents and now
for you. These characters are so vivid and so exciting that they literally jump off
the page and into your life. And it's completely up to you what they look like.

They're Puffin Classics for a reason.
It's because they're the best.

Puffin has been publishing the most innovative and imaginative children's
literature for generations. From Mowgli to Merlin, Peter Pan to Pollyanna, no
matter what your age or what you're into, wherever you see that little bird
you'll be introduced to a whole host of new faces and amazing places.

PUFFIN CLASSICS

THE MOMENTOUS YEARS
1919–1958

The Atom Bomb, 1945

THE
MOMENTOUS YEARS
1919 – 1958

By

H. E. PRIESTLEY, Ph.D., M.A. M.Ed.

AND

J. J. BETTS, B.A.

(Senior History Master, Hendon County Grammar School, N.W.4.)

J. M. DENT & SONS LTD.
BEDFORD ST. LONDON W.C.2

AUTHORS' NOTE

THE mere fact that we already know scraps at least of very modern history will make it easy to read this book with interest. 'From the known to the unknown' is a very good guiding principle in all kinds of study. How often are teachers of history struck by the quick response of students to any 'digression' into modern affairs!

This book makes no greater claim than to tell the story of the years 1919–58. It avoids, as far as possible, the use of difficult words and phrases.

The old argument that present-century history is too confusingly 'near' or too controversial to be introduced into our schools and colleges has got to give way before the over-riding need for information on the world of our time. Teachers can at least give a fair general view of recent events. If they make no attempt to do so the inquiring student picks up a mass of tit-bits from films, magazines, and conversations, which, however valuable, is hardly likely to make up a proportioned picture.

It has not been found either desirable or necessary to give this book a marked point of view. The simple assumption that good is better than evil is sufficient guide to judge many of the actions of modern statesmen.

In the chapters on the Second World War we have been reluctant to attempt any strict appraisement of the relative contributions of the Allies to victory. 'I was walking along Oxford Street when I met another Englishman,' said the radio comedian in 1944. The remark may be remembered to illustrate how inextricably interwoven were all our peoples, and how difficult, perhaps undesirable, it would be to disentangle these 'war efforts.' So Australians with memories of New Guinea, South Africans of the desert, Indians of Italy, and Canadians of Caen and Arnhem, are asked to read Chapter XXX with a tolerant understanding of its limitations, and the rest of the war-story with a still more general and generous regard.

The authors are gratefully indebted to Mr. H. W. Marsh of Messrs. J. M. Dent & Sons, Ltd., for his many valuable suggestions in regard to fact, style, and stress.

H. E. P.

J. J. B.

CONTENTS

APPENDICES

ILLUSTRATIONS

* ix

MAPS AND CHARTS

MAPS

TIME-CHARTS

	The Struggle for Peace	Germany, Italy, Japan	Russia
1919	**Treaty of Versailles**	Weimar Republic	Third Comintern formed
1920	League of Nations meets		
1921			
1922	Washington Conference	Fascist march on Rome	
1923		Stresemann versus chaos	
1924	Geneva protocol		Death of Lenin
1925	Treaties of Locarno		
1926		Germany joins the League of Nations	
1927			
1928	Briand–Kellogg Pact		
1929		Italy makes peace with Pope Death of Stresemann	Five-Year Plan
1930	Briand's plan for a 'United States of Europe'	Military occupation of Germany ended	

WORLD TRADE DEPRESSION

	The Struggle for Peace	Germany, Italy, Japan	Russia
1931		Japan attacks **Manchuria**	
1932	Disarmament Conference fails		
1933		Hitler Chancellor Germany withdraws from League of Nations	
1934			Joins the League of Nations
1935	Partial Sanctions against Italy	Italy attacks **Abyssinia**	
1936	Britain and France urge Non-Intervention in Spain	German troops enter Rhineland Civil War in **Spain**	
1937		Anti-Comintern Pact (Rome–Berlin–Tokyo)	
1938	Munich Agreement	Germany seizes **Austria** (Mar.) Germany seizes **Sudetenland** (Oct.)	
1939		Germany seizes **Bohemia** and **Moravia** (Mar.) Italy seizes **Albania** (April) Germany attacks **Poland** (Sept.)	Russo-German Pact of Neutrality

THE SECOND WORLD WAR

CHAPTER I

THE LIGHTS GO UP

AT eleven in the morning of the 11th November 1918, the sounding of maroons and the firing of guns all over England announced that the fiercest and cruellest war the world had ever known until then had come to an end. For the rest of the day there was no more thought of work. Churches were opened for thanksgiving, streets were crowded with merry-makers out to celebrate the coming of peace again. Most of the schools had been closed for some time owing to a severe epidemic of influenza. When at the outbreak of war in 1914 Sir Edward Grey had said that the lamps were going out all over Europe, he had no idea how literally true his words would be. The first air-raids of history had brought a black-out to the English towns and countryside. But on 11th November 1918 there was no further need for it. The lights went up again.

The imperialist designs of Germany had for the first time been defeated by a world alliance and her great empire brought to its knees. On 8th November a delegation from the German Government arrived at the Forest of Compiègne in France where Marshal Foch, commander of the Allied armies, had his headquarters in a railway carriage.

'"What do you want, gentlemen?" he asked.

"Your proposals for an armistice," they replied.

"But we are making no proposals," answered the marshal. "We are quite happy to go on fighting."

The German delegates were desperate. "We must have terms," they insisted. "We cannot continue the conflict."

"Oh, you have come to ask for an armistice," said the marshal. "That is a different thing."' [1]

The terms were presented and the delegates sent a messenger

[1] *War Memoirs of David Lloyd George* (1936), vol. vi, p, 3321.

back to Germany with them. In the meantime mutiny and disorder were spreading all over the country. The German emperor was forced to abdicate and he fled to Holland. The delegates received telegraphed instructions to accept the armistice, and they signed it at four o'clock on the morning of the 11th. At eleven o'clock all firing ceased on the Western Front, and the 'Great War' was ended.

The terms of the armistice were such that the Germans could not hope to renew the war. In January 1919 a Peace Conference began its long deliberations on the future of the world. There were many varying points of view and many disagreements, but in June the final terms were presented to the Germans. The famous Hall of Mirrors in the Palace of Versailles, where the first German emperor had been crowned, was prepared for the ceremony of signing the treaty. There, in the presence of visitors and journalists, the statesmen of the various powers gave their assent to the most important political document ever framed.

CHAPTER II

THE Hall of Mirrors has a great place in German history, for there, forty-eight years before, the first German empire had been founded after the defeat of France.

By the Treaty of Versailles, signed on 28th June 1919, Germany was disarmed, and had to surrender her ships, big guns, and tanks. Her army was reduced to 100,000 men, her navy to 15,000, and her air force was abolished altogether. Alsace and Lorraine were returned to France, and Germany was cut off from East Prussia by the famous 'Polish Corridor,' which gave Poland access to the sea. Some outlying areas on the borders of Denmark, Poland, and Belgium were allowed to detach themselves from Germany by popular vote and join these states; others, like Danzig and Memel, were handed over to the newly constituted League of Nations to administer.

The Germans were deprived of all their colonies. Great Britain was entrusted with the government of German East Africa. German South-West Africa was given to the Union of South Africa, the German portion of New Guinea to Australia, while Togoland and the Cameroons were given to France, and the German-owned islands in the Pacific to Japan, Australia, and New Zealand, all under League of Nations mandates.

To the Germans one of the most galling provisions of the treaty was the one in which they were compelled to admit the responsibility of their country for causing the war. This having been done, measures of punishment followed as a matter of course. A commission was appointed to decide how much Germany should pay. As a security the left bank of the Rhine was to be occupied by allied troops for fifteen years. The French, who had been the greatest sufferers

3

from the ravages of war and occupation, were given possession for fifteen years of the important coal-mines in the industrial district of the Saar, which was to be administered by the League of Nations. At the end of this period the people themselves were to decide by vote whether they would become part of France or of Germany.

New York Times

Famine in Germany, 1919

Such in brief were the provisions of the Versailles Treaty. Some of the richest districts in the country, some 26,000 square miles in all, were taken away, and Germany lost about 6,000,000 people through this transfer of lands. In addition, the prospect of paying the vast sum which was demanded as reparations, a hundred million pounds a year for sixty-six years, was staggering.

After the flight of the German emperor in 1918 the country passed through very troublesome times. A German republic was proclaimed in Munich, but there were fights in Berlin

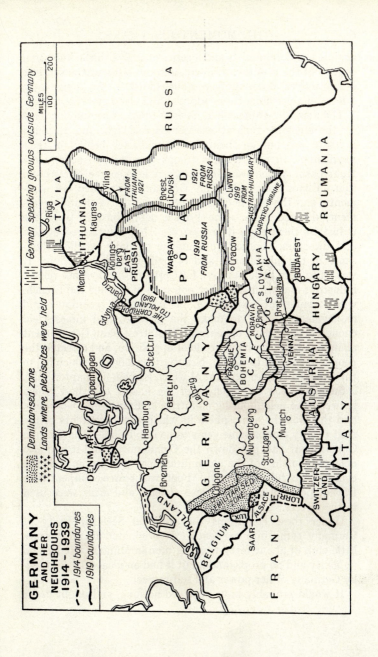

GERMANY
AND HER
NEIGHBOURS
1914 - 1939

---- 1914 boundaries
—— 1919 boundaries

Demilitarised zone

Lands where plebiscites were held

German speaking groups outside Germany

MILES
0   100   200

RUSSIA

LATVIA

Riga

LITHUANIA

Vilna
FROM LITHUANIA 1921

Kaunas

Memel

Königsberg

EAST PRUSSIA

Gdynia

Danzig

THE CORRIDOR (TO POLAND) (1919)

POLAND

Brest Litovsk

1921 FROM RUSSIA

Lwow

1919 FROM AUSTRIA-HUNGARY

WARSAW

1919 FROM RUSSIA

Cracow

CARPATHO-UKRAINE

Stettin

BERLIN

Danzig

Hamburg

Copenhagen

DENMARK

Bremen

Cologne

GERMANY

Nuremberg

Munich

Stuttgart

HOLLAND

BELGIUM

LUX.

DEMILITARISED ZONE

SAAR

ALSACE

LORRAINE

FRANCE

SWITZER-LAND

ITALY

Prague

BOHEMIA

Brno

MORAVIA

CZECHO

SLOVAKIA

Bratislava

VIENNA

AUSTRIA

HUNGARY

Budapest

ROUMANIA

against the Communists and a series of strikes in the industrial centres of the country. Slowly, and not without the sacrifice of many lives, the republic established itself. In August 1919 a form of government was adopted and elections were held.

The new Government had no easy time. The amount fixed by the allies for reparations seemed too high, and although pressure was put on them the Germans fell behind in their payments. In 1923 French troops were sent to occupy the Ruhr basin, which was Germany's richest source of coal and iron. Chaos followed. The Germans suspended all payments, and the people of the Ruhr, by order of their Government, downed tools. The French determined to work the industries themselves if necessary. They imprisoned owners and directors, deposed government officials, expelled thousands of the inhabitants, and brought in French labour. It was all to very little purpose, for Germany had lost her richest industries and with them her power to pay, while the French, with insufficient experience in industrial technique and management, failed to make the factories and mines yield enough even to meet expenses. The Stresemann Government abandoned in 1923 its attitude of opposition, and directed the people to go back to work. Negotiations followed which led to the Dawes Plan, an account of which is given in Chapter VIII.

Such was the tragic effect of the hatred that had grown between the neighbouring countries of France and Germany, and this was the atmosphere in which the discontents of the next twenty troublesome years came into being. The German Government had put down the Communists, and it had also defeated a rising of the old military party in Berlin, but the country was full of turmoil. Food was scarce, tempers were frayed, political meetings were violent, and arms were used in the streets.

Under these conditions the National Socialist Party of Germany came into existence. It originated in an obscure little club of about forty working men in Munich. It had no publicity and no propaganda, but it had an idea—the recovery by Germany of her power and self-respect.

It would probably have achieved nothing, and might never

have been written about in history books had it not one
evening been visited by a stranger. His name was Adolf
Hitler, and he had been sent by the Bavarian army commander to find out if there were any Communist activities

E.N.A.

Adolf Hitler

going on in the society. He listened to the discussion and found
that the theories of the party were very much to his liking.
Soon the man who had come to spy not only became a member
of the party himself, but persuaded his superiors, Captain
Röhm and Colonel von Epp, that Germany could be reawakened by 'National Socialism.' Thus began the political

career of the man who was one day to become 'Führer' or 'Leader' of Germany.

He had had a chequered career. Born in 1889 in a little village on the Austrian border, he had lost his parents when young, and had drifted from one menial job to another in Vienna and Munich. On the outbreak of war in 1914 he joined the German army and fought as a corporal on the Western Front. The armistice again found him without work, and it is as a political spy that he first found his way into the turbulent post-war history of Germany.

The secret of Hitler's power is that he taught the Germans what they most wanted to believe. A life of penury and semi-starvation had filled him with hatred and bitterness—the same bitterness that was then latent in the German masses after the crushing defeat of their armies. They needed to be reassured, to be told that they were still the master-race, the *Herrenvolk*. Hitler could do this in bursts of passionate oratory, proclaiming the greatness of the 'Nordic' man and the 'Aryan' race from whom all the benefits of mankind had sprung. What matter though in cold, scientific fact neither of these existed? The Germans would believe if they were told often and often enough. Hitler, too, could point to the nation's enemies. The Communists, according to him, had betrayed an unbeaten army, had stirred up mutiny in the fleet in 1918, and were even now 'selling out' the State to Bolshevik Russia; while the Jews, the enemies of honest labour, were living by their wits and growing fat on the sweat of the poor.

With Hitler in charge of propaganda the party made some progress. A newspaper, the *Völkischer Beobachter*, or *Popular Observer*, was bought, and administered National Socialist doctrine in daily doses. The roughs who flocked into the party were given uniforms, and were organized in bands to throw opponents out of meetings, to 'beat them up' in the streets, and to take part in the noisy processions with much waving of banners, 'Heil-ing' the Führer, and singing the new party songs. The new name, 'National Socialist German Workers' Party,' was adopted, and its members were later to be known universally as 'Nazis.'

Von Epp and Röhm were followed into the party by many other German officers of the last war, including Hermann Göring, the famous flying ace, and even the great General Ludendorff. Rich industrialists, whom Hitler visited and harangued, gave him their support, thinking that they could use him to further their own plans. Soon there was no lack of funds in the National Socialist Party. Meetings grew in size, and the new swastika emblem was saluted by thousands.

In 1923 the members of the party thought they were strong enough to attempt to seize power in Munich. An important speech was to be made by the head of the Bavarian Government at the now famous Munich Hall, when the storm-troopers surrounded it. Hitler entered and announced to those assembled that a new Government was to be formed by force, with himself and his friends in power.

Next morning, when the leader, accompanied by Ludendorff, attempted to lead a procession through the city, they were met by the police and checked. There was a skirmish and the procession was dispersed with casualties. Hitler fled to some friends in the hills but was captured, and at his trial he was given a five-year term of imprisonment. Within a year he was free.

While in prison he had written the first part of a book which was later read by every German—*Mein Kampf* (*My Struggle*). What this book preached and how its doctrines were carried out by the National Socialist Government which he finally established must be left to a later chapter to describe.

CHAPTER III

THE LEAGUE OF NATIONS

THE statesmen who drew up the peace treaties of 1919 were bound to create some sort of a League of Nations. Such a body was needed to see that the treaties were kept. The chief statesmen of the world, led by President Wilson, had pledged themselves to it, and the hopes of peoples everywhere were centred in the creation of an organization which would stop further war.

The idea of world-wide co-operation and brotherhood was not by any means new. In every age there had been dreamers and prophets who longed for it. The Roman Empire had imposed peace upon its own world, the Catholic Church had at least tried to establish unity and peace in the Middle Ages, and in the early nineteenth century the Holy Alliance had provided a league of princes and governments, if not of peoples, whose object was to give Europe peace. Many writers had produced books on international law, i.e. rules which civilized nations ought to keep. An International Law Court had even been set up at The Hague at the end of the nineteenth century, but it had no power to enforce its decisions or to compel nations to bring their quarrels to the court.

After the terrible waste and suffering of the Great War many people in all countries of the world argued in this simple way: 'In former days wars between such places as Lancashire and Yorkshire were common: nowadays these districts are ruled by the same Parliament, so that wars between them are impossible. Could not a world parliament similarly stop wars between the nations?' But there were many other people who did not argue this way. Some were content not to think of the problem. Some said: 'There has always been war, and I suppose there always will be.' Some perhaps even liked war because it brought excitement and profits. A large number of people wanted to abolish war, but refused to give up their 'sovereign rights,' i.e. their complete power in their own country, and were suspicious of a 'Parliament of Man.' We shall see in this chapter how in the years after the Great War an effort was made to enable the nations to live and work together, and to settle their quarrels. And behind the story of the world of 1919–39 we must picture the struggle between the masses of men and women who believed in the League ideal, and the masses who were indifferent or hostile to it.

The Peace Commissioners in Paris were hampered by many fixed ideas among the nations. Britain was anxious to keep her power on the high seas in order to maintain the security of her empire. France was so bitter against Germany that she feared to disarm. For a century America had proclaimed the Monroe Doctrine, i.e. her refusal to let any outside nations interfere in the American states. So the conference had to be very modest in its proposals.

THE CONSTITUTION OF THE LEAGUE OF NATIONS

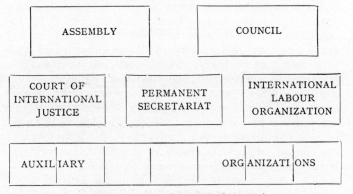

(Health, Finance, Communications, etc.)

After great labour on the part of such statesmen as President Wilson, Lloyd George, Lord Robert Cecil, and General Smuts, the League was hammered into shape. Geneva was chosen as its headquarters, both because it was a beautiful place, and because it was in Switzerland, a small country of which no other state could be jealous. The Allied nations together with thirteen neutrals were invited to join,[1] and although enemy states, such as Germany, and countries without settled government, such as Russia and Mexico, were left out, they could enter later if two-thirds of the Assembly agreed.

The 'Covenant,' or list of promises which the members signed, showed the way in which peace and the rule of law were to be established. Article 8 planned steps towards the disarmament of the nations. The 'Heart of the Covenant,' as President Wilson called Article 10, said that the League would protect its members against attack and guarantee their independence. Under Article 12 states promised to settle their disputes by discussion or in an international court of law. Article 16 provided for 'sanctions' to punish any country which made war; the guilty state was to be immediately boycotted by the rest of the world, so that it lost all its trade, and could get help from nobody.

The work of the League was to be carried out by four main bodies or organs of government, viz: (1) the Council, (2) the Assembly, (3) the International Court of Justice, (4) the Secretariat. Besides these there were various other organizations, such as the International Labour Office, which dealt with particular problems. The Council was the most important. It represented chiefly the Great Powers and met at least three times a year. Its chief task was to settle disputes between states and so prevent war, or to decide how to stop any war that had broken out. Its decisions had to be unanimous. The Assembly was a meeting of all the members of the League, and in it all states, great and small, were equal. It selected representatives of the small states on the Council, it had power to admit new members to the League, and it discussed all matters affecting the world at large. The International Court of Justice was designed as an improvement on the older Hague Tribunal with a staff of brilliant

[1] Thirty-one Allied states signed the Covenant as part of the Treaty of Versailles: the U.S.A. and Ecuador withdrew, the little country of Hejaz became swallowed in Saudi Arabia, but China added her signature. There were altogether forty-two members at the first Assembly in November 1920.

E.N.A.

Switzerland, the Home of the League

judges to settle arguments between states on the meaning of treaties, international rights and customs. The International Labour Office was established to help all the states of the world to improve the lives of the workers, and gain a better standard of civilization and comfort for all. The Secretariat was the Civil Service which acted as the office for all the daily work of the League.

The League of Nations was created mainly to prevent further outbreaks of war. But its most urgent task was to heal some of the wounds of the Great War, and in this it was most successful. Largely through the enthusiasm of Dr. Nansen, a Norwegian scientist, over 400,000 prisoners of war were sent safely to their homes. The League cared for many Christian refugees turned out of Turkey. It drew a health barrier across Europe to stop the spread of typhus from Russia. It took steps to stop the trade in dangerous drugs and the sale of arms to native tribes. Scientists and teachers from all over the world were brought together to exchange ideas and information.

One of the chief problems which the League felt obliged to face was the starvation and bankruptcy of Austria, a little state with a large capital—'a mighty heart in a tiny body.' By borrowing large sums of money the League was able to rescue Austria from complete collapse, and to get her industries and agriculture working again.

One part of the work of the League needs special attention, as it was something new in the history of mankind. The Peace Conference had awarded many backward territories and conquered lands to certain of the powers to be ruled and developed, not as possessions, but as a 'sacred trust' of civilization. Such places, e.g. Syria, Palestine, Mesopotamia, Togoland, German East Africa, and many Pacific islands, were termed 'mandated territories.' The League of Nations was the body which watched over the interests of these backward countries, and received a yearly report from their guardians. Similarly it watched over the rights of minorities, e.g. the rights of Poles living in Germany, or Germans living in Poland. Another particularly difficult task was the control of the Saar basin. The wealthy coal-mines of this part of Germany were awarded to France as compensation for her war damage. In 1935 the people of the Saar were to be allowed to decide their own future. The League governed the district well and fairly despite the bad feelings that prevailed there, until its return to Germany after the plebiscite. Likewise there was the unpopular task of governing Danzig, a German town which had been made into a free city because Poland had to have an outlet to the sea.

Up to 1923 the League of Nations made great headway. It grew in numbers from the original forty-two members to fifty-five. In 1924 there were present at Geneva seven prime ministers and sixteen foreign secretaries, and it really seemed that the ideal of a world parliament was to be achieved.

Yet the League suffered from certain weaknesses which were ultimately to prove fatal to itself and to the peace of the world. The first major disaster in its short history was the refusal of the United States to join. President Wilson had been the finest architect of the Covenant. When he returned home he found that the prophet was without honour in his own country, and to his bitter grief the Senate objected to 'entangling alliances,' and wished to keep out of the affairs of Europe. The United States helped in some of the welfare work at Geneva, and later, in 1926, joined the Court of International Justice; but its general absence was a very serious handicap.

Soviet Russia did not receive an invitation to join the League, as some nations would not willingly co-operate with it. Germany, as the defeated nation, was in a peculiar position. She was uncertain whether to join, and her late enemies were uncertain whether to ask her to join until the period of good feeling and high hopes when the Locarno pacts were signed in 1925 led to her entry.

The first great weakness, therefore, of the League was that it was a 'League of *some* nations,' not of all. Its second was that it had no military power of its own to enforce its decisions. It resembled a law court which had to *persuade* people not to fight, and had no policemen to *compel* them to keep the peace.

The League had acted successfully in settling many disputes between small states. Would it be strong enough to deal with any great power that defied it and went to war?

E.N.A.

Aristide Briand

The third weakness—and this was to prove the most serious of all—was that states which were dissatisfied with the peace settlement of 1919, especially Germany, Italy, and Japan, were coming to regard the League with suspicion or even hatred. They were beginning to view it as a league of the 'haves' against the 'have-nots,' as an alliance of the victorious powers to prevent any changes in the arrangements made at Versailles. As conference after conference failed to get the chief states of Europe to disarm, so Germany, Italy, and Japan became more and more suspicious and determined to rely on their own arms.

How did the League stand after its first ten years of life? We have seen that in many small matters it succeeded. The period of 1922-5 had been especially promising, when Germany, led by Stresemann, seemed on the road to becoming a friendly member of western Europe, and after signing the splendid treaties of Locarno had herself joined the League. Small wonder that Sir Austen Chamberlain had joyfully described this time as 'the real dividing line between the years of war and of peace.'

Yet in 1930 the League was far from secure. Its great weaknesses had not been remedied. Attempts to get the nations to reduce their armies and navies had so far failed, while Germany, disarmed by the Treaty of Versailles, was growing impatient of the failure of the Allies to cut down their own forces.

M. Briand, one of the wisest peace-lovers of his day, realized that the League was at the cross-roads. It must either become strong or collapse; either establish the rule of law or let the nations follow the old way of national independence, national armaments, and national wars. Everything depended on the peoples of the world. Were they now educated to support the League or were they still content to call it a 'League of Notions'?

'Unite to live and prosper' was Briand's message as he urged Europe to form a federal union within the framework of the League. We shall see in ensuing chapters how this message was not heard, and how, in consequence, the next ten years saw the world rushing down the slope to destruction like the Gadarene swine in the Bible story.

CHAPTER IV

MODERN TURKEY

IN the nineteenth century the Turkish Empire was called 'The Sick Man of Europe.' In 1920 the sick man was almost brought to his death.

The Turks had joined the Germans in the war of 1914–18, and had been defeated in a long campaign in Egypt and Palestine. On 10th August 1920 they had to sign a peace at Sèvres in France, which deprived them of their large empire and handed it over to the League of Nations. Great Britain was given the government of Mesopotamia and Palestine, France was to administer northern Syria and south-east Anatolia, and Italy south-west Anatolia. The valuable port of Smyrna and the land behind it was ceded to the Greeks, and a strip round the Dardanelles was to be made into a free international zone, ruled by the Allies.

What was to happen now to Turkey? It is one of the miracles of our day that it was transformed in ten years from a corrupt, oriental empire, to a virile and efficient national state.

The hero of the story is a soldier, Mustapha Kemal, one of the most popular of all the Turkish generals. He had won fame as the man who had driven the British from the Dardanelles in 1915. He was the son of poor parents and had been educated at various military schools, where he learnt not only to be a good soldier, but also to hate the sultan and his corrupt government. He believed fervently in a Turkish national state, free from the tyranny and oppression which was sapping the country of all its strength. As a young man he had joined a secret society and had been imprisoned. Nevertheless when the Italians attacked the Turkish land of Tripoli in 1911 he had been one of the few who had smuggled themselves through Egypt so as to get to grips with the enemy.

In 1920 the affairs of the country reached their lowest ebb. The Greeks were already in Smyrna; the British, French, and Italians were garrisoning every town of importance in the

empire, which was already being broken up in Paris to be
handed over to the various powers under a series of mandates.

Mustapha Kemal's name was on the list of those to be
arrested, but the Turkish Government got him away on a

E.N.A.

Kemal Atatürk

special mission into the mountains of Anatolia.   Here he
energetically set about organizing a movement of resistance.
He knew that the vast empire which Turkey had held would
certainly be lost, but to give up Smryna would mean certain
destruction.

Mustapha Kemal now became the acknowledged leader of

the numerous guerrilla bands operating in Asia Minor. He armed them with rifles stolen from the enemy and drilled them in the fastnesses of the mountains. He travelled the length and breadth of the land, talking to the peasants and townspeople about their beloved country which was so near to destruction. Even the general of the sultan's army came over to his side. When he held his first National Congress delegates arrived secretly from all parts of Turkey, many on foot, some even in disguise. They decided to support him, and formed a provisional Government to replace that of the sultan in Constantinople. Kemal now ordered that all government communications going through Asia Minor should in future be sent to him.

These were bold steps, amounting to open defiance, both of the sultan and of the Allies. The sultan ordered his recall to Constantinople, but he defied the order, and remained with his few thousand ill-armed volunteers.

With the news of the Turkish losses at the Treaty of Sèvres, Kemal's small army rapidly grew to a national revolutionary force which set all Asiatic Turkey aflame. Here was a puzzle for those who had drawn up the Peace Treaty. The Allies, tired and war-worn, could do little beyond holding the Dardanelles and the strip of land around the capital. The only people who would wage war seriously were the Greeks, who still had a powerful and well-equipped army, and were supported by the naval might of England and France. They attacked in the west, occupying Thrace and marching on Constantinople. At the same time Greek forces cleared the coast of Asia Minor and advanced into the very heart of the country. Kemal waited for them in front of his headquarters at Ankara.

On 24th August 1921 began the furious battle that decided the future of Turkey. It lasted fourteen days, and was fought with passionate hatred and without quarter by two races which had been enemies for centuries. Time and again the Greeks attacked and were flung back. In the end, with no more strength left, they retreated, scorching the earth as they went.

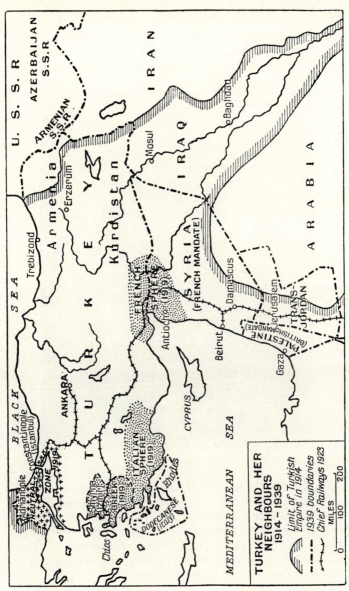

TURKEY AND HER
NEIGHBOURS
1914 ~ 1939

///// Limit of Turkish
Empire in 1914
—··— 1939 boundaries
·+·+· Chief Railways 1923

MILES
0   100   200

MEDITERRANEAN SEA

BLACK SEA

U. S. S. R

AZERBAIJAN
S.S.R

ARMENIAN
S.S.R

Armenia

IRAN

Erzerum

Trebizond

Constantinople
(Istanbul)

Adrianople

NEUTRAL
ZONE

Smyrna

GREEK
(1919)

ITALIAN
SPHERE
(1919)

Chios

Rhodes

DODECANESE
(Italy)

ANKARA

T U R K E Y

Kurdistan

Mosul

Baghdad

IRAQ

FRENCH
SPHERE
(1919)

Antioch

SYRIA
(FRENCH MANDATE)

Damascus

Beirut

Jerusalem

PALESTINE
(BRITISH MANDATE)

TRANS-
JORDAN

Gaza

CYPRUS

ARABIA

B

His army exhausted and his equipment sadly depleted, Kemal had not the military strength left even to pursue the defeated enemy. But his victory had one important effect, at

E.N.A.

A Peasant of Izmir

least, for the French and Italians who had hoped to secure spheres of influence in Turkey now quietly made their exit. The Turks were jubilant. Mustapha Kemal was given the title of 'Ghazi' or 'Destroyer of the Christians.' Many urged him now to make peace, but he would have none of it. For a whole year he worked tirelessly, drilling and re-equipping his army for the last fight outside Smyrna.

Stealth and surprise were his chief weapons. In August 1922 Mustapha Kemal met his commanders and with great secrecy made the final dispositions. On the night of the 26th a ball was to be held at his house. Amid the preparations for these festivities he moved his army up to the Greek positions and attacked suddenly in the very early morning.

The Greek Army was broken, the soldiers scattered and fled. Within a fortnight, and after scenes of savagery never surpassed, the Turks occupied Smyrna. In three more weeks Mustapha Kemal had persuaded England and France to get the Greek Army out of Thrace. In November a Peace Conference was sitting at Lausanne, and in July 1923 a treaty was made. All foreign troops moved out of Turkey, and the conquest of Smyrna was ratified.

Out of the ruins of a corrupt and discredited empire Mustapha Kemal was making a nation. 'Turkey for the Turks' was his cry, and it has guided the country's rulers ever since. Constantinople, with its unpleasant associations of Ottoman rule, gave place to a new capital at Ankara. There, in spite of every obstacle of terrain and climate, a splendid city has been built. Turkey now became a republic with Mustapha Kemal as its president. He introduced universal franchise (votes for all men and women). This was even more democratic than the franchise in Great Britain at that time, but Turkey could not be described as a democracy. Kemal's power over his own party was so great that he was able to act as a dictator.

Never has a state been reconstructed with such fury and speed. Old customs were ruthlessly cast away, and new manners, names, and dress introduced by force. First of all, the Turks had to realize that they were a nation. All foreign words were struck out of the dictionary and Turkish ones substituted. Towns were renamed. Constantinople became Istanbul, and Smyrna, Izmir.

At the same time the country was completely westernized. The reforming fury of Mustapha Kemal penetrated into the very households of the people. It reminds one of Peter the Great of Russia who shaved off the beards of his nobles.

Kemal was quite as thorough. He made it illegal to wear the old Turkish fez, and compelled everybody to wear a hat. Policemen rode through the streets confiscating every fez they

E.N.A.

Turkish Dancing Girls

saw, and people rushed to the stores for hats—any kind of hats, flowered or plain, so long as they had brims. The president himself appeared in public in a lounge suit and straw Panama. He forbade women to wear the veil, and men to have more than one wife. He abolished the salaam as a greeting and taught the Turks the handshake. They were soon raising their hats in the streets and doing the latest ballroom dances.

Whatever was outworn or inefficient he abolished, and introduced something better to take its place. He made every Turk take a surname, changing his own name to Kemal Atatürk, which means 'Kemal, Father of the Turks.' When

The Harvesters: Modern Turkey

Kemal abolished the old Turkish script and introduced the Latin alphabet he travelled the length and breadth of the country with blackboard and chalk teaching poor people how to write their own names. Prizes were given for good work, and penalties imposed for laziness.

The Turkey of to-day is nothing like the clumsy empire

which was once called Turkish. Its boundaries are much smaller, its national character is much more pronounced. Atatürk had no desires for conquest, as other people had. He merely wanted to be left alone to shape the destinies of his new nation. He was succeeded on his death in 1938 by his only friend and right-hand man, Ismet Inönü. Since then Turkey has kept to her long-held policy, to do only that which would keep her out of dangerous situations, and allow her resources to be fully developed. For five years, while other powers were fighting the Second Great War, the Turks managed to remain neutral.

Turkey was the first power to upset the provisions of the treaties concluding the war of 1914–18. She was also among the first to establish a one-party state, and a virtual dictatorship. But this dictatorship has differed widely from those of Italy and Germany in that it has never sought to embark on a career of conquest. Its only concern has been the reconstruction of the country. New industries have sprung up and old ones have been modernized. Machinery has largely taken the place of hand labour. National education and the freeing of women from oriental slavery have been in the forefront of this great movement. The small but efficient army and navy, together with the mountainous nature of the country, made it a sufficient barrier against German expansion during the critical years of the war, and guarded the flank of British armies operating in Syria and Egypt. The long neutrality of Turkey, persistently and cleverly maintained by her statesmen through difficult years, proved a great contribution to the victory of the Allies.

CHAPTER V

ITALY: THE RISE OF FASCISM

In the early part of the nineteenth century 'Italy' was but a geographical expression, not the united State which we know to-day. Thanks to the efforts of such men as Cavour the statesman, Mazzini the poet, and Garibaldi the soldier, and the goodwill of Liberal ministers in Britain, the many Italian states were combined under King Victor Emmanuel II. This new Italy had a Parliament on the English model, and was democratic. A small empire was gained, consisting of part of Somaliland, Libya, and a few islands, but, like Germany, Italy was late in the 'grab' for colonies. During the Great War the Italians fought with the Allies, hoping to gain what the Treaty of London in 1915 promised, the Brenner frontier, Dalmatia, part of Albania, and a part of Turkey.

The Treaty of Versailles left Italy indignant. Having lost 652,000 dead, she gained only the Brenner Pass, Trieste, and Istria, and nothing to speak of in the Adriatic, the Mediterranean, or Africa. Italians felt that President Wilson was a friend of the Czechs at their expense, and in disgust Signor Orlando left the Peace Conference for a time.

D'Annunzio, the romantic soldier-poet, lover of war, and extreme patriot, expressed this disgust of the Italian public when he seized Fiume, claiming it as an Italian port, although it was necessary to the Yugoslavs as an outlet to the sea for their trade. And though his own Government expelled him, the affair showed clearly the dissatisfaction of his countrymen at the terms of the peace settlement.

Though fortunate in some respects, the Italy of 1919 was, in the main, a sorry country. Its population of 40,000,000 was 60 per cent agricultural. There were a few large industries in the north, but these depended on foreign supplies of coal and iron. Many trade unions and co-operative

27

societies existed to benefit the people, yet they were not fully developed or secure institutions, and were sometimes destructive in their aims. The Parliament was meant to resemble the stable English Government, but the large number of parties made this impossible. Returning soldiers from the front found neglect and unemployment awaiting them, strikes and violence in the country, trade and communications breaking down, bribery and profiteering everywhere, parties without leaders, and governments without strength or courage. The Socialists might have saved the country if quarrels had not weakened them; some looked to Moscow and the Third International for guidance, while others were anti-Russian.

Italy needed a leader who would bring good government, justice, trade, and education to a chaotic land. It found a strong man. It failed to find a good one.

Benito Mussolini was born in 1883, the son of a Socialist blacksmith and a simple, devout mother. Poverty and temperament made him unhappy and rebellious even as a child. For a short while he taught in a village school, but it was not in his nature to play the part of a humble, obscure man for long.

In Switzerland he came into contact with many energetic rebels and Socialists. His large jaw, dirty agitated appearance, and the restless ill nature in his black eyes attracted attention. Short, intelligent, conceited, he acquired a rare gift of violent oratory. He was often in trouble with the police, and even went to prison for offences, such as falsifying his passport, avoiding military service, and publishing wild articles in the newspapers. Back in Italy again he rose rapidly as a Socialist leader, organizing strikes and noisy demonstrations. 'A rag to be planted on a dunghill' was his description of the national flag.

During the Great War Mussolini started as a pacifist, but soon changed his mind and urged that Italy should join the Allies. His enemies claimed that he had been 'bought' by a newspaper, and expelled him from the Socialist party. As Corporal Mussolini he fought in the trenches for thirty-eight days, sent many photographs of himself 'in the front line' to his paper, was wounded during army exercises, and claimed to have opened the road to Trieste 'with my own blood.'

Such was Mussolini in 1918. Renounced by his party he still called himself a Socialist. But 'What is right?' worried

E.N.A

Benito Mussolini

him less than the question 'How can I get on?' Dreams of himself as a new Caesar ruling a new Roman Empire haunted him. He was prepared to adopt any political programme which would offer him a ladder to fame.

A year after the close of the war Mussolini formed the 'Fascist Party,' so named from the bundle of rods carried by

*B

the policemen of ancient Rome. Its attempts to win power through elections failed miserably. In Milan only 5,000 votes were gained out of 346,000. So the party turned to violence. Workers were organized in armed bands to create strikes. Soon, however, it was found more profitable to turn against the Socialists and help smash up the trade unions and co-operative societies. The weak Government of Rome was afraid of the Socialists and Communists, and in its feebleness even assisted Mussolini and his growing number of followers in their street battles.

In October 1922 the Fascists marched on Rome, their leader demanding control of the Government. The king did nothing to oppose him. In all but name Mussolini became Dictator of Italy, for although he did not at once destroy Parliament, from the first he used terror and murder to put down opposition. Members of the party were schooled to rid the country of critics by shootings, vulgar insults, beatings, and imprisonment. Both inside and outside Italy civilized opinion was shocked by the assassination of Matteotti, the most fearless and outstanding of the Socialists, but the storm which followed abated when the Duce cleverly worked up an agitation against the Communists. By fair means or foul, people were made to vote for the Fascists, until in 1924 an overwhelming majority was obtained in Parliament.

During the next five years Mussolini refashioned the country to secure his complete dictatorship. He took all the chief ministries into his own hands, and power to decree laws himself. Italy was made into a 'totalitarian' state, i.e. a state without opposition parties. At the head was the dictator, assisted by the Fascist Grand Council. These chose the Senate or Upper House. The House of Commons was made to represent not districts, but the industrial corporations, which were trade unions of both employed and employers. The corporations elected 800 men, and from this number the Fascist Grand Council chose 400. Government, it was argued, was not a business for amateurs, but for trained men of industry, agriculture, and the professions, representing their own callings. The effect of all these arrangements was

Fascist Public Works: a City formerly a Marsh

that Mussolini ruled the party, and the party ruled the country. Free discussion and free elections were thus abolished in what was now called the 'Corporate State.'

A definite success for the dictator was his settlement with the Church. Since 1870, when the Union of Italy had deprived the papacy of its extensive lands, the quarrel between

Associated Press Photo

Fascism captures Youth

the Pope and the Italian Government had persisted. In 1929 Pope Pius XI agreed with Mussolini upon a settlement which pleased all Roman Catholics. The small Vatican City in Rome, with its population of 528, was made independent. The Church kept its rights over religious education but was not to interfere in politics or trade. Roman Catholicism was recognized as the State religion.

The teachings of Fascism were designed to create order at home and 'greatness' abroad. The individual was to exist only for the State. Whatever was done in the name of Italy, even the tearing up of treaties, or murder, was right. War and military glory were made romantic and attractive—'War puts the stamp of nobility upon the people.' Women

E.N.4

Fascist Youth and its Idol, Napoleon

were to have no political rights, but were to concern themselves with domestic duties. The free press was muzzled, and newspapers became organs of the Government.

There was much that Mussolini could point to, to show the advance of Italy under his dictatorship. Roads, railways, and other public works were greatly improved; laws controlling wages, hours of work, and national insurance showed some progress; and the large numbers of citizens who could not read decreased. All leisure and cultural societies were organized in the *Dopolavoro,* or 'afterwork' institution, and youths were trained to develop sturdy bodies and Fascist minds. Impressed by the new buildings, by the fact that Italian trains now ran punctually, by the apparent contentment of the people, and by the attraction of uniforms, grand parades, and mass demonstrations of patriotism, many foreigners were willing to forget the gangster methods which the Duce had used in his rise to fame, seeing only the triumph of a splendid youth movement. Beyond the Alps, Germany, distressed and hungry for unity, order, and greatness, watched the work of the dictator with a mixture of bewilderment and envy.

But Liberals abroad, including many Italians who had fled their native land, considered that Fascist Italy was rotten at the core. In place of free discussion and self-government they saw tyranny and the grip of self-seeking, black-shirted officials. Most ominous of all was the use of deceit and force in international affairs. These methods had been tried and found successful in 1923 when Mussolini demanded an indemnity from Greece for the murder of some Italian officers on the Albanian frontier. The island of Corfu was bombarded by the Italian fleet, and though the Greeks appealed to the League this did not save them from Italian aggression, and they had to pay a large sum of money. Though herself a member of the League of Nations Italy was daily praising war and making demands on the rest of the world for colonies and the right to expand, a policy which was bound to lead sooner or later to international strife, and, if unchecked, to world chaos.

CHAPTER VI

IN 1914 Russia found herself aligned with France and Great Britain against Germany. The Allies had great faith in the power of her arms and her millions of men. While they were withstanding the furious German onslaught in the west, the 'Russian steam-roller' was moving over the borders of Poland into Germany itself. Victory in the east seemed in sight, when suddenly the collapse came. General von Hindenburg turned the tables, and the Russians were driven back with immense losses into their own country. It was then that the true state of affairs began to be known. The huge Russian armies were badly trained; their supplies were either inadequate or non-existent. At last, after two and a half years of defeat, the Russian people, impatient at the corruption in high places and the unending misrule and misery, could hold out no longer. Risings occurred in Petrograd and every other large city in the country. Thus began Russia's march into a new life.

The tsar, the last representative of a line which had held undisputed sway in the country for hundreds of years, had to give up his throne. A Liberal Government took office. Its aim was 'to restore peace and security, to carry on the war, and to satisfy the people of Russia that the old state of affairs would be changed.'

It did not last long, for the grievances of the Russian people were too many and too old to be remedied by anything short of complete social changes. Hundreds of years of repression had brought about the existence of many revolutionary parties and doctrines. Among these were the Communists, who had been exiled and persecuted for years. The revolution brought them home from their retreats in Switzerland and America, and from their prison camps in Siberia. Among them was the Russian thinker and statesman, Lenin.

Lenin and his party, the Bolsheviks, as they were called, came into power. They promised the workers and the soldiers peace with Germany and the possession of their lands and factories. The sailors mutinied and murdered their officers, the soldiers deserted and returned home to claim their lands. Manor houses were burnt, many landowners were murdered, and the peasants entered into possession with the backing of the new Bolshevik Government. Peace with Germany was

E.N.A

Russia, Land of Many Races: a Turkoman Girl

quickly concluded at the Treaty of Brest-Litovsk (March 1918), and the revolution was complete.

But it still had to be defended. Many of the officers in the army had taken up arms against the revolution. Petrograd and Moscow were imperilled by anti-Bolshevik or 'White' armies, the British had occupied Archangel and Murmansk in the north, and a series of anti-Communist movements in Siberia threatened to overwhelm the whole of that vast land. It was three years before these civil wars were finally won by the Government, and in them Russia suffered a double share of massacre, starvation, and famine.

The Bolsheviks were now faced with the task of building

up the resources of their ruined country. They believed that the State should own all the industries, and began to put their beliefs into practice. Factories were taken over and handed to committees of workmen to organize, peasants were forbidden to trade, and all their produce, save that which was estimated to cover family needs, was taken for the use of the State. The result was appalling. Industrial output fell rapidly. The peasants produced only what they were forced to produce to keep them going until the next year. Some even consumed the corn which should have been saved for the following spring sowing. There were peasant risings, transport broke down, and both town and country starved.

It was obvious that some of these Bolshevik ideals would have to be sacrificed if Russia was to live. There was no way open to Lenin but to relax the stringent laws that had been made to control trading, and to allow the peasants again to own private property. Under this 'New Economic Policy' more goods were produced, shops gradually opened again, and the land was better used.

The Government was now completely remodelled on the 'Soviet' system. There was to be only one political party in the whole of Russia—the Communist party. It was, and still is, highly exclusive, and even to be a member of it is thought to be a great distinction. In a country of over one hundred and fifty million people it has scarcely ever been more than a few million strong. Its members are hand-picked by a close scrutiny of parentage, education, and political beliefs, and every member is devoted to the cause he serves, putting its welfare before his own life if need be. The country, or rather the group of countries (for Russia is a federation of many states), is governed by this party and the bodies which govern it are known as the Soviets of the various states.

The word 'soviet' means a council, and was first used in 1905, when, during the first revolution, a body, elected by the manual workers of Leningrad (then St. Petersburg), met together. The idea was again adopted after the 1917 revolution, and a second soviet of workers', peasants', and soldiers' deputies came into being. This assembly took control from

Russian Ballet Dancer

the Liberal Government and has existed ever since. Hence the term Soviet Government which we use to-day. In 1936 the Government of Russia was remodelled, and the soviet idea runs through it completely. Every town and village has its own soviet to deal with local affairs, all persons over the age of eighteen having a vote for candidates who are acceptable to the Communist party. No other candidates are allowed. In the same way every district, province, and republic has its own soviet, and above them all is the Supreme Soviet, elected in precisely the same way. It consists of two houses. The first, or the Soviet of the Union, is elected on a basis of one member per locality of about 300,000 people. The second, or Soviet of Nationalities, exists with the object of preserving the rights of the many races inside the Soviet Union, and is elected on a basis of so many members per state.

The Supreme Soviet elects about fifty of its own members who form what is called a 'presidium.' This body carries on the business of the State when the soviet is not sitting, and it chooses the Council of Ministers, which is the parallel of our Cabinet, except that the ministers are called 'People's Commissars.' Each of these has a State department under him, and is responsible for one branch of State activity.

In July 1923 the U.S.S.R., or 'Union of Soviet Socialist Republics' was formally established. The U.S.S.R. is now a federation of independent states, and it contains a central government (the Supreme Soviet), and for each state a smaller independent government, with its soviet, its commissars, and its presidium. The Central Government, through its commissars, is in charge of all matters affecting the whole federation, such as defence, finance, communications, health, food, and planning.

The story of the development of the New Russia is closely associated with the life of Joseph Stalin. This famous statesman is, strictly speaking, not a Russian by birth, but was the son of a Georgian shoemaker, and was brought up in a village in the distant Caucasus Mountains. A hatred of the tsarist regime, a keen intelligence, and leanings towards Communism brought him into the revolutionary camp where, during his

The Constitution of the Union of Soviet Socialist Republics

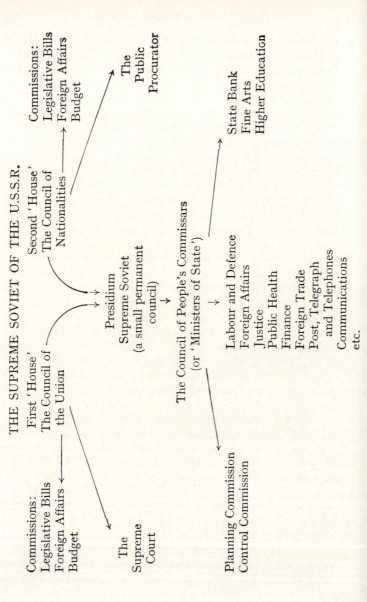

THE SUPREME SOVIET OF THE U.S.S.R.

Commissions:
Legislative Bills
Foreign Affairs
Budget

First 'House'
The Council of
the Union

Second 'House'
The Council of
Nationalities

Commissions:
Legislative Bills
Foreign Affairs
Budget

The
Public
Procurator

Presidium
Supreme Soviet
(a small permanent
council)

The Supreme
Court

The Council of People's Commissars
(or 'Ministers of State')

State Bank
Fine Arts
Higher Education

Labour and Defence
Foreign Affairs
Justice
Public Health
Finance
Foreign Trade
Post, Telegraph
  and Telephones
Communications
etc.

Planning Commission
Control Commission

youth, he became an agitator. During the war of 1914–18, while Lenin was exiled in Switzerland, Stalin was imprisoned in Siberia. He returned with the revolution, and quickly

E.N.A.

Joseph Stalin

re-established his influence in the party. Under Lenin he was given the post of Commissar for Nationalities. In this he did a great work by recognizing the right of the many nations which comprised the Greater Russia to their own languages, customs, culture, and government. By this he completely destroyed the old idea of subject races, and did much to make the old Russian empire into a harmonious confederation of states.

In 1924, when Lenin died, his work was incomplete. The dispute as to the future leadership of the Communist party, and hence of all Russia, had been going on while he was alive.

Associated Press Photo
Leon Trotsky

It now came to a head. Stalin's most formidable rival was Leon Trotsky, a brilliant apostle of Communism, whose ambition was to spread the revolution over the whole world. Stalin, on the other hand, was a grim, hard-headed realist, who rightly saw that Russia must first establish herself. He had powerful adherents, young patriots fired with zeal for their country's safety and progress. By them Trotsky was expelled, first from the presidium, then from the party, and finally from Russia altogether. From exile in Mexico and Sweden he never ceased to preach world communism. After many years he fell by the hand of an assassin.

Stalin was now secretary of the party, and leader in fact, if not in name, of all Russia. He appointed as premier his great friend Molotov, and began piece by piece to build his state.

Russia was alone in the whole world, living under a system which was almost universally hated and feared. There was very little food, machinery, industry, or trade. There were no weapons to guard her vulnerable frontiers, and the only defences were the vast spaces of her domains. If Russia was to exist it must be by forcing the powers of her people to the utmost, by ruthless severity with no mercy for opponent or idler. But, above all, it must be by teaching the workers in factory and on farm something of what the future could hold for them, and thus creating around the members of the Communist party a solid people, marching with enthusiasm towards the ultimate goal of self-sufficiency and power.

These were the ideas behind the famous five-year plans. The first one was begun in 1928. Every industry, every state, had its plan, to be studied not only by the government experts, but by all the people themselves down to the most insignificant worker. The farmer had to grow more corn for export so that more machinery could be bought in exchange. The foreign technicians who came with the new machinery were in time to be replaced by young Russians, who in turn would teach others how to build and maintain it. If production lagged behind schedule, whatever the cause, punishment would follow. If production exceeded the estimates, public recognition and encouragement must be given. Graphs and charts were exhibited in factories, schools, and public places so that Russians, even those who could not read, should *know* what was being done and what still remained to be done. Throughout the period every part of the plan was to be kept under review, mistakes rectified, and the foundations laid for the second five-year plan.

At the end of this first term industry was on its feet, Russian technicians were coming out of the colleges, and a hundred new manufacturing towns had sprung up. But, above all,

Planet News

A Collective Farm Meeting

the idea of self-sufficiency through industry had permeated to the very centre of Russian society. Stalin even felt strong enough to abolish private farming, a thing which Lenin had tried to do and failed. Many industrious peasants who had accumulated property were dispossessed. The sufferings of some of them were terrible, but the process went on. It has been stated in some quarters that millions were either shot or sent to forced labour in Siberia. Many of these private farmers killed off their cattle and livestock rather than give it up, but even the threat of famine was not allowed to stand in the way. If the first harvest suffered, or even the second,

Pictorial Press

The Lesson: a Glimpse of Russian Education

many people would starve, but in time the motor tractor stations would bring in a new era of plenty.

By 1938 the second five-year plan came to an end. The people were feeling the benefit. They now had boots and shoes, more and better food and clothing, but, above all, they had security, guaranteed by comprehensive State insurance for everybody. They had free education, free dental and medical treatment, clinics, sanatoria, crèches for children whose mothers worked in the factories, and public amenities of all kinds. This was not yet universal, but it was more than a good beginning. These advantages were not gained peaceably. As with the other dictatorships, oppression and cruelty were used to stifle opposition. Labour camps, purges, and secret police (the Ogpu, now the NKVD) were employed to further the plans of the Bolsheviks.

The new Russia had at first no place for the Church. The orthodox religion practised under the tsars had been very corrupt, and when Bolshevik rule came everything short of complete prohibition was done to stamp it out altogether. Churches were closed or converted into social centres and anti-religious museums. During the perilous years freedom of thought was not allowed, for it might have entailed danger to the State. But when the dangers passed away the natural piety of the Russian people was allowed free rein. The Orthodox Church is again recognized by the State.

What does the average Russian peasant or citizen think of all this? Experience of his bravery in war, and his determination to defend his country with his own life if need be, shows us that he values the new system immensely. Since the early days of the U.S.S.R. a new generation has grown up, cradled and reared in the atmosphere of Russian Communism. From comparing their own state with that described in the tales told by their grandfathers they cannot but pronounce it good. It is inevitable that their knowledge of the rest of the world will be incomplete, and that their picture of such societies as the English and American will be distorted as long as their education, books, radio, and films are so censored that only propaganda favourable to Communism is given them.

The events which brought Russia into the war, and the miracle of the Russian endurance under blows of Nazi Germany, will be described later. It was to be hoped that one of the results of five years of comradeship would be a complete understanding within the United Nations.

CHAPTER VII

THE FAR EAST

JAPAN is the most densely populated country in the world. Its rapid industrialization dates from 1868. Thirty years later a Parliament was created, but it was in no sense democratic as the emperor remained a divine ruler, and the descendants of the old feudal and military aristocracy retained most of the power in the land. Japan became virtually owned by the army and navy chiefs, and some eight business families such as the Mitsui and Mitsubishi houses. The bulk of the people became very poor factory workers, or remained even poorer peasants. Their religion, a mixture of ancestor worship and patriotism, kept them obedient, though individual assassinations have always been common.

China is the largest country, and has the oldest civilization, in the world. Her peoples, numbering almost one-quarter of the human race, are chiefly un-military, patient, and good-natured peasants. The nineteenth century saw the entry of white traders, and the growth of large industrial ports with the worst slums in the world.

Towards the end of the nineteenth century Japan began to expand. From then on the Government did all in its power to increase the population, and then claim more 'living space.' Hence wars became inevitable. After conflicts with China and Russia from 1894 to 1904, a foothold was gained in Korea and in Manchuria, and railways were built with troops stationed to guard them. During the World War of 1914–18 China was in a state of civil war; Russia was soon in the throes of revolution. Japan noticed with satisfaction how weak the central Chinese Government was in Manchuria, where thirty million people lived in a rich, undeveloped country.

The Manchu dynasty, with its palace at Pekin, lasted until 1911. Then, inspired by the teaching of Sun-Yat-Sen, the Chinese created a republic, accepted many western ideas, and began to strive against foreign exploitation. Many civil wars broke out as rival military governors, or 'war lords,' made themselves semi-independent in the provinces. Out of

Associated Press Photo
Japanese Types: the Newspaper Boy

the chaos came two governments, one at Pekin in the north, the other, the 'Kuo-Min-Tang' or 'National People's Party,' in the south at Canton.

After 1925 General Chiang Kai-Shek, successor of Sun-Yat Sen, and destined to become the leader of China in World War II, extended the power of the Kuo-Min-Tang over central

China, the rich Yangtse valley, and, gaining control over the northern Government, renamed Pekin 'Peiping' or 'Northern Peace.' He was now the foremost leader, but Communism was spreading fast among the peasantry, and Chiang was a Nationalist, not a Communist. From 1927 to 1937 most of his energies were taken up in campaigns against the 'Reds,' who trekked west to the interior where they established soviets in the remote provinces. As a result of the increasing menace of Japan, Chiang and the Communists drew closer together. China was thus unified under Chiang Kai-shek and the Kuo-Min-Tang, but this unity was far from complete.

While China had been struggling painfully within its own frontiers, Japan had planned and achieved the conquest of Manchuria. In 1927 the Japanese Prime Minister wrote a statement which might be called a miniature Japanese version of *Mein Kampf*. It said: 'Japan must adopt a policy of blood and iron. . . . In order to conquer the world Japan must conquer Europe and Asia; in order to conquer Europe and Asia Japan must first conquer China; and in order to conquer China Japan must conquer Manchuria.' How did Japan gain her first object?

Manchuria in 1928 was ruled by a Chinese war lord, Chang-Tso-Lin, who tried for a time to gain power over all China, but had to give way before Chiang Kai-shek. Chang was assassinated on the Japanese-owned railway, and his son came to an agreement with Chiang Kai-shek, much to the anger of the Japanese. The year 1931 was ripe for action. The Western Powers were staggering under a worldwide trade depression, poverty, unemployment, and bankruptcy. In September 1931, therefore, the Japanese staged the 'Mukden Incident,' and claiming that Chinese bandits had attacked their railway, invaded Manchuria. China appealed to the League of Nations.

This was a real test for the League. Its decision might mean a turning-point in the history, not only of China, but of the whole world. Unhappily Britain was worried by her own affairs, and was not able to fight for the protection of China. The U.S.A. was, of course, deeply concerned in the problem, although she was not a member of the League. She followed throughout the policy which she called the 'Open Door,' i.e. no special privileges for any state, but equal

Associated Press Photo

Woman Field Worker in Manchukuo

opportunity for all countries to trade freely with China. But America would not move without Britain. So, although the Western Powers condemned Japan's action, they hoped to appease her and limit the war as far as possible. Later chapters in this book will show many more attempts on the part of peace-loving nations to appease those governments which threatened war, and how the story proceeds from Shanghai to Addis Ababa, Guernica, Rotterdam, Coventry, and other scenes of devastation.

Generalissimo Chiang Kai-shek

The League of Nations did, however, send a commission under Lord Lytton to study and report on the war in Manchuria, and could not do otherwise than pronounce Japan guilty of aggression. Japan defied this report, conquered Manchuria, renamed it 'Manchukuo,' set it up as an 'independent' state under a puppet emperor, and proceeded to develop the wealth of the country. Then it left the League of

Nations, claiming that it had broken no treaties because it had never declared war. The Japanese general, it is said, wept because the League of Nations would not agree that the occupation of Manchuria was peaceful.

From 1932 to 1937, when Japan and China were supposed to be at peace, Japan conquered Jehol, gained a foothold south of the Great Wall, and intrigued to separate the five provinces of north China from the south. Soon she made fresh demands, ordering China to suppress Communism, and to compel Chinese people to buy Japanese goods and cease their boycott, while she continued to stir up one war lord against another so that she could say to the rest of the world: 'We are compelled to interfere in China to keep the peace.' This undeclared war, or 'China Affair,' as it was called by Japan, might have gone on indefinitely, but with the progress of Chiang Kai-shek in reaching agreement with the Reds, Japan had to act again if she were to keep China weak.

Japan was now fast becoming very like a Fascist state. The China war had given more power to the army and navy chiefs, whose aim was to make Japan a totalitarian state. Between 1933 and 1936 the police arrested 50,013 people charged with 'dangerous thoughts.' In 1936 she made an alliance with Germany and Italy which soon developed into the famous 'Rome-Berlin-Tokyo Axis.' Like her allies she worked up hatred against Russia and the Communists, and even propaganda against the Jews, although the average Japanese peasant scarcely knew what a Jew was. She began to talk of her 'divine' mission in east Asia, of the 'New Order,' and the 'East Asia Co-prosperity Sphere'—a vague term by which Japan implied that she intended to conquer and possess the whole of China, the lands as far as the frontiers of India, Australia, and all the islands of the Pacific. Within her borders she prepared the people for one object only—war, using the 'gravity of the situation' and the 'national emergency' as the excuse to override all opposition.

On 7th July 1937 Japanese troops in Tientsin were holding night manœuvres when they 'lost' a private who had gone off drinking and flirting. They blamed the Chinese and immediately sent a huge army to Shanghai. China had been patient, but now Chiang Kai-shek decided that she must either resist or become a slave-empire of the Japanese. 'Even a Buddha will get angry if slapped in the face often enough' says the Chinese proverb.

In the north Pekin quickly fell. Farther south in the heart of China, Shanghai was taken after fierce battles in which the

E.N.A.

Poverty in China. Street in Shanghai

Chinese lost 450,000 casualties in three months. Nanking followed, and the Japanese considered the war as won.

Chiang Kai-shek and his masses of ill-equipped peasants, however, did not collapse. Slowly they retreated inland, every defeat of the Chinese costing the Japanese dear. In 1938 the Japanese forces in the north met those coming from Nanking. Hankow and Canton soon fell. Yet far in the north Chinese armies held Shansi, while in the centre they retreated up the Yangtse River, and made Chungking their new capital. By June 1940 the Japanese controlled the river

C

The Great Wall of China: View from the Nankow Pass

as far as Ichang. Nevertheless, despite their enormous advantages in material, despite the fact that China was practically sealed off from the rest of the world, despite the 2,000,000 or more Chinese casualties, Japan could not end the war. China was like a huge sponge which could absorb its conquerors, and the war was uniting its people as never before.

From 1939 onwards Japan became more and more concerned with her further aims of expansion in the south seas, and more and more involved in ultimate war with Britain and America. She made desperate efforts to get China to surrender. The Chinese held on.

So when in December 1941 the Japanese attacked Pearl Harbor, China's lonely struggle became part of the world-wide war.

CHAPTER VIII

THE NAZIS

ADOLF HITLER was in the fortress prison of Landsberg in Bavaria. He did not find prison life irksome, for he had two well-appointed rooms on the first floor, above the ordinary prisoners, and in company with his friends. He was allowed to receive as many visitors as he wished, and was deluged with presents from his admiring followers. Here for almost a year he watched events in Germany, received reports, and dictated to his secretary the first part of *Mein Kampf*, the book which later became the gospel of the Nazi party.

What had Hitler to give to Germany? *Mein Kampf* tells us, for in this story of his life and hopes he reveals his formula for the redemption of his country. Germany had been broken in 1918, he said, but not through the defeat of her armies. The country had been betrayed to the enemy. Sects had arisen which were tearing each other apart, and which would destroy the State if they were allowed to go on existing. The only remedy was a united Germany, a Germany only for the people of German race, and purged from all impurities, such as the Jews and the Slavs who were inferiors. The Jews in particular were bitterly accused of cornering Germany's wealth, and of conspiring with Jews all over the world to control world trade. Thus in his idea 'International Jewry' was responsible for all the evil.

It was, therefore, one of Hitler's main objects to dispossess the Jews in Germany, to create there the new state of the pure 'Nordic' man. The Germans themselves must rise under his leadership to create this state.

With the newly forged weapon of a united nation Hitler would then reverse the decisions of the Treaty of Versailles. The Polish Corridor, Alsace-Lorraine, Austria, Bohemia, and the colonies would be brought back to the Reich. Freedom would be won in the teeth of the enemy. Germany, a

regenerate nation, would spread eastwards into the wide
lands of the Poles and the Ukrainians, to conquer 'living
space' for the expanding 'master race.' Germans the
world over would return their allegiance to the mother-
country. America, north and south, would have its little

E.N.A.

Gustav Stresemann

colonies of Nazis who, when the time came, would become
reunited to their kindred, one people, members of one state,
and under one leader. Thus the power of Hitler would
become world-wide.

At first his gospel found few adherents, apart from his old
admirers, for Germany was then passing through a phase
which might well have led her to democracy and peace. The

French had had little profit from the occupation of the Ruhr coalfield, and M. Poincaré, who had been responsible for this, had lost favour and resigned. At the same time there arose in Germany an enlightened statesman, Gustav Stresemann, who was anxious to cure the terrible evils by coming to terms.

Thus in 1924 a new scheme of reparations was introduced. It was known as the 'Dawes Plan,' after the American general who had been chairman of the Committee of Investigation. Germany by this plan was to pay £50,000,000 the first year, rising to £125,000,000 in five years, and in order to help her to re-establish her industries, and thus to pay her debts, she was to have substantial loans. The plan gave considerable satisfaction, and in five years the Germans paid about £400,000,000. The French were accordingly withdrawn from the Ruhr, and the way was made clear for more friendly relations.

In the next year, 1925, a sincere attempt was made by the Governments of Germany, France, Great Britain, Belgium, and Italy to make a war in the west impossible. They signed a treaty at Locarno, in which France and Germany promised not to attack each other, and if either broke this agreement, the other three promised to go to the aid of the power which was attacked. This was the one time between the wars when the prospect of a lasting peace seemed possible, and for this bright period Dr. Stresemann, M. Briand, the French Foreign Minister, and Sir Austen Chamberlain were responsible.

Dr. Stresemann died in 1929 and M. Briand in 1932. It is very doubtful, had both of them lived longer, whether they would have been able to put off the day of rearmament or disperse the gathering clouds of war.

In December 1924 Adolf Hitler was a free man again. He had no organized party now, and no money, but he still had a few ardent supporters, and a certain number of sympathizers, especially among the youth of Germany. There was also a vast German public which for six years had looked in vain for salvation from distress and civil strife. They were like an army without a leader. Could National Socialism supply this need?

This is what Hitler and his friends decided to do. At first

he was forbidden by the authorities to speak at meetings, but there were other men like Hermann Göring, and the newspaper editor, Josef Göbbels, who were eager and able to do it for him. The party was re-founded in February 1925, and Hitler began again the work of organization. Until the death of Stresemann the results in membership were not startling,

E.N.A.

Joseph Göbbels

but the country was being prepared in mind and mood for the great Nazi revolution.

Hitler's methods were sensational and successful in capturing the imagination. Mass meetings in which the swastika was paraded, the famous greeting 'Heil Hitler,' the raised arm in salute, files upon files of young, brown-shirted enthusiasts in procession through the streets, vigorous denunciation of the Jews and foreign enemies, repeated declarations about Germany's rights and future; all these combined to draw to the party standard the younger and more virile elements of the German public.

Nazi methods were ruthless. The leaders of the movement

established a guard of picked men known as the S.S. (Schutz-Staffel) whose special work it was to protect them, and to keep order in their meetings. Those who heckled or opposed the speaker were thrown out, and sometimes injured. People known to be unsympathetic towards the Nazis were dealt with in the same way, sometimes in the street, sometimes in their own homes. If they were too powerful or beyond

E.N.A.

The Symbol: Storm Troops salute the Swastika

attack, their names were kept 'in the book' until the favourable day. All the while a war was going on in the streets between the Nazis and their enemies, the Communists.

With such methods the Nazi party captured the eye and ear of the general public. Many young people enrolled under the swastika, and gave their oath to fight for the new Germany, putting it before friends, family, and everything else. Its publicity grew. It permeated all classes and all professions. Money began to flow in again. Many respectable and peace-loving Germans, seeing in the movement at least a promise of order and progress after years of strikes, dissension, and semi-starvation, gave the movement their sympathy. These believed in all sincerity that if it was at all possible to put Germany on her feet again, Adolf Hitler would do it.

E.N.A.

Hermann Göring

After the death of Stresemann the National Socialist Party increased in membership by leaps and bounds—100,000 members in 1928, double the number in 1930, double again in 1932. In the elections of that year the party polled nearly fourteen million votes, and became the largest in Germany.

*C

Propaganda flooded the country. Photographs of Hitler were everywhere. Processions became longer and more martial, mass meetings were more frequent and more impressive. The Nazi songs were sung everywhere. The attention of the whole country was focused on this one man who was now being called 'Der Führer.'

The president of the German republic was the old Field Marshal von Hindenburg, the hero of the war of 1914–18, but now over eighty years of age. He sent for Hitler and offered him a place in the Government. But Hitler was sure that if he waited he would gain absolute power. He refused the appointment. One Government followed another, but none could hold on for long. In January 1933 von Hindenburg had again to summon the 'Austrian corporal,' the man whom he despised, and Hitler was made Chancellor.

From Chancellor to Dictator was an easier climb for one so ruthless. The chief obstacles to be eliminated were the Communists, the constitution, and Hitler's own personal rivals.

In the following month the House of Parliament, the Reichstag, was burnt down. This, of course, provided an excellent excuse for an onslaught upon the Communists. Some 4,000 were arrested, and all their newspapers suppressed. In March orders were given for the Nazi swastika to be flown alongside the black, white, and red standard of Germany. The Reichstag itself gave up to the Chancellor its right to make laws. In June 1934 Captain Röhm and a number of Nazis were concerned in a plot against Hitler. This was discovered and they were executed. According to Hitler they were wicked, vicious men, and the State had to be 'purged' of them.

Next there was the enormous task of wiping out all opposition among the general public. To achieve this the force of secret police, known as the 'Gestapo,' was organized to watch every German. Nazis were put in charge of the newspapers, broadcasting, the cinema, the theatre, schools, and universities; indeed everything that could possibly influence the opinions of the people. Similarly was begun the building of concentration camps, prisons which were soon to be the scenes of torture and murder affecting many millions of Jews, Communists, Christians, and other opponents of the regime. And at the same time everything possible was done to court popularity among the true 'Aryans' by schemes to promote employment, the building of houses, and entertainments of the mass-demonstration type.

Henceforward German democracy was dead, for the future was entrusted to the hands of one man—the all-powerful Führer.

CHAPTER IX

At the opening of Chapter III we told how the statesmen of 1919 created the League of Nations mainly to prevent war. In the same frame of mind they hoped to reduce the huge armed forces maintained by every country. Would the nations boldly disband their armies and put their trust in the new league?

Most people already realized that large armies owned by rival states are bound one day to clash; that weapons breed fear and hatred among neighbours, and lead to an armaments race which can only end in war; that the people who profit by manufacturing arms are tempted to want wars; that the ordinary citizen is crippled by taxation which is spent on waste and destruction. The years before the First Great War had shown how utterly false was the old Roman saying: 'If you wish for peace, prepare for war.'

Lloyd George had urged without success that the Allies should agree upon reducing their forces before signing the Covenant. His advice was not heeded. But with the completion of the peace treaties the way to disarmament seemed clear. Part 5 of the Treaty of Versailles compelled Germany to give up the bulk of her fighting power; and it looked forward to a 'general limitation of the armaments of all nations.' By Article 8 of the Covenant, members of the League agreed that peace required the reduction of national armaments to the lowest point consistent with national safety.

So Germany was disarmed, and the victors let it be understood that they would follow suit. Yet as months and years passed they showed increasing reluctance to do so. Worried by the failure of the U.S.A. to join the League, by the unrest in Germany, and by the claims of discontented states to extend their boundaries, the Allied governments feared to lay down their arms.

The story of the disarmament conferences in the years following 1919 is therefore mainly one of tragic failures. Again and again it was pointed out that 'collective security'

E.N.A.

Georges Clemenceau: One of the Architects of
the Treaty of Versailles

was necessary before the nations would dare to disarm; i.e. that the peace-loving peoples must band themselves together so firmly that no burglar-state would dream of attacking any one of them. France, more than any other nation, took this logical view. If the League of Nations had weapons to enforce its will, the countries of the world could do without separate armies. To blame the unsuccessful disarmament conferences instead of the faulty world organization, is like blaming the spots instead of trying to cure the measles.

The first commission on armaments set up at Geneva was composed chiefly of naval and military men who were more interested in increasing the number of their guns than in abolishing them, and consequently they did little more than

E.N.A

An Unfortified Frontier. Canadian Buses wait for
American Arrivals

collect information. One useful piece of work, however, was soon accomplished. In 1921 the U.S.A. called a conference at Washington to ensure peace in the Far East. The result was a naval treaty by which the leading sea powers of the world agreed to fix the maximum sizes of their battle fleets; those of the U.S.A., Great Britain, and Japan were to be in the ratio of 5 : 5 : 3.

From 1922 to 1925 the outlook became steadily brighter. Germany, under Stresemann, a man of great goodwill, seemed anxious to heal the breach with her old enemies, and asked for agreements to renounce all war and to settle her disputes with France and Poland peaceably. The resulting treaties of Locarno in 1925 really appeared to give Europe a great measure of security, so that many men thought it possible that disarmament could be achieved.

The League set up a preparatory commission to work at the problem. A multitude of difficulties, however, great and small, prevented its progress, all combining to show how little sense of safety the nations had, and how nervous they were of giving up their arms. 'If we weaken ourselves, how can we be sure that nobody will attack us?' said some. 'Shall we feel certain that other countries will not just pretend to disarm?' said others. 'Are soldiers on the reserve to count as forces?' said still others. When M. Litvinov of Russia suggested the complete abolition of all armies, navies, air forces, and war materials, he was distrusted as a dangerous Bolshevist and ignored. By 1927 nothing had been settled.

In 1930 Mr. MacDonald, the Labour leader of Great Britain, led the way in further efforts to fulfil one of his life ambitions. At a meeting in London of the chief naval powers, it was decided to limit the size of certain large ships, but on other questions, such as the abolition of submarines, no agreement could be reached. He accomplished little except to weaken Britain's navy without any compensating progress in collective security. For although in 1928 many states had signed the Kellogg-Briand Pact 'to abolish war as an instrument of policy,' this had been no more than a promise, and had made no real advance.

The work of the League to bring about disarmament came to a head in 1932. Hundreds of officials in Geneva and elsewhere had striven to make the world conference a success, not the least its chairman, Mr. Arthur Henderson, now an old and sick man. The resulting failure was tragic in the extreme. From the start until its end in 1934 it battled with an impossible task.

The death of Stresemann in 1929 and the rapid rise of Hitler had seen Germany passing from a mood of co-operation to one of defiance. Japan was openly defying the League in the Far East. Mussolini was daily parading the glories of war. So long as Germans demanded the right to equality and the right to tear up the Treaty of Versailles, France would not hear of disarmament. Britain, anxious for the success of the conference, yet wished to retain some bombing planes to keep unruly natives in order where the security of her colonies was at stake. To these difficulties was added a worse—the economic blizzard which swept through the world at this time, bringing poverty, misery, and unrest to all nations alike.

The humiliation of the world disarmament conference brought added insecurity to the nations and bitter blows to the League. Japan, Germany, and Italy either left Geneva or threatened to do so. News soon leaked out that Germany was secretly rearming on a large scale. Whatever his protestations, the author of *Mein Kampf* was hardly likely to labour for the success of disarmament and peace. And to his delight, other powers, anxious to preserve their independence, lost faith in the idea of collective security, and neither disarmed nor rearmed themselves sufficiently to withstand alone the attack of a strong aggressor.

CHAPTER X

WE have seen how the Italians were disappointed at the peace treaties, and how they felt that the promises which had been made to them in 1915 had not been fulfilled. The rise of the Fascist Government had been the outcome of this disappointment, and it had made Italy a power, for the time being, of the first magnitude.

It was the burning desire of Mussolini to see his country greater than she had ever been, and to have his own name go down to posterity as her great deliverer and the builder of the Italian empire. If he failed miserably, we must remember that it was partly due to the poor materials with which he worked. Italy in Roman times had been the centre of the world, the all-powerful land from which the Roman legions marched to build a civilization which spanned the whole of the then known world. All the riches and glamour of ancient days had supported the pomp of the imperial Caesars. But it was different in the nineteenth century, for with the coming of machines, wealth and trade passed over to countries which had iron, coal, and oil to make and work them. Italy has none of these. The people are for the most part hard-working peasants, with little to spare for building up a mighty state. Her industrial centres in the north, great as they became, were entirely dependent on materials brought in from abroad. Greatness and empire, in these modern days, can hardly exist on such flimsy foundations.

But this was what Mussolini wanted. He dreamed of the Mediterranean of the future, controlled by Italy and policed by Italian ships and planes, with Italian colonies fringing its southern shores. He taught his people to call it 'Mare Nostrum'—'Our Sea.'

Such a policy, if pursued to its limits, was bound to bring Italy into conflict with the French, who held Morocco and Algeria, and with the British who had for over two hundred years maintained an almost unbroken naval supremacy in the Mediterranean. All the lands on its southern shore were ruled by these two peoples, apart from Libya, which had been taken by the Italians from the Turks in 1911, and the small strip of Spanish Morocco. Indeed, in the whole of Africa there

The Emperor Haile Selassie   *E.N.A.*

remained only one totally independent country, and that was Abyssinia.

This land lies in the north-east of the continent, bordered by the Sudan on the west and by British and French Somali-land and the Italian colony of Eritrea at the southern end of the Red Sea. It is vast and for the most part barren and mountainous. For these reasons, and because of the warlike nature of its inhabitants, it had been left alone in the great scramble for Africa at the end of the nineteenth century. For years it had been the battleground of warlike chieftains until the coming of the Emperor Menelik stopped the civil wars for a time, and brought some semblance of unity to the country. When he died in 1913 it seemed that anarchy would return. In 1916, however, his cousin, Ras Tafari, was elected regent for Menelik's daughter, and later he became the Emperor Haile Selassie.

The European powers had long been interested in Abyssinia. In 1891 Great Britain and Italy had marked it out into 'spheres of influence,' Great Britain taking the west, where Lake Tsana feeds the river Nile, and Italy the north-east. Five years later the Italians tried to extend their influence by force of arms, but their army was destroyed by the Emperor Menelik at the battle of Adowa. It was obvious that Haile Selassie would have to set his country rapidly in order to prevent its falling into the hands of the new Italy.

This was no easy thing. The chieftains were semi-independent, but he defeated them one by one. He tried to abolish slavery and to raise a national Abyssinian army, but these things were almost impossible. The people were ignorant, there was no national spirit, the chieftains were turbulent, arms were scarce, the natives hated the idea of being Europeanized, and there were not enough educated young Abyssinians to stand at the emperor's side. Long before Abyssinia could ever hope to have a well-equipped national army the Italians were ready to strike. For two years they deliberately built up resources in Italian Somaliland and Eritrea for the great venture.

On 5th December 1934 a joint Anglo-Abyssinian frontier commission found a detachment of Italian soldiers encamped at a place called Walwal in the south of the country, and, as the maps showed, some distance over the Abyssinian side of the border. There was a fight, with casualties on both sides.

Abyssinia had been a member of the League of Nations since 1923, and the emperor now appealed to the League to take action against Italy for this act of aggression.

From that time onwards everything connected with Abyssinia

became front-page news. Mussolini had little difficulty in securing the goodwill of the French, who were beginning to fear the growing power of Germany. The British hesitated, for their Government was loth to offend Italy.

Associated Press Photo

An Abyssinian Family

To play for time Mussolini employed every possible ruse. He was preparing to attack when the rains ceased in October 1935. Great Britain, France, and even the League of Nations offered alternative solutions to an Italian conquest, but he rejected them all. Already the Italians had 400,000 men massed in Eritrea, and on 3rd October 1935 their army under General de Bono invaded Abyssinia.

It is strange that the affairs of a backward African state should loom so large as to be the first question in European politics. The importance of Abyssinia in the relations between the nations at that time was out of all proportion to its importance as a country. The Abyssinian affair was a second test case (Manchuria had been the first) as to whether the nations would be ready to support the principles laid down in the League Covenant, pledging them to 'take any action that may be deemed wise to safeguard the peace of nations.' This dispute was infinitely more serious to western Europe, because one day the soaring ambitions of Italy, and perhaps Germany, might set the great powers of Europe one against the other.

There appeared to be only two courses. The first was to allow Italy to go on. This would mean the end of the League's power altogether. The second course was to put into motion the machinery of sanctions (see above, p. 12). This would, if successful, mean the end of Italian ambitions, and preserve the independence of Abyssinia. No wonder, therefore, that this was the first question of the day.

The British Government had sought every way out of the difficulty short of the application of sanctions. The French were ready to make terms. Hitler, now securely placed in the Chancellery in Berlin, was pleased to see the bickerings of the other powers, for they would give him valuable opportunities, and perhaps an ally.

The League of Nations acted promptly. On 11th October the Italian aggression was condemned and sanctions were agreed upon. Largely owing to the energy of the British representative, Mr. Anthony Eden, it was decided to withhold supplies of arms from Italy and to grant them to Abyssinia, to deprive Italy of all loans, and to stop trading with her. But there were many obstacles. Some of the states concerned did not apply the sanctions they had promised, and the League was not willing to apply the vital oil sanctions or to call for the closing of the Suez Canal. Many believed that such sanctions would have put a speedy end to Italian aggression, but it was feared that either of these measures might bring about a general European war, which the League most desired to avoid. Moreover, Italy had already accumulated huge stocks of materials, and had time to obtain much more before 18th November, the date when sanctions were to become operative. It soon became apparent that the attempt to stop Italy would only quicken the enthusiasm and obstinacy of the Fascists.

The contest was unequal from the beginning. The emperor, in the hope of obtaining League support, had avoided any gesture which might be interpreted as military action. General de Bono was thus able to occupy Adigrat and Adowa without opposition. Thus the defeat of 1896 was avenged bloodlessly. Far away to the south the Abyssinian bands were slowly joining together without unified plan. The Italian advance was continued as far as Makale. Behind their lines the engineers were building roads and bringing the supply bases nearer to the front line.

Meanwhile the question of sanctions was still being debated at Geneva, but with little result. In December M. Laval and Sir Samuel Hoare, the foreign ministers of France and Great Britain, produced a peace plan that was acceptable to their two governments. They proposed that the emperor should be urged to cede to Italy almost the whole of northern Abyssinia, and to allow Italians to settle in the south. The plan was reported in the newspapers before any official announcements were made, and the result was an uproar. The British Government was almost universally condemned by public opinion for making terms. Sir Samuel Hoare resigned, and the war went on.

For Mussolini the sooner it could be ended the better. The rainy season in Abyssinia begins in May, and the Italians ought to be in Addis Ababa by that time. The Duce now put in command Marshal Badoglio, Italy's most able and distinguished soldier. The advance then began. The Abyssinians were no match for the trained and mechanized Italian forces. The artillery created havoc among them, the tanks ran them down, the aeroplanes sprayed mustard gas on them, and bombed any of their columns which were visible by day.

In a few weeks the whole of the north as far as Lake Tsana

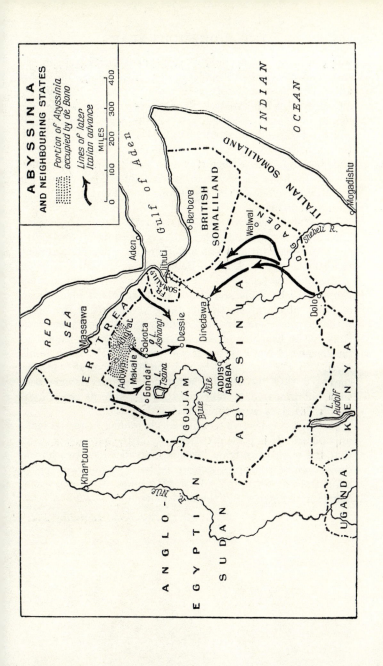

ABYSSINIA
AND NEIGHBOURING STATES

Portion of Abyssinia occupied by de Bono

Lines of later Italian advance

MILES
0   100   200   300   400

was conquered. The bulk of the Italian forces were in the east, and in March the emperor went in person to direct his army in the last desperate attempt to block the enemy advance on Addis Ababa. On the 31st a fierce battle was fought near Lake Ashangi, in which the Abyssinian imperial guard flung itself repeatedly at the Italian lines, only to be turned back by withering fire, and at last broken by artillery and bombs. The emperor, whose own country was now hostile to him, managed to reach Addis Ababa, and on 1st May took one of the last trains from there to Jibuti in French Somaliland.

The Italians entered the town on 6th May. Three days later Marshal Graziani, who had advanced from the south, reached Diredawa, and was met there by a detachment sent from the capital by Marshal Badoglio.

Mussolini had had his way. The King of Italy became Emperor of Ethiopia, and Marshal Badoglio was made Duke of Addis Ababa. One by one the governments of the world withdrew their sanctions and commenced to trade again with Italy. The Emperor of Abyssinia made a moving appeal to the League of Nations, but it was too late. Mr. Eden, in his speech to the Assembly, voiced the feelings of all when he confessed that the League had failed because its members were not prepared to take risks for the sake of peace until they themselves were threatened with war.

The idea of collective security was becoming more and more unpopular. It is part of the tragedy of the succeeding years that the world was again becoming divided into two hostile camps, whose principles were to be hotly disputed on many a neutral battleground. First Manchuria, then Abyssinia. Where and when would the next blow fall?

CHAPTER XI

THE treaty makers of 1919 made a fatal error in creating the small independent state of Austria. Following their admirable principles of constructing national states as far as possible, they split up the Austro-Hungarian empire, described by Lloyd George as 'ramshackle.' But they had no wish to make a strong Germany, so despite its German character Austria was made into a separate country. This fact was to bring great harm to Europe. It was to provide Hitler in 1938 with a 'reasonable excuse' for smashing the treaty and seizing Austria, and his success in this was to lead him far beyond 'reasonable' ventures, to aggression after aggression, and finally to world war again.

In 1919 Austria was a small land-locked republic, with a population smaller than that of Greater London. It consisted of Vienna, the lovely capital of the old empire, and some Alpine provinces. Separated from the Czechoslovakian minerals, Hungarian wheatfields, and the Adriatic sea-routes on which it had learned to rely, Vienna could not feed itself. Only loans from the League of Nations could rescue it from bankruptcy.

From 1921 to 1929 this Catholic state was ruled mainly by the Christian Socialist Seipel, who realized that Austria had a difficult course to navigate between Berlin, Moscow, and Rome. Schober, Chancellor in 1929, took steps to make a customs union with Germany, but this desirable action was stopped by France, Italy, and Czechoslovakia, and even forbidden by a decision of the Hague Court. In 1931 bankruptcy in Vienna started the landslide of world economic depression.

Dr. Dollfuss, who was Chancellor from 1932 to 1934, found difficulties multiplying. To the north was Germany, where the growing power of the Nazis threatened; to the south

Christian Austria: in this Church *Silent Night, Holy Night*
was first sung, 24th December 1818

Italian Fascist interference increased. In Vienna itself the industrial workers were ardent Socialists. Dollfuss represented the Catholic peasantry.

Such was the position in January 1933 when Hitler's triumph in attaining the dictatorship in Berlin brought at once a clear menace to Austria. He was himself an Austrian, and in *Mein Kampf* claimed 'the union of my beloved homeland to the common Fatherland, the German Reich.' Soon all the tricks and weapons of the Nazi technique were brought into play to stir up trouble in Austria. Broadcasts hurled insults at Dollfuss. Leaflet raids by air carried propaganda. Numerous Nazis moved into the country to gain key positions, to arouse hatred against the Jews, Communists, and the Treaty of Versailles, and to make thorough lists of every citizen's political opinions.

February 1934 saw Dollfuss make a fatal mistake in crushing the Socialists in violent street battles instead of allying with them against the inroads of Nazis and Fascists. The Chancellor built a Fatherland front to protect Austria, relying increasingly on Italian support to meet the German threat. In March Mussolini, Britain, and France made it quite clear that Austrian independence would be defended.

The first of the Nazi blows was delivered in July 1934. Dollfuss was murdered, and Nazi Brownshirts of Vienna tried to capture the government. Except in Carinthia and Styria, however, the revolt fell flat. Mussolini, jealous of his upstart German imitator, moved troops to the Brenner frontier, and the Nazi gangs proved insufficient to overawe the peasants and Socialists.

Hitler for a while held his hand. Apart from allowing the murderers of Dollfuss to be reckoned as heroes, he refrained from direct action for a while, relying upon smooth words and underground schemes. He spoke of Italy as 'a state with which we otherwise have no conflicting interests.' In July 1936 Germany guaranteed the independence of Austria, and promised not to interfere with her, directly or indirectly, if only she would recognize that she was a 'German' State. This was a most reasonable request, and Chancellor Schuschnigg,

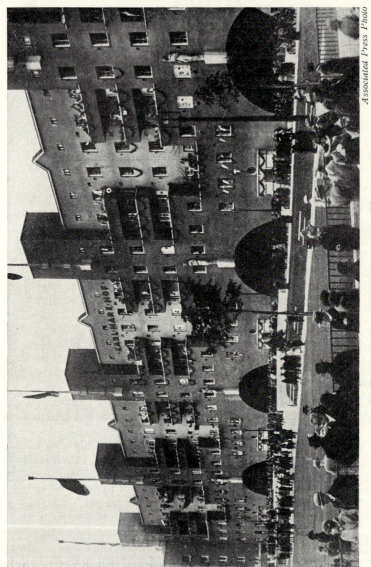

successor of Dollfuss, agreed to allow Nazi organizations in Austria provided that they did not seek to influence Austrians by propaganda.

The world was yet to learn what Hitler meant by a German State.

Month by month Hitler watched his plans mature in Germany, inside Austria, and in all the embassies of Europe. Many Austrians favoured a return to the Hapsburg monarchy as a means of keeping their freedom, but the hostility of the Little Entente (i.e. Czechoslovakia, Yugoslavia, and Roumania) and of Italy prevented this. During 1937 Italy, bitter against the western powers over their attitude to the Abyssinian campaign, and deeply involved with Hitler as an ally in the civil war in Spain, signed with him the Anti-Comintern Pact against Russia, and fell more and more under his influence. In England Chamberlain was pursuing a policy of appeasement, hoping by reasonable discussion to keep peace and honourable friendship with Italy and Germany. Anthony Eden, the Foreign Secretary, disgusted with Nazi and Fascist treachery in Africa, Spain, and Austria, refused to 'surrender to blackmail' any longer and resigned, so it appeared to Hitler that Chamberlain and Halifax could be reckoned on to do little more than protest.

Moreover, Hitler was already finding by experience that aggression paid dividends. In 1933 Germany had left the League of Nations, in March 1935 conscription had been re-introduced, in June Britain had signed a naval treaty with Germany which allowed her to break one part of the Treaty of Versailles, and a year later Germany had gone farther and marched into the Rhineland. In 1937 Hitler had openly defied the peace treaties by repudiating that clause which proclaimed Germany guilty of the Great War. And as regards breaking promises, had not Japan and Italy recently shown how successful that could be?

So the Führer felt safe to move. In January 1938 came a second attempt of the Austrian Nazis to seize power, the failure of which resolved Hitler to throw aside all caution and use German armies to compel Austria to submit. Those generals in the Reich who either disliked plunging into war, or thought the army insufficiently prepared, were got rid of. Ribbentrop, a Nazi after Hitler's own heart, was put in charge of the foreign ministry, and his master himself assumed control of all the armed forces. The stage was set for the death of Austrian independence.

From his pleasant mountain retreat of Berchtesgaden Hitler could look towards the snow-covered peaks of Austria, scenes full of memories of his unhappy youth, of imagined insults, of burning hatred and dreams of power. Thither he invited Chancellor Schuschnigg to meet him, and on 12th February 1938 was enacted one of the most extraordinary dramas in diplomatic history. With rolling eyes and in a screaming, frenzied torrent of words, the head of the Reich demanded that Austria should virtually be handed over to the Nazis. Overwhelmed and wretched, Schuschnigg agreed to the ultimatum, placing the full control of the police and the entire direction of Austrian foreign policy in Nazi hands.

Many have argued that Schuschnigg ought to have turned his back on Hitler and broadcast an appeal to the world. It is difficult to blame him, however. In view of the weakness of England and France at this time, and the friendship of the two dictators, to whom could he turn?

Despite the surrender the Austrian leader continued to preserve what he could of his country's independence. To give the people the right to decide for themselves a plebiscite was called for 13th March. Hitler, of course, feared the result of a free vote, and decided to forestall it. On 12th March the German army invaded Austria with 700 planes and 200,000 troops, and Hitler marched in triumph through the streets of Vienna.

As he expected, Britain, France, the League of Nations, and Italy did nothing. Mussolini received a telegram of thanks, saying: 'I will never forget you for this.'

Considerable sympathy with German claims to unite all Germans within the Reich probably helped greatly, and to some extent accounts for the failure of the democracies to act. But what disturbed the civilized world was the method by which the union had been created, the deceit, the violence the terror, and the success of the whole campaign.   Now that the fall of Austria had laid open the Danube and all routes to south-east Europe, would Hitler stop?

While the world was asking 'What next?' the Nazis were busy with the immediate settlement in Austria.   The Jews were robbed and tortured, 7,000 people were killed, and Austrians, willing or unwilling, were driven to vote in a Nazi-conducted plebiscite in favour of union.   Hitler proudly boasted that 99·73 per cent of the population of Austria said 'Ja!'

CHAPTER XII

THE FRENCH PUZZLE

AFTER her victory in 1919 France stood alone, alone in her desires and alone in her fears. Her desire was for security, and her fears were that the future would see a re-establishment of German strength which might again bring destruction and war on her countryside. Unless we remember this it is hard to understand the feelings of Frenchmen between the two wars. Twice in living memory their land had been invaded by the Germans, causing much sorrow and suffering.

The coming of peace revealed great differences between the former allies. The United States were glad to be rid of European commitments and to put the war behind them, absorbed in the visions of a future of prosperous isolation and safety. Even the British were willing to let bygones be bygones, and, having made a peace treaty, to wait upon events and deal with each situation as it arose. But the French were convinced that leniency towards the conquered would bring great dangers. They were therefore ready to press the Germans to the last penny in conformity with the terms of the treaty. Hence the occupation of the Ruhr in 1923. Whether the Germans were able to pay was to the French beside the point. They had caused the war and they must take the consequences.

This unbending attitude was largely the cause of France's troubles. When it became clear that Germany could not face such heavy demands a wave of disappointment swept the country. Here was a victory which was not a victory, for its fruits were bitter. England had been an ally, but was now withdrawing from European commitments, while at the same time urging France to be moderate in her demands. But there was no English Channel between France and Germany to protect her. Who, in face of such dangers, could be moderate?

Fécamp: the Fair Land of France

D

By 1924 French disillusion was complete. The Ruhr experiment had failed, and France had to accept a modified scale of reparations payments under the Dawes Plan. These payments were by no means as large as had been expected. Hardly enough could be found to pay the expenses of government, and one Cabinet after another grappled unsuccessfully with budgets which would not balance. For three years the famous statesman Poincaré succeeded in holding off the crisis by fixing the value of the franc at a level low enough to allow French trade to compete in world markets with that of other countries. When he retired in 1929 French prosperity again began to wane.

The worldwide economic crisis had meanwhile plunged America and then Great Britain into unemployment. Japan was casting greedy eyes on Manchuria, and the League of Nations was experiencing its first major defeat. Germany's growing strength was a matter for deep concern. France built the famous Maginot line on her eastern frontier as a defence against Germany. It was a great drain on her finances, and could not be met without heavy taxation and salary cuts. No wonder that between 1929 and 1933 there were no fewer than eight changes of government in France.

Half the country was now feeling that parliamentary government had been a failure. Some, seeing the proud rise of Italy and Germany from the bitterness of defeat, dreamed of a Fascist France, and founded a party called the Croix de Feu or Fiery Cross. Others wished to imitate Russia, and the Communist party became much more active. Political quarrels increased in bitterness, there were demonstrations, strikes, and riots in the streets. When it was found that the Prime Minister, M. Doumergue, was showing sympathy with the Croix de Feu, and demanding almost dictatorial powers so that he could settle the trouble, all the popular parties combined against him. Thus was founded the famous Popular Front of 1935.

The hero and guiding spirit of the movement was the French Socialist, Léon Blum. He was the son of a rich manufacturer in Alsace, and had been a political journalist for many years.

Of all his ideas the greatest was that of bringing together the popular parties to work out a common programme. The time for this had now come. In the many meetings of 1935 the Radicals, Socialists, and Communists laid aside their differences and concentrated on ousting Fascism and saving France. 'We solemnly pledge ourselves,' declared its members, 'to remain united for the defence of democracy, for the disarmament and dissolution of the Fascist League, to put our liberties out of reach of Fascism. We swear to defend the democratic liberties won by the peoples of France, to give bread to the workers, work to the young, and peace to humanity as a whole.'

In the Popular Front there was new hope for the future. In May 1936 its members presented to the country the election programme, which included proposals for abolishing violence in politics and corruption in the newspapers, for nationalizing the armaments industry and the Bank of France, restoring salary cuts, starting unemployment relief and pension schemes, and reducing working hours. In its scope it may be compared with President Roosevelt's New Deal, for not only were most of the proposals carried into effect, but they were also supported by the majority of the workers of France, who received great benefit from them.

People in France were now working a forty-hour week and were receiving a fortnight's holiday with pay a year. There was a feeling of optimism throughout the country. Had conditions been the same as they were in America such optimism might have been justified, but the new reforms cost money, and the rearmament programme in addition was a crippling load for a poor country like France to bear. Prices soon began to rise steeply and unemployment increased. Many schemes of public work which had been started in the general wave of optimism had to be abandoned because of the expense.

Meanwhile the external situation was rapidly becoming worse. The Italians had succeeded in conquering Abyssinia, and were now deeply involved with the Germans in the Spanish adventure. Hitler had re-fortified the Rhineland, and was on the eve of presenting further demands. France's allies, Poland and Czechoslovakia, were facing serious dangers, and the League of Nations, to which France had pledged her support, was failing as a force for international security.

This was a time when the French, in immediate peril from their German neighbours, needed to work, yet there were large numbers of unemployed. France needed money but could not get it. France needed unity above all, but was crippled by strikes and the struggles between her many political factions.

The Popular Front broke up in 1938. It had failed in many things, but it had at least preserved the country from the dangers of Fascism. When, however, the storm broke over Europe in the following year, there is little wonder that France could not weather it.

CHAPTER XIII

THE SPANISH CAULDRON

'THERE has scarcely been a traveller to Spain since 1600 who has not thought it his duty to preach a sermon on the theme of the "lazy Spaniards." If a race of such magnificent natural energies as the Spaniards has continued for generation after generation to live in this way, it is only because it has been waiting for an idea, a plan of work that will move their imaginations.' This conclusion of Gerald Brenan, author of *The Spanish Labyrinth*, admirably sums up the unhappy story of Spanish history in the past century.

No single country in Europe has suffered so much from divisions of all kinds. Geography shows it to be cut up by mountain barriers into different and sometimes hostile provinces. In addition there are all the class and political groups which are to be found in other modern states: Roman Catholics, the Army, Monarchists, Anarchists, Socialists, Liberals, Republicans, and recently Communists and Fascists. The Roman Catholic Church and its missionary Order, the Jesuits, which for centuries were powerful as a means of keeping the country united, have retained an extraordinary grip over politics, education, vast trading concerns, and estates. As the priests opposed all reform, usually allying themselves with the monarchy and the landowners against the poverty-stricken peasantry, a large number of Spaniards became anti-clericals.

The army of Spain, too, over-staffed with underpaid, idle, and discontented officers, normally supports the grandees, and has frequently acted like an independent political party, using its weapons to make and unmake governments. Rival monarchs left a legacy to the twentieth century of violent supporters, such as the Carlists of the Pyrenees. These and others who still hanker after the 'good old days of Crown, Church, and Aristocracy' are often referred to as Traditionalists.

Much of Spain's unhappiness is due to the troubles of land ownership. Land hunger among the miserable peasants of sunny Andalusia, bad management of the vast estates owned by the grandees, unfair rents which the Galicians pay to absentee landlords, endless disputes among the vine-growers of Catalonia, and the barrenness of central Spain, these are some of the causes of discontent. Only the Basque cultivators with their medium-sized farms seem to have been reasonably well-to-do.

The Cortes or Parliament was only a shadow of democratic government during the later nineteenth and early twentieth centuries, for the elections were always 'managed' by the provincial governors or the local landowners. Even a whole cemetery of 700 dead men was given votes on one occasion. The continual changes of Liberal and Conservative ministries were scornfully referred to as the 'changing of the guard.'

Some regions of Spain are so independent by nature that they have often fought to break away entirely from the Government of Madrid. In Catalonia the Anarchists believed that all laws were evil, and that all men were by nature good, and should be free to live happily together without restrictions or policemen. To gain freedom they used violence of all kinds. By 1936 this movement had achieved little but bloodshed.

As nearly half of the people of Spain in the twentieth century are engaged in industry, it is natural that a strong Socialist movement should have grown up. The chief trade union tried to win power through the Cortes, but this was difficult, as there was not an honest or genuine election from 1874 to 1931. Yet during the post-war period the party grew under the leadership of Caballero, a Madrid plasterer, who learned to read when he was twenty-four years old. While Anarchism wanted no government at all, Socialism aimed at a strong central government working for the common people.

Later we shall see how shortly before the civil war two more extreme parties grew up—Communist and Fascist.

With this background we can now consider the recent history of Spain and understand the explosion of 1936. From 1898, after the loss of the Spanish colonies, Parliament, under the monarchy, was occupied with a three-cornered

E.N.A.

General Primo de Rivera

struggle between Church, Liberals, and Anarchists. Strikes, executions, and assassinations multiplied, and very few good laws were passed. In 1923, after the king's muddled interference in the Moroccan War, Primo de Rivera declared himself Dictator of Spain. He accomplished a small measure of progress in decreasing strikes and building roads and irrigation works, but the Church and Army prevented real reforms. 'In a country where half the population sits in cafés and

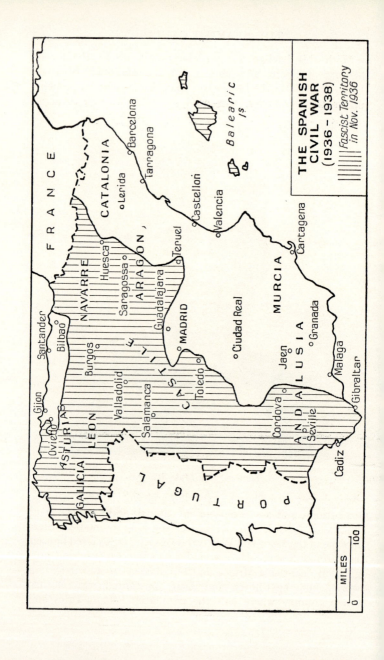

THE SPANISH
CIVIL WAR
(1936 – 1938)

Fascist Territory
in Nov. 1936

FRANCE

CATALONIA

Barcelona
Tarragona
Lerida

Balearic
Is.

Castellon
Valencia

Cartagena

Huesca
Saragossa
Teruel

NAVARRE

ARAGON

Guadalajara

MADRID

Ciudad Real

MURCIA

Santander
Bilbao
Burgos

CASTILE

Toledo

Jaen

Granada

Gijon
Oviedo
Valladolid
Salamanca

ASTURIAS

LEON

ANDALUSIA

Cordova
Seville

Malaga
Gibraltar

GALICIA

PORTUGAL

Cadiz

MILES
0   100

criticizes the Government, no dictator can last for long.' [1] So in 1930 Primo was overthrown, and fifteen months later King Alfonso fled.

The republic of 1931 was a veritable witch's cauldron of seething interests. At first the Government was Socialist and anti-clerical. It abolished Jesuit schools, but without substituting others, stopped State payments to the clergy, gave Catalonia independence, and established slightly better wages and rents for agricultural workers. Even these small measures, described by Caballero as 'an aspirin to cure an appendicitis,' provoked street battles. The problem of splitting up the large estates was not solved. The worldwide trade depression made matters worse. In a land where there were no unemployment benefits, starvation and bloodshed followed. Prisons were full, the country was police-ridden, and new anarchist and terrorist clubs grew. In these circumstances Spain swung again to the right, in support of a new party of Monarchists and Clericals under Gil Robles, which promptly undid the work of the Socialists. This in turn led Caballero to strive to join the chief trade unions in a Popular Front. Soon it was clear that Gil Robles was planning to overthrow the republic.

From 1934 to 1936 these disorders spread. Disgusted at the tortures that followed the suppression of the revolts of the Asturian miners, public opinion returned the Socialists to power once more.

It was now that foreign influence made itself felt. Gil Robles began secretly negotiating with Italy and Germany. Caballero, hailed by Moscow as the Spanish Lenin, looked to Russia for support. Two small extreme parties blazed up like a prairie fire. The Communists filled the bookshops with Russian literature and set out to capture the Socialist movement. The Falange, founded in 1932 by Primo de Rivera's son on the model of Italian Fascism, using the street technique of beatings, battles of rotten eggs, and hooliganism, won over the support of the Army, the Traditionalists, and all who feared

[1] *The Spanish Labyrinth*, by Gerald Brenan.

*D

Devastated Spain

Communism.   Throughout the summer of 1936 international undeclared war was waged in Spain.

On 13th July Calvo Sotelo, the leader of the Traditionalists, was shot.   Three days later the army in Morocco rose to

E.N.A.

Francisco Franco

overthrow the republic, and on the 18th the Government distributed arms to the people to resist the generals.

The civil war was to last two and a half years.   General Franco, leader of the rebel army, expected to be master of Spain in a few days, but the rising of the peoples in Madrid and Barcelona and the loyalty of the Navy prevented this. The Nationalists soon took one-quarter of the country, parts of

Galicia, Asturias, Leon, Castile, and Aragon (excluding the northern coast), and set up a Fascist Government at Burgos. Then General Varela advanced from the south, gaining a wide corridor of land from Cadiz to the outskirts of Madrid, while the northern coastal belt, in republican hands, was reduced to a stretch of two hundred miles. The Madrid Government, now largely controlled by Workers' Committees, soon gained strength from the International Brigade, consisting of Russians, French Communists, and other volunteers from many nations.

November 1936, therefore, saw half the peninsula in the possession of General Franco. In the following spring his forces broke the 'iron ring' round Bilbao, and by October 1937 victories at Santander, Gijon, and Oviedo had reduced the northern coast. Many Basque and Asturian refugees escaped by sea back to Barcelona. Europe heard with horror of the devastation of Guernica and other small towns which experienced the first onslaughts of modern bombing.

On the Madrid front there was violent fighting in the suburbs but little change for over two years. The region of Cordova and Granada in the south likewise saw little fighting for a long period. In Aragon, though, the Republicans were driven back to the Huesca–Saragossa road in October 1937, so leaving the Nationalists in control of two-thirds of Spain, the north and west.

Early in 1938 came the great Aragon offensive when, despite the titanic efforts of the Republicans at Teruel, their enemies broke through to the Mediterranean down the valley of the Ebro, thus cutting them in two and isolating Barcelona. Conditions in that city became desperate, as the Nationalists, well supplied with Italian and German aircraft, were free to bomb almost unopposed. For several months there was stalemate on the Ebro front, but in December came the final offensive on Tarragona and Barcelona. In January 1939 starving Barcelona fell, and streams of refugees passed into France. In March Madrid capitulated.

The civil war was undoubtedly a victory for the Axis Powers, and part of their general plan to crush Communism

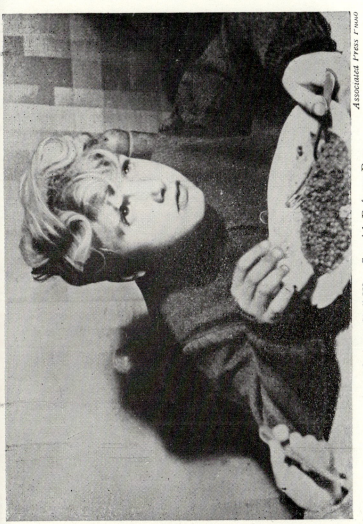

After the Civil War: Spanish Refugee Boy

and dominate Europe. From the start they supplied technicians, troops, and weapons to the one side, while Russia, handicapped by distance, yet sent much to the other. The democracies, striving for peace against the trickery of the Axis diplomacy, did their utmost to limit the war. Twenty-seven nations were represented on the Non-Intervention Committee in London. In March 1937 Britain and France established coastal patrols to prevent the sending of troops to Spain. A few months later, after many attacks on British ships, thought to be made by Italy, the Nyon Conference made Britain and France the guardians of neutral shipping in the Mediterranean. Further efforts to get foreign troops withdrawn were only partly successful. But Britain consistently refused to be drawn into the conflict, and in the end Spain was conquered by Fascism. The civil war has been well termed the dress rehearsal of the Axis for a bigger struggle.

CHAPTER XIV

BRITAIN AND THE EMPIRE

FOR Great Britain, the period after the First World War was like the end of a storm, with the ship of state, badly buffeted, striving to ride seas which were still perilous. In the first ten years the worst dangers were negotiated, and then, when men could reasonably hope for a period of calm security, there followed ten years of anxiety and preparations against the menacing storm clouds once more growing on the horizon.

The Coalition Government of Liberals and Conservatives under Lloyd George, which lasted from 1918 to 1922, partly solved the most pressing problems. Huge numbers of men were demobilized from the armed forces. Although there was insufficient building of 'homes fit for heroes,' and many ugly slums were allowed to remain, yet some progress in reconstruction was made.

The worst feature of post-war Britain was the industrial unrest which culminated in the General Strike of 1926. Four factors combined to create conditions which almost approached civil war. First, the prosperity of those who had made huge profits from the war aggravated the jealousy felt by the rest of the community. Secondly, there was widespread unemployment and insecurity. In 1921 2,500,000 people were without work, owing to the industrialization of foreign countries, the poverty in world markets, and the closing of war-time industries. Thirdly, distress among agricultural workers followed the resumption of imports of foreign corn and the consequent abandonment of arable land which had rendered good war-time service. Fourthly, the spread of Socialist and Communist ideas led to the demand that such great undertakings as coalmining and transport should be taken out of the hands of private owners and placed under public control.

Disputes and strikes therefore increased. Attempts were made to settle these by small improvements in wages and by setting up wage tribunals to act as umpires, but the chief demand for nationalization was not met. If this demand had been general it could scarcely have been refused; but many of the workers in mines and factories appeared to want, not control for the community, i.e. State Socialism, but

David Lloyd George on his Farm

Fox Photos

'Syndicalism,' i.e. control for themselves, perhaps against the interests of the public.

After the resignation of Lloyd George in 1922 a Conservative Government, under Bonar Law and Stanley Baldwin, hoped to cure the distress by giving up free trade and establishing duties on foreign goods coming into the country in order to protect English manufacturers. In 1924 the general election rejected this scheme, and the Labour party under Ramsay

MacDonald formed a ministry, which depended on the support of Asquith and his group of Liberals. Too weak in the House of Commons to venture upon any large plans to satisfy the trade unions, it made friendly gestures to Russia and provoked the wrath of the Conservatives, who accused that country of scheming to create a revolution in England.

The heated election which followed hard upon the Zinoviev letter charges returned Baldwin with a large majority. During the ministry of 1924–9 various small measures were taken to bring back prosperity. The gold standard was restored to give foreign traders confidence in English money, improved unemployment insurance and widows' and orphans' insurance schemes were adopted, local government was improved, factories and farmlands were relieved of most of the burden of rates, and finally the vote was extended to include all women. Many of these acts, however, had the appearance of 'papering over the cracks,' and the trade unions grew more and more hostile. Strikes increased until ultimately the unions used their strongest weapon to defeat the Government. In 1926 the miners', railway, and transport unions declared a general strike.

Volunteer labour prevented a complete breakdown of the life of the country. Although there was widespread sympathy, especially with the claims of the miners, yet the man in the street felt that in a democratic state the right way to gain good laws was by the use of persuasion and of the vote. So the general strike was defeated by the Government and the general public.

The Conservatives were now in a strong position, but there were no sweeping punishments or bloodshed. The miners had to work a longer day of eight hours. The mines were not nationalized, but a step in this direction was taken later when royalties, i.e. rents paid by the mines to the landowners, were purchased by the Government. In 1927 the Trade Disputes Act left the unions the right to strike over their own affairs but made it illegal to strike against the State. Relations with Russia were broken off.

A short Labour ministry followed in 1929, again scarcely

strong enough to be effective. The economic blizzard which swept through the world during the next few years blotted out every other consideration. In England unemployment figures rose to 3,000,000. Ramsay MacDonald decided that the Government must economize or go bankrupt, so in 1931 he joined with the Conservatives to form a National Government to weather the storm. Slowly world trade recovered. Britain abandoned her century-old policy of free trade to protect her industries from foreign competition and to give her empire special preference. There was no quick return of prosperity, but the worst days seemed past.

While the economic storm was subsiding anxious eyes turned eastwards where the rumble of war could be heard from Manchuria, Abyssinia, and soon Europe. Thereafter English history became inextricably woven into the tale of world events.

The story of the British Empire and Commonwealth of Nations is, in the main, a happy one. Little need be said of such countries as Australia, Canada, and South Africa where the firm foundations of self-government had already been laid, and where the growth of nationhood was combined with that of friendship with Britain. Mention must be made, however, of difficult problems elsewhere.

Relations between southern Ireland and England were far from satisfactory. Over two centuries of bitterness and the recent Easter Rebellion of 1916 had left their mark in hatred and unwisdom. Southern Ireland, which was mainly Roman Catholic and anti-British, demanded complete separation from Britain, whereas Northern Ireland would not hear of it. A Home Rule Act, passed in 1920, was not complete enough to satisfy the south. Civil war followed. In 1921 the south was made into the Irish Free State, and was given a status similar to that of Canada (later known as 'dominion status'). All the same, extremists in Dublin continued to press for a republic and wanted the north to do likewise. De Valera, the Irish leader, treated England in every way as a very foreign country. In 1937 the Irish Free State, as part of its plan to foster its own language, took the name of 'Eire.'

In Egypt Britain still held a half-control of the government as she was anxious to safeguard her trade routes, but the people were striving for full freedom. After a rebellion in 1922 self-government was achieved, Britain retaining only the right to defend the canal and to supervise the Sudan.

Recent Indian history has been dominated by the claim of the vast population to manage its own affairs. Many steps towards this goal had already been taken, and Britain had publicly proclaimed that as education and experience grew, and as quarrels between the rival religions were settled, India would advance to full dominion status. But the Indian Congress was angry and impatient at delay and would not consider 'steps.' After years of inquiry and Round Table conferences, Britain offered in 1935 a scheme to embrace all states, creeds, and classes. There was to be an All-India Federation; the separate provinces were each to have self-government; both the central and provincial governments were to be responsible, i.e. were to have full authority, apart from certain special powers left to the viceroy. Even this plan was not accepted.

So at the coming of war in 1939 the Indian problem was still unsolved. Congress, consisting mainly of Hindus led by Gandhi, worked for an undivided India, free from Britain; the Muslim League wanted 'Pakistan,' or separate nationhood for Muslims; the princes wished to keep their rights over their native states. Meanwhile in the east grew the menace of Japanese power, making it impossible for the British to leave India disunited and unprotected.

The empire as a whole saw two interesting developments during these twenty years. As the dominions grew to maturity they became more independent. In 1931 the Statute of Westminster recognized them as self-governing states united only by the Crown into a commonwealth. After this the dominions realized more keenly how strong were the sentiments and interests which bound them to Britain, and found it easy and desirable to work in harmony with her. In 1939 they voluntarily and without question followed her into battle.

CHAPTER XV

PRESIDENT WILSON had fought a losing battle at the Peace Conference. During the last year of the war he had made known his 'Fourteen Points' which, he said should form the basis of a just and lasting peace. His insistence on *justice*, on considering the wishes of *peoples*, and on not giving rein to the victors to plunder the vanquished, had given him great prestige in Europe, and played a large part in helping to end the war. But the peacemakers at Versailles did not keep strictly to these principles as the chiefs of the Allied Governments feared to throw away the advantages of victory. So the President's great reputation suffered a rapid decline.

He was weakened, moreover, by the opposition of the Republican party in his own country. Many Americans had objected to the President's attending the Peace Conference at all, because they held that an American president should stay in his own country. Although they had pursued the war with vigour while it lasted, they still regarded the European struggle, not as their own, but as one in which they had had to take part mainly to ensure their freedom to develop in their own way, unhampered by threats from outside. When the last American soldier left Europe it was to many of them the end of a distasteful but necessary episode. Hence their great disappointment when they found that their President was becoming more and more embroiled in European politics. When the League of Nations was established as a result of his actions he became very unpopular.

Laws in the United States of America are made by two Houses. The first of these is the House of Representatives (sometimes called Congress) and is elected on much the same basis as our own House of Commons, the parts of the country which are most densely populated having the greatest number of members in this House. The other House, known

Beautiful America

as the Senate, is composed of two delegates from each state, and the members of it are, therefore, fairly equally distributed over the whole of the United States. Broadly speaking, the densely populated areas of the north and east, engaged in industry and bound by trade ties to Europe, were in 1919 behind the President. The other part of the country in the south, middle west, and west was mainly agricultural, knew little about Europe, and cared less. The trouble for President Wilson was that these states in the south and west had equal representation in the Senate with the others. It was therefore in the Senate that he found the greatest opposition. In vain he visited the states of the middle west to secure support. When the time came for the Senate to ratify the treaty and approve the League of Nations there were not enough votes.

To a venture as bold as the world had ever seen it was a lamentable ending. The President retired at the end of his term, broken in health and with but a short time to live. America chose the way of isolation as the way to prosperity. It was to take a second world war and another tireless and able President to bring to her people the realization that the United States could not live in wealth and safety cut off from the troubles of the rest of the world.

Things went well at first, for the country was richer than ever. Industrial concerns grew to gigantic proportions and business barons counted their money in millions of dollars. The Machine Age seemed to have brought prosperity even to the poorest of homes. Work was plentiful and well paid. The working man was able to fill his house with the latest labour-saving devices and to own his 'family' car. Indeed the automobile industry, symbolized by the famous magnate Henry Ford, grew to enormous proportions, and with it the film industry, both of which became outward signs of American efficiency and progress.

Yet while on the surface all seemed well it was far from this in reality. Wilson had been succeeded by President Harding, and he by President Coolidge, both of whom believed in giving a free hand to 'big business.' The only indication at first that all was not going well was the series of business scandals which came to light during this period, and hints at the corruption that was going on.

The idealism of Wilson's days seemed to have passed away. In 1920 the sale of alcoholic drinks had been prohibited

Unemployment in America

throughout the whole country and a widespread trade grew in illicit liquor. These were the days of the bootlegger, the speakeasy, and the more sinister gangster, whose trade often covered many other things besides alcohol, and in some places became a menace to ordered society. But America was still confident of the reality of the boom. It became the fashion to speculate. Everybody joined in the buying and selling of stocks and shares. The price of stock gradually rose and many lucky people made fortunes by buying and selling again at a profit.

Poverty in Agricultural America during the Slump:
Destitute Pea-pickers

Then suddenly came the crash. People began to sell out and prices slumped. It was the South Sea Bubble all over again but on a gigantic scale. In the three days beginning 21st October 1929 over twelve million shares had changed hands. The unsound concerns dragged down the prices of the sound ones and millions of investors lost all they had. Firms had to close down, banks failed, and, worst of all, there was a large-scale stoppage in industry owing to lack of capital. The unemployed could soon be counted in millions. There was no system of relief, such as we have in Great Britain, and vast numbers of people nearly starved. Their only means of subsistence was the bread-line, the soup-kitchen, and the garbage bin. The great distress of the country even found its way into the popular songs:

> Once I made a railroad, made it run,
> Made it race against time,
> Once I built a railroad, now it's done,
> Brother, can you spare a dime?

and the greatest film star of the day, in his picture, *Modern Times*, showed that machine production, in spite of the great abundance which it brought, could be a very evil thing.

All this happened during the presidency of Herbert Hoover, and the depression lasted a long time. It was the next President, Franklin D. Roosevelt, who found a way out of it. He refused to believe, as Hoover did, that 'things would right themselves' under private enterprise, however much help the Government gave. He held that the one thing necessary was to get American citizens back to work, to put the dollars into their pockets. Only then would they begin to buy things, and again start the wheels of industry running. To this end the President bent all his energies. The value of the dollar was fixed, the salaries of many public servants were cut in a vast economy drive, plans for emergency relief were set up so that starving people could get food, and a beginning was made with schemes for the unemployed, the sick, and the aged.

The most spectacular achievement of the New Deal, as it was called, was the development of hundreds of local projects to get people into employment again. The greatest of these was the magnificent Tennessee Valley scheme to develop one of the biggest interior basins of the country by making dams and increasing the productivity of the land. This was followed by many smaller ones in the far west. These were

The Boulder Dam, Nevada

accompanied by a programme of expenditure on all kinds of public works, housing, bridges, roads, railroads, oilfields, and drastic reforms in the organization of industry and agriculture. Even popular entertainments and the arts were not left out. Writers, artists, and musicians were given employment and the life of the citizen was in this way enriched considerably.

In spite of all criticism, when President Roosevelt in 1936 stood for a second term of office, he certainly had a great deal to show in the way of achievements. It is small wonder he was elected. By this time the European sky was darkening, and much thought had now to be given to America's attitude towards Adolf Hitler and Benito Mussolini. Japan had already invaded China and was threatening American interests in the Pacific.

While Germany was rearming in Europe and Japan attacking China the Americans held their hand. They still believed that by isolating themselves from the rest of the world they could keep out of war. Only their most enlightened statesmen seemed to realize that with interests stretching over the whole world, they could not remain immune from attack.

Isolation, which had been so fervently preached, was a false hope. In 1939 war broke out in Europe. In 1940 President Roosevelt was elected for a third term of office, not this time to save his country from economic disaster, but as the man who was most likely to see it through the dangers of a possible war.

CHAPTER XVI

THE bloodless conquest of Austria was Germany's first step to power. Hermann Göring hastily assured the surrounding nations that they need fear no further territorial demands in Europe. Events were to prove how false this assurance really was, for behind the closed door of Nazidom the next step was being prepared.

On the northern border of Austria was the small state of Czechoslovakia, created after the war of 1914–18 and inhabited by a vigorous people with democratic leanings. It was mainly composed of two nations of Slavonic descent: the Czechs of Bohemia, who numbered seven and one-half millions, and two and one-third million Slovaks who lived in a long strip of land among the foothills of the western Carpathians. These two races had agreed to found a single state and their claim had been recognized by the treaty makers. Their country had grown in power and prestige, ardently supported by the western democracies. But within its borders there were also three and one-half million Germans who constituted the most numerous minority in Europe.

Since 1933 it had been one of the chief aims of Nazi policy to gather together all German-speaking peoples under Hitler's leadership, to make them conscious of the fact that, whatever country they lived in, they were first and foremost Germans. A special government department had been set up in Germany, part of whose work it was to keep in touch with Germans all over the world.

There were no friendly feelings, therefore, between the new Germany and the Czechoslovaks, for this little state stood in the way, not only politically but also geographically. If Hitler was to reach the fertile lands of the Ukraine and take them from Russia, it could only be by first getting rid of the obstacle of Czechoslovakia. But the little state had powerful friends. Her twenty years' alliance with France and her friendship with Great Britain seemed a good guarantee of safety from aggression. Her heavy fortifications in the

E.N.A.

Masaryk: the Father of Czechoslovakia

mountains bordering on Germany were very formidable. Her great armaments plant, the Skoda works at Pilsen, was producing the finest arms in the world.

Nazi methods were equal to this problem. In the first place, the fall of Austria had laid the southern border open to

German attack and had by-passed the formidable mountain barrier of the north. In the second place, the Nazis had for years been sowing discontent among the German minority.

The Sudeten Germans, as they were called, lived in the

E.N.A.

Dr. Beneš in 1919

mountainous districts to the north and east. Here their ancestors had migrated from Germany in the Middle Ages. Although they were an alien race, and had not been granted complete citizenship, they had been reasonably contented. They had their own representation in the Czech Parliament, their own schools and law courts, and had been treated far better than any minority in Europe.

The Sudeten Germans had by now their own Nazi party. At the head of it was Konrad Henlein, a former bank clerk and gymnastics instructor. At first he had been very moderate

E.N.A

Sudeten Types: German Girls dancing round the Maypole

in his views, but since the rise of a strong Germany he had become much more outspoken. The number of his followers was now increasing greatly. While German newspapers, in April 1938, were fulminating against 'Czech atrocities,' Henlein announced a series of sensational demands. These included full self-government for the Sudetens, complete liberty to profess and practise the Nazi doctrine, and a clear definition of the boundaries of the Sudetenland.

Under the lash of German propaganda the tension and excitement grew rapidly. Early in 1938 there was an incident in which two Germans were killed. German troops were already massed on the border ready to attack, but the Czechs showed fight and mobilized their armies. Hitler decided that it was not yet wise to risk a *blitzkrieg* (lightning war), for Great Britain and France had made it quite clear that they would help Czechoslovakia in the event of a German attack.

The crisis was over, but only for a time. During June, July, and August the flames of resentment were kept burning. Hitler now transported thousands of labourers to the western frontiers of Germany to build the Siegfried line which, while protecting him from France and Great Britain, would give him a free hand to settle the problem of Czechoslovakia in his own way.

Meanwhile Mr. Chamberlain, Prime Minister of Great Britain, sent Lord Runciman on an unofficial visit to attempt mediation between the Czechs and the Germans. This proved impossible in view of the German determination to keep the quarrel open.

By September 1938 Hitler, having fortified his western border, felt strong enough to deal with the Czech problem. The Nazi Government had the power, through its control of the newspapers, of printing stories at any time which were designed to inflame the people against any nation or class. This control of the press was a powerful weapon. During August all this propaganda had been turned on the Czechs and on President Beneš in particular.

When the time was ripe Hitler and Henlein demanded that the whole of the Sudetenland be handed over to Germany. At the Nazi rally at Nuremberg Hitler, in violent language, accused the Czechs of torturing, robbing, and seeking to wipe out their German neighbours. Lord Runciman was helpless before such a show of anger, and reported to London that the only way out of the difficulty would be to transfer the German-speaking areas in Czechoslovakia immediately to Germany.

Henlein fled from Czechoslovakia and put himself under Hitler's orders. German troops again massed on the frontier. This time the Führer had definitely committed himself. Not even Great Britain and France could prevail on him to withdraw and war seemed certain.

It was on the 16th September that the British Prime Minister made his spectacular effort. The country was thrilled by the news that he had flown to Berchtesgaden, Hitler's mountain fastness, to see the Führer personally. Hitler demanded a high price for peace. This included the cession to Germany of all districts containing over fifty per cent Germans, a vote of the people in all other districts where there were Germans to decide to which state they would belong, the abandonment by Czechoslovakia of the French and Russian alliance, complete neutralization of the country, and an Anglo-French guarantee of the new frontiers when they were decided on. Chamberlain flew back to London where he met the French Prime Minister, M. Daladier. There they decided that these terms must be accepted. On this the Czech Cabinet, and President Beneš, resigned.

Mr. Chamberlain flew back to Germany, this time to Godesberg, on the Rhine, taking with him the Allied reply. When he arrived there he was shocked to find that Hitler had prepared new demands, and had even asked for slices of Czechoslovakia to be given to Poland and Hungary. 'I bitterly reproached the German Chancellor,' said Chamberlain, 'for his failure to respond in any way to the efforts I had made to secure peace.' He came back to London for further consultations, while all Britain prepared for war. The fleet was mobilized, trenches were dug in the London parks to meet possible sudden air attacks, and plans for evacuation were put into effect. France and Russia, too, prepared for war. The Czechs strengthened their defence lines and mobilized their army.

Hitler realized that he had gone too far. At the instigation of his fellow dictator, Mussolini, he agreed to a conference of Germany, Italy, France, and Great Britain to be held at Munich on 29th September. Again Mr. Chamberlain flew to Germany and there an agreement was made. Czechoslovakia,

E

still ready to fight if necessary, was not consulted. Large
tracts of her land were handed over to Germany for immediate
occupation. In the rest of the disputed territories the people

E.N.A.

Czechoslovak Industry: Painted Vases

were to decide which country they would belong to. The
result gave Hitler all that he had asked for at Godesberg.

Mr. Chamberlain was at that time the most popular man in
Europe. Even the Germans cheered him in the streets of
Munich. The plan for the evacuation of British towns was
shelved and the trenches in the parks were abandoned. Mr.
Chamberlain came back to London, bringing with him a

document signed by Hitler and himself in which both avowed their intention not to go to war. He was wildly cheered in the House of Commons, and popular opinion almost elevated him to the position of a national hero who had, at great price, secured 'peace in our time.' And yet behind the feeling of intense relief that war had been averted there were doubts and uneasiness at this policy of appeasement. A few outspoken voices, notably that of Winston Churchill, even called the Munich agreement 'an unmitigated defeat for Great Britain.' Would time prove them the truer prophets?

It was a tragic peace for the Czechs who had to give way. Hitler now declared that with the solution of this problem he had 'no more interest in the future of Czechoslovakia.' But in England and elsewhere there were a few who did not believe his words. The next blow, they declared, could not be long in coming.

They were right. At first peace indeed seemed assured, but gradually the German newspapers again assumed an offensive tone, and began to abuse the British for rearming after having made an agreement to keep the peace. Soon Hitler himself was publicly reviling 'warmongers' like Mr. Duff Cooper, Mr. Churchill, Mr. Eden, and other prominent Englishmen who did not disguise their distrust of the Nazis.

It soon became clear that Hitler would be satisfied with nothing but the complete destruction of Czechoslovakia. The way had been prepared by German agents who had entered Slovakia and urged the people to demand independence of the Czechs. The country was thus split into two warring factions, and Hitler, having created the disorder, had provided himself with an excuse to interfere and quell it.

He now summoned the Czech President Hacha to Berlin, and by threatening to send a fleet of bombers to Prague compelled him to sign away the independence of his people. In a single day in March 1939 the German armies moved forward and occupied the capital. Bohemia was made a part of Germany, Slovakia became a protectorate, Poland and Hungary also obtained large tracts of land. Thus the well-armed, independent, and virile republic came to an end.

How long could Hitler keep up this career of unprincipled aggression? His armies had occupied first the Rhineland, then Austria, and now Czechoslovakia. Russia had expected Britain and France to come to the help of the small Republic. Britain, it is true, had never guaranteed to protect Czechoslovakia as France and Russia had done, although by some people she was reckoned to be equally her guardian. So Russia now retired into isolation, and by that very act played into the hands of Hitler.

The failure of the two western powers to agree with each other on the measures to be taken had caused them to drift apart. America was looking on these strange developments with disapproval and disdain. Thus the powers which should have kept the peace were divided among themselves. It seemed now as if nothing on earth could stop the forward march of an invincible Germany.

POSTSCRIPT TO MUNICH

The seizure of Czechoslovakia had its postscript. On Good Friday, three weeks after Hitler's success, Mussolini sent 100,000 troops to occupy Albania. That small country, where King Zog ruled a million poor shepherds and peasants, fell an easy prey. For years Italians had forced their influence upon Albania, but had not dared to annex it. Now, perhaps jealous of the Nazi advance, perhaps emboldened by his fellow dictator's example of triumphant burglary, the Duce seized the useful ports of Durazzo and Valona and proclaimed the Adriatic an Italian lake. The democratic countries heard the news with mixed anger and contempt—anger that Italy had gained such strategic advantages in the Mediterranean, and contempt for the act as a cheap imitation of the German model.

CHAPTER XVII

ASSAULT

ADOLF HITLER had a set formula for all his speeches. He invariably began with a recital of the misdeeds of the peacemakers who drew up the Treaty of Versailles, then went on to tell the story of how he, an unknown soldier, had mourned the lost splendour of Germany, and determined to build up the country on new lines and to restore its self-respect. He then described the struggles of the National Socialist party against the villainies and plots of the Jews, the Bolsheviks, the effete, so-called democracies, international Socialism, British plutocracy, and so forth. His speeches ended by dealing with the particular problem of the day, glorifying German strength, and violently denouncing and threatening all who stood in the way of the next step to expansion.

Many people, both in England and elsewhere, were ready to acknowledge that there might have been some injustices in the Treaty of Versailles. Up to March 1939 there was a sincere desire on the part of many people to cultivate the friendship of Germany. But the unprovoked invasion of Czechoslovakia had altered all this. Within six months of Hitler's cry: 'I want no Czechs,' he had proved his insincerity by enslaving *all* Czechs and by submitting them to the rigours of Nazi discipline. A programme of conquest like this could only be met by resistance. The question was no longer 'Will war come?' but '*When* will war come?'

Germany had by the Treaty of Versailles been severed from East Prussia by a band of territory inhabited chiefly by Poles. This Polish Corridor, as it was called (see map, p. 5), had been created to strengthen the new Poland and to give the country an outlet to the Baltic Sea. The only port in this region was Danzig, which, being largely German, had been put under the government of the League of Nations. Poland had therefore built a new and magnificent port called Gdynia only some seven miles away.

Within a few weeks of the fall of Czechoslovakia the Führer was planning to absorb not only Danzig but the whole Polish Corridor. Since 1936 Danzig had become predominantly

E.N.A.

Race Persecution

Nazi, and it was only necessary to send 'tourists' from Germany in 1939 to bring the question to a head. When they arrived, and increasing disturbances were reported, the problem became serious for the whole of Europe.

Hitler believed that he could do again what had been done in 1938, but unfortunately he took no account of the changed British attitude. Mr. Chamberlain in March announced that should the independence of Poland be threatened Great Britain would support her. Further guarantees to Roumania and Greece, the introduction of conscription, and a programme of rearmament showed that at last the country was in earnest.

Hitler was given to understand that his next move would not go unchallenged.

Perhaps for that very reason he pursued his programme with the greater speed. Announcing that Great Britain was

E.N.A.

Neville Chamberlain

attempting to encircle Germany, he put an end to the Anglo-German Naval Treaty of 1935 and denounced the pact he had made with Poland the year before.

The greatest problem was Russia. If Germany was to win any war Hitler believed that this could only be done by fighting on one front at a time. It seemed that now the front would be in the west. But before war could be allowed to break out Russia must be detached from the Anglo-French friendship.

The Evacuee

a small British Expeditionary Force. While the German armies were overrunning Poland the French advanced some miles into Germany, but this was little more than a diversion. Within two months the position on the western front was almost what it had been at the beginning of the war.

Elsewhere there was little to report. The German sub-marines were everywhere active and many ships were sunk. On the other hand, British naval patrols were daily bringing in enemy ships as prizes and neutral ships to be searched for contraband. A very effective blockade was set up on all German exports and imports over such seas as were controlled by the British Navy. Official secrecy often draws a veil over the most gallant actions of war because of the need to prevent vital information from getting into enemy hands, and the long watch of the Navy, the constant braving of mine, raiding aircraft, and submarine rarely found its deserved place in the newspapers. Only now and again some deed of outstanding heroism appeared in the news headlines. Of such character was the gallant stand of the converted liner, *Rawalpindi*, which was sunk by the pocket battleship *Deutschland* on 26th November 1939.

The greatest thrill of the war during these early days was the destruction of one of these surface raiders, the *Graf Spee*, by three British cruisers. The German pocket battleship type had been specially designed for sea raiding. Its eleven-inch guns were sufficient to deal with anything but the heavily armed battleship, and with its speed it could outrun all the big ships except the cruisers. It was strong enough to attack and disperse whole convoys and was therefore a constant menace. On 13th December the cruisers *Exeter*, *Ajax*, and *Achilles*, after an exciting chase, sighted and engaged the *Graf Spee* in the south Atlantic. By a series of skilful manœuvres they compelled the damaged battleship to seek harbour in the river Plate, there to refit for the second round of the battle. According to international law a belligerent ship is only allowed to remain in a neutral port for twenty-four hours, but the *Graf Spee* stayed there for four days and even then was not in a fit state to give battle again. On Sunday, 17th

December, her crew brought her out to the shallows and scuttled her. The long dreary winter was broken by a period of great rejoicing that British heroism and skill should thus defeat an enemy superior in arms.

The only other important area at this time was Finland. We have seen how the Russians had come to an agreement with Germany. This agreement, though it safeguarded them for the time being, did not rule out the possibility that the Germans would one day attack them. In anticipation of a move like this they had pushed the frontier half-way into Poland, and had thus put a valuable barrier between Berlin and Moscow. Lithuania, Latvia, and Estonia were soon afterwards forced to give up their independence and make way for Russian supremacy in northern Baltic waters.

But it came as a surprise when on 31st October the Russians demanded that the Finns should withdraw their border from the vicinity of Leningrad and take a part of Russia elsewhere in exchange. At that time the rest of Europe hardly dreamed that Finland might one day become the tool of Germany and threaten the northern gateway to Leningrad. Premier Stalin was more realistic. When the Finns refused to consider this request war broke out.

From the first the sympathy of the Allies was with Finland. They even planned to send a force to assist against the Russians, but the Swedish Government refused permission for it to pass through that country. From November to March Finland thus struggled alone against a state at least forty times its own size. Although the Finns fought well and inflicted severe defeats on the Russians, numbers and equipment prevailed in the long run. Finland was invaded at many points, and in the main assaults on the Mannerheim line between Lake Ladoga and the sea, Finnish armies were eventually forced back to their last defence lines before Viipuri. On 12th March 1940 hostilities between the two countries ceased. Russia secured a frontier farther removed from Leningrad and bases which controlled the entrance to the Gulf of Finland.

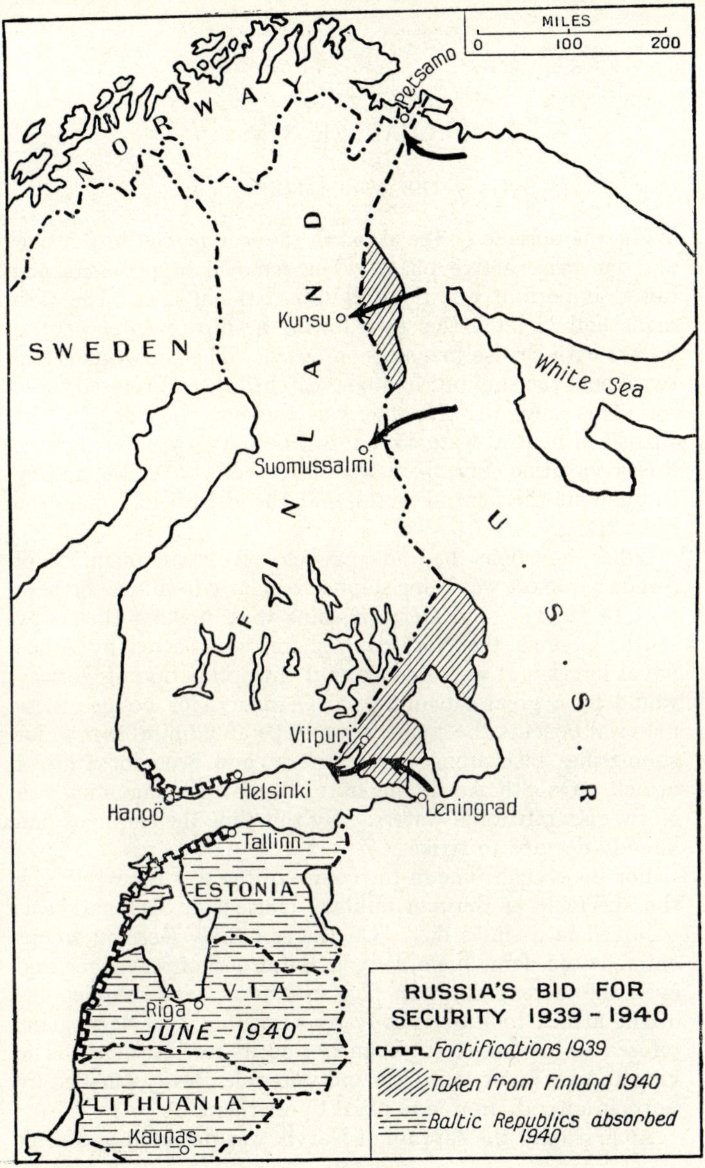
MILES
0
100
200
NORWAY
Petsamo
FINLAND
SWEDEN
Kursu
White Sea
Suomussalmi
U.S.S.R
Viipuri
Helsinki
Hangö
Leningrad
Tallinn
ESTONIA
LATVIA
Riga
JUNE 1940
LITHUANIA
Kaunas
RUSSIA'S BID FOR SECURITY 1939 - 1940
Fortifications 1939
Taken from Finland 1940
Baltic Republics absorbed 1940

CHAPTER XIX

THE AXIS STRIKES

WITH the episode of the *Altmark* the war passed into a new and far more active phase. The removal of prisoners had raised important questions of international law. The Germans had violated this by allowing a ship to enter neutral waters with British prisoners on board. The Norwegians had twice held the ship but had not searched it, and refused to do so. This ship, the *Altmark*, was therefore boarded by the British in neutral waters on 16th February 1940. This, too, was a violation, but there was nevertheless a strong feeling throughout the neutral world that the British had done the right thing.

Other questions had also arisen. A great quantity of Swedish iron ore was being shipped regularly from the northern port of Narvik, and German ships were making their way south, hugging the Norwegian shore, unmolested by Allied naval forces. It was obvious that the occupation of Norway would be a great advantage to Germany, for besides these material benefits the country would be an admirable base for submarines blockading Great Britain and even for a direct attack. On 8th April, therefore, the British laid mines in Norwegian territorial waters. By this time the Germans had already decided to strike.

For the second time in the course of the war the world saw the spectacle of German military efficiency. Denmark was occupied in a single day. On the same day German troops entered Oslo, Trondhjem, Bergen, the airport of Stavanger, and even the distant northern port of Narvik. The suddenness of the attack took everybody by surprise. The Norwegians refused to hand over the country and its fortifications. The king and his family left Oslo and were relentlessly pursued by German aircraft from one place to another.

At first only the capture of Narvik was disputed and after

an action between naval forces a landing was made. British and Allied troops were later put ashore at many points on the coast, chiefly in an effort to occupy Trondhjem and to join their Norwegian comrades who were resisting the German armies advancing up the valleys from Oslo. This was, however, impossible in face of superior German numbers, equipment, and air power, and the forces were ultimately evacuated.

Peaceful Norway

For a while the Allies held on to Narvik. They had landed men on the fjords around the town and captured it on 28th May. They even cleared all the land as far as the Swedish frontier, but the continual landing of German parachute troops in the area made their hold more and more precarious. By this time events of greater importance were taking place elsewhere, and on 11th June the Allies left Norway to the Germans.

The Chamberlain Government could not withstand the

indignation which now burst forth in the British Parliament. Assailed on all sides and with few to defend him, the Prime Minister had to bear the full blame for the reverses the country

Norwegian Girl

had suffered. After a vain attempt to form a new government he resigned on 10th May. The king summoned Mr. Churchill to Buckingham Palace and made him Prime Minister. Thus was brought into being the Government which, under Churchill's presiding genius, carried the country through the days of peril which were to follow, and finally led it to complete victory.

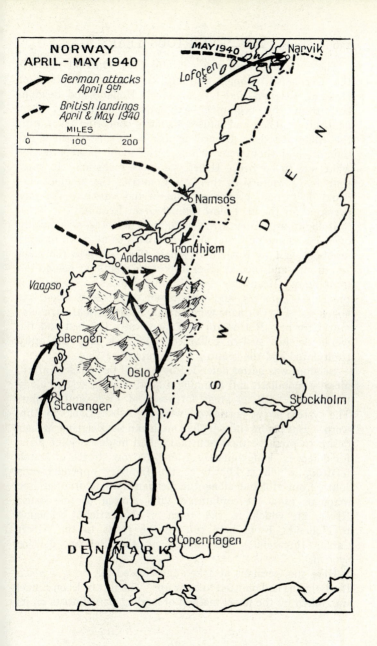

The 10th May 1940 was a fateful day. On that morning the Germans, without warning, crossed the frontiers of Holland, Belgium, and Luxembourg. Holland and Belgium had from the beginning scrupulously maintained their neutrality. They had refused to make concerted plans with the Allies for their defence against a possible German onslaught, and they were therefore the more unprepared for what was to happen. Hitler was more realistic. He knew that by a victory in the Low Countries the Maginot line could be turned, France put out of the war, and the way prepared for the final blow against Great Britain.

Holland, a country with few natural defences, was quickly overrun. Parachute and airborne troops came down in large numbers, first at Rotterdam where they occupied the main aerodrome, and then at other important points far behind the front lines. Meanwhile direct frontal attacks were made on the Dutch defences, and within four days the position was hopeless. The Germans were already in Maastricht, Arnhem, and Utrecht. Rotterdam was mercilessly bombed and the whole defence system collapsed. On 15th May the army capitulated and the country was occupied.

Belgium was better defended by a small but efficient army, already mobilized and manning a good defence system along the Meuse, with its great fortresses of Liège and Namur. The system swept north-west with the Albert Canal to Antwerp. But before the war the Dutch and the Belgians, in their desire to preserve their neutrality, had made no joint plans for defence. Unfortunately a long, narrow stretch of Dutch territory which is known as the Limburg appendix runs south from Holland along the Belgian-German frontier (see map, p. 145). It contains a vital stretch of the Meuse River, on which is the town of Maastricht belonging to Holland. From here run all the roads to the Albert Canal, threatening the whole of the Belgian defence system.

Here the Germans attacked and crossed the bridges which the Belgians had omitted to blow up. The fort of Eben Emael was taken by the novel method of landing parachutists on its flat roof. From these vantage points the Germans fanned out and in two days had penetrated far beyond Liège.

By this time British troops had crossed the French frontier into Belgium and had met the enemy a few miles east of Brussels. The French advanced down the Meuse and were between Brussels and Namur. Here both armies met the full spate of German armour backed by squadrons of bombers. At the same time a large German army swept through the hills and forests of the Ardennes towards Sedan, through country which had been thought almost impossible for an invader to penetrate, and which was, therefore, only lightly defended. At Sedan the Meuse was crossed and France lay open to invasion.

The German armies pressed on everywhere, led by tanks and mobile columns and supported by aircraft. Brussels and Antwerp had to be evacuated, but the most serious break-through had occurred between Namur and Sedan where the Germans had forced a large bulge in the French and British lines. This 'battle of the bulge,' as Mr. Churchill called it, rapidly became the 'battle of the gap,' which split apart the Allied armies. The northern groups, including some French, most of the British and the Belgians, were in retreat towards the coast in the Calais-Dunkirk area. The southern groups, almost all French, were being pushed well back into France.

The position of both British and Belgians was now desperate, cooped up in that coastal strip. First Boulogne fell, then Calais, held at first by the Rifle Brigade against enormous odds. The Belgians, completely exhausted by repeated withdrawals, could not hold on. During the last days of May they were mercilessly punished and in peril of complete destruction. To save them King Leopold surrendered.

It was a bitter blow to the beleaguered British force and the small French army hemmed in with it. Mr. Churchill warned the country to expect 'hard and heavy tidings,' for the Germans had forced these armies into a little pocket no more than twenty miles broad around Dunkirk and daily growing smaller and smaller. There was desperate fighting to hold them off until ships could arrive off the beaches to take away the army to the safety of England.

Already the German communiqués were proclaiming the imminent annihilation of the British forces. But at that time came the greatest rearguard action that military history has ever recorded, the evacuation of Dunkirk. Over two hundred British naval craft assembled off the beaches to protect all the little ships, nearly seven hundred of them, which sailed

The Evacuation of Dunkirk

out there, some of them many times, to take off the forces waiting in orderly sections on the beaches. They were manned by volunteers, yachtsmen, fishermen, owners of pleasure boats. Day by day and night by night they carried out their task of rescue in face of enemy bombing, protected only by the fire of the bigger ships. In six days 335,000 men had been brought home.

France lasted little longer than a fortnight, for the German armies now turned south along roads crowded with refugees, rounded the now useless Maginot line, took Paris, and prepared to impose terms of peace. On 22nd June French delegates were summoned to meet Hitler in the very same railway carriage where twenty-two years before Marshal Foch had received the surrender of Germany.

The terms were severe. They included total demobilization, disarming of all forces on land, sea, and air, occupation by Germany of over half the country in the north and west, the release of all prisoners of war, and many other items.

Meanwhile the Italians had only been awaiting the moment when it seemed that France was already defeated. On 11th June their troops crossed the frontiers. They were held on the Alps but advanced along the coast as far as Mentone. This, however, was only a 'token' invasion. Nevertheless, before the armistice with Germany could come into effect, French diplomats had to journey by aeroplane to Rome and conclude a second armistice, involving demilitarization of French strong points and large parts of the French colonial empire.

Worse for France perhaps than its military defeat was its moral defeat. In deference to the wishes of its conquerors the Third Republic soon voted itself out of existence. Under the weak and aged Marshal Pétain and his more active but treacherous vice-president Laval, the Government of un-occupied France was set up at Vichy. For the time being the mass of honest Frenchmen, dazed and bewildered by the suddenness of the fall and still more by the realization of how corrupt and disloyal some of their leaders had proved to be, had to obey the orders of the 'collaborationists' who fawned upon the Nazis.

What was the cause of this sudden and complete collapse? The course of the war had shown many great weaknesses on the side of the Allies. There was the lack of mechanization, the overwhelming superiority of the German Air Force, and the want of a concerted plan of defence. When the situation had become serious the French failed to keep off the roads that endless procession of refugees in cars, trucks, lorries, and on foot which prevented the effective use of military force and only presented targets for low-flying German planes. But there were other things far more serious and deep-seated.

The French had not wanted war and had feared its outbreak. They had prepared themselves a defence in the Maginot line which would in any case have been ineffective in a long

Topical Press

Pierre Laval

struggle even had it not been turned from the north. Again, during the last years of peace when the Germans were forging ahead and creating a seemingly invincible force, united under Hitler as never before, the French statesmen were still struggling with internal problems left to them by the last war and experimenting with new plans for industry which brought about a decrease in production. But probably the chief cause was the failure of Great Britain and France to work together, and the suspicions which each had of the other during those pre-war years of international crises. Many books have been and will be written on this subject alone. It is enough to say that between 1940 and 1944 the French reaped a hundredfold the bitter fruits of despair, while Great Britain was left to struggle alone against an enemy which now threatened to overwhelm her completely.

CHAPTER XX

DEMOCRACY IN PERIL

'WE shall defend our island whatever the cost may be. We shall fight on the beaches, we shall fight on the landing-grounds, we shall fight in the hills; we shall never surrender.'

Mr. Churchill's speech on 4th June was a call to the whole British Empire. The Germans had gained the Channel ports. They had but to mass their armies there, send over their fleets of bombers, put British aerodromes out of action, clear the Channel of shipping for a brief time, and cross over. 'There are no islands,' Hitler had once declared, and it seemed now as if what he had said was true.

Why did this invasion never take place? It may be because the German commanders struck through France too quickly, and could not rally their immense forces speedily enough to wheel them round and attack Britain when she was at her weakest. It may be, too, that Hitler thought that with the surrender of France the French fleet would fall into his hands, and with its help he could hold the Channel long enough to put his mechanized armies across. Whatever may be the reason it remains true that he was somehow prevented from taking a chance which never came again.

The French fleet did not fall into German hands. Those ships which were in British ports were boarded and prevented from leaving. A battleship, four cruisers, and many other smaller ships were immobilized at Alexandria. At Oran in Algeria there was more opposition. The battleships *Dunkerque* and *Strasbourg,* with many others, were anchored there, and when the French admiral refused to surrender them they were fired on. Only the *Strasbourg* escaped, badly damaged, to Toulon. At Dakar in West Africa lay the greatest French battleship, *Richelieu,* which was also put out of action.

There was still the German Air Force whose immense power had not yet been fully exploited. During the month of

Britain's War Premier: Winston Churchill

August a series of raids were therefore carried out on the south-coast ports. Southampton, Portsmouth, and Weymouth were heavily attacked but not without stiff resistance. Over the Straits of Dover and the Channel the Germans suffered far more numerous losses than did the small forces of Spitfires and Hurricanes which rose to defend the convoys sailing there.

'England, we are coming!' the German radio and press vauntingly proclaimed. They came, but they received a violent shock. In many days of bitter fighting the pilots of the R.A.F. shot out of the sky far more enemy bombers and fighters than they lost. On one day alone, 15th August, at least seventy-six were destroyed. Broken and burntout raiders studded the fields of the southern counties. Then, towards the end of the month, came the attacks on the aerodromes with the object of destroying the R.A.F. at its bases, but this, too, was just as costly a failure.

Gradually the focus of attack changed to London itself. Day raiding had begun, and the nights had been for some time disturbed by 'nuisance' raiders which zoomed above and prevented people from sleeping. Occasionally a bomb dropped. Hitler now (4th September) declared that if Great Britain still defied him he would destroy her cities and on the 7th he began in earnest.

At about five o'clock in the afternoon a great force of bombers escorted by fighters began a large-scale attack on London. Many bombs fell and before the 'all clear' sounded the sky was black with smoke from the docks and warehouses on both sides of the river. The attack was taken up again in the evening and was carried on all through the night, guided by the fires which were now blazing fiercely. Damage was widespread and serious.

We are told that Göring came to France personally to direct these air attacks and that they were intended to be a prelude to invasion. They continued, heavy by night and intermittent by day, for a period of three months. Not only was London affected, but in November German aircraft made

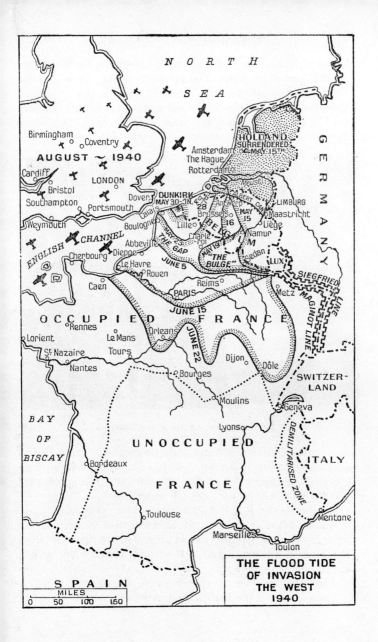

THE FLOOD TIDE
OF INVASION
THE WEST
1940

heavy night assaults on Coventry, Birmingham, Southampton, Bristol, and Plymouth. The probable object was to put the chief communications and industrial centres out of action. Whatever the object it did not succeed. War workers became used to the 'alerts,' 'spotters' took their places on the roofs of high buildings, fire-watching was organized, damaged sites

Keystone Press

Roof Spotters on the Law Courts

were quickly cleared up, and daily business was carried on as nearly as possible in a normal way. The raids went on with lessened frequency and intensity into the spring of 1941 and then for a time they ceased altogether.

Meanwhile the R.A.F. had not been idle. Time and again it had smashed at the German invasion fleet waiting on the shores of Europe, striking, too, at air and submarine bases from Bergen to Bordeaux. And as the fear of invasion diminished it took more offensive action deeper into the industrial centres of Europe—the Ruhr, Berlin, Bremen, Genoa, and Milan.

The security of the British Empire was now being seriously

threatened by Italy. Mussolini in his ambitions to make the Mediterranean Sea into 'Mare Nostrum,' had filled Libya with Italian troops and had built the great Via Mussolini (a road eastwards along the coast to threaten Egypt). Italian armies crossed the Egyptian frontier and advanced as far as Sollum. Another force from Abyssinia invaded British Somaliland and drove the small British garrisons out. In October Mussolini picked a quarrel with Greece in the hope that a successful invasion of the country would give him good bases for attacking the British in the eastern Mediterranean. Here he did not have it all his own way. Italian armies pushed into Greece but were badly mauled by the defenders. Within a few weeks the Greeks were even invading Albania! Meanwhile the British Fleet and Air Force were striking hard at the Italian Fleet. In one attack on the naval base of Taranto by Fleet Air Arm machines over half the ships were put out of action. Enemy supply ships that crossed the south Adriatic were continually harassed.

In December 1940 the Army of the Nile, under General Wavell, suddenly moved forward to the attack in the Libyan Desert. Helped by the guns from the British ships which bombarded the Italian shore positions, they advanced from one town to another with lightning rapidity. Sidi Barrani and Sollum fell. The British Army now swept forward through Tobruk, Derna, and Cyrene, finally capturing Benghazi, the Italian base. In two months over 110,000 prisoners were taken.

The British then turned their attention to Abyssinia, Italian Somaliland, and Eritrea. Men and supplies had been collected in Kenya and upper Egypt, but these were small considering the vast nature of the enterprise that was undertaken. First Italian Somaliland was invaded and its capital, Mogadishu, fell after two pitched battles. The South African columns began their long march into Abyssinia. Within six weeks of taking Mogadishu they were in Addis Ababa, a distance of over eight hundred miles, and this in face of difficult country and an enemy vastly superior both in numbers and equipment! Meanwhile at other points Abyssinia had been entered and the Addis Ababa force linked up with all the other invading bands. On 5th May 1941 Haile Selassie re-entered his capital. The broken Italian divisions were rounded up in all parts of the country. Eritrea, with its

Abyssinian Sentinel

port of Massawa, fell. British Somaliland had been retaken by a landing near Berbera and an expedition from the west. All East Africa was thus cleared of the enemy, Great Britain formally occupied Italian lands, and at last the Red Sea was open. British and American armaments in vast convoys passed through and the successful pursuit of the war in Libya was made possible. In the Mediterranean the Italian Navy was defeated a second time at the battle of Cape Matapan.

Hitler's plans led on to the Balkans and the Mediterranean. In February 1941 the Roumanians had joined Germany. It

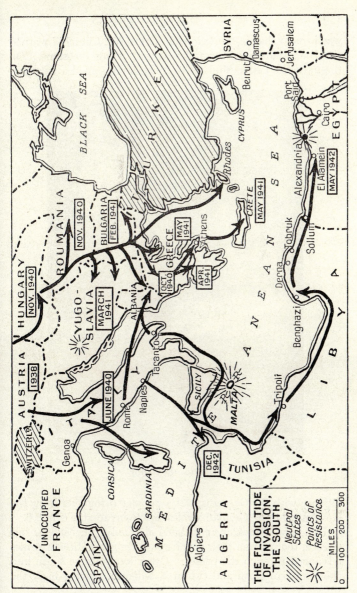

THE FLOOD TIDE
OF INVASION,
THE SOUTH

Neutral States

Points of Resistance

MILES
0   100   200   300

F

was in vain that in the following month Mr. Churchill warned the Bulgarians over the radio against doing the same. On the 25th the Prime Minister of Yugoslavia signed a treaty of

Fox Photos

General de Gaulle

alliance with the Germans, but a popular rising overthrew the Government and German armies had to invade the country.

This new attack overwhelmed not only Yugoslavia, but Greece, too. From their new bases in Bulgaria Hitler's armies advanced through the passes. Other forces drove south into the Thracian plain and captured Salonica, driving back the

British who had been sent to help the Greeks. The Allies had to retire and the whole Albanian line collapsed. By 27th April German armies were in Athens.

Several of the Greek islands had now been occupied and control of the Aegean Sea had been obtained by the Germans. In May Crete was attacked by parachute and glider troops who occupied the aerodromes. The British and the Greeks had little air cover and had to evacuate the island in June.

Spring 1941 was a black period for Allied hopes. Hitler had already taken a hand in the North African campaign. In March it was established that German crack troops, the famous Afrika Korps, were landing in Tripoli. On 4th April they advanced to Benghazi and were soon in occupation of almost the entire north coast of the province. Only Tobruk, invested on all sides, still remained to the British.

All these enemy successes had done much to neutralize British supremacy in the Mediterranean. British convoys had to fight hard to get through its narrow seas. Egypt was in danger for the second time. Only Malta held out, a hostile base for ever threatening German sea transport.

Elsewhere the struggle pursued its up-and-down course. General de Gaulle, who now stood as the representative of Free France, attempted with British support to take the French port of Dakar in West Africa but failed. Farther east, in Iraq and Syria, the Germans were checked. When in Iraq the Government was seized by Said Rashid Ali, an Axis sympathizer, British troops were landed. After a brief campaign they occupied Baghdad and all the other important places. In Syria the growing danger of German infiltration brought about the British decision to attack first. Columns advanced from Palestine and Iraq. Damascus was taken on 21st June 1941, Beirut on 9th July. In the end General Dentz, the French commander, signed an armistice and the country was occupied. The German advance was thus stemmed and Egypt was protected, at least on her northern and eastern borders.

CHAPTER XXI

ON TO THE EAST

HITLER'S treaty with Russia had brought certain advantages to both, but once his hands were free of the west he did not hesitate to fling the whole of the German might against the Soviet Empire.

We know now how valiantly and stubbornly Russia resisted and eventually beat the Germans down, but nobody could have guessed in 1941 that such would be the case. With Great Britain forced out of the war in Europe Hitler had one of two choices. Either he could invade Britain and risk a Russian attack while he fought in the west, or he could fall on Russia, and by a lightning stroke put her out of the war before the British could recover; then, completely free from all other commitments, he would be able to give his whole energy to the next venture across the English Channel.

The Royal Air Force had proved that an invasion of England was not going to be easy. We can now understand, therefore, why he chose to attack Russia. Within her boundaries were the rich cornfields of the Ukraine, the heavy industries of the Lower Don, and the oilfields of the Caucasus. They would give the Germans food for years, armaments and oil almost without end, millions of slave labourers, and a second air force to help to darken English skies. A new assault in the west would then be twice as strong as before and Great Britain would certainly be conquered.

The Germans attacked on a fifteen-hundred-mile front on the morning of 22nd June 1941. The general's order read: 'Full of confidence in the Führer, we shall beat the old Bolshevist enemy of National Socialist Germany and thereby secure final victory over Britain.'

The Germans held the initiative because they had had the advantage of surprise. They were bound to gain ground.

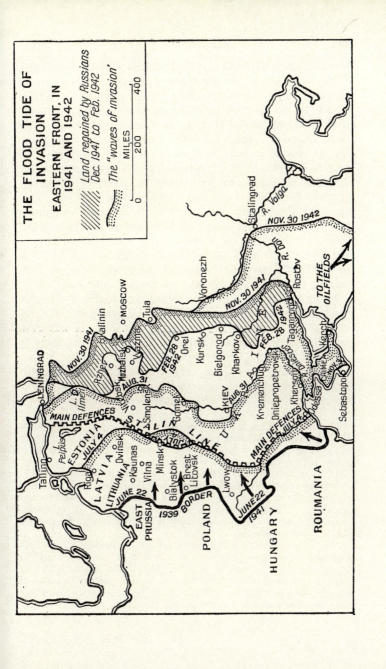

THE FLOOD TIDE OF
INVASION
EASTERN FRONT, IN
1941 AND 1942

Land regained by Russians
Dec. 1941 to Feb. 1942

The "waves of invasion"

MILES
0   200   400

But this was no repetition of the Polish and French campaigns. There was obstinate resistance everywhere. The panzer divisions surged forward leaving behind them vast tracts of land to be 'mopped up' later, but these were held by Russian troops. There was fighting in all directions with no stable front whatever. Brest-Litovsk, Minsk, Smolensk, and many other towns on the way to Moscow fell to the invaders in the first few weeks of war. An attack was also made in the direction of Leningrad from bases in Finland, now on the side of the Germans. Lithuania, Latvia, and Estonia were occupied in turn, Hungary and Roumania were now fighting for Germany in the south and advances had been made there. Everywhere the Russians were compelled to retreat, but after one month's fighting the Germans had failed to take the main objectives of Leningrad, Kiev, and Moscow, and, what is more, the Russian Army remained unbroken.

Hitler had hoped that once he attacked Russia the British would either look on impassively or would even join him in his attempt to 'liquidate the Bolshevik menace.' It was even said that Rudolf Hess had landed in England by parachute to induce the British Government to do this. It was a very grave mistake, for on the very evening of 22nd June Mr. Churchill broadcast to the country a message in which he welcomed Russia as an ally against German aggression.

No one has been a more consistent opponent of Communism than I have for the last twenty-five years [he declared]. I will unsay not a word I have spoken about it. But all this fades away before the spectacle which is now unfolding. The past, with its crimes, even follies, and its tragedies, flashes away. . . .

We are resolved to destroy Hitler and every vestige of the Nazi regime. From this nothing will turn us. . . . Any man or state which fights against Nazidom will have our aid. . . . It follows, therefore, that we shall give whatever help we can to Russia and the Russian people. . . .

We have offered to the Government of Soviet Russia any technical or economic assistance which is in our power and is likely to be of service to it. . . . The Russian danger is our danger and the danger of the United States, just as the cause of any Russian fighting for his hearth and home is the cause of free men and free peoples in every part of the globe.

Mr. Churchill's promise was kept. Supplies began to reach Russia from Britain, first in small quantities but later in much greater bulk. German submarines and aircraft failed to stop the convoys. American materials were sent through Iran, where miles and miles of railway track were laid to accommodate the traffic.

The Persian Route to Moscow

The Russian losses were severe. In September Hitler's armies were before Leningrad and made an unsuccessful attempt to encircle it. On 19th September they captured Kiev, the capital of the rich Ukraine. In October a violent attack was made in the central sector which brought the Germans to Mozhaisk, only seventy miles from the capital. The important industrial area of the Dnieper was completely overrun, and the Russians, true to their policy of destroying everything of value so that the enemy could not make use of it, blew up the famous dam at Dniepropetrovsk which supplied power to this extensive manufacturing area. By the end of

October the large town of Kharkov had been evacuated. Odessa had been cut off from the rest of Russia and the Government had been compelled to move from Moscow to Kuibishev, five hundred miles east. At the end of November the whole of the Crimea had fallen with the exception of the naval base of Sebastopol.

In November 1941 the Germans had pushed to within twenty miles of the capital and were making determined efforts to encircle it on the north and south. Had they been able to do so they would have inflicted a serious blow on the Russians. But it would not necessarily have been a mortal one, for Russia's immense resources, especially of manpower, were now being slowly brought into action. Marshals Voroshilov and Budyonny had been withdrawn from the front and were now training the vast new forces. Indeed, by February 1942 some of them, coming into action for the first time, delivered counter-attacks all along the front. They pushed the Germans back a hundred miles from Moscow and freed large areas.

This was the first time that the Russians had regained any extensive ground. The short lightning stroke which Hitler had planned was now giving place to a long war in which Russia, backed by the resources of Great Britain and America, would wear him down and eventually bring him to a desperate last stand with his back to Berlin.

CHAPTER XXII

THE WORLD IN ARMS

On the morning of Sunday, 7th December 1941, the Japanese, without warning, launched a heavy air attack on the main American Pacific base of Pearl Harbor in the Hawaiian group of islands. Over two thousand people were killed, a thousand wounded, many aeroplanes were destroyed, three warships were sunk, and others damaged.

Since 1937 China had suffered alone, with Japan occupying all the most important towns near the coast and all the main waterways. The Chinese commander, Marshal Chiang Kai-shek, was carrying on a brilliant campaign on the most scanty material resources from his inland hill capital of Chungking.

Japan's first stepping-stones to power had been crossed as a result of British goodwill, and the First World War had found her among the Allies against Germany. Her rewards, the mandated Pacific islands, were very valuable as potential bases for a thrust into south-east Asia and the East Indies. Japan has few natural resources, but there are tin and rubber in Malaya and coal and metals in China. Only by acquiring these could Japan rise to greatness.

In the military dictatorships of Germany and Italy Japan saw natural allies. The great enemy of all was Soviet Russia, against which country they made a pact known as the Anti-Comintern Pact. Great Britain and America, both well established in the Pacific Ocean, prevented Japanese expansion there until the favourable chance occurred.

Then came the war of 1939. Japan took immediate advantage of the fall of France by occupying French Indo-China in 1940. Almost too late, the Americans, seeing the growing peril, stopped the supply of certain classes of goods to Japan and negotiations followed. It was during these that Pearl Harbor was attacked.

Japan had chosen the right moment. The British Navy

Pearl Harbor, 7th December 1941

was engaged in fighting submarines, supplying the forces in Egypt, and policing the trade routes. American industry was concentrating chiefly on peace-time commodities and would take long to put on a war footing. There were, too, many American isolationists. A quick, well-placed blow by Japan had a chance of crippling the United States, and this, followed

Photo: Paul Popper

The Great Buddha at Kamakura

by a sudden attack on south-east Asia, would bring some of the most coveted lands in the world under Japanese sway. This would be the first step in the 'liberation' of east from west.

Most of the islands of the Pacific as far south as New Guinea were in Japanese hands already, but there was one important line of bases crossing this zone which belonged to America. Before anything further could be done most of these had to be occupied. They consisted of Hawaii, Midway, Wake Island, Guam, and the Philippines. Hawaii was so far from Japan that it could not be taken, but Wake and Guam were seized. General MacArthur resisted the Japanese landings in the Philippines but faced overwhelming odds. Manila, the capital, fell on 2nd January. The Americans withdrew to the Bataan Peninsula where they held out until April. In May

Planet News

General MacArthur

the island of Corregidor, the last American stronghold, was taken. General MacArthur escaped by boat and plane to carry on the campaign from Australia.

The first objective of the Japanese in China was the British port of Hong Kong. It had little chance but held out until Christmas Day, 1941.

December of that year was a black month for the Allies. Eighteen months of occupation had turned French Indo-China into a powerful Japanese base, and strong forces set out from there towards Burma and Malaya. Thailand (or Siam) was soon forced into allowing troops to pass through the country and cross the Burmese frontier. Landings were made on the east coast of Malaya and a rapid advance was begun towards the south.

At the very southernmost tip of the peninsula is the important town of Singapore. For a century it had been a British outpost and had carried on trade with the East Indies, collecting all kinds of produce from the neighbouring islands for distribution throughout the world, and shipping the tin and rubber, the main products of the Malay States. During the last fifteen years before the war docks had been constructed to take the heaviest ships. A navy based on Singapore could control a great part of the China Sea and all the outlets from there to the Indian Ocean. But its value depended on the safety of the Malay Peninsula which lay behind it. On this peninsula the Japanese had now gained a foothold.

The advance was swift. Crossing to the west coast the Japanese captured one town after another, always resisted by vigorous rearguard actions. The invaders were more numerous and better equipped for jungle fighting. On 11th January the last big town, Kuala Lumpur, was evacuated and the enemy approached Singapore.

The British were not ready to meet these overwhelming forces. On 10th December the Navy had lost two of its biggest ships, the *Prince of Wales* and the *Repulse*, off the east coast of the peninsula after an attack by torpedo-carrying aircraft. The army was retreating rapidly and one by one the airfields were being lost. On 31st January the mainland was evacuated and a stand was made on the small island on which the town is situated. The Japanese made landings at various points, seized the main reservoirs, and the island opposite the naval base. On 15th February the British surrendered unconditionally. It was a severe loss, not only of the great naval base but of all the men and equipment in it.

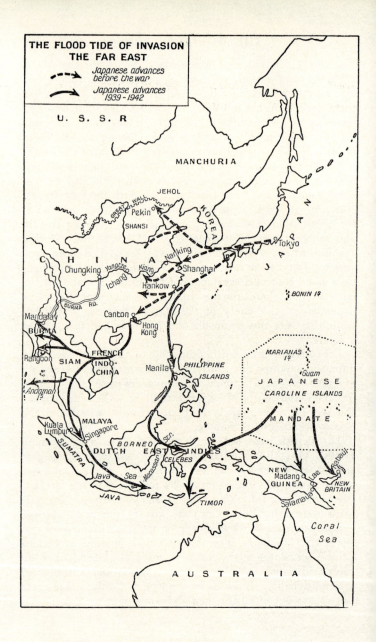

THE FLOOD TIDE OF INVASION
THE FAR EAST

- - → Japanese advances
      before the war
— → Japanese advances
      1939 - 1942

U. S. S. R

MANCHURIA

JEHOL

GREAT WALL

Pekin

SHANSI

KOREA

Nanking

Tokyo

C H I N A

Chungking   Yangtze

Kiang

Shanghai

Ichang

Hankow

BURMA RD.

BONIN IS

Canton

Hong
Kong

Mandalay

BURMA

FRENCH
INDO-
CHINA

Manila

PHILIPPINE
ISLANDS

MARIANAS
IS

Rangoon

SIAM

Guam

J A P A N E S E

Andaman
Is

CAROLINE ISLANDS

MALAYA

Kuala
Lumpur

Singapore

BORNEO

DUTCH   EAST   INDIES

Str.

M A N D A T E

SUMATRA

Java
Sea

Macassar Str.

CELEBES

JAVA

TIMOR

NEW
GUINEA

Madang

Lae

Rabaul

NEW
BRITAIN

Salamaua

Coral
Sea

A U S T R A L I A

The Japanese were now making landings on all the most important East Indian islands. Sumatra, Borneo, Celebes, the Moluccas, and Timor fell. For a short time they were held in check by a spirited action in the Macassar Straits, but after a second action in the Java Sea they landed at many points in the island of Java. By the end of March it was practically all conquered.

One by one the other south sea islands were occupied. Rabaul in New Britain, Madang, Lae, and Salamaua in New Guinea fell in rapid succession, and the Solomon Islands were overrun. A serious threat to Australia was developing. Allied aircraft raided enemy bases while the Japanese flew over north Australian towns dropping bombs. It seemed as if the attack would soon be delivered when a Japanese fleet sailed into the Coral Sea. It was met by American ships and planes and completely defeated. From that time the threat to Australia gradually disappeared.

The Americans were now beginning to recover. General MacArthur was conducting land operations, while the fleet under Admiral Nimitz attacked Japanese bases in the Marshall and Gilbert Islands. These attacks were the first of a series which eventually forced Japan from her island bases and threatened her communications with the newly won lands in the East Indies.

Another line of advance was towards India. We have seen how, in cutting off the Malay Peninsula, the Indian Ocean had been reached through the long strip of Burmese territory that extended down the west of the isthmus.

One of the main objects of the Japanese thrust in this direction was to cut the road to China. With the capture of the Chinese ports, the main sea routes to Marshal Chiang Kai-shek's army had been blocked up. The Chinese had, therefore, in a very short time constructed a road south-west from Chungking. For hundreds of miles it wound its way through the mountains and ravines of south-west China till it reached the Burma border. Along this road from Mandalay a constant stream of supplies was reaching the Chinese. For a short period, in deference to Japanese wishes, the British had

Photo: Paul Popper

An Old Chinese Peasant

closed the road, but it was now open again. The Japanese now moved to take the southern end of it and cut off the Chinese Army entirely.

Striking west from Thailand they captured the port of Rangoon and advanced up the rivers Irrawaddy and Sittang. The British, and Chinese forces which had been sent to help them, were pushed back far up the Chindwin River in the very heart of the country, and a second Japanese force captured Mandalay and Lashio. By the summer of 1942 the Japanese had occupied practically the whole of the country and forced the British into Assam.

The Japanese had hoped that certain sections of the Indian people would help them to defeat the British. But this did not happen. India remained loyal in face of the growing threat. Meanwhile the Japanese made an effort to gain control of the Indian Ocean. They captured the Andaman Islands, raided various points on the coast of India and Ceylon, and sank some British ships.

The Germans were now making their thrust in Russia towards the Caucasus oilfields. If the Japanese could control the Indian Ocean it would be possible for the two powers to forge a link across the world. This would cut the Allied eastern communication lines with Russia and bring to Japan a wealth of raw materials. If this link could be strongly held an Allied defeat would surely follow.

But by now the Japanese drive had spent itself and the Germans were soon to be turned back at the approaches to the Caucasus. Meanwhile the Allies were slowly building up their resources in Russia, in India, in America, Australia, and the Pacific.

In 1942 Axis expansion reached its limit. The years which followed were to see the process reversed, first very slowly, then with more and more momentum as the months rolled by, until the threats from Hitler, Mussolini, and Tojo were dispelled and their empires crumbled before the growing and finally overwhelming strength of a world in arms.

CHAPTER XXIII

SEA POWER AND AIR POWER

WHEN the Germans divided France into two parts they retained possession of the whole Atlantic coastline. This not only assured them ample U-boat bases but also established contact with neutral Spain, the source of many supplies. The unoccupied part of the country was in the centre, south, and south-east and was governed from Vichy by a group of men under Marshal Pétain, who for various reasons believed in non-resistance to Germany. Among them were Admiral Darlan, Flandin, and the more famous and sinister Laval. The idea of collaboration with Hitler's New European Order marked a complete break with the tradition of freedom and democracy which France had so long cherished. Many who believed in Free France escaped and joined the Allied forces. Others became active saboteurs, destroying, when they could, industrial plants, bridges, vehicles and doing anything, however insignificant, that would hinder the Germans and their Vichy collaborators.

From the harbours of Bordeaux, Brest, Lorient, and St. Nazaire submarines preyed on the British shipping, and from the western airfields of occupied France bombers scoured the eastern Atlantic on the watch for merchantmen. The number sunk was very great, and for a long time it appeared that the British people would be starved out and their industries stopped for lack of materials.

In the Bay of Biscay the battle of supplies raged for months. U-boats and bombers attacked merchant ships, British fighters attacked U-boats and bombers. German fighters came out to deal with the British fighters. It was a perpetual game of hide-and-seek, tense and confusing. Farther out in the Atlantic German long-range bombers patrolled the sea routes waiting for Allied craft.

The British were at a disadvantage, for their bases were

too far from the scene of action. They had occupied Iceland when Denmark fell in 1940, but apart from that their nearest points to the great struggle were in Northern Ireland and Cornwall. Eire was approached to allow the use of bases there but the Irish refused. So the struggle had to go on against very heavy odds.

Fox Photos

Convoy in Line

Surface raiders continued to be troublesome long after the battle of the river Plate and many ships went down with guns blazing before their superior armaments. It was therefore all the more thrilling when, in May 1941, it was learnt that the *Bismarck*, Germany's newest and greatest battleship, had been sunk in the Atlantic. After her discovery she had sunk the British battleship *Hood* but was chased by the cruisers *Norfolk* and *Suffolk*. British ships converged on her from all quarters. After being lost for a day and a half she was

sighted again by a flying boat, making for France. Her
speed was reduced by torpedoes from the air, she was heavily
damaged by the big guns of the *Rodney* and *King George V*,
and finally sunk by torpedoes from the *Dorsetshire*. The loss
of the *Hood* with practically all its crew was serious, and the
great triumph was mingled with mourning for the gallant
men who had gone down in achieving it.

At this time the *Scharnhorst* and the *Gneisenau*, two more
commerce raiders, were shut up in Brest. To prevent them
getting out heavy bombers attacked the docks night after
night. On one occasion the Germans sent out the *Scharnhorst*, putting a dummy ship in its berth, but it was located at
La Palisse, 240 miles away, bombed, and was soon back again
in Brest for repairs. While there the two raiders were more
of a liability than an asset, and on 12th February 1942 an
effort was made to get them away. The Air Force located
them near the French coast not far from Boulogne on their
way to Kiel.

Once they were found, a large air battle developed, the
British aircraft firing torpedoes, the German fighters and
the ships' guns trying to hold them off. Slowly they passed
the Straits of Dover, the Belgian and Dutch coasts, the Fries-
ian islands. At last, having sustained considerable damage,
they were berthed in the Kiel Canal.

Germany never gained control of the sea. On the other
hand, British forays and raids on the Continent were frequent.
Not long after Dunkirk a small body of soldiers landed on the
French coast and brought back prisoners. At the end of 1941
the Lofoten Islands and Vaagso in Norway were attacked and
valuable enemy installations destroyed. In August 1942
Dieppe was attacked by commandos. They stayed on French
soil for a night and a day. An assault was also made on the
submarine base at St. Nazaire and again troops were landed.
The work of these small expeditions equalled in gallantry
anything seen during the war, and they were a constant
reminder to the enemy that the British forces on land and sea
and in the air were continually on the alert.

British air power was now growing fast. In the Churchill

Cabinet Lord Beaverbrook was Minister of Aircraft Production. His abilities as an administrator and his power to get things done quickly began to bear fruit. During the whole of the time the Luftwaffe was raiding British towns small forces of bombers were going nightly over the Reich. Göring had boasted that his country would never be bombed, but Londoners, sheltering in their cellars and 'Andersons' at that

Keystone Press

The Boyhood of ——?

time, derived some comfort from the news that their own air force was active too.

Munition works, industrial plants, railway marshalling yards, docks, aerodromes, power stations, and the like were the targets of this nightly air offensive which grew in intensity as the war went on. Bold sweeps were made on well defined targets. One day in summer a small fleet of heavy bombers flew at tree-top height over France and Germany to bomb an important plant at Augsburg where submarine parts were being made. In 1943 another force of torpedo-carrying bombers attacked the Eder and Möhne dams, bursting the floodgates and paralysing industry for miles around. Meanwhile the large towns were feeling the growing weight of air attack. Hamburg, Cologne, Munich, Stuttgart, Düsseldorf, Bremen, Duisburg, and even Berlin were paid frequent visits with increasing loads. Targets nearer home were not neglected. Almost nightly Coastal Command aircraft laid mines in enemy waters and attacked supply vessels. Fighters were sent out daily on offensive sweeps over France to draw the Germans to combat and to bring home valuable information. Because of this a great part of the Luftwaffe, which in June 1941 had gone away to Russia, had to be brought back to defend the west. For a time air raids on Britain ceased almost completely.

Long before America declared war her influence in the battle of the Atlantic was helping Britain. Her patrols were covering the west of the ocean from her own coasts to Iceland, jointly occupied by the two countries. The Americans also sent a large number of destroyers in return for the occupation of certain Atlantic and West Indian bases. But for the complete conquest of the submarines full co-operation was necessary.

CHAPTER XXIV

THE ENGLISH SCENE

IN three years the face of England had altered. The first reaction to war conditions had been to evacuate the mothers and children, to black out the country, to paint white lines along all the main roads, and to insist on everybody carrying a gas mask.

Britishers took the war seriously enough, but they did not realize how intense the struggle would become, nor what they would be called upon to sacrifice to gain victory. The deprivations, of course, came gradually. First, petrol was rationed to the private motorist, and he was allowed only a few gallons a month. Many people who could hardly imagine themselves without cars had to cut down their journeys, and eventually 'put up' their cars for the duration. At the beginning of 1940 food rationing was introduced. At first it was very simple and covered only staple commodities such as tea, butter, sugar, meat, and bacon, but later an ingenious system of 'points' was worked out to ensure a more even distribution of little luxuries, such as dried fruits, tinned goods, and cereals. Late in 1940 tropical fruits, such as bananas, oranges, and grapefruit disappeared altogether, and apples, brought mainly from Canada, became scarce. In 1941 rationing was extended to cover jams, sweets, and even clothing. In addition, as scarcity always leads to high prices, the Government fixed the prices of many goods and services to ensure fairness to everybody. They also stabilized rents.

Human energy has to be kept up especially in war-time, and under these conditions something had to be done to ensure that the worker had a good midday meal. Accordingly, in every town, 'National' or 'British' restaurants were established with the support of the Ministry of Health. They were usually situated in large halls and patronized by all classes of people. They gave a good meal, well cooked and served, at a very low price.

Education, which had suffered terribly at the outbreak of war through evacuation, began to recover. The air raids, feared in September 1939, had not come to pass and many children returned home to their families. Schools were re-opened in the big towns again and were kept going later in spite of raids. Greater provision was made for feeding in schools, and under a nation-wide scheme milk was brought into school and sold to children at the price of a halfpenny for a third of a pint. Special measures were taken to ensure supplies of nutritious food for children so that their health should suffer as little as possible from war-time privations.

At a time when production, both of food and armaments, had to be kept at a very high level unemployment almost ceased to exist. National defence absorbed a great deal of labour, the services drained offices and workshops of their staffs leaving only the 'key' men. The age for conscripting men for the Army went up step by step to fifty. Everybody who could be of use had to register for national service, and the conscription was applied to women. The Auxiliary Territorial Service (A.T.S.), the Women's Auxiliary Air Force (W.A.A.F.), the Women's Royal Naval Service (W.R.N.S.), and the Women's Land Army (W.L.A.) came into being and released men for the fighting forces. Women did things which they had never done before, such as ferrying aircraft, manning predictors on anti-aircraft gun sites, receiving and checking ships' cargoes. In time almost all the clerical and catering sides of service life were covered by them.

The same applied in industry. Girls who chose could enter, and it was a common sight to see them come away from the factories in boiler suits after a day's work among oil and metal. Married women with no dependants under fourteen years of age were called on for part-time and full-time work in factories and shops, filling up the gaps left by the numbers of skilled and unskilled workers who had left for the forces.

Under the direction of Mr. Ernest Bevin, Minister of Labour, the output of the country for military needs rose until it was greater in volume per person than that of any country in the world. The importation of machine tools from America contributed greatly to the drive towards mass production. Firms which had before the war manufactured luxuries and

The Ploughgirl

even the little comforts of life were switched over to war production, and the country first experienced the scarcity of such commodities as fountain pens, press studs, hair grips,

British Council Photo

On Munitions

plastic ware, crockery, and cosmetics. Large new armament plants sprang up where there had previously been heath, field, or common, but the small manufacturer, too, was given a chance to produce 'parts' which were later assembled at other great centres.

New camps, new training grounds and aerodromes appeared all over the country, and military traffic which had been so

The Old Campaigner   *Central Press*

rarely seen at one time now filled the roads. Tanks and
armoured cars rattled along with their crews fully armed and
wearing their steel helmets covered with netting. Motor
cyclists in leather coats and crash helmets were a common sight.

In 1940 the Local Defence Volunteers (L.D.V.), later
known as the Home Guard, was formed. Men who had
imagined their fighting days to be over, men who were held in
reserved occupations, and boys who had not yet been called
up were invited to enlist. It was from the beginning a popular

institution, and so useful that two years later conscription for this part-time army was introduced. Rigorous training made it into a formidable force, and its members were soon manning A.A. guns and guarding important points. This force constituted a second army, releasing thousands of men for more important duties abroad.

Meanwhile the youth of the country were not forgotten. In 1941 the Air Training Corps was founded for boys of sixteen. Here air crew aspirants learnt signals, navigation, aircraft recognition, and mathematics, completing the first part of their training before being called up. Their blue R.A.F. uniform with chrome buttons was a familiar sight in every town, especially in the vicinity of secondary schools, from which many members of the A.T.C. were recruited. The Home Guard also had its own cadets and so had the Navy, especially in the coastal and port towns. There were organizations for girls, such as the Girls' Training Corps (G.T.C.) and the Women's Junior Air Corps (W.J.A.C.). All these uniforms, together with the N.F.S. (National Fire Service) and the various branches of the Civil Defence, such as the A.R.P. (Air Raid Precautions), wardens' services, and the Red Cross, made up somewhat for the colour that had been lost when war came.

A less picturesque kind of work was to be found in the mines. The country needed fuel to feed its rapidly growing armament industry. While the householder was urged to save, and was even rationed with coal and coke, an attempt was made to encourage young men to go into the mines instead of the services. Mining had never been a popular occupation outside the coalfields and the response was disappointing. Eventually Mr. Bevin introduced conscription in the same way as for the army, and prospective miners were picked out by lot just before the time of their call-up. They were assured that everything would be done to teach them all that was possible about the coal-mining industry. There was some dissatisfaction among these 'Bevin Boys,' as they were popularly and somewhat inconsiderately called, but it was a great and worth-while experiment.

Everywhere there was the greatest scarcity of workers, but

this was most serious in the hospitals. Domestic work has never appealed much to the Englishwoman for it has never had a very high standing. It is a pity that the charwoman, the assistant cook, and the cleaner have not been given in this country at least the dignity which their labour merits. For want of the people to do the menial work many hospitals had to close down whole wards and the efficiency of the health services was impaired.

Another direction in which the scarcity was felt was in the schools. Teachers to replace those who had been called up were at a premium, and with the many additional burdens that fell on the schools during war-time this was keenly felt. Owing to the lack of staff it was found impossible, after the passing of the Education Bill, to raise the school-leaving age as early as had been planned.

After three years of war the cities of Britain had had their appearance altered considerably. In some of them whole areas had been levelled by bombing, and when a site had been cleared it often appeared as a 'gridiron' of streets with no houses at all. Gay blossoms of tall willow-herb grew on the rubbish heaps, but in some places industrious 'diggers for victory' had planted tidy gardens where houses and offices had once stood.

Many of the city buildings had an appallingly secondhand look. Some were clean cut by bombs, the inside walls showing, with the inevitable static water tank where the other half of a building had stood. Clock faces which used to adorn shop frontages were either completely blown out or remained at the same time they had shown when the blast of a bomb had put their works out of order. Shop windows were boarded up leaving only small panes of glass fixed in wooden frames through which the passer-by could peer. Illuminated signs were no longer illuminated and glass name-plates were broken. Even in places where buildings were undamaged there was that forlorn aspect which comes from lack of paint. The appearance of the English town had altered from its pre-war smartness to an air of grim waiting until the Army released the builders and decorators, and the factories and brickyards could again supply the paint and bricks for ordinary human needs.

During this time the posters of Britain provided a certain amount of humorous relief. 'Be like Dad, keep Mum,' they

Fox Photos
A Bombed Corner of the House of Lords

told the passer-by. 'Is Your Journey Really Necessary?' they asked the would-be traveller at a time when trains were few and far between. The comic 'Shanks's Pony' urged you to walk short distances and let the war workers use the buses. 'Coughs and Sneezes spread Diseases' told you to use your handkerchief and check the 'flu germ. 'Dig for Victory'

Piccadilly in Wartime: the Flower-seller

rallied a growing number of allotment holders to ease the food situation, and many of the government posters advertised the dangers of the black-out, the necessity of telephoning less, and the need to eat more carrots.

Amid all this there was a certain amount of pageantry,

especially at reviews of youth and processions inaugurating savings weeks. National Savings were one of the chief means of raising money. 'Spitfire Week,' 'Tank Week,' 'Warships Week,' and 'Salute the Soldier Week' were held at intervals in every town, and at some of these the money lent to the Government averaged many pounds per head. There were civic processions and speeches to open them. Towns adopted warships, tanks rumbled through the streets, planes were put on the public squares and opened for inspection to encourage these savings drives.

In the later days of the war the supreme thrill was to walk along Piccadilly or to sit in Green Park, for there the growing strength of the United Nations was symbolized. Belgium and Norway, Free France and Canada walked arm-in-arm. Loose-limbed Americans stood in groups talking at the doors of their clubs. Australians, New Zealanders, Poles, and Indians displayed their picturesque uniforms. Schoolboys on a day's jaunt in town strained to read the names on their shoulders or gazed at their rank badges and medal ribbons. Red-tabbed staff officers, generals, and admirals frequented the streets round Pall Mall. Commandos, parachutists, and air-borne soldiers were often met. The elderly private of the Home Guard with a row of ribbons, the spick and span pilot officer with outspread wings and perhaps a D.F.C. ribbon on his breast, the 'Waaf,' 'Wren,' 'Ats,' the Land Girl, the Heavy and Light Rescue, the smart Lady Warden, and the N.F.S. elbowed each other at the doors of the crowded Corner Houses seeking a place for tea. There seemed to be more service men and women than civilians, and what civilians there were no longer carried gas masks.

It was certainly true that there was now a job, and in most cases an interesting job, for everybody. Above all, there was an alertness, an air of up-to-the-minute efficiency which contrasted oddly with the badly weathered paintwork and broken buildings around. This, if anything, gave one the sure feeling that Great Britain and the United Nations were on the way to winning the war.

CHAPTER XXV

DEMOCRACY RISES AGAIN

AT the beginning of the war most Americans would have said that, although they sympathized profoundly with Great Britain, the struggle across the Atlantic was none of their concern. But before long many of their leaders realized that it would not be easy for America to stand aside.

This did not necessarily mean the employment of armed force. The idea of war was far from the minds of many Americans when Mr. Roosevelt became president for the third time. But it did imply that the peril to America had been realized, and that the way to combat it was to give all material aid possible to Great Britain. Thus at the end of December 1940 Mr. Roosevelt, in one of his 'fireside' talks, acknowledged that the United States must be the 'arsenal of democracy.' America could provide large numbers of tanks, guns, planes, and munitions if her industries were turned to war production and if the seas could be kept open.

Since 1937 the laws of the United States had forbidden citizens to help any nation at war by selling munitions. Even non-military supplies could be bought by such nations only provided that they paid for them 'on the barrel-head' and carried them away in non-American ships. The embargo on the export of arms was lifted in the first month of the war, but even so, these 'cash and carry' laws were preventing America from being as much help to Britain as Roosevelt wished.

Mr. Roosevelt's declaration was the beginning of a new policy. It led to a measure in March 1941 called 'lease-lend,' by which the U.S.A. consented to lend these materials to Great Britain and her allies for an indefinite period and to wait for repayment until circumstances permitted it.

Among other measures were the occupation of Iceland, Greenland, and the Atlantic bases, the closing of the German and Italian consulates, the freezing of German and Italian assets, and the stocktaking of all foreign property. When the Red Sea was opened American supplies flowed to Egypt and

Associated Press Photo
Children the World over: a Nazi Youth practises
his Music

later through Iran to Russia. The speed with which American-built ships took the place of those sunk by U-boats was a vital factor in winning the battle of the Atlantic.

Great Britain and the United States were now working together and some declaration to the world was necessary as to what they were working for and what they intended to do once Germany and Italy were defeated. It was a world sensation, therefore, when in August 1941 Mr. Churchill went out in the battleship *Prince of Wales* to meet President Roosevelt. The result of their talks was a document known as the Atlantic Charter. This statement gave in very broad outline the joint policies of the two countries: (1) to seek no increase of territory for themselves, (2) to consider the wishes of the people concerned when making territorial changes, (3) to restore self-government to all peoples in the form which they desired, (4) to give all states equal access to such of the world's materials as would make for prosperity, (5) to seek to improve the standards of labour and social security through- out the whole world, (6) to establish peace and security, (7) to facilitate freedom of travel, and (8) to ensure safety from aggression through the reduction in armaments over the whole world.

The Charter was well received and all the Allied nations, including Russia, signified their agreement with its aims. The conference between Churchill and Roosevelt was followed by a series of talks in Moscow, in which the Russians gave particulars of all the materials they needed for carrying on the war. America promised these, and to ensure the supply Great Britain gave up the share which had been allocated to her. They were conveyed through the rough waters of the Arctic Sea, and taken by rail on the newly constructed lines through Iran to the distant Caucasus.

Four months after the framing of the Atlantic Charter, America was at war (see p. 157) and Mr. Churchill again went to see President Roosevelt. On that occasion (December 1941) his short stay in America and Canada was a triumph. He spoke to the two Houses of Congress in Washington and to the Canadian Parliament. A year later, in January 1943, many other states had joined the allied cause.[1] These, now calling themselves 'The United Nations,' pledged their word

[1] U.S.A., Great Britain, Russia, China, Netherlands, Australia, Belgium, Canada, Costa Rica, Cuba, Czechoslovakia, Dominican Republic, Greece, Guatemala, Haiti, Honduras, India, Luxembourg, New Zealand, Nicaragua, Norway, Panama, Poland, Salvador, South Africa, Yugoslavia.

to stand by each other against Germany, Italy, Japan, and their allies and to make no separate peace until the common enemy was vanquished. Arrangements were made for the unifying of Allied commands and for the pooling of all resources of war materials.

Meanwhile the results of this steady collaboration were already beginning to show themselves. The North African campaign had gone badly at first. A second British advance into Tripolitania from the Egyptian border had relieved Tobruk in November 1941, even passing through Benghazi, but at the beginning of 1942 the march was again reversed. After fierce tank battles the enemy was checked at El Alamein, the very last outpost before the river Nile. Here between the sea and the impassable Qattara Depression, on a line only fifty miles long, both armies were regrouped. By October 1942 the Eighth Army, now fully equipped with British and American armaments, attacked again.

CHAPTER XXVI

THE TABLES TURNED

TOWARDS the end of 1942 the Germans were as near to complete success as they had ever been. Field Marshal von Hoth was facing Stalingrad with a powerful army which threatened to cut Russia in two by occupying a stretch of the Volga. Southwards the enemy was overrunning the Kuban valley and forging ahead towards the rich oilfields of the Caucasus. In the eastern Mediterranean the halt of the Germans and the Italians at El Alamein seemed but a prelude to the final attack on Egypt.

Things were happening, however, which seemed to indicate that the war had reached a turning point. Nothing illustrates this better than the fact that although the Germans had obtained complete mastery of North Africa they could not occupy the island fortress of Malta.

When in 1940 Mussolini joined Hitler, Malta suddenly came into the war picture. It lies only fifty-two miles from Sicily, on the direct route between Italy and her empire in Libya. It also lies on the route from Gibraltar to Alexandria but it is nearly a thousand miles from either of them. Its capture by the Axis would have closed the Mediterranean to the Allies.

The story of its resistance and final triumph is one of the most thrilling in the annals of the war, and ends with the award to the island of that high military distinction, the George Cross. The Italian Navy alone could not take it. When Rommel and the Afrika Korps came to Italy fleets of bombers could not shake its resolution. Instead, its active fighter forces, built up from four machines in 1940, harried the Axis supply lines and forced convoys to sneak across the narrows by dark and creep along the Tunisian coast towards the harbour of Tripoli. No wonder that the Italians called Malta the 'Isola del Diavolo'—the Island of the Devil, or that the

British sailors escorting their precious cargoes of supplies through these dangerous waters named them Bomb Alley.

In the later months of 1942 the enemy tried every method short of direct assault. Large groups of bombers escorted by fighters appeared almost by time-table, but were driven off with heavy losses. Civilians took refuge in caves and underground shelters, anti-aircraft guns flashed, and Spitfires darted

E.N.A.

Haulers on the Volga

out to bring down the attackers. In face of almost impossible odds escorted convoys sailed in with food and munitions. The island came very near to starvation, but when General Montgomery attacked at El Alamein at the end of October the Luftwaffe found other work to do. The raids on Malta became less intense and the critical period drew to a close.

At the other side of Europe the defence of Stalingrad was exciting the admiration of the world. The German armies, from the bridgehead they had thrown across the Don, had advanced to the city, and had reached the banks of the Volga north and south of it. Hitler had boasted loudly in one of his speeches that Stalingrad would be taken. All that the Germans succeeded in taking was heaps of ruins, defended pile after pile by desperate soldiers and civilians. Furious fighting among these ruins lasted for two months.

The city of Stalingrad stretches for twenty miles along the west bank of the Volga. It was never completely occupied

Malta under Fire

by the Germans and the river was never crossed. In November the Russians, having gathered all their available forces, suddenly struck to the north-west and the south. They made a complete break through, took the German forces in the rear, and in the end surrounded a large number of them. A hundred miles to the north-west strong armies crossed the Don, drove due south, and recovered the whole of the Don elbow with about five thousand square miles of land. A huge German army was left isolated, either to starve or surrender. Thus ended the long series of Russian defeats.

In the Mediterranean the gallant resistance of Malta was soon to be justified. Rommel, now before El Alamein, was far from his supply bases, while the British had assembled in the Nile valley large quantities of materials. They attacked in the last week of October 1942 after air and artillery bombardment. In a week the Axis line was broken and soldiers were streaming away to the west. Thousands of them, especially Italians, and vast quantities of stores were taken. In little more than a month General Montgomery's forces were at El Agheila.

A few days only were allowed for reinforcements and regrouping, and the advance was continued along the shores of the Gulf of Tripoli. At the end of January 1943 the British were in the town itself.

It seemed now that the Axis supremacy in Africa must come to an end. On 8th November 1942 British and American forces, commanded by General Eisenhower, had landed in French North Africa at many points, taking the enemy completely by surprise. There was some resistance, but Casablanca, Oran, and Algiers were soon occupied. Admiral Darlan was made head of the Government there, and when he was assassinated the power passed to General de Gaulle and General Giraud.

Hitler's troops now advanced into unoccupied France, but before they could enter Toulon and take the French Fleet, lying in the harbour there, the admiral commanding it ordered all the ships to be sunk. Among them were the battleships *Dunkerque*, *Strasbourg*, and *Provence*, three cruisers, an aircraft carrier, about twenty-five destroyers, and twenty submarines. Of the whole fleet only three submarines escaped. The greater part of the fleet went to the bottom.

Frenchmen who had once been doubtful now joined de Gaulle. After French North Africa the whole of French West Africa came over, with its naval base of Dakar, a valuable acquisition which had previously been withheld.

Unless the Germans could occupy Tunis, where the Allies were now advancing, they would be turned completely out of Africa. Airborne troops were quickly landed and established

The Two Leaders: Eisenhower and Montgomery

themselves on the coastal strip to a depth of about sixty miles. For two months neither side made much headway, but at the end of March the Eighth Army began its drive from the east through the strongly held Mareth line. In April it joined hands with the Americans and a general attack was begun on all the enemy positions. Soon only the tip of land behind Tunis was in enemy hands and this was gradually lessened. On 7th May the Americans entered Bizerta and the British took Tunis. The last of the Axis forces were trapped in the Cape Bon Peninsula. There was no retreat, and General von Arnim was one of the 248,000 prisoners taken.

The peril to Malta was now over. The Germans and Italians were completely out of Africa. Well might Mr. Churchill say: 'We have struck the enemy a blow which is the equal of Stalingrad.'

CHAPTER XXVII

THE ROAD BACK

SOMETHING had gone wrong with the German war plans. The knock-out blows that had been aimed at Great Britain and Russia had not had the expected effect. Instead, Germany was now like a boxer in the ring who, having exerted himself to the utmost in the first rounds, is beginning to tire as his opponent gathers strength.

Hitler, the apostle of 'audacity,' was now finding that his methods were bringing new and stronger enemies into the field against him. The American war potential was steadily rising. Men, tanks, planes, and materials were crossing the oceans in spite of all that German submarines and planes could do. The rate of ship construction, thanks to mass methods, was more than making up for the number sunk. The increased efficiency of counter-measures, especially in the number of aircraft patrols, was making submarine warfare more dangerous to the hunter than to the hunted. In October 1943 Portugal granted the United Nations the use of the Azores Islands as an anti-submarine base, and with that great asset the whole of the convoy routes could be effectively patrolled and protected.

The German situation in Europe was gradually deteriorating. In the occupied countries the Underground Front was becoming more active and its members were in touch with the Allied Powers outside. The flames of national liberation had not died in these lands. Marshal Tito in Yugoslavia was waging open war on the Germans, who had never gained full control of the country since they occupied it. Guerrilla bands in Greece were operating on the enemy supply lines. In Poland, Belgium, Holland, Norway, Czechoslovakia, and France, sabotage was carried on in exploits which varied from blowing up war plants to letting the petrol out of the tanks of lorries. Even in Denmark, which had been extolled as

Hitler's model republic, the people had turned against repression, and sabotage was widespread in spite of everything that was done to stop it.

The Germans had imported millions of workers from the rest of Europe to keep their factories running and to free Germans for the fighting forces, but they were by no means so efficient

Marshal Tito's Headquarters

in their work. When, in addition, night by night thousands of R.A.F. Halifaxes and Stirlings attacked these plants with bombs German war production fell off rapidly. In 1943 Flying Fortresses of the United States Army Air Force began their heavy daylight raids, and sent down thousands of tons, especially on ball-bearing factories, synthetic oil plants, and aircraft assembly plants all over the Reich.

Hitler, then, with decreasing power both in machines and men, was now having to face enemies, not only on the Russian front but in the south and in the occupied countries as well, with a strong probability of more fronts being opened. This was not what he had advocated in *Mein Kampf*.

The freeing of Stalingrad and the occupation of the Don elbow was followed by more striking Russian advances. The capture of Rostov-on-Don cut off the Germans in the Kuban. Other forces pursued them as far as Kharkov and Bielgorod.

Winter Campaign.   Russian Troops advancing

In the German counter-attack of spring 1943 these two towns were again lost, but in August the Russians mounted their first summer offensive. It proved that they were at last more than a match for the Germans in men, material, and leadership. In the north both Smolensk and Briansk, 'half-way houses to Moscow,' were taken. Kharkov was freed again on 23rd August, and in the Ukraine the Russians got a strong foothold in the Donetz bend, occupying Poltava and Stalino.

The summer of 1943 was no less eventful on the south front. In June the Italian islands of Pantellaria, Lampedusa, and Linosa were taken. In July the Allies landed strong forces on the south coast of Sicily. The British took Syracuse but were held before Catania. The Americans reduced all the west of the island. A final joint thrust conquered the north-east corner. On 25th July came the news that Mussolini had resigned. In one country, at least, Fascism was in its death-throes.

On 3rd September Allied forces landed on the toe of Italy. Five days later Marshal Badoglio, now Premier, surrendered unconditionally to the Allies. The Italian Fleet came over to Malta and the Germans hastily prepared to leave Sardinia. On the mainland they continued to resist. The main Allied force pushing up the toe of Italy made contact with others which had been landed at Reggio and Salerno. On 1st October Naples fell.

Common peril had forced the Allies to co-operate. Joint success now made contact more and more necessary. The plans for the invasion of Italy had been agreed on by Churchill and Roosevelt at Casablanca six months before. In October another conference met, this time in Moscow, between Eden, Cordell Hull, and Molotov to agree on the future of Italy. In December a notable assembly met at Cairo to discuss the prosecution of the war against Japan. Here, for the first time, Churchill and Roosevelt met Marshal Chiang Kai-shek. All the important generals, ministers, and chiefs of staff were present to consider their own particular parts of the plans.

From Cairo, Churchill and Roosevelt flew to Teheran, in Iran, and there met Marshal Stalin to discuss the measures to be taken against Germany. What was said will remain secret for a long time, but we may be sure that it included plans for the invasion of Germany's 'European Fortress' and preparations for peace.

Victory [said Mr. Eden, after this conference] is only a means to an end, and that end a peace that will last. This recurrent threat of war can only be met if there is an international order firmer in strength and unity than any enemy that can seek to challenge it. Is there now then, not the possibility of creating such an order? Do the foundations exist? Six months ago I could not have given you any certain answer. It might have been so, it might not have been so. But to-day I can give you the answer. It is an emphatic 'Yes.'

Meanwhile advances on all sides were continuing. In Italy the line of the Sangro River had been reached. In Russia Kiev, the old capital of the Ukraine, had been captured and this was followed by the taking of Zhitomir and Korosten beyond it, and of Gomel, a key-point farther north. In December and January Leningrad was freed from danger of

War's Destruction. Monte Cassino after Bombardment

encirclement and perpetual enemy shelling. From February to April 1944 strong attacks were again made in the Ukraine, freeing the whole of south Russia including Odessa and the Crimea.

The Germans in Italy had now fortified a belt of country round Cassino and the Sangro which they called the Gustav line. In January 1944 a landing was made by the British and Americans at Anzio with the object of drawing forces away and taking the line in the rear. Until May the fighting continued; there were desperate struggles by the British to hold the beach-head, and by the Germans to hold Cassino the

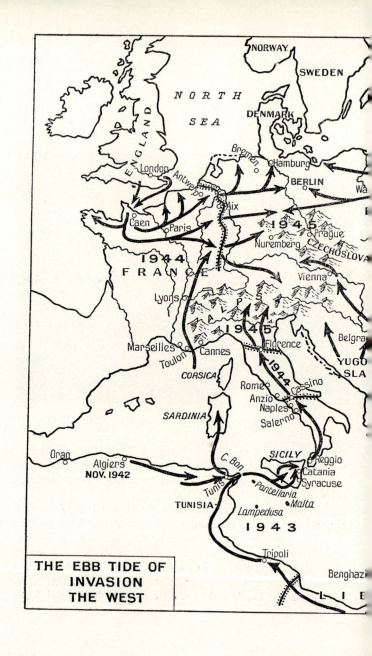

NORWAY

SWEDEN

N O R T H
S E A

DENMARK

ENGLAND

London
Antwerp
Bremen
Hamburg
BERLIN
Wa

Aix
Caen
Paris
1 9 4 5
Prague
CZECHOSLOVA
Nuremberg

1 9 4 4
F R A N C E
Vienna

Lyons

1 9 4 5
Belgra

Marseilles
Cannes
Florence
YUGO
SLA
Toulon
CORSICA
1 9 4 4
Rome
Cassino
Anzio
Naples
SARDINIA
Salerno

Oran
Algiers
NOV. 1942
C. Bon
SICILY
Reggio
Catania
Tunis
Syracuse
Pantellaria
TUNISIA
Malta
Lampedusa
1 9 4 3

Tripoli
Benghaz

THE EBB TIDE OF
INVASION
THE WEST

L I B

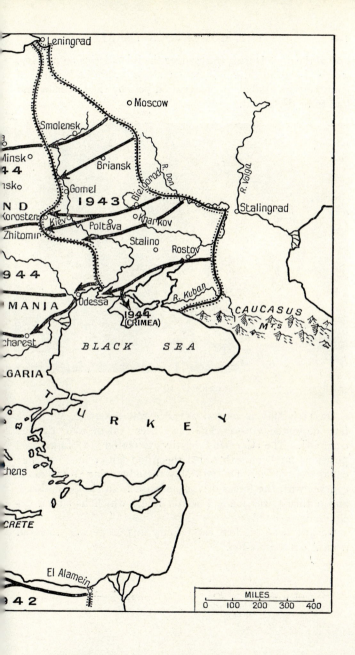

hub of the line. During the fighting the Benedictine monastery, which stood on the hill commanding miles and miles of country, was used as an observation post by the Germans and had to be destroyed.

Franklin D. Roosevelt

On 11th May a general advance was ordered. Within a few days the Gustav line had been taken and Cassino occupied. The Germans hastily retreated to improvised positions farther north called the Adolf Hitler line, but they could not hold it. On 25th May the advancing troops made contact with the forces driving forward from the beach-head, and a thrust was made towards Rome which had been declared an open city.

On 4th June the first capital city in Europe was liberated from Axis domination.

CHAPTER XXVIII

THE END IN THE WEST

On 6th June 1944 the greatest military operation of all time was begun. For two years, since the slogan 'Strike now in the West' had appeared on walls and hoardings, the British people had waited, some of them very impatiently, for the day when their wish to bring relief to hard-pressed Russia would be gratified.

We now know what a long and tedious period of preparation was needed to work out every detail of this gigantic enterprise, how new military methods were studied and adapted, how details of equipment and arms were worked out down to the waterproofing of vehicles and the issuing of rations. Special springs had to be made for protecting vehicles from road shocks, special tyres which even if punctured would bring a vehicle safely home, special lifting disks to put under the wheels of 100,000 cars and trucks for embarking them. Shirts had to be prepared so that they would not harbour vermin, and bags had to be supplied in case of seasickness. We have since heard of 'Pluto,' the pipe-line which was ready for laying across the Channel to take petrol, and of the 'Mulberry' ports, floating harbours which were to be assembled as soon as the first bridge-heads were established, but we can hardly imagine the magnitude of the task of drilling, provisioning, arming, and equipping such a colossal number of men. All over the south of England were the concentration areas where men were kept ready, then nearer the coasts the marshalling areas where they were organized for transport, and finally the embarkation points. Every precaution had to be taken in case any hitch should occur in the execution of the main scheme—air raids at embarkation points, high winds and storms at sea, successful resistance on the French coast. But the planners were driven by one overriding consideration —that the invasion *had* to succeed. On 24th December 1943

General Eisenhower was made supreme commander of all the invasion forces.

On the whole the British civilian bore the burdens with goodwill. In 1942 he was impatient. In 1943 he was in-

Planes by the Thousand.   American Production

terested. He knew something important was happening. He heard of secret landing rehearsals at lonely points on our coast, of landing barges being made in large numbers, of equipment on the secret list, and he guessed what was going on in the large areas of Devon and East Anglia that were evacuated and screened off for military operations. In spring 1944 there was tense expectation. Hitler was boasting about the impregnability of his West Wall, the British man in the street was speculating on the exact date of 'D Day,' and saying to himself as the tanks rumbled towards the south coast and the marshalling areas filled with fresh troops: 'It can't be long now.'

April passed, and then May, and nothing happened. D Day had to be postponed to eliminate 'snags' in the organization and to carry out minor rehearsals. The final decision depended on the weather reports. On 6th June the B.B.C. announced that parachutists and airborne troops had been dropped at certain points and this had been followed by landings. It is hard to say whether the Germans were surprised or not, or if they expected the attack to be made on the Normandy coast. The first operations were successful. Several beach-heads were established round the small town of Arromanches, and the huge Mulberry harbours were towed across the Channel and put together near the beaches. The following fortnight was full of tension. The weather deteriorated, high winds rose and interfered considerably with the landings, damaging one of the artificial ports. By the time the weather cleared London and the south coast were undergoing a peculiar ordeal of their own.

It had been proved now that Hitler's European fortress was not impregnable. In the summer of 1944 the Russians practically cleared their country of the enemy; in August they made a large-scale assault on Roumania through the Carpathian gaps. At the end of August they captured Ploesti, the much-bombed oil centre, and entered Bucharest. By the middle of September Roumania was out of the war.

Meanwhile the Allied armies in Italy, under Field Marshal Alexander, were advancing north of Rome. In July the Americans took Leghorn, in August the Germans evacuated Florence, and before the end of the summer the Allied armies were overlooking the valley of the Po and were within striking distance of the main industrial centres of north Italy.

Life in southern England and particularly in London was

Corner of the 'Mall-ganj'

not easy during that summer. Göbbels had long promised the British a secret weapon which would put an end to any attempts at invading the continent. The flying bombs were probably intended for the south-coast ports to stop embarkation. Launching sites had been under construction for some months but had been held up by British air attack and the German secret weapon was too late. Its full force was then turned on London. The first flying bomb (V1) arrived during the night of 13th–14th June and they continued until the end of the war in the west. They were fired at first from launching sites in France and Belgium. London was protected through the summer of 1944 by a wide balloon barrage, and by squadrons of fighter planes which shot down large numbers of them. Nevertheless they did great damage and destroyed many thousands of homes.

By July the Allies were well enough established to carry out a great offensive in France. The plan was to use British and Canadian troops to bear the heaviest shock of the German attack in the Caen region, while the American line, using Caen as a pivot, should sweep in a wide arc southwards, eastwards, and then northwards up to Paris. This was the plan which General Montgomery, Commander of the Allied land forces in France, had drawn up a month before D Day. Its development kept surprisingly true to pattern. The German High Command concentrated on holding the British and Canadians in the Caen sector. This enabled the Americans to capture Cherbourg and break through the German lines near Saint-Lô. American armour under General Patton secured the Brest peninsula, then turned east and swept rapidly across France. The powerful German forces at the pivot held for a time at Falaise but were surrounded and annihilated.

From that point the German cause in France was lost. On 15th August a second landing was made, this time from the Mediterranean near Cannes, and within a few days British and Americans were advancing up the Rhône valley, liberating towns and bringing arms and relief to the Maquis. These patriots, who from their mountain retreats had long resisted the Germans, now came out in large numbers and joined the invading armies. The German defence collapsed completely. Paris fell on 23rd August. General Eisenhower, in whose hands had been the preparation and execution of this vast project, now assumed direct command of all Allied armies fighting on French soil. General Patton's mechanized forces joined up with the armies from the south, and the northern group advanced across the Seine and pressed on into Belgium, taking in their stride the flying-bomb installations near the French coast. For a short period London had respite from attacks.

On 3rd September Brussels was freed and the British advanced towards the German and Dutch frontiers. On the 17th the British 1st Airborne Division landed near Arnhem in the hope of liberating Holland before the winter, but before they could be reached by the main forces many had been killed and taken prisoner. The rest had to be withdrawn. Elsewhere the advance went on. On 11th September the Americans crossed the German frontier north of Trier. In October the United States 1st Army received the surrender of the town of Aachen. In November, after air attacks and landings, the island of Walcheren and the port of Flushing were taken.

Here the advance was halted along the whole front because of the approach of winter and the vast length of the Allied supply lines. In little more than three months the British and Americans had swept through France and carried men, arms, and supplies for many hundreds of miles. Optimists in England had predicted that the war in the west would be won before Christmas, but they were disappointed. Beyond the Rhine and behind the Siegfried line the Germans succeeded in re-forming the remnants of their armies for the last great struggle. In December Marshal von Rundstedt opened a counter-offensive in the Ardennes, with the object of enveloping the whole British Army by striking at Liége, Brussels, and Ostend. In six days he made a penetration of forty miles, but the position was restored by the end of January with great losses inflicted on the Germans.

The advances of the Russians were quite as spectacular.

The latter part of 1944 was taken up with a series of campaigns which ended in freeing the lower Danube completely from German domination. In September the Russians crossed into Bulgaria. Within a month they had effected a junction with the Yugoslav patriot forces under Marshal Tito, and captured Belgrade, the capital of Yugoslavia. The

Yugoslav Boys

end of the year saw their armies in the neighbourhood of Budapest, the Hungarian capital.

During these days the advances of all the allies were complicated by the existence of 'pockets of resistance' left behind by the Germans as the advancing armies swept forward. In the west the isolated garrisons in such places as Brest, Saint-Nazaire, and the Channel Islands still held out, but in eastern Europe the problem was much greater. The Russian advance up the Danube left large numbers of Germans behind, and these had to be dealt with. The reconquest of Poland in 1944 led them to the gates of Warsaw, but left wide tracts of land in Latvia and Lithuania to be 'cleaned up.' In January 1945 the Russians under Marshals Koniev and Zhukov made a dash from the Polish bases into eastern Germany. Within three weeks they advanced to the river Oder, only fifty miles from Berlin, and overran a large part of Silesia. Here they made a halt to give themselves time to overcome resistance in East Prussia and to 'mop up' the German forces left behind in Torun, Poznan, and the Silesian towns of Glogau and Breslau.

Meanwhile the Allies in the west had been seeking to put their own supply position in order. In November the channel leading to Antwerp had been cleared and equipment was being sent through Antwerp to supply the armies. All was ready for the general advance early in 1945.

In March of that year the line of the Rhine was reached below Cologne by the Americans from Jülich, and by the British and Canadian armies fighting their way through the dense Reichswald forest. General Patton's forces also took up the offensive and cleared the German Army out of all the land west of the Rhine between Cologne and Strasbourg.

Here the advance did not end. The Germans left a bridge intact at Remagen, and the Americans stormed over it, establishing a bridge-head many miles deep. On 25th March a combined assault was made on the lower Rhine by the 21st Army Group (i.e. the British 2nd Army, the American 9th Army, and the Canadian 1st Army). Their preparations had been hidden by a smoke-screen sixty miles long. At the appointed time landing craft crossed, airborne forces were carried over, and bridge-heads were secured. Almost at the same time other armies crossed further upstream, sweeping away all resistance. Within a week the invasion of central Germany was in full swing.

The winter of 1944–5 began in Britain with disappointed hopes. Germany had not collapsed and a new peril had arrived in the south. After the flying-bomb sites of the Germans had been taken there was for some two or three weeks a spell of quiet. Soon, however, the city was shaken by a series of mysterious explosions which shattered buildings and claimed many victims. These were caused by projectiles known as V2, which were later found to be immense rockets fired from sites in Holland and aimed at London. They arrived at all times of the day and night, without warning, and travelled faster than sound. Day after day throughout the whole winter they continued, and did not cease until the Allied invasion of Germany at the end of March 1945 cut the supply lines.

On 7th February it was officially announced that Mr. Churchill, Marshal Stalin, and President Roosevelt were in conference at Yalta in the Crimea, and five days later the decisions made at this momentous conference were made known to the world. They made it clear that Germany's position was hopeless and that only unconditional surrender would be accepted. Plans were made for the future government of Germany, for the assessing of reparations, for building up the life of liberated Europe, and for the setting up of governments in Poland and Yugoslavia. But by far the most important decision was that the foreign secretaries of Great Britain, Russia, and the United States would meet every three or four months. Part of the declaration reads:

Our meeting here in the Crimea has reaffirmed our common determination to maintain and strengthen in the peace to come, that unity of purpose and action which has made victory possible and certain for the United Nations in this war; we believe that it is a sacred obligation which our Governments owe to our people and to the people of the world. Only with continued and growing co-operation and understanding among our three countries and among all the peace-loving nations can the highest aspirations of humanity be realized.

The complete collapse of German resistance was now only a matter of time. In the west the large towns fell one by one to the rapidly advancing armies. The British struck north-east and cut off Holland, the Americans swept across central Germany towards Bohemia, while the French advanced in Württemberg. Meanwhile the Russians, now in Austria, captured Vienna and other Russian armies swept on to Berlin. A rapid advance in north Italy completed the picture, for from 21st April, when Bologna was captured, news poured in of the successive liberation of Milan, Turin, and Trieste, of the execution of Mussolini by Italian partisans on the 28th, and finally of the surrender of all the German armies in Italy to Field Marshal Alexander, the Supreme Allied Commander, on 2nd May. In Germany 26th April saw the Americans and Russians effect a junction at Torgau and Berlin was surrounded. On 2nd May the capital of Germany surrendered to

Brutality. The captured Commander of the Belsen Concentration Camp (note British Troops in the Background)

the Russians, but Hitler, with Göbbels and other prominent Nazis, had already committed suicide. On 7th May all German forces surrendered and the war in the west was ended. Many of the Nazi leaders who had not committed suicide were captured or gave themselves up, to await trial as war criminals at Nuremberg.

The 9th and 10th of May were general holidays in this country in commemoration of VE (Victory in Europe) Day. Bonfires were lit, parades and celebrations took place in all the towns. The searchlights which in earlier days had been used for grimmer purposes now swept the sky in whirling, circling patterns. The factory hooters and ships in dock sounded for hours the well-known V (· · · –) sign. For two days the country relaxed after nearly six years of 'blood, sweat, toil, and tears.'

There was a sordid side to victory in the disclosures which were made when the Nazi concentration camps were captured, and stories of mass suffering too horrible for belief were found to be true. Millions of people had died through ill-treatment or starvation during the long Nazi rule.

There was also a sorrowful moment in the hour of victory. On 13th April, less than a month before the final collapse of Germany, the world was deeply shocked to hear of the death of President Roosevelt. More than any other American, past or present, he had come to be regarded as a friend of all men everywhere. He was an idealist who refused to let the beastliness of war and the selfishness of greedy men blind him to the vision of what might be if all behaved as good neighbours. His idea of a New Deal for Americans had widened into one of a New Deal for mankind. Expressed in the simple words of the 'Four Freedoms,' it had given the common man hope and a goal for which to fight.

CHAPTER XXIX

THE END IN THE EAST

In August 1942 it looked as if Japan had won the first round. The conquest of the whole of the East Indies within a few months seemed stupendous. But there were many factors which made it possible for Japan to lose the second round.

Let us look at the position at the end of 1942. By this time the Germans had been checked at Stalingrad and the British advance from El Alamein had begun. This meant that Japan and Germany would not link up across the Indian Ocean nor would they drive the British out of the Near East. In the second place India and Australia were still unconquered, and American production was mounting in a way that must at some time have powerful results in the Pacific. Meanwhile the first trickle of British troops was arriving in India with the idea of preparing for a large-scale invasion of Burma, and the Chinese were still occupying Japanese attention.

Having made such large gains the problem now was how to hold them. If by doing so the Japanese could exploit their tremendous resources in oil, rubber, tin, metal, and rice they could probably sustain a long war with hopes of tiring out their adversaries. That is why they fortified every available island and coral reef in the south-east Pacific, and held on to Burma, blocking any line of supply to China and any possible attempt by the British to reach the China Sea.

The struggle was long and tedious. For three years the Australians maintained a campaign in the jungles of New Guinea, in New Britain, and on Bougainville in the Solomons, driving the enemy back slowly over the most difficult country. During this time the Americans had to develop an entirely new technique of attack—the amphibious operation known as 'island-hopping.' It began in the Gilbert Islands in November 1943 when the island of Tarawa with its airfield was taken by assault in the face of determined enemy resistance. This was the pattern of American attack: from the Gilberts to the Marshalls (February 1944), the Admiralty Islands (March

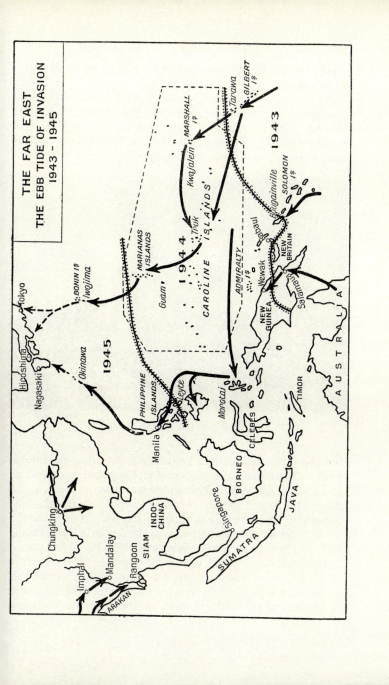

THE FAR EAST
THE EBB TIDE OF INVASION
1943 - 1945

1944), the Carolines (June–September 1944), and the Marianas (July 1944).

At the end of 1943 Lord Louis Mountbatten, chief of the south-east Asia command, launched the British offensive in Burma. Here throughout the whole of the following year violent fighting went on and dangerous thrusts were made on both sides. The British made progress on the Arakan front,

Black Star Photo

Building the Burma Road

but the Japanese isolated a British force defending the Imphal plain. These had to be reinforced and supplied by air. Two and a half divisions were flown in and they held the position. In August the British and Americans captured Myitkyina, the most important Japanese base in northern Burma. Now without a doubt India was safe, and Japan would be beaten in Burma as she had already been on the Solomons and in the Pacific islands.

The year 1945 opened with great promise. The recapture of the Solomons was complete, American landing parties had by-passed the Japanese in New Guinea by capturing the island of Morotai which could be used to dominate the Moluccas.

The defence of New Guinea had been costly to Japan; its isolation was a disaster.

But the greatest blow of all was that of the landing of American troops on the island of Leyte in October 1944. In December a second landing was made on Mindoro Island. Within three months the whole Philippine group had been

War in the Jungle

overrun and Manila captured. It had taken General Mac-Arthur three years to make good his promise to return to the Philippines as victor.

With every new advance the peril to Japan increased. Super-Fortresses in ever greater numbers were sent out to bomb Japanese supply centres and to paralyse war industries. Nearer and nearer came the American amphibious forces supported by ever increasing naval and air power which Japan, with her dwindling resources, could not possibly meet. Iwo-jima in the Bonin Islands was taken in February. From

H

there it was only 680 miles to Tokyo. In March a combined assault was made on the island of Okinawa, 440 miles from Nagasaki, with complete success. Here the Americans repaired and built airfields. The obvious next move was to gather all available forces to invade the mainland of Japan itself. Everybody expected it. The newly won Japanese empire could not now last. It had been completely severed from its centre. It seemed as if the destruction of Japanese forces in New Guinea, in the scattered East Indian islands, in Malaya, in Burma, and in China would go on piecemeal until resistance ceased entirely.

On 7th May came the victory in Europe, and while during the hours which followed everybody rejoiced, they still thought with sorrow about the boys who were out in Burma, and those who since 1942 had been held prisoners in Japanese camps and from whom news had been scanty and infrequent. What was happening to them? When would they be free? 'Not for a year at least,' said some. 'Japan may have lost her empire, but there's plenty of hard fighting to do. Those Japs won't give in without a terrific struggle.'

There was no invasion of Japan, but her leaders were urged to surrender to avoid further unnecessary bloodshed and suffering. The Japanese determined to go on with the war. On 6th August the world heard with bewilderment about the dropping of an 'atomic' bomb on Hiroshima, and read in their newspapers something about its devastating effects. The Japanese leaders replied that they would still go on with the war. Three days later a second atomic bomb was dropped on Nagasaki and that was the end. On the 10th the Japanese made an offer of unconditional surrender. An armistice was announced on the 14th and orders were flashed to all parts of the Far East to put an end to the fighting. One by one the fronts became quiet. On isolated islands of the Pacific sundry Japanese garrisons gave themselves up when they heard the news. Prisoners of war were liberated or released from camps, occupying forces moved into Japan and into all the places where Japanese sway had been exercised. London again rejoiced, this time for VJ Day (15th August 1945).

CHAPTER XXX

1. CANADA

DURING the days of destruction in London the reserved Englishman experienced many a moment of warm pride and satisfaction on finding himself sitting opposite a staunch Canadian face in a railway carriage, or perhaps bumping into a Canadian 'voice' in the black-out.

Within a week of Britain's declaration of war Canada had followed suit. Under Mr. Mackenzie King and his Liberal Government the country marshalled its resources in men and material for the common struggle. Far removed from the fighting, Canada became a source of strength and wealth, invaluable to the mother country and her allies.

A few facts and illustrations can give some idea of Canada's war effort. Some three-quarters of a million men were called to the forces. That was about 35 per cent of all men between the ages of eighteen and thirty-five, and of these, volunteers in large numbers were sent to fight overseas. Starting almost unarmed, during the course of the war Canada became the third largest naval power and the fourth largest air power of the United Nations.

After a period of intensive training, and more tiring waiting, Canadians played prominent parts in many theatres of war. On land the Canadian 1st Division saw some of the heaviest fighting in the thirty-nine-day campaign for Sicily, where they drove through the centre between British and Americans. On the Italian mainland, Canadians, now organized in a self-contained corps attached to the British 8th Army, figured notably in the attack on the Hitler line which opened the way for the advance up the Liri and Sacco valleys to Rome. In late 1944 they shared in the drive through north Italy breaking the Gothic line near the Adriatic. Again, in Normandy, the Canadian Army actively contributed to the cracking of the Hitler fortress. The Canadian 3rd Division, part of Montgomery's 21st Army Group, wrote a stirring chapter of its history at Caen, the pivot on which swung the great advance of the Americans through the Cherbourg peninsula. During September 1944 listeners to the radio

Canadian Forestry Corps at work on the shores
of Loch Ness

heard with exciting frequency the news of successive captures of the Channel ports by the Canadians, British, Dutch, and Belgians, who worked together so successfully in the Canadian 1st Army, capturing 73,000 of the enemy, and then proceeding to operations in the Low Countries where they cleared the Scheldt estuary and held the western end of the Allied line in the push into the Netherlands.

At sea Canada rapidly acquired strength. In four years her small navy was increased fiftyfold, and many new naval bases were built on the east and west coasts and in New-foundland. Canadian shipping gave considerable help in the Atlantic convoys and Canada even built ships for Britain.

It has been said that the British Commonwealth Air Training Plan was the major contribution of Canada to the Allied cause. By D Day over 100,000 air-crew personnel from all parts of the empire and commonwealth had been trained in Canadian skies, where climate, security, and available space made this possible. Canada's own air force, as well as the Canadians serving with the R.A.F., played no small part in the bombing of Germany's vital industrial towns, coastal fortifications, and communications that preceded the invasion of Europe. In the raid on Duisburg, for instance, on 14th October 1944 over 500 Canadian Halifaxes and Lancasters helped to deliver a 10,000-ton bomb assault.

The effect of the war on Canadian industry and agriculture was surprising. Despite the direction of men to the forces production leaped ahead. This enabled Canada to give unstinted help to the Allies in food and materials of all kinds, and later to become a pillar of strength to the U.N.R.R.A.[1] organization in finding food for stricken countries.

2. AUSTRALIA AND NEW ZEALAND

Of all the dominions Australia was most directly 'in' the war. But well before the threatened invasion of Australia by Japan her people had shown that the defence of civilization was the concern of all.

In 1939 Australia, with her small population of 7,000,000, had an army of 80,000 men. Volunteers for the A.I.F., enlisted for service in any part of the world, swelled its numbers, and by 1944 reached nearly half a million. With the conscription of others for home defence, some two-thirds of Australia's active male population were engaged.

Australia had her own efficient Navy and Air Force. In connection with the latter it is interesting to note that she arranged for the training of 26,000 men in the Empire Air

[1] United Nations Relief and Rehabilitation Association.

Training Scheme. These, as well as the volunteers in Britain's services, were of the utmost value. Yet the major assistance of Australia to the Allied efforts was the work of the Army in many theatres of war. In the first offensive in the Western Desert no small part was played by the 1st Division. In Greece and in Crete the 6th Division fought stubbornly in impossible situations. In Syria the 7th Division were among the armies which helped to forestall the Axis. At El Alamein, the crucial battle of 1942, Australians displayed that quality of courage and toughness for which they were famous. As the British official report stated: 'The 9th Australian Division fought themselves and the enemy to a standstill, till flesh and blood could stand no more. Then they went on fighting.'

Three months after the Japanese attack on Pearl Harbor it appeared that only a miracle could save Australia from invasion and defeat. Already Japanese bombs were falling. Many of the trained troops were fighting far afield in the Middle East. There were 12,000 miles of coast to defend and military roads to the north were lacking. In these circumstances Australia reacted very much as Britain had done after Dunkirk. Men were recalled from abroad, delaying actions were fought in Malaya, Java, and Timor, a Home Guard was formed of men between eighteen and sixty years of age, roads and aerodromes were built by civil construction corps mainly made up of elderly men. Even then the Australians strove to build industries such as shipping and aircraft manufacture, which had never been a characteristic part of the country's economy.

With the defences of Australia in such peril the obvious policy was to fight off the Japanese before they could attempt an invasion. The resulting campaign in New Guinea, though fought with the help of other forces, was the outstanding feature of the Australian part in the war. On 31st August 1942 the first land defeat was inflicted on the Japanese at Milne Bay. Shortly afterwards the Australians drove back other Japanese forces which had crossed the Owen Stanley Range and were only thirty-five miles from Port Moresby. This campaign helped to clear the enemy from New Guinea and began the process of rolling back the tide of Japanese invasion. To quote an official writer on the campaign: 'This involved years of hard fighting in the worst imaginable type of country, where roads were virtually non-existent, and where, in the most crucial days, every ounce of equipment and food had to be man-handled over slimy precipitous tracks through disease-infested jungle.'

The story of New Zealand is closely linked with that of Australia. A young and happy country of 1,500,000 people, she realized at once that her civilization and security depended on the outcome of Britain's struggle. The year 1939 found New Zealand engaged in housing schemes, pension schemes, medical schemes, and similar projects for the betterment of citizens. But the wealth and activities of this small nation were immediately directed towards the war effort of the commonwealth. An army was trained for service at home or abroad. The young New Zealand Air Force grew rapidly until by 1944 it had a strength of 42,000 men trained at home or in Canada. Like their Australian neighbours, New Zealanders were invaluable in the Middle East campaigns and in the Pacific. Apart from the purely New Zealand forces thousands of them were to be found as volunteers in Britain. Not least in the hearts of Englishmen were these 'young men who had travelled 13,000 miles to fight with the Allies.'

3. SOUTH AFRICA

The coming of war found South Africa in some uncertainty as to the part she proposed to play in the European strife. But with the defeat in Parliament of General Herzog and the coming into power of General Smuts the doubt was dispelled. War was declared on Germany and South Africa took her share in the struggle, a share 'conditioned by her geography and special problems.' Though somewhat hampered by the two opposition parties of General Herzog and Dr. Malan, General Smuts, perhaps the most respected statesman of the whole British Commonwealth, guided his country through the difficult years of war with honour to South Africa and to the incalculable benefit of the Allies.

again assured India that British policy was to lead her by steps to dominion status. But progress was almost impossible so long as the strife between Hindu and Muslim continued.

Yet recruits to the Army poured in. The normal peace-time army of 200,000 grew in a few months to 500,000. Those parts of India still ruled by princes were foremost in placing all their reserves at the service of the Government. The Royal Indian Navy, small but efficient, quickly trebled its size. Indian merchant seamen formed a quarter of the total in the empire and commonwealth.

By autumn 1940 600,000 Indians were serving beyond the 'dark waters,' in Malaya, Aden, the Middle East, and Somaliland. Thanks largely to the viceroy's policy of including more and more loyal and capable Indians in the Executive Council and the National Defence Council, the war was gradually recognized as 'India's war' despite the illogical and stubborn policy of Congress.

With the resources of Britain strained as never before, the products and manufactures of India became of vital importance to the eastern half of the empire and commonwealth. Particularly needed now was her output of steel and pig-iron. India not only provided 90 per cent of her own military requirements but was able to send many kinds of necessities to Britain.

The war spread relentlessly. In 1941 Indians were fighting with the Allies in Libya, Syria, Abyssinia, and Somaliland. The following year was possibly the most dangerous in the history of India, at least in recent centuries. The fall of Burma, defended only by one division of British, Indian, and Burmese troops, saw the Japanese on the borders of Assam.

The Indian paradox was again incomprehensible. In the very month when Rangoon fell to the Japanese (March 1942) the British Government sent Sir Stafford Cripps, one of its ablest statesmen, renowned for his anti-imperialist views, to visit India in order to settle the question of the future constitution of the country and to plead for unity in face of the threat from Japan. Yet his offer that at the end of the war India should have an all-Indian constitution, was described by Gandhi as 'a post-dated cheque upon a crashing bank.' The Hindus wanted immediate independence and a flat refusal of 'Pakistan' (see p. 103); the Muslims objected because Pakistan was not expressly promised. The failure of the mission was followed by accumulating troubles. Gandhi continued to wreck the war effort. Food shortages, arising from

Fox Photos

Mahatma Gandhi

the recent increases in population, the loss of Burmese rice, food hoarding by the speculators, cyclones and tidal waves, brought hunger and starvation to parts of India. Fifth columnists working for Japan did their best to disrupt the State. Japanese raids on Ceylon and serious losses to the Fleet added to the gloom. India had sent her best men abroad and had not even a single fully trained division for her own defence. April 1942 was, according to Field Marshal Wavell's later dispatch, 'India's most dangerous hour.'

Yet in this very month Wavell issued instructions for the

reconquest of the whole of Burma to be planned. Disorders in India seemed to have a rallying effect on the vast masses of loyal people. In the extreme north the hill tribes rendered valuable help to the British and Indian troops. The empire was soon able to fight back in the Arakan area 'amid physical obstacles of jungle-covered hills and swamps, some of the most formidable in the world.'

The year 1943 saw the critical period over. Lord Wavell now became viceroy, while General Auchinleck took his place as Commander-in-Chief, and the planning of the coming offensive against Japan was handed to Lord Louis Mountbatten, chief of the south-east Asia command. India could now point with pride to its army of volunteers numbering two millions, fighting in theatres of war all over the world. The Royal Indian Navy, formerly five small vessels, now numbered ninety ships. Renewed famine in Bengal, the result largely of misgovernment in that province, called for vigorous action by the viceroy, who insisted on an all-India food policy and the appointment of an experienced Australian statesman, Mr. Casey, to the governorship of the province.

Wars are won, as the British people well know, by the workers, as well as by the fighters. While Indian troops were engaged overseas, Indian labour reconstructed in eight months the old Persian land route by which supplies were sent to Russia. While, in 1941, the rest of the British Commonwealth of Nations was thinking of training aircrews, making precision tools, and turning out tanks, the Indians were able to send to England 700,000,000 sandbags. Many a thoughtful British civilian, seeing the array neatly piled up against the public buildings in London, must have wondered where they had all come from.

In the closing years of the war India became the base for the overthrow of the Japanese on the Burma front (see p. 212). Although little progress was made at that time in solving the problem of finding a constitution acceptable both to Hindu and Muslim, the average Indian could look back with satisfaction at much of the work that his countrymen had done during the years of world chaos.

CHAPTER XXXI

NEW PROBLEMS

1. UNITED NATIONS

THE war of 1939–45 affected the lives of more people than any other war in the history of the world. For six years men's energies had been turned to destruction. The battlefield, bombing, starvation, execution, mass murder, evacuation, and forced labour had brought death and suffering to millions. When peace came there was further scarcity of food, sickness, and homelessness.

The energies of man had now to be turned firstly towards the establishment of permanent peace, and secondly towards the alleviation of suffering both in the lands scarred by war, and in those whose standards of living had been reduced by the exhausting effort put out by both sides. Thirdly, the powers which had been victorious in the war would sooner or later have to decide on the future of the defeated countries. This was not likely to be easy, for in 1945 relations between the wartime allies underwent a change. During the war the first and foremost object had been victory. Now that it was over the nations inevitably separated into two groups, one round Soviet Russia and the other round the United States of America. These two groups differed widely in their political systems and each sought to safeguard itself and spread its ideas in a war-torn world. Thus, whatever may have been the high ideals voiced in the Atlantic Charter (see p. 183), the Russians were determined to set up Communist governments wherever possible and the Western powers, surprised and shocked at the Russian hostility which had become apparent even before the last shot was fired, were equally determined to defend free parliaments, free speech, and free business institutions.

Finally, almost the whole world had been forced into a

supreme war effort. Africans and Asians in large numbers had fought side by side with white soldiers, had picked up their ideas of liberty and democracy, and had returned to their homes anxious to hasten the day when they would govern themselves. Among almost all, the desire was to get free of the control of the Western states, and this desire produced leaders who preached independence and the need to make an end of 'colonialism.'

Such were the problems with which the world of 1945 was faced. The greatest of all was how to preserve peace. The atomic bomb had not only been discovered, it had been used, and already there was talk of bigger and more deadly weapons of mass destruction.

Why had the League of Nations failed? That was the question now uppermost in the minds of the allied statesmen. This time it must be reconstructed on more solid foundations; it must become the 'Forum of the World'; it must have power and resources. Yet it must still be a league of nations, and not a world government, for it might be many years or even centuries before the people of all lands would be willing to join together in one world state.

In July 1945, at San Francisco, delegates from fifty nations signed the United Nations Charter, the preamble to which is given in Appendix III. This is a statement of the aims of the United Nations. In it the prevention of war is given first place. Other factors like equal rights of people and nations, respect for treaties, social progress, and tolerance all contribute towards achieving the prime object. After the preamble comes the body of the Charter which describes in detail what is to be done and what bodies are to be set up to do it.

From this Charter the whole structure of the United Nations has grown. Once a year its General Assembly, composed of delegates from all member states, meets to discuss the chief questions of the day which have to do with peace and progress. The United Nations Organization was given headquarters in New York where it now has a wonderful new building. Its work is carried on in five official languages (English, French, Spanish, Russian, and Chinese). All delegates and visitors may wear headphones and listen to speeches which are translated simultaneously.

The day-to-day business of the United Nations is, however, carried on by other councils, one of the most important of which is called the Security Council. This is made up of eleven

Fox Photos

The United Nations Building, New York

members. Five of these, China (Nationalist), France, Russia, Great Britain, and the United States of America, are permanent members; that is, they are always on the Council. The other six are elected by the General Assembly for two-year periods.

The Security Council may consider any quarrel between nations, or any situation which may lead to a quarrel. It may recommend ways of settling a dispute, and if necessary it may call on member states to stop trade with, or even to take up arms against, any state which is found to be breaking the peace. But in drawing up the Charter, Russia insisted that decisions of the Security Council should be unanimous. The power thus given to any one permanent member to veto a decision of the others was to have the most disturbing effect during the years that followed. It was used many times, especially by Russia.

The United Nations is kept going by funds contributed by all the member states. Its permanent staff of officers, experts, clerks, lawyers, inspectors, interpreters, and typists is called the Secretariat, and it is under the control of the Secretary-General. From 1946 to 1952 the Secretary-General was Mr. Trygve Lie of Norway, and from April 1953, Mr. Dag Hammerskjöld of Sweden.

Some of the greatest things the old League of Nations did were acts of mercy such as caring for all the people who were made destitute by the war, helping refugees back home, checking the spread of disease, and fighting the slave trade. The work was taken up again and put into the hands of the Economic and Social Council, composed of members elected from the Assembly. Its work is so vast that it has to be divided up between a large number of departments known by the name of Specialized Agencies. Each has a director, an office, and a staff of experts with headquarters in various capitals of the world, e.g. Paris, Rome, and Geneva.

In 1947 a serious epidemic of cholera broke out in Egypt. Immediately the World Health Organization appealed for help to all member states of the United Nations. Doctors and drugs were sent, vaccine was flown out, and the epidemic was stamped out in six weeks. All the other Specialized Agencies do work which is very important to the welfare of the people of the world. The Food and Agriculture Organization works to teach people of all nations how to get the best crops from the land, how to deal with pests, and how to prevent soil erosion. Where one part of the world produces too much of a particular crop for its own needs, this organization tries to find ways of transporting what is not wanted to people who are short of it.

The International Labour Organization exists to improve the conditions of workers. It cannot compel any government to make rules, but every year a conference is called for the exchange of information between countries. The United Nations Educational, Scientific, and Cultural Organization (U.N.E.S.C.O.) carries on a campaign to help people of all nations to be able to read, sends out experts to the various governments, advises them on the training of teachers, and collects scientific information. It knows, as one of its leaders said, that 'war begins in the minds of men,' and so it carries on a more noble war of its own against ignorance, misunderstanding, and hatred among the nations. The International Refugee Organization found homes for more than a million and a half refugees between 1947 and 1952. Other Specialized Agencies deal with aviation (International Civil Aviation Organization), world postal services (Universal Postal Union), telegraphic services (International Telecommunications Union), weather information (World Meteorological Organization), and many other matters.

In 1946 there were large numbers of children, especially in central Europe, who were in great need of food, clothing, and care. To help them the United Nations started a United Nations International Children's Emergency Fund (U.N.I.C.E.F.). Many governments made grants towards this work, and in various countries appeals were organized. By the end of 1950 the total amount of money received was over £50,000,000. This went to help child victims of the warfare in Palestine (1948), of the earthquake in South America (1949), of the floods in Italy (1950), and of a typhoon in the Philippine Islands (1951). Everywhere where children are in want, the fund is available for their help. Milk, cod-liver oil, vaccines, medicines, food, and clothing have been provided; campaigns have been run to show the value of vaccination, and instruction has been given in general hygiene as a means of preventing disease. Many ordinary people have laboured in schools and churches to help this fund. Much of its success has been due to the understanding of helpers such as Danny Kaye, the famous comedian who toured the world and made films for U.N.I.C.E.F.

Thus, although the chief task of the United Nations Organization is the political one of preventing war, almost equally important is that of removing the causes of war, by rooting out ignorance, fear, want, and disease.

2. COLD WAR

The work of peace-making had begun during the war. The meeting at Yalta early in 1945 had gone a long way towards defining the spheres of influence of the various allies. Then in May came the collapse of Germany. The Russians were well established over all the eastern part of the country and had, in the opinion of some, come perilously near the Rhine. In July 1945, at a conference in Potsdam, Germany was divided into British, French, American, and Russian zones. It was a shock to the West to see how quickly Poland, Bulgaria, Roumania, and Hungary emerged with Communist governments. For some time Czechoslovakia, inspired by Jan Masaryk, son of the great statesman of the inter-war years (see p. 113), held out, but after his untimely death in 1948 another Communist government established itself. Thus the land occupied by Russia and the countries since called 'satellites' included and still includes much which was once considered part of Western Europe.

The process of peace-making went on until 1947 and treaties were signed with Bulgaria, Roumania, Hungary, Finland, and Italy, but it was some years before they could be concluded with Austria and Japan. Germany and its possible reunion has been a troublesome problem ever since. After 1947 further treaty-making was found to be impossible, normal relations across the frontier became difficult, and this split became symbolized by what has since been known as the 'Iron Curtain.' By 1949 this iron curtain could be said to run across Europe, dividing the Communist-ruled states of Poland, Czechoslovakia, Hungary, Bulgaria, and Roumania from the rest. Yugoslavia under Marshal Tito, though remaining Communist, broke away from Russian control.

The effects of this cold war, as it was called, were sometimes as devastating as a real war. Berlin was one of the key points of the struggle. The city itself had been, like Germany, divided into zones, but the western zones were connected to West Germany only by one motor road stretching for many miles through Russian-held territory, and by a narrow air corridor. In 1948 the Russians, hoping to get control of all

Berlin, stopped the traffic along this road, and Berlin had to be supplied for eleven months by air alone. This Berlin air-lift was one of the greatest post-war achievements, and a dramatic lesson to the Russians. Another effect was the distressing flow of refugees from East to West, sometimes at the rate of a thousand a day. All these had to be fed, looked after, and eventually housed in Western countries. As Russia continued to tighten her grip on East Germany, the British, Americans, and French combined their three zones, gave them a new stable currency, and encouraged the West Germans to build a Federal Parliament for themselves at Bonn. In reply the Russians created a separate state in East Germany.

Since that time Europe has settled down to an uneasy peace. Changes in leadership have occurred in Russia, and some slackening of international tension has at times permitted courtesy visits between notabilities. Mr. Malenkov, once head of the Russian state, and subsequently Mr. Krushchev and Marshal Bulganin have all visited this country. Russia too has been opened up to a certain extent to British tourists and delegations, but no better proof that the cold war still continues may be found than a view of present-day Berlin, that city of contrasts, where armed guards of West and East face each other across the streets, and where two monetary systems, two trading systems, and two ways of living exist in the same city.

Periodically we hear of purges in the government of the Communist countries, some no more than the normal changes of leaders, to be occasionally expected in any country; others involving executions, long prison sentences, and denunciations of former ministers as traitors. The imprisonment of religious leaders such as Cardinal Mindszenty, Primate of Hungary, has served to underline the intolerance of the Russian system and the power of what Mr. Churchill called 'The Fourteen Men of the Kremlin.' Riots of workers as in Germany and Poland reflect the discontent of peoples who feel that their governments are but puppets, and that they as individuals have to serve only the needs of the new Russian Empire.

In Asia, especially in the lands bordering on the U.S.S.R., the impending spread of Communism was feared. The peril from Japanese imperialism in China was now past, but another bitter struggle had arisen between Chiang Kai-shek and the rapidly growing Communist strength under Mao Tse-tung, assisted by Russian arms. In 1947 the Nationalists were being driven back on the coast and into the south of the country by vastly superior numbers. In 1949 the war ended with the complete expulsion of Chiang Kai-shek to Formosa. There he has remained up to the present time, protected by an American alliance, but lord only of his island and the small off-shore islands of Quemoy and Matsu. Meanwhile the Chinese Communists claim Formosa as an integral part of their dominions. The Americans and the Nationalists deny this claim, saying that the island has never been part of Communist China. The expanding state of Mao Tse-tung is still, largely through the influence of the Americans who refuse to recognize it, debarred from a place in the councils of the United Nations.

Communism, with its stress on the abolition of private property and privilege, has always been an attractive doctrine to peoples of under-developed lands where food is scarce and poverty widespread. In states which have achieved their independence, Communist aid is offered for development schemes, and thus Russian influence not only permeates into neighbouring countries but also takes root across the seas, in Africa, Indonesia, and South America. Strong measures have had to be taken in Malaya where Communist infiltration might at one time have led to a full-scale civil war. Even to-day, after Malaya has been granted its independence, the struggle still goes on.

In Korea the Russians in the north and the Americans in the south had organized governments, and by 1949 had withdrawn most of their forces. During the year which followed there was occasional fighting along the 38th parallel which marked the border of the two states. Then, on 25th June 1950, the armed forces of North Korea made a surprise attack on the South Korean Republic. The United Nations Security Council met immediately and, in the absence of the Russian delegate who had decided to boycott the meeting, ordered the North Koreans to withdraw. They did not do so. Before long a United Nations army, drawn from twenty-two nations, was fighting in Korea, and the North Koreans were joined by the Chinese Communists who poured thousands of so-called volunteers into the peninsula. For three years the war dragged on with heavy casualties on both sides and the usual toll of misery and death among the civilian population. On 26th July 1953 an armistice was agreed upon with little gained on either side. But one all-important fact now stood out clearly. Unlike the old League of Nations, the United Nations had decided to resist aggression by force of arms.

Since then the uneasy peace has continued. Much in future will depend on the attitude of the two powers, the U.S.A. and the new China, towards each other.

3. THE RISE OF NEW STATES

After the spread of the German arms across North Africa, and especially after the occupation of almost the whole of south-east Asia and the East Indies by Japan, the position of the European powers in their foreign dominions could never be the same again.

Nationalism in India was generations old. The Indian National Congress, aiming at Hindu self-government, had been in existence since 1885, and the Muslim League since 1907. It was partly owing to the Indian contribution to the victory of 1945 that the Labour Government of Great Britain granted self-government to this vast subcontinent. India thus came to be made up of two states known as India and Pakistan. Both in time became republics while still remaining in the British Commonwealth. Gandhi, who had led the nationalists, was assassinated by a Hindu extremist in January 1948. In the following July, Mr. Jinnah, the Prime Minister of Pakistan, died. They have been followed by discerning and moderate statesmen, and both countries have grown in importance and nationhood despite the chaos at first caused by the flight of refugees from one to the other. Their bitter quarrel over Kashmir was discussed at the United Nations, but India refused to allow a plebiscite there. So Kashmir remains partitioned, and India continues to rule over much of the country in which a large majority of the people are Muslims. Apart from this painful problem, the first decade of India's history has been one of great progress and of growing reputation in the world. Mr. Nehru, the prime minister, and his gifted sister, Mrs. Pandit, are figures of nobility and moderation, occupying an uncommitted and peace-making role among the great powers.

In other parts of the British Empire the wise example of granting independence has been followed. Ceylon became a dominion but Burma chose independence and separation. In Malaya 31st August 1957 became *Merdeka*, or Independence Day, amid great rejoicing. In Africa the former Gold Coast became the modern Ghana in 1957, and is now busy on a programme of self-education and reform. The same is happening in Nigeria, which became independent as recently as 1960. Kenya has passed through troublesome times owing to the rising of the Mau Mau. The states of central Africa, Southern and Northern Rhodesia, and Nyasaland have been bound together in a federation with a special African Affairs Board to safeguard African interests. In 1958 the first Parliament of the West Indies was opened.

The one part of the Empire on which the post-war period has imposed great racial strain is South Africa. In May 1948 General Smuts was defeated in the elections and was replaced by Dr. Malan. Since then a succession of nationalist prime ministers and their cabinets have attempted to solve the racial problem by trying to bring in a state of *apartheid*, with white, coloured, and black inhabitants living as much as possible to themselves. This policy has met with great resistance both inside Africa and in the debates of the United Nations. It is argued by the South African Government that to give power to the numerous native peoples would bring disaster to the country and that the Europeans are carrying a great burden of responsibility for their less developed dependants. All who cherish the ideal of a multiracial Commonwealth are, however, anxious and troubled about the future of South Africa.

Elsewhere, both within the Commonwealth and without, the

march towards independence has gone on with varying results. The Indonesians refused to accept their former Dutch rulers, and four years of intermittent fighting and negotiation ended in their independence.   Self-government has brought problems.   Serious rioting amounting almost to civil war has harassed the young republic, and continued attacks on those energetic and efficient Dutch residents still left have weakened the state.

In the Near East the seven states of Egypt, Saudi Arabia, Iraq, Syria, the Lebanon, Transjordan, and the Yemen banded together in the Arab League.   This was originally an instrument for assisting the stream of allied supplies to the Middle East, but it ultimately became much more.   In 1948 the British withdrew from Palestine, and Israel proclaimed herself a sovereign state.   Into this land many Jews had already arrived from all parts of the world.   The new state was therefore a conglomeration of people with varying backgrounds and languages, but with one aim in common—Jewish nationhood. This kept the state alive against the bitter opposition of the surrounding Arab states.   Fighting and terrorism ensued, in which the unselfish mediator, Count Bernadotte, was assassinated.   In 1949 armistice agreements were signed and the new state of Israel was recognized, though still hated by the Arabs, many of whom had fled as refugees from lands now occupied by Israel.

The Arabs, previously a loose and often disagreeing confederation, now found some unity of aim.   In 1952 a military revolution occurred in Egypt which resulted in the abdication of King Farouk and the establishment of a republic in the following year.   The leaders, firstly General Neguib and later Colonel Nasser, quickly became the spearhead of this Arab movement.   To-day, though these Arab states are by no means united in aim and have different kinds of governments, some of them have been joined together in the United Arab Republic with Colonel Nasser at its head.

In 1956 Colonel Nasser nationalized the Suez Canal, an event which profoundly affected the interests of both Britain and France.   On 29th October 1956 Israel, whose ships had been for years shut out of the Canal, and who had been engaged in constant small battles near her frontiers, launched an attack in the Sinai peninsula. Britain and France immediately landed troops to protect the Canal zone. This for a time brought the world dangerously close to a general war. At last, under pressure from America and the United Nations, Britain and

Camera Press

North African learns to write

France withdrew on condition that the United Nations formed an international force to restore peace. This was done, but Colonel Nasser was allowed to retain the Canal and appeared to the Arab States to be triumphant.

The Communist powers made great capital out of the event, and since that time the Near East has been a continual battle-ground of ideas waged by 'hate broadcasts' and other means of propaganda. This has been accompanied by uprisings, assassinations, and interventions of various kinds both by East and West. Iraq had a revolution in 1958, during which its king was murdered; out of these happenings the Communists hoped for advantage. Another uprising in the Lebanon almost resulted in a revolution. This was forestalled by the landing of military units by America and Great Britain in the Lebanon and Jordan respectively. They were withdrawn when the position in both places had been more stabilized. In the meantime the Middle East, with its rich resources of oil and its extremes of poverty and wealth, remains precariously in the balance. It might well be turned into a happy and prosperous community if the United Nations could organize technical assistance on a vast scale, using perhaps the expert knowledge of the thousands of Jewish doctors and scientists of Israel. But political and religious hatreds are still to be overcome.

Farther along the coast of Africa France felt the full force of this Arab revival. After much trouble, first Morocco and then Tunis became detached and independent. It was otherwise with Algeria which for over a century had been regarded as an integral part of France. This country is largely Muslim, and malcontents gathered together in the mountains there to wage for years a war of liberation. The wealth expended by France, first on the disastrous war in Indo-China, then on this long struggle and the internal dissension it brought with it might easily have brought about the complete collapse of the state had it not been saved by General de Gaulle. In 1958, after establishing a new constitution in France, he set himself to the critical task of pacifying North Africa. He announced generous new plans for the improvement of Algerian education and opportunities for Algerians as citizens of France.

In the north-east corner of the Mediterranean lies Cyprus. This island became British in 1878, ceded by Turkey. It is inhabited mainly by Greeks and Turks in the proportion of about four to one. Here, after the war, the demand for union with Greece was raised by the Greek Cypriots, and was led by their archbishop, Makarios, of the Greek Orthodox Church. It was not long before British refusals to grant 'enosis,' as it was called, led to shooting episodes and the rise of a secret society known as Eoka. For years the island has been terrorized by gunmen. The deportation of Archbishop Makarios and the increase of British vigilance had little effect. Then came his liberation and the experiment of increased leniency by Governor Sir Hugh Foot who, in an attempt to gain confidence, ran great personal risk. This too failed to bring peace. Communal clashes became frequent, and Eoka continued its campaign of terror with little respite. The Turks wanted to divide the island, the Greek Cypriots insisted on complete union with Greece. Independence was finally granted, but the British, reluctant to abandon this important military outpost, retained their bases for defence on the island.

The new nations of the world present a fascinating picture of variety. Some, like India, have built stable democratic parliaments. Others, like Pakistan, have failed to do so and are trying other experiments. Some have obtained self-government too soon and have still to create bodies of honest civil servants without which no government can function. All have to provide good laws and good government or face the spread of Communism among their people. In many the roots of Western civilization have already gone deep, and their future promises well.

4. RUSSIA AND CHINA

The war of 1939–45 started as a purely European war, which but for certain events might have begun and ended in Europe. It spread, and never in history has the world been so quickly transformed as between 1939 and 1949.

Hitler had intended to destroy Russia. He failed, and Russia came out of the struggle, even if exhausted, with a prestige never before equalled, a foothold in western Europe, a number of dependent states on her borders, and the certainty of becoming one of the world's foremost powers. Her prime minister, Joseph Stalin, was the only one of the three prime ministers of Russia, America, and Great Britain, both to survive and to remain in power. At home he removed mercilessly every rival and even every critic. Abroad, though he was an ally of the West, his formal alliance hid a rooted hostility. This attitude led him into many almost absurd

mistakes in statesmanship, of which the attempt to expel the
Western allies from Berlin was one. These mistakes were one
of the factors which helped to prevent the spread of Communism among the rank and file of other countries. Even before
his death Yugoslavia had broken away. He died at the age of
seventy-three, surrounded by fear, uncertainty, and hatred
even among his immediate circle. Two months before he had
arrested fifteen leading doctors on criminal charges, and
appeared to be contemplating savage action against many of
the leaders of the state.

With his death in March 1953 it was expected for a time that
things would change. Malenkov, who succeeded him, was
more liberal, and his early pronouncements seemed to presage
a relaxation of tension. In the struggle for power among the
Soviet leaders, however, he soon resigned and was succeeded
by Krushchev and Bulganin. We do not know the moves and
counter-moves which went on in the Kremlin, nor the reasons
for the purges which killed one man and spared another, or
which raised unknown men to the top and relegated world-
famous figures to obscure posts in distant republics. The
world shed few tears over the disappearance of Beria, the
hated chief of police under Stalin, but the astonishment was
great when Krushchev, emerging to supreme power, violently
attacked the memory of Stalin, the whole 'cult of personality'
and the myth of his greatness as a military commander. It
seemed that at last a new liberal and humane voice at the head
of Russian affairs might now be heard.

Materially Russia was fast recovering from the wounds of
war. Progress in scientific fields has been immense. The
world was startled in 1957 by the launching of Sputnik I, the
first artificial satellite made to circle the earth in space. All
this has gone on at the same time as widespread industrialization and improvements in agriculture.

It remains true that no country can live to itself, though this
realization was late to dawn on the minds of post-war Soviet
statesmen. Since Stalin died, however, exchanges of visits
between Soviet citizens and those of the West have gradually
increased in number, and there are signs that a sense of pro-

portion is slowly entering into the Soviet conception of science. It is too early yet to say how far literary men are likely to be permitted to voice criticisms of the state, but it may be that the Soviet intelligentsia of the future will not stand up to the dragooning and dictatorship of ideas that their fathers did.

Outside Russia proper all the satellite powers except Yugo-slavia have been kept faithful, at least in appearance. The Warsaw Pact countries, however, as they came to be called,

Camera Press

Krushchev visits Mao Tse-tung

showed increasing signs of restlessness after Stalin's death. Control from Moscow seemed less rigid. Workers in field and factory could see or hear of the full shops in nearby Western countries. In 1956 serious riots in Poznan, Poland, were suppressed only with difficulty. While remaining faithful to Moscow, the prime minister, Gomulka, managed, however, to obtain a considerable measure of freedom. It was a more dramatic and more terrible story in Hungary. In October 1956, at the very same time as the Suez dispute, a rising broke out against the Hungarian Communist Government. It was so sudden and so strong that for a brief space of time Russian tanks left the capital, only to return again a few days later to restore order and a Communist Government with much bloodshed. Thousands of Hungarians escaped to the West, while others died in the attempt.

Beyond Russia lies the Chinese People's Republic with its five hundred million inhabitants. Mao Tse-tung, using the same methods as Stalin did, is regimenting the once easy-going Chinaman into supreme efforts to attain industrial efficiency and military power. Only a few years ago China was regarded as being Russia's poor relation, but there are already signs that Chinese influence is being brought to bear to stiffen Russia's attitude towards the West. Perhaps the cartoons in the newspapers are to some extent right when they show Krushchev playing second fiddle to Mao.

China is undoubtedly making stupendous strides in modernization. It is still, however, widely separated from the West in outlook and understanding. Some progress has been made between the West and Russia in learning to live together. Much greater progress between China and the West must come in the immediate future if the many matters in dispute are to be settled peaceably. To this end U.N.E.S.C.O. has recently launched a ten-year project for getting schools and colleges to pursue East-West studies.

5. Recovery in the West

Twice in this century Great Britain has passed through great disasters, but in spite of this we see in 1958 a country new, fresh, and with every visible sign of wealth and industry. Its people on the whole are well off and its children are well fed and healthy.

The end of the war saw a period when stocks of food, clothing, and other necessities had become so small all over the world that everybody wanted everything at once. Labour was scarce, wages and prices went up. Britain had been in the front line of the war, had sold much of its overseas property, and closed down many of its most productive sources of income at home. The whole country realized that the export trade must be revived. This necessitated the help of American capital and a good deal of sacrifice. Rationing of food lasted well into the 1950's, and prices of goods not regarded as dire necessities were kept up by the purchase taxes.

The Labour Government under Attlee, which came into office in 1945, had the tasks of constructing the fabric of social insurance on which the Welfare State was to be built. Near-free medicine, dentistry, and surgical aids are now becoming so commonplace that we have almost forgotten the dread of illness that faced our fathers. The educational system too has been reconstructed but not with such success. The 1944 Act gave secondary schools for all, but the expansion of education has not kept pace with the need. Only recently have public authorities, shocked at the enormous developments of education in Russia, awakened to the need to spend much more of our national income on science teaching and technical education in particular. Public services, nationalized by the Labour Government, remained so, apart from Road Transport which was handed back to private enterprise when the Conservatives came into power.

To-day we appear to be on the threshold of a wonderful new Industrial Revolution. The word 'automation' is on all lips. Factories which can almost run themselves are now realities. The opening of Calder Hall, the world's first atomic power station, on 22nd May 1956, may prove to be one of the great industrial landmarks in man's history.

France too has developed her industries and agriculture, but politically has been less fortunate. Since 1945 the country has been assailed by conflicts within and without, by disputes between the many political parties, by recriminations and accusations; and abroad a disastrous campaign in Indo-China and warfare in Algeria. One prime minister succeeded another without reaching any solution. In 1958 General de Gaulle took office and began a radical series of reforms. His Algerian policy, though it has not yet stopped the war, has at least forged some sort of public unity.

So far there are few signs of the reunification of the two parts of Germany. The allies in 1945, determining that the Germans must never again be able to wage war, dismantled some West German industries. The post-war division of the world into two camps, however, proved to them that Western Europe, and indeed the Western world, could not do without the support of its most productive industrial area. Since that time Western Germany has moved rapidly ahead, not only in manufactures and trade, but in complete integration with the Western world, including its military forces. The recovery has astonished all who have seen her new towns, busy factories, and prosperous shops.

The doctrine of European Union is an old one which again came to the fore during the last war. When the fighting was over and Europe in ruins, General Marshall announced his plan for sending American aid, provided that the European powers united to restore the prosperity of Europe. This gave rise to several bodies, including a customs union of Belgium, the Netherlands, and Luxembourg (familiarly known as Benelux), and an organization called the Schuman Authority for the pooling of European coal and steel. Later Benelux was joined by France, Germany, and Italy, who in 1958 signed a treaty establishing a common market between them by which tariffs would be gradually reduced and finally abolished. Great Britain, which at first remained aloof from both these bodies because of her fear of weakening the Commonwealth, is now showing greater support for them and is putting forward other proposals for a free trade area for the whole of Europe.

Lastly, beyond the Atlantic lies the wealthy and powerful United States of America, whose rulers refuse to stand by and allow the nations of Europe, all weaker than herself, to fall prey to Russian Communism, either by direct conquest or by infiltration. American aid has flowed out to smaller countries in spite of the protests of large sections of American citizens. America is the backbone of the North Atlantic Treaty Organization, formed in April 1949, to co-ordinate the efforts of all member states for common defence. It includes not only states which have seaboards on the Atlantic, but also others, such as Italy, Greece, and Turkey. All these have agreed that 'an armed attack against one or more of them shall be considered as an attack against them all.' President Truman, who followed Roosevelt, concluded his term of office at the close of 1952 and was succeeded by General Eisenhower, who has already held office for nearly two terms. His policy and that of his government has throughout all this time been one of watchful preparedness.

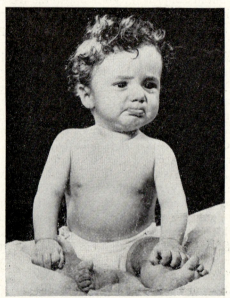

Pictorial Press

Citizen of To-morrow

N.A.T.O., created to defend Europe and America from the vast armies of Soviet Russia, which were never disbanded after the war, has naturally aroused bitter hostility among the Communist powers who formed the Warsaw Alliance in reply to it. Thus in 1958 the world continues to be divided into two armed camps, both rich and becoming richer, but still living under the shadow of war.

What of the future? Among all people on earth the will to

peace continues, but the securing of peace is a matter to test the skill of the cleverest statesmen. The years since the end of the war have seen purges in the Soviet Union, inquiries into Communist activities in Great Britain and the United States, flights of sympathizers from East to West and from West to East, requests for political asylum, abductions of important and sometimes unimportant people, spying activities which put the writers of thrillers to shame, bitter speeches and more bitter newspaper comments.

Conference after conference on disarmament has broken down. Russia demands the abolition of nuclear bombs but refuses to allow inspection within her borders. The West, too, wishes to abolish nuclear weapons, but will not do so until Russia agrees to reduce her mighty conventional armaments of tanks, submarines, and guns. Thus we all live under what Churchill called the Balance of Terror. Many well-informed people are saying that the splitting of the atom has been the best preventative of war so far devised. Neither side, they say, would dare to use the hydrogen bomb and it is therefore the perfect deterrent.

Meanwhile statesmen fly from one capital to another, heads of governments meet together, and there is much talk of summit conferences. Throughout the whole of the human race rises hope, that hope which makes men rebuild devastated cities, plan great welfare schemes, seek employment for all, educate and nourish the young, care for the aged, and encourage the useful spending of leisure. We hope and believe, therefore we work.

We inherit from the Momentous Years a task such as mankind has never had before, on a worldwide scale, and concerning all men and women alive. May we be equal to it.

APPENDICES

I. THE COVENANT OF THE LEAGUE OF NATIONS
(*The Preamble*)

The High Contracting Parties,

In order to promote international co-operation and to achieve international peace and security;

By the acceptance of obligations not to resort to war;

By the prescription of open, just, and honourable relations between nations;

By the firm establishment of the understandings of international law as the actual rule of conduct among Governments; and

By the maintenance of justice and a scrupulous respect for all treaty obligations in the dealings of organized peoples with one another:

Agree to the Covenant of the League of Nations.

II. AFTER DUNKIRK

(Extract from the Prime Minister's Speech to the House of Commons on 4th June 1940)

. . . Even though large tracts of Europe and many old and famous states have fallen or may fall into the grip of the Gestapo and all the odious apparatus of Nazi rule, we shall not flag or fail, we shall go on to the end, we shall fight in France, we shall fight on the seas and oceans, we shall fight with growing confidence and growing strength in the air, we shall defend our island whatever the cost may be, we shall fight on the beaches, we shall fight on the landing grounds, we shall fight in the fields and in the streets, we shall fight in the hills; we shall never surrender, and even if, which I do not for a moment believe, this island or a large part of it were subjugated and starving, then our empire beyond the seas, armed and guarded by the British Fleet, would carry on the struggle, until, in God's good time, the new world, with all its power and might, steps forth to the rescue and liberation of the Old.

III. THE UNITED NATIONS CHARTER
(*The Preamble*)
(*Signed by fifty Nations on* 26th *June* 1945 *at the San Francisco Conference*)

We the peoples of the United Nations,

Determined to save succeeding generations from the scourge of war, which twice in our lifetime has brought untold sorrow to mankind;

to reaffirm faith in fundamental human rights, in the dignity and worth of the human person, and in the equal rights of men and women of the nations large and small;

to establish conditions under which justice and respect for obligations arising from treaties and other sources of international law can be maintained;

to promote social progress and better standards of life in larger freedom;

to practise tolerance and live together in peace with one another as good neighbours;

to unite our strength to maintain international peace and security;

to ensure, by the acceptance of principles and by the institution of methods, that armed force shall not be used, save in the common interest;

to employ international machinery for the promotion of the economic and social advancement of all peoples;

have resolved to combine our efforts to accomplish these aims, have agreed to the present Charter of the United Nations, and do hereby establish an international organization to be known as the United Nations.

	Europe	Mediterranean and Africa	Russia	Far East
1939 Aug.			Pact of Neutrality with Germany. 23 Aug.	
Sept.	Germany invaded Poland. 1 Sept. Great Britain and France declared war on Germany. 3 Sept. Poland partitioned between Germany and Russia. 22 Sept. Warsaw surrendered. 29 Sept.			
Nov.			Russia invaded Finland. 30 Nov.	
1940 Mar.			Finland signed peace terms. 12 Mar.	
Apr.	Germany invaded Denmark and Norway. 9 Apr.			
May	Germany invaded Low Countries. 10 May Holland surrendered. 15 May Belgian Army surrendered. 28 May			
June	Evacuation of Dunkirk. 3 June	Italy declared war on Great Britain and France. 10 June		

	Europe	Mediterranean and Africa	Russia	Far East
June	France capitulated. 22 June			
July		Great Britain attacked French ships at Oran. 3 July		
Aug.	**Battle of Britain.** 8 Aug.–31 Oct.			
Sept.				German - Italian-Japanese pact for new World Order. 27 Sept.
Oct.		Italy invaded Greece. 28 Oct.		
Nov.		Attack on Italian Fleet at Taranto. 11 Nov.		
Dec.	'The Fire of London.' 29 Dec.	British Offensive in Western Desert. 9 Dec.		
1941 Jan.		Malta dive-bombed		
Feb.	Roumania joined the Axis	Italian Somaliland occupied. 26 Feb.		
Mar.		British Somaliland regained. 23 Mar. Battle of Cape Matapan. 28 Mar.		
Apr.		Addis Ababa occupied by British Imperial troops. 5 Apr. Greece and Yugoslavia invaded by Germany. 6 Apr. Axis invasion of Egypt. 26 Apr.		Russo - Japanese pact of neutrality. 13 Apr.
May		Battle for Crete. 20 May–1 June		
June		Syria entered by British and Free French. 8 June	Germany invaded Russia. 22 June	

	Europe	Mediterranean and Africa	Russia	Far East
Aug.			Britain and Russia entered Persia. 25 Aug.	Japan orders general mobilization. 11 Aug.
Sept.			Kiev taken by Germany. 21 Sept.	
Oct.			**Battle for Moscow.** 5 Oct.–6 Dec. Kharkov taken by Germany. 29 Oct.	
Nov.		British Offensive in Western Desert. 18 Nov.	Rostov taken by Germany. 27 Nov. Russian Counterattack in the Ukraine. 27 Nov.	
Dec.			First Russian Winter Offensive began. 6 Dec.	Japan attacked **Pearl Harbor.** 7 Dec. Hong Kong taken by Japan. 25 Dec.
1942 Jan.		Second German Counter-Offensive began. 21 Jan.	Mozhaisk regained by Russia. 19 Jan.	Manila taken by Japan. 2 Jan. Japan invaded Dutch East Indies. 11 Jan.
Feb.				Japan captured Singapore. 15 Feb.
Mar.				Japan captured Rangoon (Burma) 8 Mar.
May	R.A.F. Bombing Offensive against Germany increasing		Kerch taken by Germany. 16 May	Japan captured Mandalay. 4 May Air-Sea Battle of the Coral Sea. 4–8 May Philippines surrendered. 6 May

	Europe	Mediterranean and Africa	Russia	Far East
June				Air-Sea Battle of Midway Island. 4–7 June
July		Axis reached El Alamein. 1 July	Germany captured Sebastopol. 1 July Rostov again taken by Germany. 27 July	
Aug.			Voroshilovsk, Krasnodar, and Maikop taken by Germany. 5–9 Aug.	Japan defeated at Milne Bay (New Guinea). 27–31 Aug.
Sept.			Battle of Stalingrad begun. 5 Sept.	Japan crossed Owen Stanley Range. 9 Sept. Allied Counteroffensive in New Guinea. 29 Sept.
Oct.		Battle of El Alamein. 23 Oct.		
Nov.		Allied landings in French North Africa. 8 Nov.	Russian Winter Offensive in Stalingrad area. 19 Nov.	
Dec.				British Offensive in Burma. 19 Dec.
1943 Jan.		Tripoli taken by Britain. 23 Jan.	Surrender of German 6th Army at Stalingrad. 31 Jan.	Australians captured Buna. 2 Jan.
Feb.	'Round the Clock' Bombing of Germany begun		Russians captured Kursk, Krasnodar, Rostov, Kharkov. 8–16 Feb.	Japan evacuated Guadalcanal. 9 Feb.
Mar.			Germany again took Kharkov. 15 Mar.	
Apr.		Allied Offensive in Tunisia. 7 Apr.		

	Europe	Mediterranean and Africa	Russia	Far East
May		Axis forces in Tunisia surrendered. 13 May		Americans landed on Attu (Aleutians). 11 May
July		Sicily invaded by the Allies. 10 July	German Offensive in Kursk area. 6 July	
		Fall of Mussolini. 25 July	Russian Counterattack. 12 July	
Aug.			Russia regained Orel, Bielgorod, Kharkov, Taganrog. 4–30 Aug.	U.S. took Munda (Solomons). 6 Aug.
Sept.		Allies landed in Italy. 3 Sept.	Russians took Novorossisk, Briansk, Smolensk. 16–25 Sept.	Australians landed in Salamaua and Lae. 12–16 Sept.
		Italy surrendered. 8 Sept.		
Oct.		Naples taken by Allies. 1 Oct.	Russians crossed Dnieper. 7 Oct.	Americans landed on Treasury Islands. 27 Oct.
		Allied Offensive on Volturno River. 13 Oct.		
		Italy joined the Allies. 13 Oct.		
Nov.		Allies crossed Sangro River. 23 Nov.	Kiev regained by Russians. 6 Nov.	Americans invaded Gilbert Islands. 20 Nov.
Dec.			Russians opened Offensive west of Kiev. 24 Dec.	
1944 Jan.		Allied landings at Anzio. 22 Jan.	Blockade of Leningrad lifted. 27 Jan.	Americans invaded Marshall Islands. 31 Jan.
Feb.		Bombardment of Cassino. 15 Feb.		Japanese Offensive on Arakan front broken. 28 Feb.
				Americans invaded Admiralty Islands. 29 Feb.
Mar.			Russian Offensive in the Ukraine on 3 fronts	

	Europe	Mediterranean and Africa	Russia	Far East
Mar.			Russians entered Roumania. 31 Mar.	
Apr.	Increased		Crimea liberated. Apr.–May	Australians took Madang. 24 Apr.
May	Bombing Offensive on	Allied Offensive across Rapido and Garigliano rivers. 11 May		
June	west Europe			
	Allied landings in Normandy, D Day. 6 June	Rome captured by Allies. 4 June	Russian Offensive on Karelian front. 11 June	
	Flying-bomb attacks on Britain began. 13 June		Russian Offensive on Central front. 23 June	
July	Allies captured Caen. 9 July	Leghorn taken by Allies. 19 July		
Aug.	German retreat from Normandy. 12 Aug.		Russians entered Bucharest. 31 Aug.	Allies captured Myitkyina (Burma). 4 Aug.
	Allied landings in south France. 15 Aug.			
	Paris liberated. 25 Aug.			
Sept.	Brussels liberated. 3 Sept.	Gothic line broken. 2 Sept.	Russians entered Bulgaria. 8 Sept.	
	Rocket attacks on England began. 8 Sept.			
	Battle of Arnhem. 17 – 26 Sept.			
Oct.		Allies landed in Greece. 4 Oct.	Russians entered Belgrade. 20 Oct.	Americans re-landed in the Philippines. 20 Oct.
Nov.	Belgium cleared of Germans. 3 Nov.			
Dec.	German Counter-attack in the Ardennes. 16 Dec.			British captured Kalewa (Burma). 3 Dec.

	Europe	Mediterranean and Africa	Russia	Far East
1945 Jan.			Russians overran Hungary. Jan.–Feb.	
Feb.			Russians entered Warsaw. 17 Jan. Russians 50 miles from Berlin. 1 Feb.	Americans landed on Iwojima. 19 Feb.
Mar.	Allies crossed the Rhine. 7 Mar.			Mandalay recaptured by British. 20 Mar.
Apr.	Germany overrun from west. Ruhr area cut off. 1 Apr. Russians and Americans met on Elbe. 26 Apr.	Allies reached river Po. 23 Apr. Milan liberated by partisans. 26 Apr. Surrender of German Armies in Italy. 29 Apr.	Russians took **Vienna.** 13 Apr. Germany overrun from east.	Americans captured Okinawa. 1 Apr.
May			Berlin surrendered. 2 May	Rangoon recaptured. 3 May
	UNCONDITIONAL SURRENDER OF GERMANY 8 May 1945			
June				Australians landed in Borneo. 10 June
Aug.			Russia declared war on Japan, and invaded Manchuria. 8 Aug.	First **Atomic Bomb,** dropped on Hiroshima. 6 Aug.[1] Second Atomic Bomb, dropped on Nagasaki. 9 Aug.
	UNCONDITIONAL SURRENDER OF JAPAN 14 August 1945			

[1] 6 Aug. 1945, at 8.15 a.m. (Japanese time).

INDEX

Francisco J. Uriz

¡A ESCENA!

EDELSA / EDI 6
Colección LEER
ES FIESTA

1 © **ALBERTI,** Rafael, 1962, págs. 19-20, *«Roma, peligro para caminantes»*; págs. 21-22, *«Los ocho nombres de Pablo»*; págs. 23-25, *«Poemas escénicos»* (Ed. Aguilar, Obras completas)

2 © **ALEJANDRO,** Julio, pág. 7, *«Breviario de los chilindrones»* (Periódico «El día de Aragón»)

3 © **AZORÍN,** págs. 58-61, *«Cuentos anarquistas»* (Ed. Taurus)

4 © **BORNEMANN,** Elsa, pág. 15, *«Tinke, Tinke»* (Ed. Plus Ultra)

5 © **BUENAVENTURA,** Enrique, págs. 80-83, *«La maestra»* ("Primer Acto", revista de teatro española)

6 © **CANDIA,** César di, págs. 49-52, *«Entrevista a Obdulio Varela»* (Semanario "Búsqueda")

7 © **CAMPOAMOR,** Ramón de, págs. 16-18, *«Antología Poética»* (Alianza Editorial)

8 © **CELA,** Camilo José, págs. 43-48, *«Conversaciones españolas»* (Ed. Plaza y Janés)

9 © **FERNÁNDEZ MOLINA,** Antonio, págs. 33-34, *«Arando en la madera»* (Ed. Litho Arte)

10 © **GARCÍA TOLA,** Fernando, págs. 8-9, *«Cómo hacer absolutamente infeliz a un hombre»* (Ediciones Temas de hoy, S.A.)

11 © **GÓMEZ,** Albino, págs. 68-70, *«Los grandes»* (Ed. Kraft)

12 © **GONZÁLEZ ABREU,** Teresa, págs. 53-55, *«Monólogo de Manuela»* ("Cine Cubano", revista cinematográfica)

13 © **LANZA,** Silverio, págs. 62-65, *«Autobiografía»* (Hyspamérica Ediciones Argentina S.A.)

14 © **MARQUÉS,** Josep-Vicent, págs. 40-42, *«La no conversación»* ("El País dominical")

15 © **MASLÍAH,** Leo, págs. 10-11, *«Democracia en el bar»* ("Conjunto", revista de teatro cubana)

16 © **MAURICIO,** Julio, págs. 75-79, *«Teatro breve argentino contemporáneo I»* (Ed. Colihue, Colección L y C)

17 © **MIHURA,** Miguel, págs. 35-39, *«El negociado de incobrables»* (Ed. de la Torre)

18 © **PIÑERA,** Virgilio, págs. 56-57, *«Muecas para escribientes»* (Altea, Taurus, Alfaguara)

19 © **RESINO,** Carmen, págs. 84-92, *«Teatro breve y el oculto enemigo del profesor Schneider»* (Ed. Fundamentos)

20 © **SÁENZ,** Dalmiro, págs. 12-14, *«¿Quién, yo?»* (Juan Goyanarte Editor)

21 © **SÁNCHEZ FERLOSIO,** Rafael, págs. 71-74, *«El Jarama»* (Ediciones Destino)

22 © **TOMEO,** Javier, págs. 26-27, 28-29 y 30-32, *«Historias mínimas»* (Ediciones Mondadori España, S.A.)

23 © **UMBRAL,** Francisco, págs. 66-67, *«Travesía de Madrid»* (Ediciones Destino)

Diseño de colección y cubierta TD GUACH
Fotocomposición GRAMMA
© Francisco J. Uriz • EDELSA / EDI 6
General Oraa, 32
28016 MADRID
I.S.B.N.: 84-7711-064-6
Depósito legal: M. 28.381-1991
Imprime: Gráficas Rogar, S. A.
C/ León, 44. Pol. Ind. Cobo Calleja
FUENLABRADA (Madrid)